The OUTLINE of LOVE

Also by Morgan McCarthy

The Other Half of Me

The OUTLINE *of* LOVE

MORGAN McCARTHY

TINDER
PRESS

First published in Great Britain in 2013 by
Tinder Press
An imprint of HEADLINE PUBLISHING GROUP

1

Cataloguing in Publication Data is available from the British Library

ISBN (HB) 978 0 7553 8877 6
ISBN (TPB) 978 0 7553 8878 3

Typeset by Palimpsest Book Production Ltd, Falkirk, Stirlingshire
Printed and bound in Great Britain by Clays Ltd, St Ives plc

For Cian.

ACKNOWLEDGEMENTS

I'd like to thank Cian for his unfailing love and belief in me. Huge thanks also to Nicole, Gemma, Diane and Sue for reading and sound advice, and to the rest of my friends and family for their encouragement. I'm so grateful to Leah, Emily and the team at Headline for the always-unerring editorial judgement, support, and hard work. I'd also like to thank Jo, Carrie and everyone at Conville and Walsh, for being absolutely brilliant.

PART ONE

Persephone and her friends disport themselves in the bowered arches by the lake of Pergus, where the grass bows under their milky feet like the most sumptuous velvet and flowers put out their colours like flags waving for a celebration: lilies, irises, violets. The perfume of the flowers is so pervasive that hounds lose their trail of scent, falter and scatter, leaving the hunters to curse and return home. And so no male voice is heard in the glades, and no rough note disturbs the aural tapestry of rustling leaves and soft soprano song.

Ivy Ford
Persephone and Hades

I am sitting in the garden, without moving – because there is no point in moving – feeling the slow progression of a chill rising up over me; the last light drawing back over my face, the square of lawn between the stone walls filling up with shadow like a cold bath. When the shadow reaches the top of my head, I tell myself, I will get up and go inside. On every side of me, any direction I could look, the crumpled land rolls and folds, holding nothing. I have lived in the Assynt Peninsula my whole life but even I know it's a strange place: even stranger after two thirds of a bottle of wine, consumed alone. At the borders of the horizon the mountains sleep, like titanic dinosaurs that have been dreaming for so long that they have sunk into the land, ossified, and will never heave themselves free. A heavy silence descends from them, lifted only by the wind, which comes to rustle and hiss through the dead heather and the dry grass, then exhausts itself.

Our house is the only human-built structure within this empty land-bowl. There are three other houses within a half-hour's drive, the first belonging to Mrs Farquhar (of whom more later), the second to a misanthropic farmer, and the third to nobody, having been empty for years. It is only really crofters – their predecessors having been exiled here in the days of the Clearances

– who live outside the villages here at this tip of the Highlands.

'How do they do it?' I'd once asked my father when we drove past their small farmhouses, overseeing the sheep scattered across the stony clutter of the land, as if distributed by some hurricane from greener pastures. 'How can they stand it?'

'The same way that we do, I suppose,' was his answer, mildly spoken.

'But *I* can't stand it,' is my reply, never spoken.

We live here, my father and I, because my great-grandfather's brother was a geologist and was disappointed in love. He was left waiting at an American altar by his flighty bride and so he decided to move somewhere that would ensure that he never met another living woman to trouble him again. The land here, created by glaciers many thousands of years ago, has enough rocky riddles and rewards to keep a geologist occupied for an entire career, which is exactly what happened. After the death of my great-grandfather's brother, the house he built was passed sideways and downwards through the generations, becoming ever more dilapidated, and would probably have merged back into the landscape if my mother and father hadn't decided twenty-five years ago to 'get away from it all'.

The ordinariness of our house – its square white shape, evenly placed windows, pointed roof – and our neat little green garden with its one tree and line of washing is made bizarre by its presence in this landscape. Like a Magritte joke it sits jauntily in the towering tables and shelves of rock and the grim plains, where the only colours are brown, yellow and grey under the wide, grey sky. The tourist guides would have you believe that this part of the earth is dramatic or spectacular, which is wrong, because these words imply some kind of movement – a show – when all there is is stillness. The tourists call it bleak, which is also wrong. What they are actually trying to express is their own uncomfortable realisation: the bleakness of their own transience that the massed land causes them to notice.

'And you're only here for a weekend,' I say to them.

But now the time for envying the tourist buses is over: now it's my turn to take the long road east to the airport and from there, to civilisation. This is what the letter I hold tells me, informing me coolly that I will begin my BSc in management at King's College, London in early October. I have no idea what I will end up managing – or indeed, whether I want to manage anything – but it seemed like a practical sort of choice and I didn't have any better ideas. When I first opened the letter I put the envelope to my nose. It smelt of dried ink. I was disappointed; I had wanted to sniff some mysterious scent of London: a whiff of perfume, a trace of fog and gunpowder.

I have visited London only once, when I was small and my father and grandparents took me to a show in the West End. All I remember of that day were the lights, the black stone, the piercing sting of my sweets glowing fluorescent and overwhelming. The rough nap of the velvet seat, a curtain drawing momentously back. I have no idea and my father can't remember what the show was, but I know there was a princess, the white bell of her skirt moving through the dark set like a delicate man o' war. When I think of London now I remember the occult delights of that day; the sugar-fuelled unease, the unreality of it. Almost anything could happen to me, in the dream-space of London. And I want this: I want for almost anything to happen.

When I hear the first murmurings of my father's car, I drink the rest of the wine in my glass, push the cork back into the bottle, then put it in a bush. I don't rush. It takes a minimum of two and three-quarter minutes for a car to gently bump down the single track road leading up to the house, so that I could have the glass rinsed and back in the cupboard were my father suspicious enough to think of sniffing it. But, of course, he isn't. My father's worries are timid ones; they huddle in his own head, reluctant to impose themselves on others. If he found me drinking he would just be deeply and quietly sad, because he thinks drinking could be a cause of cancer. He also worries about me smoking, driving too fast, eating pink chicken, and going out without an umbrella. He knows the various ways someone might die young like a waiter knows the menu, so I try not to remind him of any of them.

Evan Triebold's fine-tuned sense of death developed in 1991, the year his wife, his father and his mother died one after the other. My mother, Sylvia, died of cancer. Then his father died in a car accident. Three months later his mother Laure was diagnosed with a brain tumour, the idea of which prompted her to kill herself. She left a note for Evan: 'I'm impatient. I'm not going to wait. Sorry.'

I don't think my father kept the note: it was horrifying to him that, after what death had done to his family, his mother would rush towards it so carelessly. I never asked about it, though secretly I would have liked to have seen the note. Never having met Laure I can romanticise her decision: the courage of it, the panache.

My father's car finally crackles to a halt on the rough drive and sighs itself quiet. Then Evan himself appears around the corner of the house, politely announcing his arrival with a small cough.

'Hello, Perse.' Wherever he turns up, whoever he greets, he always does it shyly. Then, once he is welcomed, some ease settles back over him, as if he has pulled a blanket over his shoulders. He sits down a little awkwardly on the bench next to me and plucks leaves from the creeper on the wall. My father has pebbly colour eyes, tucked under a soft fold of skin at the corners, grey eyebrows, and a lot of heavy grey hair. His face is sparse, slightly uncertain, easily understood.

'Hi, Dad.' (In his birth country of Switzerland my father would not be called Dad. He would be Papa, or maybe Vater. But Sylvia would have said Dad, and I say it too, so she is still part of our conversations.) 'Did you have fun in Inverness?'

'The pictures are selling well, apparently. They don't want the gold or silver frames though – they keep getting requests for the driftwood, the, ah, knots and natural look, I suppose. I wonder if they imagine a little old man collecting wood by the sea. It seems ironic that I have to import the wood, doesn't it?' As he talks he pulls the leaves absently to pieces. Green confetti sputters from his fingers.

My father takes photographs at places like Achiltibuie and Morar; initially it was a hobby, but now they are framed and sold to tourists. The product is, of course, tacky, but in his studio the prints hang ready to be framed all over one wall, and they are beautiful. Hundreds of sunsets, hundreds of glittering grey loch edges, sea-rims, arcs of sky.

'I got the details of my university place today,' I tell him. 'I'm living in a house rather than halls, apparently. But I don't mind where I am. So long as it's London.'

My father says, 'Oh, that's splendid, Perse,' and pats my hand, not quite meeting my eye.

'I'll be careful,' I tell him. 'I'll stay away from drugs and street gangs.'

'I know you're a sensible girl,' he says. 'I'm very proud of you.'

'You won't be lonely, will you?' I ask.

'Oh, no, no. I'll have Mrs Farquhar, and Mr Anderson, and the Cullens, and the McCleods.'

'But you hardly see any of them. You've only met Mr Anderson once. And you never go to the McCleods' dinner parties.'

'Oh, they're not really for me. I'd feel out of place.' He looks at me, blinks, and adds, 'But I'm sure I'd make the effort to go to more of these things after you've left. I'll be sociable. You mustn't worry about me.'

'It's hard not to. Just . . . make sure you see people. Do *something*.'

He nods, and I sigh, then we sit for a while longer in silence, both hoping that Sylvia will say something. But as usual, she keeps quiet, and eventually my father gives me an apologetic smile, and goes inside.

My father has maintained every possible memento of my mother in the house – her clothes, books, half-hearted attempts at decorating – as if she might, any day, walk in and say something like, 'Have you seen my reading glasses?' to which he could say, 'In the drawer, where they've always been.' If the house is her shrine, my father's stories, told over and over, have become scripture. How she loved reading, painting pictures she always threw away, experimenting with food that was always inedible, writing to her parents back in England. How in a small village of Dorset, where her family was from, she had opened a health food shop, but nobody quite understood ginkgo biloba and aloe vera back then and so she closed the shop and went travelling in Europe, where she met my father in a Swiss boulangerie.

Even our neighbours pay service to the cult of my mother. They tell me how romantic she and Evan were, that every week they had dinner by the light of a candle in a jar. They say she was easily distracted, that she was kind. They try not to talk about how she died, of the illness that took little bits of her, her hair, then her flesh, like a kidnapper, until finally becoming greedy and wanting everything.

After her death, our own lives stopped moving. It is as if there are still three of us, my father still bewildered after all these years of my mother being dead, still only partially recovered. My mother's name always in his mouth: *Sylvia*, a ferny, wraith name, soft and hushed. His own name, *Evan*, an assonant echo, forever reverential.

The next day I go to Ullapool. I intend to tell my father (who is also out and about today) that I'm posting letters, but really I need to visit the bottle bank and then the supermarket, my bush stock having run dry. In accordance with my father's curative preservation of all things Sylvia, her old red hatchback has been kept running and has now passed into my hands to travel where I like, so long as it isn't far and I slow down at bends.

The car hiccups and rocks down the uneven track from our house before I slide out on to the main road and turn south. Today the sun is out again: a dreamlike hazy disc, like a light behind opaque white glass, marooned in the featureless span of the sky. I squint at it suspiciously: up here there is no trust of the sun. Its appearance is greeted with a raised eyebrow or a bitter laugh. *Don't think we don't know what you're up to*. Here one minute, gone the next, and then days of black rain. We're wise to the routine.

The road ducks and dives through the land, slipping under the noses of the rock-trolls of the hills, cresting briefly, dipping again, like the path of one of the little brown birds that swoop over the heather. It passes the barren lakes, the stripped slopes, the occasional clutch of pines, huddled together as if knowing they are exposed, the silver birches lichened like alien trees, the needly scruffs of gorse. In the distance Stac Pollaidh lies, its distinctive mammoth humps moving slowly from one car window to another. Ullapool appears only after the person driving there has become dizzy with following the road, concentrating on every turn, and slumped into a tired hatred of the hills. Then, like a mirage, a house's garden will appear, fresh and unexpected green. Then the sheep proliferate, followed by more houses, then hotels and, finally, everything is green, the flat steely loch opens wide and turns blue, and the village appears, neat and white on the waterfront. Everything in Ullapool is small, square and white, down to the suburban road where I park: an arrangement of white houses at right angles, white fences and cherry blossom like a slow 1960s American dream, the mountains hovering in the distance above them.

A face withdraws behind a curtain when I get out of the car; a window across the road closes. I imagine children being rushed inside, their tricycles left overturned and spinning in the suddenly empty street. There is a low level of suspicion of me in Ullapool, I know: I am tolerated here, but not really liked. My name, my face, my voice all mark me out as something different and unfamiliar. I can sympathise. I'm not quite familiar with myself yet either.

Apparently, before my mother died, I used to attend parties and playgroups with the other children of Ullapool, but after my father started to worry about the sharp edges of other people's hearths and the bacteria that might be harboured in their mayonnaise, these social visits tailed off. Maybe the invitations themselves waned: perhaps I had become an awkward presence at Pass the Parcel: a half-orphaned, disconsolate four year old. After nursery school I was home schooled with the help of our neighbour Mrs Farquhar, if neighbour is the right word for someone living on the other side of the mountain.

I sidle around the aisles of the supermarket, alert for my father, whose tired blue estate I have spotted in the car park. I pick up a few bottles and go to the furthest checkout, so wary of being seen that I don't notice Kirsty McRae – chin in her palms and eyes widened with hostility – until it is too late to turn back.

I put the bottles down in front of her with a 'Hello' of apology.

'Right,' says Kirsty in response. 'Having a party?' She taps a bottle with one hot-pink nail.

I look at her warily. The most contact I have had with Kirsty McRae is hearing her mutter, 'Would you look at that whore?' as I passed by her in the street, but, like everyone else, I know who she is – a gap-toothed femme fatale in fake gold jewellery and dirty-edged white trousers, who has given blow jobs to most of the local teens. I had always imagined that she would be the first to leave the town for the bright lights of the porn industry, but she lingers on, queen of her small sexual pond.

'Just restocking,' I murmur.

'Re-stock-ing,' repeats Kirsty, as if amused by the word. As I walk away I can feel her mouth something behind me, but it doesn't matter, because I'm out in the strange flat sunlight, empty bottles gone, new bottles snugly hidden in my carrier bag, and it's only a few weeks before I'm gone for good.

As I pass a pub on the way back to the car I hear someone shout: 'Persephone!'

Here is the reason for Kirsty's dislike, and several other girl-feuds besides. The eligible males of Ullapool are sitting outside with pints of beer, sunglassed and boisterous, calling me over. Robert Lennox doesn't appear to be with them, but I don't want to cross the road. A superstitious shiver moves over me: the idea that if I step over the pub's threshold my hair will stiffen, my lashes lengthen, my skirt shrink, and I will become Kirsty McRae, sitting at the pub for ever, while the changeling Kirsty goes to London in my place.

'Got to run,' I call, making an exaggerated sad face, waving, but moving quickly. Their voices follow clearly in the thin, pure air off the Loch.

'Come back tonight!'

'Fuck that, just come over to mine!' Laughter follows this last. An old woman walking a terrier looks at me disapprovingly, as if the noise is somehow my fault.

I wait to cross the road behind an idling tourist bus, one of the many that stop here to spill out their contents: Canadian and American tourists, thinning out over the village with maps and binoculars, taking the ferry across Loch Broom, eating seafood, demanding photographs of anything in a kilt. Now that it is late afternoon the tourists are being recalled from wherever they were spending their money, reeled invisibly back to the bus. What is unusual is that my father in his battered hat is amongst them, walking next to a woman: a camera-wielding, peanut-coloured American woman.

Taken aback, I stop at the side of the road to watch them, expecting my apparent father to reveal himself as another man, a mild grey doppelganger listening to his companion. But it is my father, with his own distinctive gestures – even now moving his head in the way he does when he is interested, tilting his ear towards her, as if aligning the ear and her mouth more closely will allow him to better understand her meaning. He listens seriously for a little longer. Then he straightens, and laughs.

Realising that I am one head-turn away from being seen, I move further behind the bus, then I cross the road quickly, and walk back to the car, without looking back to find out if they have seen me.

Once I get home I lie on my bed with a magazine, wondering at my behaviour. Scuttling around town like a skittish animal, spooked by the town bike, the local boys, the tourists. It is as if that, now I know I am leaving, I can't bear to touch anything with more than the lightest of brushes, as if making contact with the Assynt will trap me somehow, fix me in place. Not that this explains, of course, why I avoided my father, who appears to be faithfully and promptly obeying my instruction to see people, to *do something*.

I listen out for his car, the sound of the door opening and closing, its faint, familiar whine, and get up from the bed to go downstairs. But the next sound isn't something I expect: another car door, opening and closing, followed by the sound of two voices – one Evan's, one American, and female. I sit back down, blankly, and stay where I am without moving. Exit routes unroll in my head. Out of the window and down the tree? Out of the door, into the bathroom and out of the window?

I am still sitting on the bed when my father comes to tap on the door, before putting his head around it.

'Hello, Perse. Have you just woken up? I was calling you.'

'Really? I didn't hear you. Sorry.'

'We've got a guest for dinner,' he says festively, 'Sadie Weisner – she's holidaying here. She was going to the Summer Isles but missed her ferry so I invited her here instead. I thought I could cook venison. Come down and meet her.'

I wonder whether the headache spreading like an ink stain, blooming darkly in my temple, justifies my staying in my room while we have a guest, but give up and follow him like a sulking cat down to the kitchen.

'Hi,' says Sadie brightly, putting out her hand. The brief impression I had of her earlier was of a tall woman with a lot of matte blond hair, much younger than my father. Now I realise that she is closer to his age, with deep-colour skin and the healthy, compact look of a woman over forty who exercises and makes sure she eats plenty of fruit. 'I'm Sadie. Great to meet you.'

'Persephone,' I say. 'How do you do.'

'Oh, just great! I love it here. What a pretty name you have.'

'Sadie and I have just been for a walk around Ullapool,' Evan says.

'This area is just breathtaking!' says Sadie. She enthuses about the mountains ('So desolate and proud!'), the loch ('Haunting!') and the locals ('So welcoming!') while my father hovers proudly at her side, irradiating her oblivious left ear with his smile, as if he has personally offered up the Assynt to her, laying it down at her feet like a cape for her to tread upon.

The light slides down over the humpbacked horizon as my father cooks and I make small talk with Sadie, who, it turns out, is staying at the local bed and breakfast rather than leaving town tonight. She is travelling with a group of other Americans, something she has been doing for most of the past year. She shows us photos of herself looking cheerful in front of Shakespeare's house, Aztec temples, the leaning tower of Pisa, and so on, grinning her way through the pick of the world's sights.

Sadie had one previous husband who died a few years ago of prostate cancer: a loss which, she tells us, propelled her to start going round the world in order 'to really experience everything, and really *live*'. As she talks I have the rising, uncomfortable feeling that my father and I are about to be the new characters in *Second Chances*, the TV movie of Sadie's life.

When we sit at the table, my father brings out three wine glasses and a bottle of Beaujolais, which he puts down without comment but with the same air of 'special occasion' that has hung over him all night. Then he decides to put on music and realises his only CD – Ravel – won't do, so I am sent upstairs to find something more cheerful in my own collection.When I come back down they are sitting closely together, laughing over something they try unsuccessfully to explain.

'I'm really sorry, but I think I'm going to get an early night,' I say, cutting them off. 'I ate lunch late, and I've got a horrible headache.'

Though the headache is genuine, their concern makes me feel guilty and I go upstairs feeling both wrong and wronged, dropping down onto my bed with the weight of it. The headache keeps me awake for a long time, lying listening to the muted sounds of laughter below me, looking up at the window in which the mountain tips have become colder, grander, glinting like frost under the last of the light.

The next morning, I get up too late to work out whether Sadie's presence in the house is because she stayed over last night, or whether she has only just arrived. She and my father are sitting with coffees making plans for a drive to Dunnet Head, which I excuse myself from, saying I've already arranged to see Mrs Farquhar.

'That's such a pity,' Sadie exclaims.

'I know,' I say. 'But it was really lovely to meet you – I hope you enjoy the rest of your time in the Highlands.'

'Oh, I'll be here for a little while longer, so we can hang out again,' Sadie says. 'I can't wait!'

'Great!' I say, picking up my car keys. 'Glad to hear it!'

I drive towards Mrs Farquhar's house with no idea of what to do, as I'm almost certain that she's visiting her sister in Edinburgh. As I suspected, the tall, lonely grey-blocked house is clearly unoccupied, so I get out of the car and sit on a rock with a cigarette: another of my secret cancer-pleasures. As a concession to my father I restrict myself to only one a week, but this strikes me as a two-cigarette week.

Mrs Farquhar's house overlooks the dam, beyond which a wide, still body of water stretches into the far slopes and ends in a drifting desert haze of yellow and blue. The sky is rainless for once; an odd blue, like the blue of a Dali painting. Over the water the wind calls up a low, tuneless singing noise, like a giant blowing across the mouth of a bottle. Mrs Farquhar's house actually used to be a hotel, but it wasn't a success: the eerie whistling noise bothered the guests. Now she occupies one corner of it like a caretaker, living on her pension and money from tutoring.

I blow a long speculative stream of smoke into the warm sky, wishing I'd thought to pick up a couple of magazines. Last night Sadie said the Assynt Peninsula would suit those with an artistic or philosophical temperament ('You could just sit all day and be inspired!') but as neither an artist nor a philosopher I am sadly marooned in the hills, the great bowl of near-bare rock, graduating yellow and grey up to the sky. I don't see how anyone could be inspired here. Without a breeze the intense quietness is reflected by the blank hills and sky: pressed, layered into a silence so thick and impenetrable that it is like liquid glass. Surely it would seep into a creative thinker and stop them like an old watch; the unanswerable coma of silence.

Time here is a strange thing: I feel the land could either be very far in the past or far in the future, with nothing much changing between either time, leaving it hovering uncertainly between the two like a dream landscape. The land gives the appearance of not noticing the brief pressure of motion on its surface, the lives of people and animals vanishing in a micro-blink, too quick to register. But the things that stop and come to rest – signposts, houses, bridges, bones – become part of the land itself, they collapse and petrify, giving up their allegiance to civilisation, their function and familiarity. The flats and hills are scattered with ruins: the half-tumbled castles, the wall-traces, roofless crofting cottages, the chambered cairns – alongside those of a more recent vintage: the rusting bathtub in the field, the stranger's car broken down thirty years ago by the side of a road. The human relics have both an equality in their abandonment, and an equality with the structures that have not yet been abandoned, so that a ruined crofting cottage will sit alongside a new house as if in recognition that in very little time the occupants of the new house will be dead, its roof will have fallen in, and it will have rejoined the sleeping mountains.

Life in a place like this is a strange and small thing. Take our neighbours – the abrupt and timid Mrs Farquhar, the short-spoken farmers and gamekeepers: they all have something subdued about them, as if they understand that their presence here is as transitory as the bumble bees that skim the heather, but can't quite bring themselves to leave.

And how does someone grow up on the face of the mountain if they can't put their feet down, can't become part of their environment, if they have no sense of time accumulating but rather of its suspension, if they look out every day on the great waves of rock that no one could anthropomorphise, no matter what sort of philosopher or artist they are? I have spent my formative years here but I don't feel formed. After eighteen years I can tell I am still soft in places where I ought to have a shell, still milky and new where I should be weathered and worn.

If I think about this too much the idea of going to London horrifies me as much as it lures me. I don't feel like the world is my oyster then: I feel that I am the oyster, about to be tipped out of my casing into a wide, hungry mouth.

Despite appearances, I'm not *completely* inexperienced. So far I have had three encounters with teenage romance: not bad for a girl with twenty miles between her and the nearest male under the age of fifty. Luckily my mother, who was slender and lush-haired and a beauty by anyone's standards, passed some of that down to me, which has given me a fighting chance. I have her tea-coloured skin, her shape, her dark hair and mutable dark eyes; the irises almost black in low light, coppery brown in the sun. But my face is its own idea, a mix of ancestral features that have no resemblance to either the gentle sags and curvature of my father or the delicacy of my mother. When I was a child I wasn't pretty – all nose and eyebrows, like a baby bird – but as I grew up the rest of my face sharpened, rebalanced and came into focus. Then boys started calling to me from the windows of pubs and cars, middle-aged men coyly asked me for directions, and old men told me I was a pretty wee lassie.

Like a light switched on unexpectedly in the dark, the suddenness of this attention was disorienting. It was out of the question to consult Mrs Farquhar, who reminds me of a small white mouse, skittering around the edges of her house as if avoiding its owners. I can't even imagine her ever having a Mr Farquhar. Neither could I ask my father for advice. But despite these handicaps, making my way into the world of love clumsy and alone at the age of sixteen, I ended up on a date with Robert Lennox.

I was sitting on the shingle beach at Ullapool watching the ferries move in and out like stately turtles when Robert's shadow slid across the length of me.

'Persephone, isn't it?' he asked.

'How did you know?' I asked, though everyone knew me, just like they knew everyone else. What I meant was 'How did *you* know?' I was aware of Robert's existence in the same way that a fish might note that one of the seagulls overhead was more loud, more central than the others. Always at the head of the troupe of boys attempting unsuccessfully to get into the local pub, in the middle of the group smoking in the park, his voice distinct from the rest, his blond head twinkling, like the pound coin in a pocketful of change.

'I asked about you,' he said. 'I've been asking everyone who the hot girl is that we only see once a month. It's not fair to hide away, you know. You've got to think of us poor lads.'

I felt that it would look better if I appeared not to have noticed him before, and said, 'Who is *this* poor lad?'

He dropped down on to the shingle, gazing up at me with delight.

'Robert Lennox. So how long are you here for today? Don't tell me you're only staying the afternoon.'

'That was my plan.'

'But the nights are so much better.' And so we ended up going to a small pub for whiskies, supplied to us clandestinely by Robert's brother, who worked behind the bar. The whisky tasted like poisoned oak and decay but I drank it anyway, Robert watching me, half approving and half curious.

'Why didn't you go to school around here?' he said. 'Did you go to boarding school or something?'

'I didn't go to school at all,' I told him. 'I can't even read.'

He dipped his finger in the whisky and wrote on the dark wood of the table, *Kiss Me.*

I laughed, but then his face was abruptly close to mine and it seemed the only reasonable thing to do was to kiss him, in the solidity of the smoke and heat of the tiny pub, with the smell of old wood and ancient spirits, watched by two old men with pipes, neither approving nor disapproving. When we left we kissed again outside, and then once more at my car.

'I want to see you again,' he said. 'But I don't want to wait until next month.'

I gave him the number of the switched-off mobile phone in my bag, silently accumulating its missed calls from home.

'Bye then, Persephone,' Robert said finally, leaning down to the window. 'Where's that name from, anyway? It's foreign, isn't it?'

'Greek,' I said.

'I thought you weren't from around here,' he said, then added before I could correct him, 'I like that, you're . . . exotic. Or something. Anyway, drive safe, Persephone.'

After that night Robert did call me, but I didn't answer, because by then I'd met his on-off girlfriend Lorna, who had appeared outside the small shop where I'd been buying cigarettes, had told me I'd better stay away from her boyfriend, and had delivered a short, decisive slap to my cheek. The slap itself didn't hurt, but I was shocked, putting my hand up to my face, as if I could feel the indentations of her fingers, their scalding shape.

'Bitch,' she added, perfunctorily, before walking away.

As Lorna was the most popular girl in her school, and the school was the only one in Ullapool, my date with Robert had far-reaching consequences. The story of what had happened cast its own off-colour light over me, so that when I walked through town I was followed by the eyes of an audience, half hostile, half appreciative. The girls thought I was a boyfriend thief; the boys thought I was a possibility. Kirsty McRae saw me as a young pretender to her throne and hated me accordingly.

I didn't tell my father any of this: the idea of my pain would have horrified him, and I could imagine him responding by moving us even further from civilisation, to the outer Hebrides, or the North Pole. As it was, I think he was relieved that, after the worry of my late night home, I seemed to have lost my enthusiasm for visiting Ullapool.

Aside from the compactly clustered teens of the town, Assynt life hasn't been generous with prospects for romance, most older men having fucked off to Inverness, Edinburgh, Manchester or London. The more ambitious the man, the further down the UK they dive. The only other people I meet are those passing through, on foot, by bicycle, car or coach, making their circuitous way up the coastline to the tip of the Highlands. And so my second experience of love was with an English tourist, Alex, travelling with his family clockwise from Inverness on a night of thick rain that hit the roofs with the weight of lead droplets, loud as the mournful thunder.

Alex's family were plotting their course with the help of a ten-year-old guidebook that directed them to the 'comfortable cheer of the Dam Lodge', Mrs Farquhar's defunct hotel. I was still there, waiting out the rain, when they turned up at 11 p.m. and frightened the dry little Mrs Farquhar so much that I offered to stay and help prepare a room for them for the night.

'We can't send them down those roads to Ullapool now,' I told her, noting the arrival of Alex in the porch, water rolling off his hair, his eyelashes dark with beading.

'Thank you so much, dear,' she whispered, patting my hand with her small paw. 'Will you stay too? I don't for the life of me know what to give them for breakfast.'

So calls were made and the family were sent to their dusty high-ceilinged rooms to sleep under the watchful auspices of Mrs Farquhar's stuffed stag heads. The rain having stopped, I went outside to sit in the garden with a stolen snifter of brandy and a cigarette. The lights of the house turned off one by one, until only one upstairs window was lit, giving the wet garden an intimation of edges, vague forms. The eaves of the house dripped sonorously onto the terrace, the only sound aside from the tiny noise of my lips on the cigarette. Beyond the wall of the garden was a greater wall of black, the soft density of the Assynt night. Mountains, lochs and roads were submerged, muffled in its finality.

The door opened behind me, casting a dark cut-out in its square of light. 'Can I join you?'

Alex sat down before I could reply, so I wordlessly offered him the cigarettes.

'I don't smoke,' he said. 'I used to. But I've started studying medicine. I've seen pictures of smokers' lungs.'

'If you lived here you'd smoke.' I told him.

He considered this, then nodded.

'Having a good holiday?' I asked facetiously.

'It's got better.' We looked at each other for a while, before I put my hand up to his face, collecting water droplets on the ends of my fingers. When he kissed me, it was shyly at first, as if he didn't realise that he was the good-looking arrival from civilisation, doing me a favour. Flattered, I didn't mind the gathering force of his kiss, or the way his hand moved on to my knee and travelled, unhesitating, up the length of my thigh, reaching the skirt boundary. I didn't even consider what the hand's intentions might be until it had slipped past the elastic pinch of my thong, making me jump.

'Alex!'

He looked at me, with the vague-eyed, ruffled innocence of a child that has just been woken up. 'What?'

'That's too much,' I said.

'We can just kiss, if you want?' he offered, but I sat back with irritation, relighting my cigarette. The lovely moment was over; my face was clammy from his rainy hair, the wetness of the bench had leached into my thighs. I realised that I was cold.

'I think you'd better go to bed,' I said. 'Mrs Farquhar is still up and she's *very* traditional. The shock of seeing you out here with me could kill her.'

The next morning I avoided him, staying in the kitchen to make breakfast, crossly pushing the bacon around a heavy skillet, only emerging once I heard his family's rental car scrunching its way back on to the narrow road.

'What a nice family,' Mrs Farquhar said mildly when I brought her tea. 'That boy is going to be a doctor, Persephone. *You* could do worse than to marry a doctor.'

Experience number three was the most promising and the most disappointing of them all. It happened on a surreally hot day in the early summer. I was walking down to the end of the drive to get our post and arrived at the road at the same time as a thinned-out group of hikers, toiling snail-like under their backpacks. One of the group detached himself and came over, waving a map like a white flag.

'We're looking for the bone caves and aren't sure if we took a wrong turn,' he said as he got to me. 'Are you local?'

We both looked down at my dusty flip-flops and rolled-up pyjama bottoms, then he smiled at me.

He must have been over thirty; blond-haired and tall with rough blond hairs on his tanned forearms. His eyes were bright blue and humorous. He was good looking in a way that was far from my experience, far from boyish.

'I live in that house.' I pointed, mentally calculating how long my father would be away. 'You can all come in for a drink if you're tired? And I'll draw you a route to the caves on your map.'

'That's kind,' he said. 'I could do with refilling our water, if you don't mind.'

I stood and watched as he went back to the group, who had sat down on the scrubby verge and rocks and begun rolling up their sleeves and trouser legs. With rising excitement I saw that the hiker was gathering up their bottles rather than inviting them all to join us.

'I don't want to fill your house with scruffy hikers,' he explained.

'You all look fine,' I said politely.

'Yeah, really debonair. But then, the dress code around here seems pretty casual.' He indicated the pyjamas.

I watched as he filled the bottles one by one at the tap, standing real and sun warmed in our dimly lit kitchen, unlikely as a leopard. When I sat down in front of the map he joined me, our arms almost touching.

'If you follow this route –' I drew a wavering line in pencil – 'it's a good scenic walk and you get the best views. It's steep here, and . . . here. Then the caves are . . . here.'

'I think I fell down somewhere along the road and hit my head on a rock,' he said, and laughed. 'What the hell are you doing out here? I just don't believe in this perfect little townhouse in the middle of the mountains, with a girl like you inside it offering water and a safe path. It's like a folk tale.'

This was so close to one of my own daydreams that I felt a quick, nearly painful intimacy with him.

'The sort of story where I'd either be a witch or a good fairy?'

'Or a princess,' he said, 'ignorant of her true birthright.'

'What's your role? Are you the third son?'

'Only child, I'm afraid,' he said. 'I hope that doesn't spoil it.' I glanced out of the window, where his friends were still reclining like dropped dolls around the roadside and my father's car was nowhere in sight.

'You're a very whimisical hiker,' I observed. The map and pencil lay between us but we stayed leaning close and serious, as if there were a very important task we both had to concentrate on.

'I often let my imagination get the better of me,' he said. I was still and tense under the continuing eye-contact, not sure whether to move forward, hoping he would do something. What he did surprised me. He took my hand, quite hard, and held it for a moment. 'Thank you for your help,' he said, then switched his stare away, standing up. Confused, I folded up his map for him and followed him to the door, where he thanked me again, overly politely.

As I was closing the door I changed my mind and went out after him. 'What was that?' I asked.

He hesitated before he turned around, hands opening in apology.

'That was a married man acting like an idiot over a beautiful girl. I'm sorry.'

'No . . . it's fine,' I said, startled and suddenly awkward, the ease between us abruptly lost. I retreated, giving a redundant wave. (I draw my lips in now, remembering that earnest wave – quick and panicked, the wave of a child.) After that I closed the door, went to the window, and watched him walk down the drive, straight backed and lean, towards his friends. He handed the water out, then in twos and threes they stood up and set off in the direction I had drawn for them, cresting the next hill and vanishing, and then the last one of them turned and looked back at the house, shading his eyes, and I felt the closeness of it, like physical contact.

After that day I thought about the hiker when I was daydreaming or before I went to sleep, trying to remember him perfectly, until he got worn away with the constant handling, his face eroding like a statue's, and all that was left were the things he said, learned off by heart, and his blue eyes.

In those three little tableaux, a triptych of experience, I feel I have had a précis of young romance. The usual scenarios – the older married man, the pushy boy, the love triangle – have played themselves out even in the most remote corner of society. I suppose I should have had foreknowledge of what would happen from all the films and TV shows I've watched, but it didn't help. You don't see it coming, you don't know a situation is a cliché until it's over. Up until then you believe it will be different, because there's always one person it's different for, and why shouldn't that be you?

From my three encounters I have taken a few pieces of a man, joining other pieces accumulated haphazardly, taken from actors, singers, characters in fiction. I might be watching a film and a man will look up in a certain way, or pour a glass of something with a particular shrug of his body, or a smile, and I'll feel a sting of recognition, because it will be *his* signal, a glimpse of the man in my mind; reminding me powerfully of a future I haven't met yet. Over time my hopes have shifted, been disappointed, regrouped, and gathered, stronger than before, like so many little sequins coalescing into something radiant: something star-like. A man with the sheen of magazine pages on him, his body confined by the edges of a screen, cold and passionate and bright and dark. His features are still vague – he is a template only, an outline of love – too indistinct to see properly.

If this man is anywhere, he is in London, which has already become not the dried-ink course as detailed in my introductory documentation, but the site of my grand passion. Even now he might be standing in his steepled house, hundreds of lights at the window, wondering at the chill he feels, this touch, from my ghostly fingertips.

I am still sitting on the rock, upright but nearly asleep, when a change in temperature rouses me. Behind me the sky has given itself up to an oncoming cloud drawing near from the coast, a thick angry grey that has sunk close over the mountained horizon and billows there oppressively as if threatening to roll down the slopes like an avalanche, enveloping everything.

I have been out for over an hour, which hopefully means that by the time I get back home my father and Sadie should have left. I rub my cold arms, the skin numbed and unfamiliar with chill, and scuttle to the car under the pressure of the darkened sky.

If it is impossible to find human metaphors for the ancient rock of Assynt, it is easy to find them for the weather, which has its own changeable personality. To put it bluntly, the weather is unhinged. Flat and morose one day, brightly showy the next, its present bad mood indicates an impending tantrum, in which it will thunder and wail and splash the impassive mountains with its tears, like a woman driven mad by a man who doesn't notice her. I shut the car door and drive away from the clouds, but they follow me all the way home, comprehensively covering the horizon, so that I step out into a solid downpour. Hunched under my rain-battered umbrella, I notice that my father's car is still at the house, and so, when I walk inside, is Sadie.

'We dawdled too long and then the rain started so we decided to stay here instead,' my father explains.

'It was my fault, I've been talking away, as usual,' Sadie said. 'My itinerary will just have to wait, I guess.'

The absence of a witticism in her comment does not prevent my father from laughing enthusiastically. I look at them in dismay.

'Hon, you're soaked,' Sadie exclaims, misinterpreting my expression. 'You don't even have a coat!'

'I'll put the fire on,' my father says. 'Sit down and dry out.'

'I was just going to go to my room and—'

'No, no, stay by the fire,' they both insist, and so I am settled between them with a blanket under my damp legs and a cup of tea, feeling awkward.

'Evan's been telling me about the history around here,' Sadie says, as if history is an acquaintance of my father's. 'It's fascinating. The Highlands just seem all the more beautiful when you hear about the past. There was such sadness here.'

'I don't know the rest of the Highlands particularly well,' I say. 'You probably know more than I do.'

'We're rather lazy travellers,' my father says guiltily.

I raise my eyebrows at this, because I'm not a lazy traveller. I haven't travelled because my father won't travel, Mrs Farquhar can't travel, I have no friends to travel with, and I know he would be worried if I went alone. The only Scottish places I have ever visited outside of the Assynt are the glens, wet and green as a garden in the morning, with their cheerful stream of tourists, and Inverness: a single bright light, compared to the Christmas tree of London.

'So you read about the Clearances?' my father is asking Sadie.

'Sure, but not just that. Look!' She pulls out a guidebook with a picture of a ruined castle on the front and shows us where the pages are dog-eared. 'So many of the places I visited seemed to have a story about a witch or a seer being killed. So I started turning down the corners on every page that mentioned it.'

We all look soberly at the book with its interleaved mess of pages.

'We have Black Bridge,' my father says. 'That's not far away.' Black

Bridge is small and made from stone, crossing nothing, leading apparently to nowhere. Not far from its redundant arch a suspected witch was burned in a barrel of tar a couple of hundred years ago. 'Apparently they accused her of cursing someone's baby,' my father explains.

Sadie shudders. 'How barbaric.' I hold back my own shudder, the twitch of a different feeling, because it occurs to me that I myself – living at a remove from the community, sexually suspect, slightly foreign – would have been a prime candidate for burning not so long ago.

~

A few days later, on a night in which a bad fairy turns my father into a small note on the kitchen table that says 'Back in a few hours. Love Dad', I have an urge to look through my mother's things. This is something I haven't done for nearly a year now. Not much was actually left behind, as my father found to his dismay when she died. Sylvia disliked hoarding: disorganised by nature, she scattered discarded paper, receipts and bills like a high wind. I view the things she did keep, assembled by my father in a drawer, as important clues; old tracks showing her indentation, her outline.

My mother kept, as most people would, a dark circle of my baby hair in a locket, pressed flowers and cards that my father had given her and letters from her mother. There are hard icing roses from a wedding cake, plane and cinema ticket stubs. There are articles she had liked and cut out of magazines, a few recipes that, from the look of them, never got cooked, photographs of Sylvia when she was my age; with her thin, unicornish loveliness and blown, round scoops of hair, leaning on her elbow and laughing.

There are the things I will never understand, things which meant something to Sylvia only. A sheet of green paper with potato printing on it. A little sketch of another girl. Notes from female friends: 'Thanks for everything, Syl,' writes Lucy in blue Biro. 'Missing you much. Can't wait till the next time. The wine awaits!' Then there is a letter on the back of an envelope, which Sylvia probably never got around to writing or sending.

Dear Editors.

I feel I must object to the article titled 'How to seduce your man'. I am frankly shocked that a women's magazine would advise its reader to hide their career successes so their 'target' doesn't feel threatened. Surely this advice belongs in the fifties, not the eighties. I really think that today the emphasis should not be on how to style yourself and your body to minimise your real self in order to, in effect, trick a man into marrying you. What is so unpalatable about <u>*woman*</u> *in her natural state? And surely there are more achievements in a woman's life than marrying the 'right kind of man' – a ridiculous statement in itself.* [Some scribbled crossing-out follows, and finally a blot of tea] . . . *self-worth. Yours with concern,*

Sylvia Triebold.

I like this letter, with its endearing underlining of 'woman'. I like the idea of my mother as a feminist, jotting off passionate, random letters, even if these missives bounced harmlessly off the thick walls of their destinations. According to my father, Sylvia's caring found room for a lot of things: women, stray dogs, children in war zones, smog. Her sympathy was like a barefoot, flowery party; no guest turned away.

I put the letter and the other things away and close the drawer reluctantly. When I was little I used to leave it open, and though I know better now, I have still not lost the feeling that by closing it I am shutting my mother inside, pushing her away and alone into the dark.

~

The time until my flight to London shrinks and vanishes; the days eaten up like a spark travelling along a fuse. During this time I'm not sure what my feelings are: trying to peer into my own heart is like looking into a room with the blinds drawn. I think I can make out the edges of objects, or people, but I can't identify any of them.

My worry about leaving my father has been partially replaced with a vaguer, less reasonable worry about Sadie. In the past couple of months there has been a good deal of Sadie: picnics, dinner, walks, drinks. She has been sleeping in the guest bedroom for the last week, having abandoned first her tourist bus and guide, and finally her hotel room in Ullapool. Perhaps she thinks she is seeing the real Scotland now.

I know I am being hard on Sadie, in the way I think about her. She tries to be sensitive about her position; she has a nervous respect for the dead wife, my mother, and says hopeful, friendly things like, 'Your mom must have been a great decorator, huh?' (which is not true) or 'She was a real beauty' (which is). She wants us to be friends: Persephone, Sadie and Sylvia. I'm just not sure it's as simple as that.

We are sitting now at the kitchen table while my father is inexpertly assembling his idea of a traditional Scottish breakfast for

Sadie. The window is a dark wall of rain, as if we are living behind a waterfall. The dim roar of it surrounds the house.

'This weather is crazy!' Sadie says with approval. 'I guess you'll be one of the few people who moves to London and thinks there's less rain. Which campus are you at?'

'The Strand,' I say.

'Oh, that's so central. You'll be able to walk everywhere . . . along the Thames, to Covent Garden, Trafalgar Square, Westminster.'

I turn these names over in my head, liking their Englishness, their regal consonants.

'London's so much smaller than you expect,' Sadie continues. 'It's . . . dense. They've got these old, old houses all in rows, and inside them it's like a doll's house.'

Concerned about the smell of burning coming from my father's direction, I am finding it hard to listen to Sadie. *Daal's house*, she says.

'The people aren't very friendly,' she adds, thoughtfully. 'They're so much friendlier around here.'

'What are the people like?' I ask, amused to hear what she might reference. Stiff upper lips, queuing?

'Tribal,' Sadie says unexpectedly. 'You get tribes of business people in suits. Tribes of kids in hoodies. Tribes of Japanese tourists. They're the obvious ones. But there are so many different groups and sub-groups of people. It's not like here. You could spend all day sitting in one busy place in London and you could count endless different tribes, and every district of London you go to those tribes will change. It's fascinating.'

I wonder if I will become part of a tribe – or if I am part of one already, but just don't know it yet. Maybe I'll arrive in London and meet hundreds of girls exactly like me, all having previously thought themselves so unique. But I'd welcome that: to sink gratefully into the group, swim with the shoal. The prospect of best friends is as tantalising as that of a boyfriend. These words, so common in print and on television, so rarely said by me, who has no best friend and no boyfriend. My closest encounter with a girl is a slap, my closest encounter with a boy is pulling his hand out of my pants. Despite this, I remain an optimist.

'You look happy,' Sadie says, smiling at me.

'I can't wait,' I tell her.

My father looks over. 'Just be careful,' he says. 'Make sure you get to know people before you trust them.'

'Oh Evan!' Sadie says. 'Your daughter is going to university, not joining MI6. And now, I want a photo of you two with this fantastic breakfast!' and my father and I have to arrange ourselves for the camera, set our smiles as the flash is adjusted, avoiding each other's eye as we finally, sheepishly disband.

There is something compelling about Sadie's good humour. Her enthusiasm, with its whiff of the suburban sitcom, its corny overtones, is hard to refuse. My father certainly hasn't put up any resistance, listening to words he can't possibly have heard before – gee, bummer, goof, megabucks, neato, rinky dink – without so much as a blink.

I have noticed other changes in my father since the arrival of Sadie. Wine, for a start, which has made so many appearances on the dining table now that my cache of bottles outside has lain undisturbed for almost a fortnight. He's forgotten on a few occasions to remind me to take my vitamins. I've heard him murmuring gamely along to pop ballads on the radio. And finally – most recently – I went to get something from his room and realised that the pictures of my mother next to his bed have been moved to the sitting and dining room, shuffled out from marital exclusivity into public space.

Later that night, after I have fallen asleep, I have a dream that I am trying to steer a boat, but the water keeps roiling up and directing a vicious spray in my eyes. I half wake up, sleep again, and am back in the boat, this time with my mother. As time passes my mother shrinks, getting smaller and smaller until she is tiny, and I can't find a safe place to put her. She slips through the boards of the deck, and through my hands. Finally, she is as light and insubstantial as if she is made of paper, and when the wind catches her she flies right over the side of the boat and away in the cindery wind.

The anxiety of the dream wakes me up, and I lie feeling at first traumatised, then annoyed at the obviousness of it. *Tell me something I don't know*, I say to myself. But still, I am unsettled, and it takes me a while to reabsorb the known landscape of my room, the solidity of the black outside my window. I have been told that in cities – big cities – there is never real dark, or real quiet, just the continual electric hum of concentrated life, serviced by shops and taxis and clubs. People stay up until the day begins, and wake up before the end of the night.

I look out of my window into the soft absence, a vanished world, the silence ruffled only by the movement of the wind, and think of London. I comprehend it only as a strange place, a place of lighted windows studding tall black skyscrapers, of perpetual motion, of a noise I can only imagine as a roaring singing, a clattering, purring musical forest of voices. With the sound of London in my ears, I go back to sleep.

When the day of my early morning flight (booked because I didn't want to miss a moment of my first day, intensely regretted when the alarm shrills at three in the morning) arrives, my father and Sadie drive me to Inverness airport, where we all stand around in the terminal, my father pretending to watch the departure screens, eyes submerged, Sadie expansive with emotion, hugging me and wiping away her own extravagantly shed tears, me frightened, dry eyed and dry hearted, because I can't quite feel this as a *moment:* it is just a strange gathering at an airport, standing between the familiar and the new.

'I promise I'll look after Evan for you, hon,' Sadie says.

'I'm glad to hear it,' I say politely. I wish I were glad, but all I can think of is that by the time I come home my mother's photographs will have moved from the dining room to the drawer of her possessions, and then from there to the attic, where they will begin the process of de-charging their emotional energy, until one day they are thrown away.

I don't think Sadie *seeks* to push my mother out in this way, but her presence alone is making it happen: without intending to, Sadie will overwrite her. There is an uneven-looking wall in our house, because Sylvia used one pot of satin and one of matt when she painted it, but when she realised her mistake she just laughed and said it had character and, anyway, she was damned if she was going to paint it again. This story is being replaced with Sadie saying, '*Your mom must have been a great decorator*,' and one day my father will look at the wall and notice that it is looking shabby and repaint it, and that will be the end of that.

It is an intense relief when finally my flight number slides up on the screen and I can leave the edgily packed concourse, saying the last of my several goodbyes, waving at my father and Sadie.

'Be safe,' my father calls behind me, as I pass through the doorway. 'Be careful.'

Encased in the neutral plastic alienness of the plane, watching the dark land contract and disappear under the clouds, I find I don't have to think about my mother and father. I rub my face with a shiny and unhelpful paper napkin, sit back, and close my eyes.

I think about the local vicar in Ullapool, who put a sign up outside his red stone church: *Jesus died for our sins*. It caused a debate among a community short of debating matter: some saying that the sign was too negative because faith ought not to focus on death but on life, while others argued that to remove it would be to sugar-coat not only the death of Jesus but also the dangerous extent of human sin, an example of which being the teenagers parking in the hills above the town in order to 'carry on' in their cars. The debate ended when someone graffitied *Thanks Jesus* under the words. To replace it the vicar put up a sign that read: *We only believe as deeply as we live*, which attracted no more complaints. Mrs Farquhar, who could be surprisingly sharp about some things, said that really the quotation was from Emerson and it didn't refer to belief in Christianity or even God necessarily. 'It could mean anything,' she said.

I don't believe in God or Christianity, but I have the susceptibility of belief. I venerate something I know nothing about, sacred because it gives me nothing, and I can't see it or understand it. I believe in the ineffable future, a place that will validate all my various longings: a place where there will be something wonderful.

PART TWO

Pity Demeter! She knows that the kind of young woman her daughter has become, a maiden with a new face and bare feet and an armful of flowers, is the most irresistible kind of woman for a passing man, or a passing god.

Ivy Ford

Persephone and Hades

My first perception of London is of the change in the darkness. This is no longer the soft thick comatose dark of the Assynt, but an electrically charged dark, awake and alive. When I arrive it is not even six o'clock and I leave the airport in a freezing stupor, standing shivering in the petrol fumes of waiting cars while the taxi driver loads up my cases. My first, half-asleep vision is of a wide black river, full of swimming lights. I can't see anything other than this flickering black strip, the motorway which speeds me to the centre of the city.

After a while the daylight comes, a grey dimness which lights up the rain-specked window. I can't tell where the sun is – something I have got used to knowing without realising it – because I can't see the sky from the taxi window without putting my face against it. My sightline is a variation of concrete, glass and brick, except when the road rears up on its great columns like a centipede, overshadowing shabby little shops and houses already dwarfed by towering structures with their company names blazing above the city. As we get nearer to the centre the buildings start turning to stone; embellishments erupt on them like lichen, magnificent in the pewter light. We pass some rows of trees and parks but they look wet and cold, an off-colour green, as if the sheen of smog has tarnished them.

I feel shocked and strange. I watch the streets, trying to see everything through the window of the taxi, seeing very little. A few images distinguish themselves: a red bus, a man with dreadlocks sitting on the kerb with his feet in the road as if he is paddling in a grey river, stacked vegetables outside a tiny shop, being rained on.

And then, finally, my own narrow street, my new house – in a thin Georgian terrace with the same yellowish, patterned brick as the rest of the houses in the row. After I pay the taxi driver I stand in front of it for a moment, under a still-humming streetlight. The house looks neat and prissy, with its shiny roof and spinster's necklace of railings. It has an air of being drawn up against me and my presumptuous suitcases; as much as to say with a tucked-in mouth, 'And *who* . . . are *you*?'

Once inside, the house's frigidity collapses into a dispirited cheapness. I peer through doorways at a brown and cream kitchen, magnolia walls, dourly dark chests and wardrobes in a sitting room turned to a bedroom, hard, grey acrylic carpets. Brought out by the noise I am making, two girls come down into the hall to meet me.

Both of them, without humour, introduce themselves as Claire. Claire Hetson is a big flat-bodied girl, with pale skin, the kind which looks thirsty for light, and faint brown hair that reminds me of the pond-water tea I had at the airport. She arrived at the house first and informs me that consequently she has taken the largest bedroom. The other Claire – Claire Brayne – is small and dark with ferocious eyebrows and a thinly moustached mouth. She arrived second and now occupies the second-best room.

'You ought to put your things in the room you want, before the last girl arrives,' she advises me.

I tour the house with the Claires, while they explain the concept of the inventory to me.

'It's something we fill in to say what's damaged, so we don't get charged when we leave.'

'Maybe we could have a drink and get to know each other?' I suggest. 'Then do it later?'

'Better to do it now,' says Claire Brayne firmly.

The two Claires and I discover a dripping tap in the bathroom that has left its chalky scale mark down the pale blue sink, a patch of damp in the so far unoccupied bedroom, a damaged windowsill, and a boiler that coughs like a man dying of tuberculosis. The boiler sparks a debate between the Claires as to whether to include it in the inventory. One Claire believes it is a mechanical fault which we cannot possibly be held accountable for, though the other Claire says that her uncle, a solicitor, warns that assumptions such as this are often the ones people suffer for in court. Finally, it is added into the inventory, which has become thicker and thicker before finally spilling over into a second volume, Claire Hetson's notepad.

The two Claires ask me what subject I will be taking, and nod when I tell them, without further comment. The question itself seems to have stretched them to their conversational limits. Finally, we stand in the kitchen where Claire Brayne puts the kettle on and takes some mismatched mugs out of a dimly cobwebbed cupboard.

'So . . . have either of you got boyfriends?' I ask, having run out of other things to ask. Neither Claire has a boyfriend. 'I haven't either,' I say. 'Boys are in short supply where I'm from.' Silence from the Claires, so I forge on. 'That's the Highlands. Could you guess that from my accent? Neither of my parents are Scottish and I've always wondered if I had a Scottish accent or a combination of theirs.'

'I don't know,' says Claire Brayne. A box of saucepans sits on the worktop. One, upturned, reveals the name 'Claire' in white paint.

'Oh, your name,' I say, baffled.

'Yes, I put it on them all,' Claire Hetson says. 'When my sister was at uni, she said people just used all her pans, without asking.'

'The funny thing is that now there are two Claires!' I say.

'Well, my pans don't have my name on them, anyway,' says Claire Brayne.

'I could always add an "H",' says Claire Hetson.

I am feeling suddenly near tears. I pick up my mug of tea and peer in to see if any spiders have surfaced, trying not to think about home, where my father and Sadie will be sitting in the late sun, with a bottle of wine, no doubt; trying to miss me and failing.

It is almost afternoon before the last girl arrives. The first we hear of her is a protracted ring on the bell, as if she is leaning on it (which she actually is, having her hands full of bags). I rush to let her in and see her mother first, a vague statue-faced woman, who nods at me before turning and brusquely ditching her daughter; 'Goodbye, Camilla,' she calls. 'Work hard.'

I hear the ring of the name Camilla, prettier than the sparse Claire; a fitting evocation of Camilla herself, who rearranges her bags, takes her shoulder off the bell, and steps inside. She arrives in my vision like a cloud of petals, or confetti, something particulate and shifting, so that I can't see all of her properly. Only when she pauses and gets tangled up pulling off her two shoulder bags do I get the chance to study her unobserved, her plush, butter-cream hair hanging halfway out of a ponytail, pink cheeks and silver pumps, a striped scarf, the colour of sweets, a shirt emerging slapdash from her pullover.

Camilla shakes hands with the two Claires as if she is shaking them off her. I find my smile has leaped up before she even turns to me, and says; '*Hello*, I'm Camilla. Oh, you have such beautiful hair.'

~

A couple of weeks later, Camilla and I are sitting in her room with glasses of warmish white wine, while Camilla puts on eyeliner in a full-length mirror propped against her door. In the mirror her blue eye peers querulously at itself from under her fingers.

'Marcus said he would call me days ago and didn't,' she says. 'He's definitely been around. Sammy said she saw him drinking in the Queen's Head. Fuck!' Camilla scuffs at her eye-lid with a tissue.

'So who was he with at the pub?' I ask.

'He wasn't with a girl. Or do you think maybe he was? Do you think Sammy didn't mention it because she was being nice?'

'No, no, I meant was he with his housemates, or were James and the others there?'

'Dunno,' says Camilla, not really listening. 'Anyway, I don't see it as a competition between that stupid slutty whatshername and me. I don't even worry about her, actually. She went on one date with Marcus. That doesn't mean anything.'

I take a swallow of my wine to keep up with Camilla, who has nearly finished hers, and try to find a space to put the glass down. Camilla's loft room has gradually become like its owner; pretty, but disarrayed. A thin vanilla light turns to a haze on her clouded window pane, scatters itself like powder over the messy lavender bed, the crowded desk, the chair covered in clothes thrown down with regal carelessness, the fairy lights, collages of her sixth-form friends, wilting peace lily, violet Georgia O'Keeffe print stapled illegally to the wall, and pile of broken-backed chick-lit novels. My room is austere in comparison, furnished only with a small shelf of gleaming stiff books from the course reading list, and a laptop. My clothes hang in the wardrobe, failing to fill even the small amount of space allotted to them. The room has the temporary feel of a budget hotel room, a backstage area in which I dress, before going upstairs to Camilla's room.

In the breaks between the songs we play, the sound of the neighbours arguing can be thinly heard. It is far louder in Claire Hetson's room; which might be the largest but quickly revealed itself to be the worst located ('Karma at work,' says Camilla). When we see the neighbours outside, they ignore us apart from the occasional look of sidelong dislike. The woman is fat with crispy, banana-coloured hair, the man small and murine, having only their opaque eyes and wasteland complexions in common.

Camilla, who is proficient at placing people, has explained that the couple next door are what is known as chavs. According to Camilla, a chav is a nylony person bedecked with check patterns, hoop earrings, baseball caps, and unhealthy-looking babies. They hang around in groups, much like hipsters, emos, goths, yardies, and the many other bewildering tribes of London she is happy to describe to me.

Camilla knew exactly what to make of the two Claires, with their saucepans and facial hair. She calls them Brayne and Brawn, not entirely quietly, and in turn they bang on their ceilings when she plays music at high volume, or when our group gathers in her room after going to clubs.

I have not asked Camilla what group she belongs to. I can detect something privileged in her messiness and the muddy estate car of her mother; I notice the photographs of her riding a gleaming brown horse, her casual references to the woods or lake at 'Longthorne', which I have realised recently is the name of her house, and not a village. I have never really thought that much about class before but now I understand more fully that it is not just something you are – upper, middle, lower – but something that can be owned, so that you *have* class. Camilla and her mother have class, that is obvious.

I don't think I have class. Perhaps, just as wondering whether you are mad means you aren't, wondering whether you have class shows that you don't. My father technically doesn't have to work, which is lucky because his photography is not particularly lucrative. He was the son of rich parents, themselves the children of richer parents. Their money sat still as time passed, unlike working money, the active money of business people. The stillness of the money pervaded the house where my grandmother Laure lived, my father told me once, a thickly carpeted, velvet-curtained tall house, where the ticks of the old clocks made a soft chocking noise, absorbed by the weight of dusty fabric and silence. The money has been worn down by each generation, but it is enough to pay for the Assynt house, and for my tuition fees.

In contrast, my mother's family had a prosaic, small yet capable amount of money. When she was a child she lived in a new suburb in Dorset, with a housewife mother and a teacher father, and a new car every three years. I have no idea about my great-grandparents on her side, or what they did, which is another good indication that I don't have class by English standards.

'Persephone Triebold isn't a very Scottish name,' Camilla observed early on, in what I thought might be an attempt to place me. Then, as has happened many times since, I had to explain my English mother, Swiss father, and Greek forename. It is an unsettling process; as if my identity is scattered, and I am trying to herd up its various elements into something sensible. At first I thought these multiple origins might – as at home – prompt people to infer something shifty, shady about me. But I seem to be the only person to whom this occurs. Camilla and the other people I meet simply praise my looks or my accent, or my name, which they say is unusual, or pretty. I am accepted fast into a group of girls who fall naturally into Camilla's and my orbit, like the ball bearings in a game settling into their pre-ordained holes. It seems that I have been placed after all.

The dim light of the day outside is darkening in swathes across the sky. Through the glass I can see the wisteria that scales the back of our house; the flowers vanished from its malnourished limbs long before I came. Nearly everything I can see from the window – even the birds, the grubby, shabby pigeons – is darkly grey, apart from what is artificial; the flaring window of a bar at the end of the street, boards around a building site plastered in layers and layers of Day-Glo club posters. I can feel the cool on my back, flowing from the old sash window into Camilla's scented, overheated bedroom. October has no patience with the outgoing summer; any residual heat has been cleared out to make way for the cold, which trickles under doors and down the chimneys, finds its way through apertures in the bed sheets, gathers dripping and chilly on the bath-room window, jabs mercilessly at the exposed, white skin of Londoners at play.

'The taxi will be here in a minute,' Camilla says, tipping her wine glass up to drink its last drops.

'This top doesn't look quite right,' I say, looking at myself again in the mirror.

'It looks amazing,' Camilla says, but though I admire Camilla – her self-confidence and her pink and white loveliness – I do not exactly trust her judgement. I have already noticed that the dark turquoise of her own top doesn't suit her, something I feel guilty for noticing. I don't hunt for the flaws in others – make-up shorelines, awkward teeth, sloping breasts – but I don't seem to have any control over the way my eye picks them out, like moving points in a vista.

I notice my own faults too, inexorably; I am familiar with the process of covering them and worrying about them. My breasts that aren't large enough, the scar on my knee from a fall when I was young, my stubby fingers. I also have a birthmark on my stomach that looks like a constellation of spattered coffee, one of my lower teeth points slightly the wrong way, and if I don't wax I get a dainty moustache, the same colour as my hair.

I don't know what I would say if Camilla asked my opinion on her outfit, which she never does. Probably I would say the only thing that seems to be acceptable, among my new friends: 'It looks amazing.'

The party tonight is at Marcus's house, which is why Camilla has booked the taxi early, sighed while I changed my shoes, rushed through the wine, and hurried us out to collect the other girls from halls. She stares at her watch now like a general, one silver pump nodding impatiently.

'I thought you said you were avoiding him?' I ask. 'Until he called you?'

'Oh, I've been avoiding him all week and it hasn't worked. I haven't seen him at all! Besides, it's a party.'

In our first week of university Camilla optimistically called a house meeting to discuss with the two Claires whether we might have a party of our own.

'You can invite all *your* friends,' she said generously (meaning a few other awkward-bodied girls and Claire Brayne's new boyfriend, a bum-fluffed stumbler known to us as Wrong John). But the Claires frowned quite heavily upon the whole idea. Claire Brayne's eyebrows actually met in the middle, as Camilla observed afterwards. We were already in their bad books for changing the television channel to *Hottest Celebrity Scandals* while one of them was recording something, and for throwing out one of the frying pans. 'All the non-stick was peeling off,' I explained to Claire Hetson.

'You should have asked me before you threw it away.'

'We'll replace it,' said Camilla. 'Anyway, someone threw out my pasta bake.'

'Actually that was me,' I said. 'It was disgusting.'

'When are you going to replace my pan? It wasn't cheap,' Claire said.

'I *beg* to differ,' said Camilla.

After that, and the fact that I forgot to buy another pan, relations between ourselves and the Claires have become so strained that I can feel the atmosphere vibrating like an elastic band when we all have to be in the same room.

Fortunately, Marcus, whom Camilla met on her philosophy course, lives with three stoners and an absentee female with a locked door, and so his house has slipped into an eternal weekend; drawing in excitable students with their bottles of vodka and small plastic bags, like magic potions which will make them dance, and be funny, and have sex in other people's bedrooms.

We collect our friends Laura and Sammy from halls before the taxi rejoins the flashing traffic.

I am the only one who peers out of the window on such journeys: everyone else, sitting in the clamour of perfume and coats and handbags and clinking bottles, takes the view for granted. I look out on a London that is dim and cold and smoky. The people on the pavement, lit by white streetlights, sail along on a tide of rain and litter, the scurf of the streets that blows in as soon as it is swept up. Some people are sequinned and meandering, some shabbily blanketed and static, some suited and hurrying. The London I see is dark, and garish, and hungry, like a medieval king in exile. Like me, it seems to be looking for something.

The girls talk as our taxi pushes onwards through the traffic. We establish things; that Camilla 'definitely' likes Marcus. That Laura also likes Marcus, but this becomes a 'maybe' when she meets Camilla's eye. That Sammy wants to 'see what happens' with Ben, who may or may not come tonight. That everyone suspects that James – who has a girlfriend – likes me, after we danced together last week at Moriarty's: an oddly Victorian-feeling dance, chaste motions vivid with sexual implication, like a rehearsal for the real thing. James gave me a look that said, I want to but I can't. I gave him a look that said, Maybe you can.

'I don't think so,' I say. 'He has a girlfriend, remember.'

'Who no one ever sees,' Camilla says. 'He hasn't gone home and she hasn't visited him once. He's probably hiding her because she's some embarrassing school-girlfriend. I give it a month tops.'

The hall of Marcus's house is so full of people that at first I imagine they are queuing for something, but it turns out that every room is so overcrowded that in each doorway there are slow-moving twin currents, of people moving inwards, and people leaving. The party seems to have divided by meiosis into several smaller parties, with different music rushing from doorways and meeting other music headlong, so that in the hall there is a curious layered sound, like several orchestras tuning up at once.

We pass through what was, over a hundred years ago, meant to be a dining room, in which hip hop drums from the stereo and a group of people are tapping and trimming tidy little lines of coke on a wardrobe door balanced on two chairs to make a table. On a laptop in the corner a porn film is playing with the sound off: a Thai girl, her tennis game interrupted, lies with her legs in the air, her face serenely patient. Then we reach the epicentre of the party, the sitting room, where a joint hovers from one of the wreathed hands to the next, like a bee visiting flowers, and smoke hangs in the doorway to the kitchen like a curtain. I can't identify if any of the figures beyond the curtain might be James.

Camilla finds and starts talking closely to Marcus, who is already looking over her shoulder at an attractive girl with a Cleopatra fringe. Marcus is one of James's friends and, like him, is admired by the females of King's. He has very dark hair and sleazy eyes. According to gossip he is fabulously well endowed; his penis flits through the mythology of the university like a unicorn, rarely sighted but much discussed. Camilla says the rumour is true, claiming to have 'felt it through my jeans'.

Wanting to cross the smoke curtain into the kitchen but quailing at the idea of actually finding James, who I want but am not sure what to do with, I go out into the hall, where there is now a staircase queue for the house's sole bathroom. The queue starts straight at the bottom then sprawls drunkenly up the turn in the stairs like toppled dominoes. One girl has fallen asleep on her step. At the top of the stairs a window is open and a cold wind blows through, a wave of wintry darkness, passing over my hot face. Sammy, who is at the front of the queue, grabs my arm and pulls me into the bathroom with her. I sit on the edge of the bath and look away scrupulously while she sits on the lavatory, skirt bundled over her knees.

'James is looking hot tonight,' Sammy tells me.

'He's here?'

'He asked after you, actually.' She stands and flushes.

'Oh . . .? What did he say?' I ask.

Sammy, apparently not hearing me, is leaning her forehead against the dirty mirror. 'What am I going to do about Ben?' she says. 'I like him so much. Why did I sleep with him? Do you think he still might call me? Should I call him?'

I hesitate, alarmed. I am still not at ease with the girls' habit of asking each other questions like this. I worry that if I tell her what I suspect to be true – that Ben believes that he will be able to sleep with several more girls before term is out and is therefore unlikely to limit himself to just the one sexual partner – and advise Sammy to avoid him, this may not be the case after all and I may be obstructing the course of a great love. But then if I tell her not to give up hope, or to call him herself, her disappointment might be worse. I am too timid to take on this sort of responsibility. In any case, my friends don't really listen to others' opinions. They absorb advice eagerly, eyes shining and abstracted, mouth slightly parted, then they do whatever they were always going to do.

I settle for patting Sammy on the shoulder closer to me. 'Maybe wait until tomorrow and think about it then,' I say, comfortingly. 'Let's get another drink.'

After administering wine to Sammy until she looks more cheerful, I reach an intoxicated state where people seem to move like fireflies through my vision, and when I finally drift into the kitchen, the fluorescent light falls with what appears to be a holy haze, a halo of beatification, on James Cass. He catches hold of me and I put my arms around his neck, receiving a kiss on the cheek and a glimmer of his drowsy tobacco scent.

James meets all the usual criteria of good looks: blond hair, a muscular body and a winning smile, though his eyes aren't inspiring. He has other bad points, which I totted up yesterday with Camilla. For one, he isn't very witty. And from the way he smiles affably when people say something obscure, I suspect I might be cleverer than him. But he has a thoughtless, generous confidence, bright as a coin, and his smile really is exceptional.

Before I can ask James a few of my pre-prepared questions, Camilla appears, walking through the crowded people in the kitchen as if they are less solid than herself, brushing through them like cobwebs. As she gets closer, I can see she is not quite steady, the light in her eyes diffracted. She takes my arm.

'We *have* to talk.'

In the little garden, a cracked paved area surrounded by long grasses and bindweed, with a residual smell of the neighbouring pizza takeaway, Camilla complains that she has just seen Marcus kissing another girl.

I put my arm around her. 'I'm sorry,' I murmur.

'He's such a slag!' Camilla cries.

'Men can be slags?' I am pleased to hear it.

'Yes, or sluts, or tarts, or floozies. Did I tell you he said yesterday that he thought if he were to fall for anyone at uni, it would be me?'

'Yes.'

'And he said I had pretty eyes . . .' she sniffs. 'Oh, well, fuck this. What time is it? Let's go to Becky Myers' party.' Becky Myers is a very good example of a slut, tart and floozy, and I have no intention of going to her party. They usually end up with Becky and a few men playing strip poker, or else a premature comatose ending after Becky and her housemates take too much ketamine. Camilla is looking stubborn, though, and I can see Marcus in the window stroking the face of the girl with the Cleopatra fringe. I sigh. What appears to be James's elbow moves into the frame.

Inspiration strikes me. 'Why don't you take Sammy?' I suggest. 'She's only here because she was looking for Ben, and he's not around.'

'He's shagging that red-haired girl from your course, that's why,' Camilla informs me. She never has much patience with others' problems with men, it all having been used up with Marcus. 'Sammy needs to move on. How are you going to get home if we both go? Laura left already.'

'There are a few people I know here, I can go with them.'

'Okay, darling,' (another thing I am not yet at ease with, the terms of endearments the girls use. I feel self-conscious when I copy them and standoffish when I don't) 'just call me and let me know you're home safe, all right?

By six o'clock the party has thinned and contracted into little groups here and there: the LSD enthusiasts in the upstairs bedroom, three girls comforting another on the stairs, weed-smokers in the dining room, the mostly male lager drinkers in the kitchen, reluctant to stray too far from the black bin filled with bottles and melting ice. Marcus and the girl with the Cleopatra fringe have managed to clear the sitting room, lying haphazardly together on a flabby leather sofa, legs knitted, mouths intent. I am beginning to worry that James has left without my noticing when I meet him in the hall.

'There you are!' he says. He reaches out one hand towards mine as if to take it, then seems to realise this is not appropriate. The hand drifts back to his side, where it hides itself, embarrassed, in his pocket.

'Camilla and Sammy have gone to Becky Myers' party,' I tell him with mock despair. 'I'm marooned.'

'We'll take you back,' James says. 'You live near us, right? I think the guys will be ready to leave soon. Harry's passed out and someone's glued dried pasta on to his face. I haven't seen that before . . . it's much better than magic marker. He looks like a monster.'

I have no intention of sharing a cab with 'the guys', who to date have not taken a taxi without one of them being sick in it. 'Oh, that's really sweet of you, but I ought to go now. I've got an early seminar tomorrow.'

James hesitates, looking at me. 'I'll come with you now.'

'Oh no – you should wait for your friends,' I say, triumphant. We to and fro politely but the deal is done and he puts his beer down carefully on to the floor, like a sacrifice to the spirit of the party.

'You're not leaving, are you, James?' asks one of the girls on the stairs suddenly.

'Yeah,' he says, waving vaguely, and then we are out into the cold night, my feet skimming the ground, freezing in my insubstantial coat. I am in a bewilderment of anticipation, but as we settle into a cab diagonally opposite each other a distance falls over us and we talk with a kind of elaborate consideration, stilted and slow.

'So, when are we going to meet your girlfriend?' I ask. James never talks about her, but I'm not sure if this is an indicator of a relationship in its last stages, or a kind of love so intense he wants it all to himself.

'I don't know,' says James. He gives an uncomfortable shrug. 'She's a bit . . . stressed, with things. Me being here. But there's not much I can do about that.'

'Stress is difficult,' I say, wisely.

'I can't imagine you being stressed. You seem very calm. It's nice.'

'Well, I try not to worry about things.' I shrug.

Actually, at this moment I am worrying that I am wearing an old flesh-colour bra which under a top gives my breasts an egg-smooth roundness; but if uncovered, will look like something unfortunate and surgical. I am worrying about what to do if he tries to kiss me: whether I should do the right thing and remind him of his girlfriend, or kiss him back, take him to my house and try to get the bra off before it is seen.

James is talking about his future in accountancy, or banking: I'm not sure which and it's far too late to ask. Then he pauses, and says, 'I feel like I can talk to you. When I talk to . . . other girls, I feel like there are things they want me to be saying. Because of their plans, or some idea of the future, or whatever. But with you it's like I can say what I want to say.'

'Be careful,' I say. 'I might be judgmental.'

He treats this seriously. 'But you're not. You're—' he breaks off. 'You hear everyone complimenting you, I know.'

'Not at all,' I say. I tip my face down modestly, though my fingers are tight around each other with expectation. But James doesn't elaborate on what compliments he might be tempted to bestow on me if I were not already over-burdened with them.The taxi stops outside my house, too soon, stopping the conversation along with it. We say goodbye hurriedly and embrace, leaning awkwardly across the taxi seat. James looks both sly and unhappy. Then he is driven away, without looking back or waving.

I loiter for a moment outside in the strangely still street, under the fraudulent yellow of the lamp-post, without feeling cold: the nervous energy that built up in me during the ride home still charged, still circulating. At this time in the morning even the people arriving home late have already gone to bed and the road is as deserted as a frozen lake. Only the wind can be heard, a sandpapery noise, as if its edges are scraping the new frost off the pavement.

I try to follow the instructions of the note on the front door – 'Please come in quietly, Camilla and Persephone' – then make myself a cup of tea to take to bed. Finally I check on Camilla, who is lying on her bed with the lights on, fully clothed and snoring. Her face is crumpled sweetly in sleep and her perfume rises, faded, a prim, floral scent at odds with the wine-dotted top falling away from her breasts and the stain of red lipstick on her mouth. I pull her shoes off and put the duvet over her. Then I turn off her lamp and her fairy lights, close her door, and go to bed, where I drink my tea and contemplate the text James has sent: 'Sleep well X', as if X is either his or my secret identity.

I don't sleep well. Darkness blooms under my eyelids, but my head is dazzlingly lit. I dream I am back at the party wrapped in my duvet, befuddled and nervy, talking to James on the phone. His voice is unfamiliar and comes from a long way away, and I suspect I am not talking to him at all, but someone I don't know. In the end the dream moves on to the narrow pebbled beach facing Loch Broom, the water hissing in and out, like the artificial fog over a dance floor.

At King's College there is a distinct sensory clash between the high-minded past and the mundanity of present-day learning. The Strand campus is pale, haughty; a cold palace behind a barnacled, castellated façade. But the dingy smell of academia haunts its lofty ceilings and long corridors; its grandeur is half obscured by the influx of students, the out-of-date posters curling on scarred cork noticeboards, the cheap green carpet, yellow-paged hardbacks, dead pens and thirty-year-old plastic chairs.

I am sitting in a lecture room trying to feel with my fingers how puffy my eyes are from the previous night.

'Leadership can be separated from management,' Dr Thame is telling us, far at the front. 'But managerial leadership increases as one moves up the organisational hierarchy.'

I write this down. I have learned to write what I hear in my lectures without listening to it, to absorb it at a later date. My attention is actually on the notes from yesterday's nine o'clock lecture, about which we have a seminar later in the day. The seminar leader is Dr Bending, a slightly crazy lady who said on our first meeting, 'Persephone, eh? That's a rather weighty name. I hope not an inauspicious one!'

I frowned at her, because the name was my mother's idea. Before I was born, Sylvia wrote it into the first pages of a blank baby album, the kind with pink ribbons on the front and a little plastic window to be filled later with my face, a creased uncooked pastry bun looking like any other baby's face. When I study the photograph I can only identify myself from my eyes. Shiny, short sighted, but speculative, as if they know something is up, but not exactly what. This is what my mother wrote: *Persephone was a beautiful and much adored goddess who represented the seasons. She was loved more than anything by her mother Demeter. Even when they were not together, she was always in her mother's thoughts.*

The writing is dusty looking now, as if it might blow off the page; its black has gone grey-blue. But it is there still, evidence of life.

'Of course, there is charisma. This is important for transformational leadership, though it is hard to define and measure.'

Dr Thame's pen squeaks illegibly on the smudgy white board. I wonder if James will be at Moriarty's, our favourite club, tomorrow. I saw him outside a lecture talking to another girl and decided to walk past rather than interrupt them, but he noticed me and came over quickly, smiling, leaving the other girl where she stood. Afterwards I wondered whether that showed he was more interested in me, or whether he might already be involved in some way with the other girl, and had come over simply to prevent himself being found out.

'Think of it as the four I's. These are on the handout. Idealised influence. Inspirational motivation. Intellectually stimulating. Individual consideration.'

I circle the four I's studiously. I wonder what James's girlfriend looks like. Nobody seems to know. There was supposedly a picture of her in his wallet when he first came to university, his friends said, but it isn't there any more, and nobody has met her, not even in the first weeks of term.

'Five behavioural aspects – this is Conger and Kanungo 1998, the reference is on your handout. Now, they identified "performing unconventional behaviour", which is of interest . . .'

I wonder if the girlfriend has lost interest in James too. This is a difficult idea, because if she has lost interest perhaps there is something deficient in James, something essentially short term in his character, so that any process of getting to know him is simply a countdown to an invisible best-before date. But then – if she hasn't lost interest and he has, I am wishing for something that would hurt her.

'Okay, and finally the other side of charismatic leadership – lack of other leadership skills, for example. Which brings us to . . . turn over your handout, please . . . possible catastrophe for the followers.'

After my lecture I stand waiting for my bus under an umbrella, relieved as always to be still, better able to track the moving city around me, which is too much to comprehend when moving myself, so that I end in a blank, muffled state, focusing only on the people I need to avoid bumping into, the edges of the pavements and the mouths of the streets. In Central London there is always something in motion, a door, a sign, a car, a person. Stop anywhere and ten things will have passed you within a few minutes. Back in the Assynt, I could sit so still for so long that it would seem as if everything had stopped, paused indefinitely. But it is nearly impossible to get the measure of the places I go to in London, because from one minute to another everyone has changed.

When my bus arrives, cheerful in its red like Father Christmas, knowing it is just as hoped-for, I follow the routine of boarding like everyone else. At first I was dismayed by the buses but now I am used to them – more used to them than to the swooping, howling trains of the underground, the dead air of their black tunnels. The trains remind me of children's toys with their garish yellow, red and blue plastic: toys that have been graffitied, dented and torn by the angry children.

On the buses, unlike the underground, there is at least some regulation in how many strange people can press against you, judgement being meted out by the battered-looking drivers. Even in this the drivers are capricious; at times they sail half-empty past stops full of people, at others they stack us to the ceiling. If I get a seat, I have developed a technique for preventing people I don't like the look of sitting with me, which is simply to look them in the eye as they come down the aisle towards me. It seems to trigger some animal response and they will walk further down the bus rather than sit with me. Then when a tidily dressed woman appears I gaze intently out of the window, showing I am no threat, and they invariably settle down with their coats and bags tucked up like mine, to prevent any touching.

This technique is not so successful on crazy people, however, who take the eye-contact as an invitation to talk. And London is full of crazy people. I have no idea if they home in from the provinces, drawn by the light like distracted, dizzy flies, or whether something in the air exacerbates their various conditions, but on almost every street there is someone who jabbers, stares or intones in their own untouched circle of the pavement. And the buses are worse, presumably because crazy people are too busy being crazy to learn to drive.

I assume that the first person I see talking to himself must be using a hands-free mobile device until I realise there is no winking silver bug implanted in his ear. He is a large man, with dark eyes set in wise, fatty wrinkles like an elephant's. A few weeks later he is joined by a small, pale rubbery man and they embark upon an inexplicable conversation in which neither is listening or responding to the other. Another regular on my bus route is a young man in an unhappy parka, who sits with his leg blocking the aisle and complains clearly and loudly to a point far past the window about the people forced to push past him.

Then there is a woman I only see once, a big woman in a ratty fur with ratty platinum hair who argues with the man next to her. 'I in't 'avin it,' she says. She stabs at her forehead to illustrate her point. 'Need' – jab – 'to clear' – jab – 'me' – jab – 'fuckinead.' I can't hear the man's responses – his voice is low level, upper class. He wears a ravaged suit. The next thing I hear, they're laughing. Are they drunk? They get off the bus after only one stop, passing back into the drizzly, hooting murk of the street, like Dickensian manifestations, grotesques as weary and mad as the city itself.

When I get back home, the Claires are nowhere to be seen and my own friends are occupying the sitting room, unexpectedly quiet.

'Shushushush . . .' Camilla cautions me as I start to say hello. She pulls me on to the sofa next to her and turns the television volume up on what appears to be the news. The screen is showing a woman behind her pastel-blue desk, saying:

'. . . in Italy. But now the former Lights musician and Booker prize-winning author is back in time for the publication of his third novel—'

'He's back!' Camilla shouts.

'Who's back?'

'*Leo Ford*,' says Laura.

I have seen my friends in this state, individually; they become vague and radiant, kittenish. Now this mood has descended over them all; they lean forward as if the television image is actually three-dimensional, clutch my arm and exchange glances. Something hums between them.

An airport is shown on the screen, from the point of view of a camera, chasing a man's back like a dog, in a pack of other people holding cameras. The man is indistinct, dark haired. I expect that he will be some bland, bald-faced boy, of the kind the girls usually point out on television, but I lean forward with interest too, catching the tension like a shiver from a draught.

The camera moves around, tightens its focus, and Leo Ford appears, lit up and shimmering in the flashes going off around him. It is a particular moment of vision – startling, throwing his detail and colour into high definition. His remarkable eyes pass over the cameras in greenish disinterest; he looks away, reaches a doorway, and is gone. The leisurely motion of his exit is entrancing, his smooth shoulder under a shirt with rolled-up sleeves, the brown of his arm, the denim on his hip.

'God,' I say.

'The novel will be released before the end of the month,' concludes the voice-over, to which none of us have been listening.

'One day he will be mine,' Camilla sighs.

'Sure he will,' says Laura, sideways.

I realise my hands are clenched between my knees and I loosen them, self-conscious, though in the general excitement no one has noticed my particular reaction. But I almost want to run away with it, take the discovery away for myself. What would it be like to know a man like that – to sleep with a man like that? I try to picture it, the way I have often rehearsed kissing James, but my mind can't do it; I just can't imagine how it would feel, to be close to such terrifying perfection.

~

Dear Persephone, writes my father – he has always favoured handwriting over emails, scratching out his humble little peaks and dips of ink across a thick page, carrying out his obsolete rituals of applying the stamp, travelling several miles to the post box – *I hope your course is going well and you are studying hard, etc. etc. Your new friends sound like lovely girls. University is the best time to make like-minded friends, who last much longer than circumstantial friends. Forgive your 'old man' – it wasn't his intention to start subjecting you to platitudes, and I'm sure you'd rather be enjoying the company of your friends than reading about them. I'm just so pleased you're happy. As you know, I do worry and I'm relieved to hear none of my worries were at all reasonable (as Sadie has repeatedly told me).*

There is a whimsical note to the letter that I haven't noticed in my father before, as if it had lain in sediment since – when? The death of my mother? – and it is only now that Sadie has swirled the water and his unexpected colours, his glittering element, has risen to her pan.

Sadie has decided to extend her visit to Scotland for a while longer, which is great news. She wanted to add a note to you:

Frowning, I read Sadie's note, written in a predictably rounded hand, punctuated by smiling faces.

Hi there, hon! I wanted to reassure you I'm looking after your dad, and keeping him out of trouble. How is everything? Hope you've found time in your busy drinking schedule to get down to some galleries! And don't forget all that architecture. We'll get fixed up so you can email us some photos. We'd like to see your girlfriends – and your admirers! Your dad thinks it's too awful of me to write this, but is there anyone special . . .?

Finally, my father tells me that this Christmas he and Sadie thought it might be fun for the three of us to go on a ski trip to Aspen.

I wasn't sure at first but now I think it will be a lovely change – and the setting will be very festive. I hope you like the idea?

I can picture Christmas now: my father's reclaimed radiance, Sadie's hopeful, stylised intimacy, me sitting with them at a decorated table like a lumpen foster-child, darkening the air around me: ruining it. I don't want to ruin it. I want their happiness to set into place; I know that my presence now, as a creature of the past, could damage their new relationship.

This would be an appropriate moment, sitting at the rained-on window with a letter in my hand, to cry about my mother. But I never knew her, so instead I compose a reply to say how glad I am that they are enjoying themselves, that I am indeed managing to see the sights of London as well as socialising with friends and keeping up with my essays, and that I will unfortunately be spending the winter holiday concentrating on my studies.

'Three years ago, not long after his first novel won the Booker prize, Leo Ford was arrested for the attempted murder of the American businessman Bruce Yelland,' I read. I am sitting on the draughty bus next to a man who smells of burning tyres, a glossy newspaper supplement on my lap.

Leo had joined his sister Ivy Ford on her boyfriend Yelland's yacht for a holiday off the coast of Sardinia. Four days later both Leo Ford and Bruce Yelland were rushed to hospital; Leo with a bullet wound in the shoulder and Mr Yelland with a near-fatal wound to the chest, from a Japanese sword that ornamented his yacht. Both men survived. Leo was acquitted after claiming self-defence. Bruce Yelland recovered but fled the country before he could be formally charged. A warrant was later issued for his arrest for importing and dealing cocaine.The circumstances of the altercation between the two men have never been explained by either, and the subject is strictly off-limits in interviews with the literary lion.

When the article – '21st-Century Celebrity Arrests' – moves on to its next entry I discard it and scan through the second of my purchases, a flimsy magazine with a large picture of Leo's face on the cover, green irised, appearing both vivid and shuttered, eyes guarded even as he looks into the camera. Inside, the same picture occupies a full page, in honour of Leo having been awarded first place in the magazine's '100 Sexiest Men' feature. A hot-pink heart shape of text hovers near Leo's collarbone, exclaiming:

Number One: Leo Ford. Yes, no prizes for guessing who. He was the hottest indie guitarist ever to hide under a mop of hair and mumble shyly in interviews before he quit music and broke all our hearts. But you can't keep a sexy man down and it wasn't long before Leo was back, minus the hair and with a prize-winning, smash-hit novel that confused and delighted the critics. As if it couldn't get any more romantic, Leo is something of a bad boy, taking on drug dealers with his swashbuckling sword play. Swoon! We may not understand this literary love god's fiction but he could probably read us like an open book: Leo, we want you! We want to have your children!

I half-read the rest of the magazine, which is designed only for half-reading, taking its cheap shots at the rich and famous, revelling in its own spuriousness like the teenagers who collect around street corners, cheerfully abusing the passers-by. It even has a page for showcasing the scars, stains and spots of celebrities, each one helpfully marked with a big red ring.

I think about Leo Ford, who could never be red-ringed with mortality. Now I've heard of him it seems he is everywhere, on walls, in the press, in bookstore windows, on the television. I hear his voice in radio interviews, the low, amused sound of it. The songs from his old band, Lights, are played in bars. The magazines contain nearly unrecognisable photographs that schoolgirls take of him on their mobile phones, entering restaurants or walking along night-dimmed streets. I hear the conversations about him around me as if I am filtering the air for his name: two students in a lecture wondering whether the sword or the gun was used first, two young girls on the bus planning to camp outside his house and get his signature, two old women in the park arguing over what the ending of his novel means.

Yet despite the appetite for him that scatters his image over the city, he is on one side of a very thick glass wall: he exists in a different life, the physics of his universe are different. The artificial proximity to his face on the magazine cover gives an idea of intimacy, but though his eyes send out their green flares like northern lights, it is not a beckoning signal: it is a warning, the black lashes low against the audience, the public, of which I am a part. The picture is not of closeness but detachment. Even so, when I look at his picture I feel the cold movement of longing, for someone who isn't even real, or certainly not real to me.

When I get home with my bag the two Claires are waiting for me in the kitchen, arms folded police-like.

'Hi, you two,' I say, giving them a smile I hope is friendly yet nonchalant. I don't want to bare my molars like a frightened mule, giving their complaint about noise or mess any credence.

'Persephone,' starts Claire Brayne, 'I know you and Camilla have a *hectic* social life –' ('hectic' is used in this context as a kind of swear word) – 'but the people you bring home—'

'It's the noise too,' says Claire Hetson.

'The *people* you bring home,' repeats Claire Brayne authoritatively, 'are stealing our food. I had a loaf of bread in the fridge, specifically for making sandwiches for lunch. Then today it was gone. That's just an example. Other things have gone missing too.'

'Like my pasta sauce,' says Claire Hetson.

'I didn't eat any bread,' I say soothingly, knowing that Laura, Alistair and Marcus had eaten most of the bread with honey, and Camilla ('I *have* to have soldiers with my eggs') had made herself toast with the rest.

'Well, I didn't eat it. And Claire didn't eat it.'

'I saw her having a sandwich earlier,' I say, to be difficult.

'That was the last bit of my own loaf. I kept it in the cupboard.'

'I wouldn't accuse you and Camilla,' Claire Brayne says, looking like she would like very much to accuse me and Camilla. 'It's just that you have to respect other people's possessions, and so you have to be careful about who you bring home.'

'And can you tell Camilla . . .' Claire Hetson says.

'I think you two should tell her,' I say. 'Look at what happens to messengers,' and take advantage of the silence that follows this by retreating from the kitchen.

I am innocent of food crimes; existing during the days on toast, packets of biscuits, and a token piece of fruit (so as not to feel guilty about my diet). When I hit an energy slump in the evening, I start drinking. Then at around two or three in the morning, I have some chips, fat and salty, for supper. I don't like to spend much on food. Cartoon-like, when I see a big ham or a steak it turns illusorily into a new necklace, or a bottle of vodka. Camilla, however, helps herself to whatever food is in the fridge, with the justification that she had bought some freshly squeezed orange juice which the two Claires guzzled. This reason has lasted her a good two months.

'Anyway, I always buy the loo roll,' she says. 'Anyone would think those two are too uptight to poo.'

But then, Camilla is the queen of the house, expansive and capricious, and she knows it. She has marked her territory: a throw on the murky sofa, her tulips on the table, Japanese prints instead of Claire Hetson's picture of an uncomfortable-looking tennis player.

Her disordered femininity lies carelessly and confidently over the house like the strains of music that throb down from her imposing closed door.

The Claires ask me to confront her, casually, so as not to give away their status as petitioners ('Oh, could you ask Camilla if she's seen my CD?'). Asking Camilla directly only gets them a startled, dignified stare, followed by a bewildering medley of denial ('I didn't take your CD'), diversion ('What's *really* the issue here, though, Claire?'), insult ('It's actually not *my* kind of music'), counter-attack ('So who drank my orange juice?'), and illogic ('I thought this was a house where we could all share things. We all drink out of my mugs, don't we? I buy the loo roll! But this is how you would like things to be. Fine, I'll *get* you your CD. No, I insist. I'm going up right now. I wouldn't want to part you for more than five minutes from a CD you haven't listened to for months!'). The outcome usually is that Camilla is pressed to keep the item for a bit longer ('Just until I can make a copy').

Sammy and Laura, who knew each other at school, have rented a flat together rather than sign up to the haphazard university accommodation scheme, and we spend a lot of our time holed up there, making plans. Today we are all packed in close on the sofa with cups of tea. It's morning but the curtains are still drawn, casting a dim mink-colour light over last night's wine glasses on the querulous-legged table.

The house of the two Claires smells generally of mildew and lemon cleaner. Here, there is the sour, spicy odour of last night's Indian takeaway and wine dregs, the sullen scent of marijuana, the ubiquitous girl-perfumes: sweet synthetic coconut, green tea, jasmine, vanilla, all layered over the underlying odours of rubbish and pine bleach, then of old carpets and wood-rot: a landscape of scent.

We are writing names down to invite to a party, a process involving much laborious scratching and stabbing of names, which ebb and flow, demoted and reinstated, circled or crossed. The paper on which the list is written looks like a colony of ants has been stamped to death on a white flagstone.

'George,' Camilla says questioningly. We laugh, because George has gradually, without any of us noticing, become Laura's boyfriend.

'We should make it a condition of him being invited that he's not allowed to go home before twelve,' Camilla continues. 'Or does he turn into a pumpkin if he stays out?'

'He usually has rowing in the mornings,' Laura says, frowning.

'So that's where he gets those arm muscles,' Sammy giggles, but Camilla is not to be deterred.

'Now that I think about it, if we have a party will *you* come?' she says to Laura.

'I came out last week,' Laura says, her cheeks flushed. 'Don't forget last week.'

'How could we forget?' Camilla says, and laughs lightly. 'It was like, your annual appearance. You should produce commemorative mugs.'

Laura looks away and Camilla carries on with the list of names. Sammy and I look at each other uncertainly. She raises her eyebrows in the direction of Camilla. I shrug back.

'Okay, Becky Myers,' Camilla says.

'No!' we all shout, and the delicate good humour of the sitting room, the golden female circuit, is restored.

Getting ready to go out has become a sacred routine, of four parts. First, I eat: only a little, to make it cheaper to drink. Second, I draw myself a new and better face, with shinier eyes, darker lips, livelier cheeks. When I was a child I used to love make-up, applying it precisely and reverently: the powdery-smelling lipstick given to me by Mrs Farquhar, some old blue eye shadow of my mother's, never worn. There are pictures of me as a long-nosed six year old with big blue-lidded eyes, like a featherless baby bird. I have my hand coquettishly on my hip, a shatterproof smile.

Thirdly, I get dressed, standing in the lamplight that turns the leprous walls of my room smooth and makes my face into a renaissance chiaroscuro, dark haired, flame eyed, romancing itself in the mirror. I sing along to the music; clothes fall in swathes on the bed behind me, bras and necklaces noose the bedposts. I settle tonight on a red skirt, which hovers in a vaporous bell over my thighs, and a boned top that shores me up like a crustacean carapace. Finally, once I am all stitched together, fixed with beads and spray and pins, painted like a fetish, I go up to Camilla's room with some vodka.

Tonight we arrive earlier than usual at Moriarty's, a club with a dark-domed witch's cauldron interior, hung with star-shaped glitter balls, the lifeless winds of the air conditioning sweeping down on to the blackly sparking dance floor. With no crowds outside, the shabbiness of the exterior is noticeable; the acidic-smelling lobby has the cool shadow of a car park, the public shyness before it fills. We make our way past the bouncers: fatty, big men who gather in their black suits like old bull seals. Then we take a scrap of paper from one employee, hand it to someone standing next to them who spears it on a stack, and go in pack-like, hunting our men.

I spend the night in much the same way as every other, half having fun, half watching out for James. He has been absent from our parties and nights out for the past week, which, I've heard, is because he is 'on a break' from his girlfriend. The word *break* sounds in my ears like something physical, like the crack of a bone. And surely it can only go one way from here. Once a bone is fractured it should be fixed together in a cast to mend, not left apart.

James is one of the first people I see, turned slightly away from me, part of a larger group of people I don't know well. I notice the confidence of his body at rest, leaning against a wall, not taking an active part in the female theatre that surrounds him but somehow necessary to it, so that it would collapse in a sigh of sequins and hopelessness if he walked away. Then he turns and sees me, and smiles his desirable smile.

'You made it,' he says. 'I was just asking where you were.'

'How long can you have been here?' I ask. 'It's so early.'

'Early birds and all that,' James says, and I am not sure whether he is making an oblique reference to me being the sought-after worm, or whether he is just blankly word-associating, so I settle for smiling at him vaguely, and we stand like this – smiling at each other – for a prolonged while. Meaning flies between us.

'You're drunk,' I realise.

'I can still spell your name,' he says. 'P-e-r-s-o—'

'No . . .' We are standing nearly nose to nose. His eyes are a silky grey; I can smell the evaporating alcohol rising off his skin.

'I . . . can't spell your name when I'm sober,' he says.

After that he offers to get me a drink and I go with him to the bar, where we talk playfully and insubstantially about pointless things, made important by their heavy, exciting layer of suggestion. The barman moves several times into my peripheral vision, then moves away, ignored.

'Perse!' Camilla has joined us and clings abruptly to my arm, insistent and open-mouthed with distress.

'What's wrong?'

The three of us turn to follow her finger, which lands on Marcus in the distance, kissing a short girl in a short skirt. As the girl stretches up to him the skirt rises, revealing the lower halves of her buttocks.

Camilla starts to cry.

'Oh, no, he might see. Quick.' With an apologetic look at James, who raises his hands indulgently, I lead Camilla away, into the blue-lit, crowded lavatories. Girls come and go and repeatedly try a door without a lock, like trains pulling in and out. I take Camilla into this cubicle, where she leans collapsed against the wall, and put my foot against the door. I hold her for a moment; she wraps her arm around my neck with a force that surprises me. She smells of beer and cider and blackcurrant, of decaying perfume. One arm trapped under her, I use the other to grope behind me for tissues, then proffer them in the direction of her nose, turned downwards on to my shoulder.

'I feel like I'm under a curse,' Camilla sobs. 'The men I like are always shits, and there are people who like me, who are really nice . . . But I don't *want* them! What's wrong with me?'

This complaint is familiar to me; Camilla has said much the same thing every week since meeting Marcus. I tried to talk to her last time, telling her, tentatively, to forget about him. But it is the advice she has forgotten: she puts her head down now and starts crying again. Mascara rills down the side of her nose, stains her crumpled, shaky lips. Her skin looks like softened wax, glimmering unhealthily in the wintry light.

I stroke her arm rhythmically with my free hand until she stops crying and sniffs periodically instead, railing at Marcus's faithlessness.

Then I get some tissues and run them under the tap, scrub Camilla's face, fluff her cheeks with powder, and hand her my eyeliner so she can redraw around the shape of her eyes. The make-up turns her face back into a cheerful face and once I've promised to drink some tequila with her, she leads us out of the lavatories with something like her usual enthusiasm.

After another few drinks I have to think more carefully about how I am moving, check that my limbs are performing correctly. As we dance, a constellation of broken glass crackles under my feet like sand, a blown glitter on the black ice rink of the dance floor. The light hits the hot smoke; I can smell the alcohol vaporising off slick, pale skin, the raisiny-sharp odour. It isn't long before James appears, moving through the people on the dance floor like a romantic hero striding out of the battlefield – except – as I focus better, I see he is not striding so much as yawing.

Once beside us he takes my hand and presses it with his own, reminding me of the hiker back in the Assynt, but oddly without the enchantment, the fervour, I felt in that moment. When drunk, his good looks lose distinction, slip slightly.

'Persephone, I . . .' he says.

'You . . .'

'James, you're really drunk,' I say, sounding to myself rather like a disapproving wife in a period drama.

'No . . .' James protests. He sways a little, knocking Camilla's drink.

'Good lord,' she says. 'You're a disaster.' She rolls her eyes at me then takes his arm, her usual authority apparently restored. 'Come and sit down. You need some water.'

James allows Camilla to escort him away to the sofas, where he sits with royal grace and the bonelessness of the very drunk.

I turn back to the others and we dance, but there is a fracture in my own drunkenness, which usually hangs over me like a warm, silvery globe, a lovely moon. The alcohol drains away, leaving me in chilly lucidity. I look around and become aware of my feet hurting; that I am being jostled. The dance floor is like a scene from a Bosch, my drink is a false, clammy sweetness in my mouth, my bare arm is wet where someone – perhaps James – must have spilt their drink. I consider going home, getting out before the lights come on and reveal the general neediness, the deterioration, the awkward milling of the previously uninhibited crowds.

Then Sammy looks suddenly over my shoulder, eyes horrified. 'Oh, Persephone!'

I expect to see another scene in Marcus's Rakes Progress around Moriarty's, but I see a different tableau over at the sofas: James kissing Camilla. I am so taken aback that I turn back around straight away, like someone recoiling from a spider.

'Right,' Sammy says sternly. 'Let's go.'

'Where?' I ask, worried that she is about to march me into a confrontation.

'Home.'

Outside, the pavement is covered by students, reeling, singing, drinking from the bottles they brought out under their coats. The noise of them fills the frosty street, joining the general sensory clutter of London; voices fly raucously up over the roofs, the sullen chimneys. The stately grey buildings have vanished into the blackness above us and all that remains are the swarms and blitzes of lights and advertising, the sizzling cars exhaling their exhaust fumes, the slippery vaporisation of chip shop and curry oils, the cigarette smoke, the bitter smell of the air conditioning vents, their hot air colliding with the cold.

'Want to get chips?' Sammy asks, and I nod. We stand in silent companionship for a while outside the takeaway, a heavy, hot packet of chips in my hand, as I look inside at the other girls: their uncovered, puckered flesh appearing over waistbands and under short skirts, like creased marshmallow, collapsed sofa cushions. They eat too much, they drink too much, and I – my lips stinging with salt and my fingers slick with oil – am becoming like them.

When it starts to rain we discard the chips and get into a cab. Once in its leathery smooth interior, with its neat signs about not eating or smoking or vomiting, I feel I am enclosed in an orderly, kind little universe. The wind and sleet of the tarry sky has vanished, whirling powerlessly outside the windows. Sammy's scent, honey and almonds, is reassuring. She strokes my hair and says, 'I think you can do better than James anyway. Laura's friend was in a lecture with him and he didn't know what apartheid was.'

I lean against her and listen to her voice comforting me, its sweet crooning movement, its murmured rises and plunges. I hope that in the morning, when I am sober again, everything will become clear.

PART THREE

Persephone holds out the flower. It hovers in the air between them.

'You can't give it back now,' extemporises Hades. 'It's already picked.'

'But—'

'You picked the flower. I can't give it to anyone else now. You have entered an obligation.'

'I didn't realise . . .' Persephone falters. Hades presses his advantage.

'And I've come such a long way to meet you. Come to Hades for a few hours.'

'I have to be back before dark,' Persephone says.

'I'll make sure you are,' Hades lies, ushering her into his chariot.

Ivy Ford
Persephone and Hades

The next day I wake up in the same position I must have passed out in, lying like a felled tree heavy across the bed, arms thrown out as if in violent death, all my clothes still on. I get up and begin the melancholic process of undressing and redressing. I wipe my make-up off, watching my eyes and mouth shrink and my cheekbones recede, remembering what happened last night.

I check my bag and find a text from Camilla on my phone (*Where are you?*) which was sent around two-thirty, about an hour after I left. This turns my soft bruise of hurt into something harder and cooler. An hour with James: an hour in which I was forgotten by both of them.

I listen for the usual sounds of movement in the room above me – shuffling, bed-creaking, even a male cough – which, thanks to the age of the house, usually arrive dim but recognisable in my room. But I can't hear anything to tell me whether the silence above is inhabited by either of them. After a couple of hours I begin to worry that Camilla is upstairs alone, with alcohol poisoning, and that her last memory as she is taken away in an ambulance will be of me being angry with her, so I go upstairs with two cups of tea.

I find her in bed, swaddled like a caterpillar, face hidden. I prod the duvet uncertainly and she moans. Then her pink and white hand extends frailly from the cocoon to accept her cup of tea, and finally more and more of her face appears, plump eyed, rosy and puffy with alcohol-sleep.

'Are you angry with me, Perse?' she asks in a tragic voice.

'No,' I say.

'He likes you, not me.'

'I don't want him to like me,' I say. 'I'm not interested in him. If you like him that's okay.'

'I don't like him! I didn't mean to kiss him. I just felt shit about what happened with Marcus. Whom I've probably ruined things with now.'

'I don't think he'll mind,' I say. 'So what happened to you after . . . you know?'

Camilla pulls the pillow over her face as if to hide from the question, and groans exaggeratedly.

'Oh it was awful, Perse. I was so drunk I just didn't know what I was doing. James said "Let's forget that happened" to me, like it was a horrible thing but it was all my fault and so *I* was the horrible thing. Then he went home and I realised everyone had gone home and I was really drunk. So I was just, like, reeling around the club and then I bruised my knee tripping on some steps, and then I kissed some other guy who was really ugly just because I felt so crappy. Then I had to escape him so I got a taxi home. Oh, it was all such a *disaster.*'

I murmur something soothing and pat the highest of the peaks under the duvet, my hurt leaving my body like a resigned sigh; unable to maintain my anger at Camilla, who obviously never meant to hurt me, and has – as always – ended up only hurting herself.

Laura, who stayed home last night, calls later that day to tell us that she recorded a TV interview with Leo Ford for us to watch. We all gather in her and Sammy's sitting room, where Camilla retells the story of her awful night; her bruised knee now a cut-open knee, the ugly guy now hideous. Camilla and Laura laugh but Sammy makes enquiring eye contact in my direction. I shrug.

'Thanks for recording this for us, Laura,' I say, to change the subject.

'Oh yes!' Camilla cries, clapping her hands. 'There are *some* benefits to you two staying home like an old married couple. Let's watch the interview!'

'He never normally does interviews,' Sammy says. 'And especially not on television.'

'That just seems so unfair.'

'Yeah, he owes this to his fans. To us. Buying someone's book should give you some claim to see at least five minutes of them.'

'Five minutes of *all* of them.'

The first few minutes of the interview are missing and so the recording begins with Leo Ford sitting in a chair. He is still, but perfectly easy. One leg outstretched, shirt-sleeves pushed up. At the open neck of his shirt there is a brief dive of tan skin, mysterious solidity. The camera moves closer as if it is being drawn in, focusing on Leo's face, his eyes the colour of sea edges, horizons, mountains: distant things. I watch him with an unhealthy, leaping feeling, as if nervous of the proximity.

The woman interviewing Leo resembles a bisque doll in her structured navy dress, painted hair and unyielding eyeliner. She is held in place by her high-gloss styling but her mouth falters, her eyes are pleading, and it is obvious she has fallen for him too.

'Back in 1998,' she is saying, 'you and your best friend at university, Tom Farrell, formed the indie band Lights.'

On the screen behind Leo newspaper headlines appear, awkwardly brash. Leo turns and looks at them. The pages say, 'Fainting fans provoke health warning', 'Praise the Lord, it's Leo Ford', 'Leading Lights', 'London concert riots'. There are pictures: of his languorous-eyed grip on the microphone, his cherubic hair. The Leo of these foggy grey photographs doesn't look happy. His younger face is calmer, stiller, than his face now. He looks collected, as if he has mentally gathered everything belonging to himself, and hidden it.

'Lights was extremely successful during its brief run. It shocked the press and your fans when, a week after you completed your first major UK tour, the band decided to quit. Since then Tom has continued his career in music, while you retreated from the spotlight. Was your difficulty with fame the reason the band parted ways?'

'I think it was a large part of it,' Leo said. 'Tom probably got sick of my complaining about it. He used to draw moustaches on me every time he found me asleep, which I think was his way of expressing resentment. Even today, I still wake up at the slightest approach. It's like having SAS training.'

'You didn't foresee how famous you would become – how much interest the public would have in you?'

'I was nineteen,' Leo said. 'Foresight was not one of my strong points.'

'I get the impression you're still wary of media attention, as this is only your second television interview. Don't worry – I'm going to learn from the first and *not* ask you about your love life.'

'Ask him!' cries Camilla, anguished.

Leo laughs.

'Is it just the subject of love or do you feel uncomfortable with any sort of personal discussion?'

'It's unnatural,' Leo said. 'Normally when you talk personally it's to a friend. Except you take away one of the friends and replace them with thousands of people you don't know. And the friend isn't telling you anything – you're the only one speaking. If anyone in the world feels truly comfortable with that, I'd question their sanity.'

'And yet it's part of the bargain you make with fame,' the interviewer teases.

'That's what my publicist tells me,' Leo says, smiling.

'So with that in mind, I'm going to – tentatively – ask you about something personal.' Leo sits back slightly and watches her without speaking. She is bothered by his disapproval – her hands twitch like mice – but she presses on: 'The incident in 2005 that led to your arrest – would you say that has affected your work? Has it made it harder to write, or have you found the opposite – that it has inspired you in any way?'

The question congeals in the air for a protracted moment, in which the interviewer almost winces, and Leo frowns. Then he says: 'I think it would be misleading for me to claim that my own life doesn't influence what I write. But whether I personally understand how every environmental influence contributes to my character – and consequently to what I produce – that's different.'

'But consciously, has it affected you?' the interviewer pushes.

'No.' They stare at each other for a moment before Leo, in what I think must be a deliberate gesture, uncrosses his arms and sits more easily, as if to soften the answer.

'Has anything in your life affected your writing in a conscious way? For example, many people have commented on the remarkable female characters of the novels: Athena, Anna and now Dolores. Are any of these characters based on women you know – old loves, perhaps?'

'You're getting back to the love life question,' Leo observes.

The interviewer holds up her hands in mock surrender. 'Okay, moving on, obviously you have a rather interesting family . . . your father, William Ford, is the head of Carson's bank, your sister Ivy is a prominent academic, with a book of her own published not long ago – have any family members made it into your fiction?'

'Half-sister. And no, I don't let family into the books. Firstly because it would make them think they are more interesting than they are. Secondly, it can make Christmas dinner uncomfortable. Thirdly, it's slightly insulting to assume a writer has copied a character from life. It implies we don't have the ability to create one ourselves.' The interviewer looks chastened, and Leo changes his tone, 'Of course, we might steal a piece or two of someone, if we think we can get away with it.' They both laugh.

'God he's hot,' whispers Sammy.

The interviewer looks relieved. Leo looks amused. They are both aware he doesn't like the questions, but he is tolerating it, he is not unkind, and the interviewer is grateful.

'Will there be another move in your career?' she asks. 'Obviously you have gone from music to writing. Will you go from writing to something else entirely? Or even back to music?'

'Well, I knew the music was something temporary. I was only a singer and guitarist – Tom did all the writing. I didn't see myself as a musician. But then, I don't necessarily see myself as a writer, either.'

'Do you see yourself as an actor, perhaps? Are the rumours true that you may star in the film of your first novel, *Athena*, expected to go into production next year?'

'Not at all true,' Leo says. 'It wouldn't be appropriate.'

'It will be disappointing to many fans. Inevitably some readers, possibly people who went to see Lights perform just so they could see *you*, will buy the books as another way of seeing Leo Ford, rather than for the book itself.'

'I think that's pretty hard on the readers – and the books,' Leo says. But he knows she is right, I can tell. He doesn't like it; his eyelashes lower over his expression.

'I hope no one would read a book simply to see the author,' Leo continues. 'Because if the writer is any good, they should never be seen, even if they are writing about something they have intimate experience of. You should never become aware through a clumsy interjection or image that another person – a human being – has written what you read. It would be like the stage curtain falling down. The words and story should stand alone, impermeable, and an object in their own right. The author should be . . . someone who briefly doesn't exist. A vanishing act.'

From university I move along the rain-black streets like a rat travelling through an underground pipe, only going forward, nose lifted to the wind. In the Highlands I used to stroll, now I scurry, like everyone else around me. This part of my walk home, even on a sunny day, is not lovely: the shop lights surfing the scummy air like chemicals on the surface of a dead river, the roads choked with traffic, cars gathered up tight together against the rain, pavements crowned with litter and cigarette butts, the hard colour of road signs and damaged phone boxes and adverts and fluorescent lights blazoning themselves over the grey and cindery face of the street.

I pass the usual inhabitants of any London thoroughfare: the group of aimless teens on the corner, the loaf-faced man staring madly at the concrete bin, the foreign students with their primary-coloured rucksacks. In the traffic a growling noise creeps along behind me, a twitchy bass line and a frantic booming overlaid with male shouting.

The music reminds me of children banging saucepans. The car, a shiny four-wheel drive, gets just ahead of me and stops at the lights. Its contents, four young men, watch me when I walk past again.

'Hey, hey,' one shouts. I smile evasively and look down, neither encouraging nor hostile, then they pass on, just like everything else.

I have been in a strange mood lately. Reading Leo's first novel – lent to me by Camilla – didn't help. Despite what Leo said in the interview I spent the duration of the story trying to see him in it. It is about a woman called Athena and her lover. Athena is intelligent and sternly idealistic but it ruins her life. She sees too much around her that makes her unhappy. Eventually she kills herself. The tormented lover ends up a middle-aged family man living in a fake Tudor house in a new suburb, driving a people carrier. The cover of the book says it is an ironic fable, but I felt it as more like an odd dream, one that leaves you with a feeling not of sadness, exactly – more an absence of sadness, which is even worse.

The last couple of weeks have been stressful, with disputes in the house and an unusually high workload raining down on us. James has called a couple of times but I haven't answered, though I remind myself that to feel upset or betrayed by his kiss with Camilla is not fair, that privilege being accorded to the girlfriend on the other end of their break.

Camilla herself is in a twittering, snappy state because Marcus, with whom she has started sleeping again, didn't get her a birthday present and now she doesn't know if they are in a relationship or not. I feel sorry for her, but I am frustrated with speculating about him, bored with her seeing every television show or film as nothing more than a reflection of her own frustrated love affair. Surely she must know he just doesn't want her; not enough, anyway. Not in the way she wants him to.

Near our road there is a park I cross every now and again, and as I walk across it now I have the sense that the time I have been at university has bowed in on itself as if finally tired of travelling, tired of newness. Nothing has changed in the weeks since I last crossed the park. Even the other people passing through the park seem the same, sharing a stoic ambivalence, heads downturned. I breathe the scent of the air, the leafy chill, the smell of cooling water. It feels to me as if there is something desolate in it.

I remember the wasted, frustrated feeling that shunted me away from the empty Assynt mountains, the feeling of containment, as if I were trapped in a heavy glass, like a shot of alcohol, evaporating. This feeling has not left me since I arrived in the glare of the city, but rather has lain low, gathering force. It returns now like a kick in the heart, harsher and stronger than before.

I think of the great and vague ideas I had about coming to university; the longing for love, or excitement, for something that would clarify me. I am frightened that I am slipping further away from this, settling into a low-level existence, like a monk who has seen an unclear vision, and never again recaptures or gets close to that moment where he glimpsed something finer, and was uplifted.

The television interview with Leo Ford keeps returning to me, along with that feeling of unsettlement I had as I watched, an increasing awareness of the thick glass wall that divides public and personal. To Leo I am part of the public: I am external. The more I see of him – even if I went to a book signing and faced him across a table – the more impassable and obvious the glass wall would be. There must be a way of crossing it; like a wasp sensing its way across a pane – if I can just fall back, move a little to the side, and find the window that, somewhere, must be ajar.

*

The Christmas holidays approach, burling and bullying their way into the shops, draping themselves over the lamp-posts and windows, chiming and flashing like a fruit machine. Soon my friends will go back to their families and I will stay behind in the deserted house. To forestall my father's worries about my being alone I told him that I would be spending the holiday with my maternal grandparents in Dorset. Though I led him to believe this would be a fortnight's visit, I'm actually planning to stay with them for a week. The other week is set aside to carry out my masterful idea.

The idea, it has to be said, is not exactly original. I know that the post-box of the publishing house Bendricks and Blake is likely to be full of hormonal applications to slave over a photocopier or kettle with the promise of a glimpse – just an eye-graze – of Leo Ford. Now that he is releasing his third novel there is no newspaper or magazine without him in it somewhere, refusing to pose, yet still folded in between the pages, his eyes lifted to the reader's with a small shock of intimacy. He is credited with bringing new literacy to teenagers, or to half of them, anyway.

However, I have done my research and applied for work experience in the reference book division, which – though I can't hope to be stirring Leo's coffee – is nonetheless in the same building. I am welcomed for a week in December, in which I expect some convenient scenario will arise: being stuck in a lift together, for example, or passing him in the corridor and dropping a sheaf of papers.

'What!' Camilla says when I tell her about it. 'That's so cunning. You'll *have* to run into him. I can't believe I'm not going to be around to hear all about it. Phone me! Actually, tell him to phone me.'

Then later she looks at me, puzzled, and asks: 'Why didn't you tell me that's what you had planned?'

'I didn't want to jinx it,' I say, and she nods understandingly.

I'm not sure why I didn't tell Camilla. More often, lately, I have felt unsure around her. I can see that she hasn't changed – she is still affectionate and charming and impulsive – but the longer I know her I can also see that, like a handful of glitter thrown into the air, these things obscure some of her less appealing behaviour.

Despite this, she is still my best friend, and when she goes back to Longthorne for the holidays I miss her. Her noisily inhabited room is an emptiness directly above me, and I feel the absence of her bright head, which I have been used to seeing appear around my door at unpredictable intervals. When there is a noise I even glance up at the door, as if she will be there, loud and impassioned, asking what I make of Marcus's latest text.

I prepare myself with vigour for Bendricks and Blake: I scrub and polish and tone and curl and paint and spray. I dress in new, smart clothes bought for this purpose: clothes I tell myself are not just for this week – not at all! – they will be useful for job interviews and so on in the future. They are an investment. Despite this, I feel guilty, not so much about the clothes themselves but about my ability to pay for them.

I bought the clothes with an allowance that has been accumulating unspent since the beginning of term, because my father, not knowing how much money I need, has given me far too much. The torrential allowance comes rolling in generously and frequently, like a puppy: its eager good humour encourages me to treat it lightly. And when I do, I feel a shame made worse by my lack of accountability. It would be easier if my father knew how I wasted my money, if he could be angry with me, but he is miles and miles away, trusting and believing in my good heart, my sensible self-governance.

Despite my efforts to clothe myself in serious professionalism, I am not noticed at the office. It is hard enough for me to make friends with the strung-out inhabitants of the accounts department, where I have been initially posted, and I give up all hope of befriending any of the executives who slip in and out of the offices like poured cream, rich and silent, or the editorial high rollers who roll busily past me in the corridors. The days pass and there is no sign of Leo. I am beginning to realise that it was ridiculous of me to expect him to visit the office in person, that he would accept what his publishers offer him – proofs, advances, humble advice – over expensive lunches, or at his own house.

Trying a different tactic on Thursday, I return to smoking – a habit I haven't felt the need for since coming to London – in order to lurk outside with the others bemoaning their addictions in the festive sleet. In this they are the same as all the smokers I've ever known. In the summer, when their colds and yelping coughs are gone and they don't have to stand in the rain, they will forget what a miserable thing it is to be a smoker.

Standing with them, in any case, brings me no luck. The human resources smokers keep to themselves, the secretarial smokers keep to themselves, the accounting smokers form their own group, and so also do the two editorial assistants, huddling with black-rimmed glasses and put-upon murmurings. It seems that anyone really important has a more important place in which to smoke.

I do overhear one conversation between the editorial assistants, standing as near as I can to them with the kind of neutral face that instantly gives away one's eavesdropping.

'Sarah from publicity was complaining about it this morning,' one of them says.

'Don't they know when he'll be back?'

'Nope. Never do. He just goes AWOL and there's nothing anyone can do about it. Sarah said all the stress just gets passed down to her. She's thinking about leaving.'

'Then she should. She's shit at her job anyway. Remember that press release? She needs her own proof reader.' They laugh.

'Anyway, she shouldn't complain about him. He always comes back in the end. And he basically keeps this company afloat. Have you seen our accounts? Red, red, red; Leo releases a book, black, black, black.'

I realise my cigarette has nearly burned down to my fingers and hurriedly drop it. It's my last and so I have to leave, though by this stage the two girls are talking about where to get lunch, agreeing definitely not at the place around the corner because someone once found a fingernail in one of their panini, and wondering whether it's pretentious to call a single panini a panino, when even the place selling it calls it a panini. Of the missing Leo Ford I hear no more, not a whisper, for the rest of the week.

The only friendly person I meet in my time at Bendricks and Blake is Michael, a fellow flunky from the fiction department above, who I chat briefly to at the photocopier. We arrive at the same time:

our eyes meet over the stacks of paper. He has a stubby childlike face with small glasses and large hopeful hair: his hair actually being the most forthcoming thing about him, flopping and bounding glossily, like an enthusiastic spaniel.

'You go first,' he says politely.

'Oh, no,' I say. 'Please.'

'You must be new here,' he says, and laughs. 'I've seen some nasty scenes at this photocopier. The one upstairs is always breaking so we foray down to use this one. It's a bit of a turf war, actually.'

'I'm just doing work experience,' I say. 'I won't tell them I saw you.'

'Ah, work experience. You must be having a terrible time. I remember it as slave labour.'

'Oh, no, I love it. I was allowed to use a computer yesterday. And I've got my own pen from the box in the cupboard.' I show it.

'I'm Michael,' he says, extending a hand.

'Persephone.' I take the hand, which is new and soft. I guess that he can't be much older than me.

'And how are you liking the Underworld? Sorry – you probably get that all the time.'

'You're the first. And the Underworld suits me fine, thanks.'

'How long are you on work experience for?'

'Actually it's my last day today.'

'Ah,' he says, looking serious, perhaps disappointed. 'So, are you thinking about going into publishing?'

'I'm not sure,' I say honestly.

'Rightly so. The pay is awful. They know there are always hundreds of other graduates slavering for your job, that's the problem. But, if you ever need me as a contact . . .'

He takes out his pen and writes *Michael* and a number on the top sheet I am holding. This is the first time I have taken a number from a stranger: not knowing the protocol, I quickly write my own number down for him in exchange. He steps back, then forward again, as if in a strong wind.

'Well, I'll let you get on,' he says. 'But, even if you don't want a career in photocopying, we could get lunch sometime.' He sounds casual and humorous enough but for a moment he peers at me, quickly, in a curious way – one I have begun to recognise – and I wonder if it was a good idea to give him my number simply because he was the only person all week to be friendly to me.

'That's very nice of you,' I say, neutrally. 'Thank you.'

'See you soon,' he says, gathering his paper up. His hair gives a hopeful shrug, we say goodbye and the lift gulps him up.

I write a Christmas card to Camilla, as promised, admitting that I have nothing to report. ('What a waste of a week!' I write. 'Not so much as a sniff of Leo Ford. All I've got is this lousy pen.') But then, I don't know if I ever really expected to see Leo. He is not entirely something I can believe in. His books are there, his photographs, but Leo is what he said he wanted to be, an invisible hand, a vanishing act.

The next week I leave for Dorset to spend Christmas with my maternal grandparents. I would rather have stayed in the London house, but the rules of Christmas force me into the welcoming arms of my family. I travel down on the whining, acrid train with its wrathful plastic colours, looking out into the unfocused chill of the exterior world, the land that lies in drifts of whiteness, stripped trees poking scratchily through, like witches in a fog.

My grandfather Jack remarried a while after the death of my grandmother Ellen, to a woman also called Ellen, who my mother apparently always got on well with. When talking about them, I refer to the newer Ellen as my grandmother, often forgetting that a switch was made at all. It occurs to me that, if I have children, that is how they will think of Sadie, a realisation that is unexpectedly painful.

Jack and Ellen themselves are grey and white and quiet, their features eroded by wrinkles, the colours leached out of them. They talk about the weather and gardening and cookery. They prepare for potential heart conditions with daily walks, and invite the vicar over for Boxing Day dinner. In their red brick house everything is as conventional as it possibly could be. I sit with them and watch Christmas specials of sitcoms and soaps I have never watched, in front of the tree, which is artificial. I remember this tree from a visit when I was small; I put my nose into it and sniffed up a snuff of dust. Even the decorations are the same, brought out every year to occupy their traditional places. There is nothing in my grandparents that reminds me of my mother.

For their part, Jack and Ellen are delighted to see me; they never ask why I haven't visited them sooner. It doesn't occur to them that they should be hurt rather than grateful. They have bought me ring binders and a little pad to rest my wrists on when I type, which they have seen in one of the strange catalogues that appear in the mail, advertising shower radios, fake cats to dissuade real cats from the garden, orthopaedic slippers. They also give me a strangely horrible rainbow scarf and hat, which they have obviously decided is the kind of thing young people wear.

Jack and Ellen ask about my father and Sadie with unclouded interest. I don't know what else I was expecting from them, really – my grandfather's eyes to fire behind his glasses, Ellen to clutch her breast and denounce the American floozy? But instead they have gone online as Gramps76 and downloaded her holiday snaps from the Internet.

Later, my father calls and we all gather around the telephone as if it is an old-fashioned wireless, waiting our turns to swap pleasantries. When I take the receiver I hear a surprising amount of nothing: not the expected crackle across the miles of snow and water, the hiss of distance, just a quiet room with music playing in the background – carols, recorded bells – and my father's voice saying, 'Hello . . . hello?' as he does when I am more than a couple of seconds late in replying. 'How has your day been?' he asks, as if concerned.

'Wonderful,' I say with automated enthusiasm, conscious of my grandparents' presence, before I realise he is asking about my day not only because it is Christmas, but also because it is the first Christmas day we haven't spent together.

'I was thinking about stockings,' he said. 'And how I ought to have posted one to you. I don't know if it would be quite the same.'

'I was on borrowed time with the stockings anyway,' I said. 'I was hoping nobody would tell you they're just for children.' My father doesn't laugh, which makes my own laugh sound silly: a false squeak, a tinkle of nothing. At around this time I would normally be helping him make the roast dinner – this time for me, not for him. In America it is 8 a.m. Stocking time.

The ensuing conversation with my father and then an excitable Sadie tires me, so that when I pass the telephone on to Ellen, I only half listen to her side of the chat. Evan has always spoken softly, his consonants too gentle to penetrate the plastic of a receiver, and I can't make out his voice at all.

The most important part of my grandparents' day is watching the Queen's speech, which the Queen appears to participate in under duress, immobile, her face angrily grey. I look out of the window instead at the indeterminate view, the grey and white of the sky melting on to the land, and I can half believe I am in a floating world, the top of a cloud, which has drifted off from the rest. The snow, the wet coldness, the fake tree and the chattering television, they are enervating me, drinking me up like a spirit. I am looking forward to going back to London.

The only place I find my mother – aside from the photographs of her that hang over the fireplace in the sitting room – is her old bedroom. My grandparents have not changed it, in the way of parents whose children die young. The mattress is new but on the pine bed frame I find a little carved heart, in an unobtrusive place, done roughly, as if with a compass. I run my finger over it, imagining that it has been left for me.

The flowered brown wallpaper is old, crackling at the edges, with a thin smell of dryness; the curtains are perfectly preserved brown velvet. I can see patches on the walls where there must have been posters, and marks of Blu-Tack. I ask my grandfather if they were pictures of actors or singers. He laughs and says they were all pictures of horses, from a phase of Sylvia's.

I didn't know about the horse phase: I add it to my collection of my mother's likes and dislikes, the familiar list remembered and recited by my father like a well-counted rosary, until I could say it by heart too.

Sylvia liked the magnolia at the gate to our house, sometimes pausing when she passed it in full billowing bloom, just to stand under it for a moment. She liked Ovid and Homer. She liked to get up early in summer, when the sun was cool and glittery over the mountains, but in the winter she would hide in bed until it was light, depressed by the dark. She loved her rock records; Led Zeppelin, Cream, Jimi Hendrix, though my father tried briefly and hopelessly to get her grooving to Bach and Fauré. She liked making her own bags and bandannas, and once attempted (and abandoned) a smock. And she liked horses, at least for a while.

It seems strange to me that I can know all these things my mother liked, and by doing so feel as if I know her better, but Sylvia will never have that. She must have wondered before she died what sort of person her daughter would become. It must have made her sad to know that she wouldn't find out. I will always be a stranger to her, a blank space. My likes will be a mystery. But then, when I think about my list of likes – clothes, alcohol, men – I'm not sure that it isn't better this way.

I arrive back in London a day early, partly because I had run out of sensible things to say about gardening or cookery, and partly because sleeping in Sylvia's room was beginning to give me strange dreams. Once back I spend a lot of the time catching up on overdue work at the library, where I run into Sass, a Sloane from my course who has the mild eyes, silky hair and intelligence of an Afghan hound. I don't know her particularly well, but I quite like her, and my house is empty, and so I promise to go for a drink with her that night.

The same day I get a call from a number I don't recognise, so I leave it and wait to check the voicemail: 'Hi, Persephone, it's Michael, from Bendricks and Blake. Happy New Year. Thought I'd catch up and say, er, Happy New Year . . . which I suppose I've already said. It'd be good to see you for lunch or a drink some time.'

I don't want to leave this kind message hanging in the ether, like a rejected handshake, simply because I suspect Michael might be attracted to me, so I call and tell him I'm out with some friends tonight and we should all try to meet up. I say it casually, to communicate that this is not a date.

'Great, well we're going to a place called Spook tonight. You should really see it,' he says, so neatly that it is impossible to detect whether he is responding to my signal or whether he never intended to suggest a date to begin with. 'It's not very easy to find, so I'll send you directions. Also, there's usually a queue, so it's better to arrive early or you might not get in.'

'You're not exactly selling it to me,' I say.

'Trust me. It's worth it when you get inside.'

Spook turns out to be an unmarked door in a West End alleyway, lit by one suspended lantern, glowing chloride green. The small queue outside the door is the only indicator of its purpose, and we join its end. In the few minutes before the door opens more and more people arrive to stand behind us, forming a line all the way back to the street. I look at the clientele with interest and attempt to put them, mentally, into Camilla's tribes. A few hipsters, indie kids, scene kids, punks, rockabillies – or perhaps psychobillies – fashionistas, trustafarians, but mostly miscellaneous, drinking as they wait, apparently used to the process.

When the door opens several of us file through, past a doorman who nods without speaking for us to walk down the tight-angled set of stairs, into a long, barely visible corridor, a brick-lined midnight tunnel. I brush the wall with my hand in the darkness, checking its closeness, feeling the damp that blooms out of its pores.

'What is this place?' Sass says in my ear, and because I am thinking it too I answer more confidently than I feel.

'Oh, it's worth it when you get inside.' And then, thankfully, it is. At the end of the corridor is another door, which opens to show us the secret of Spook: a series of large, vaulted rooms that must once have been cellars. We walk through one room of silver antique mirrors and baroque sofas upholstered in a smoke-colour fabric, the lights directed upward so that a lifting veil of dark rises and falls above the room while below it we move in a clear evening, across a dance floor as reflective as a reservoir. In another room a small crowd are gathered around a dancer who stands in front of a projection of columns, veiled thickly as a lampshade, arms thickly braceleted, removing her first veil. Another room is filled with silver balloons, reflecting our own faces back at us as we wend between them: curved faces, fawn-like with surprise.

We find ourselves a seat next to an ice-cream van dispensing shots of tequila and stare around, silent for the moment.

'I guess you were right,' says Sass.

Sass and I spend an enjoyably tipsy few hours watching the mutable scenery of the club, discussing nothing in particular – university gossip – and I only remember that I am meant to be meeting Michael once we have already left. I am waving Sass off in her taxi and looking for another when Michael enters the tall mouth of the alleyway.

'Persephone! Are you leaving or arriving? You're leaving! I'm sorry we're late. I had to wait for the girls to get ready.' He gestures at the backs of some women entering Spook.

'Can I persuade you to come back? Come on. Just one drink.'

'I do have to go . . . early start tomorrow,' I say, and add, because he looks guilty, 'but I've had a really good time. I'd like to come again.'

'You like it here?'

'God, yes. I haven't been anywhere like this before. My friends and I always go to the same places every week. I thought when I left Scotland that I was going to be experiencing city life and meeting fun, new people but so far university is just another bubble. A closed loop.'

'Then you should definitely come back. Meet my friends. They may not be fun but they are at least new. And I can give you more information on publishing. If – that is to say – you're interested.'

'I think I'd rather meet new friends than discuss publishing,' I say.

'So, you decided it isn't for you?' he says.

'I don't know what *is*,' I say honestly. 'I suppose I ought to do something related to my degree. But I'm not sure my degree is for me, either.'

'What do you study?'

'Management.'

'Oh,' he says. There is an awkward pause, then we both laugh.

'It is that bad, then,' I say.

'Don't ask me. I can't even manage my own hair.' The hair in question is, today, rising up in unexpected crests before dropping again, skirting jauntily over one ear. 'Anyway, it's not the law that you have to do something directly related to your degree. Most people don't.'

'What did you study?'

'Er, English literature.' He smiles apologetically.

'Of course. I guess that'll be useful when you're promoted up from photocopying.' As soon as I say it I realise from his apparent embarrassment that he must not be the young office flunky I took him for. 'What *do* you do at Bendricks and Blake?' I ask, curious.

'I'm an editor,' he explains, 'though I really just edit Leo Ford.' The name breaks on my ears like a foamy wave, like a shower of sparks.

'Oh?' I find I am able to say, my mouth moving in my steady

face, 'I've heard of him. I suppose that does sound like more fun than photocopying.'

We laugh and he looks at the row of taxis, believing that I must still want to leave, and says, 'So, shall I call you when we're planning our next outing?' I'd like to carry on talking about Leo, but I can't do it subtly, so I don't try.

'Yes please,' I say. Nervous, I lift my hand to push my hair back. The hand is shaking, so I drop it to my side. My voice, I am grateful to hear, keeps talking, automatically and lightly. 'Is this where you usually come?'

'Fairly often,' he says. 'We have to pick our places according to how much hassle Leo gets. Things are very chilled out here. But anyway, the next drinks are on me. As an apology for my lateness.'

'I couldn't let you do that.'

'Feminist principles?'

'Exactly,' I say, though really it is more to do with Leo not seeing that his friend is buying me drinks.

'Well then, see you next time.'

In the taxi going home I am emptied with shock, until the news solidifies, becoming more real and probable to me, and I wrap my arms around myself as if to contain it. I am beginning to understand that something mysterious and wonderful has happened tonight. At last. I meet my eyes in the driver's mirror: they are wide and glittering and I look away, unnerved by their wildness.

The news continues to gain weight as I am carried through the night streets, until it reaches a point where it is genuinely true, and then I begin to worry. I thought at first that perhaps Michael was attracted to me. But now his status has been revised from a paper-carrying flunky to the editor of Leo Ford, his interest is beginning to look like charity. He made polite contact with a struggling student

– a friendly offer of help – and I told him I wasn't interested in publishing and now I won't ever hear from him again.

My other housemates arrive home the next day: Claire Hetson asking immediately where the last of her jam went, Claire Brayne noting that there is a leak in the sitting room that corresponds to the position of the bath tub above, Camilla arriving last and late just as she did on the first day we met, throwing herself into my arms with a fervent cry of how much she's missed me.

'It's been so lonely without you,' I tell her through the creamy hair in my mouth, grateful to have her back. I am not asked about how my Christmas holiday went – it being assumed that it was as uneventful as everyone else's – and I am grateful for it. In the cold light of term time the whole idea of Michael becoming my friend, and through him, meeting Leo, seems not just improbable but absurd.

The main topic of discussion has been that Marcus is now 'official' with a girl he met skiing at Christmas: information that has seen Camilla take to her bed for nearly a day, receiving only tea and biscuits and malicious rumours about Marcus's new girlfriend. But as I sit handing Camilla tissues I begin to feel exasperated with her, lying prone and sodden in her heap of pillows. All of the girls react angrily to Marcus's behaviour – 'That shit!' – but he has never pretended to be anything other than a shit. He is like a hot coal that Camilla keeps trying to hold: if she stopped trying to hold him she wouldn't get burnt.

By the next night Camilla has recovered in time for a party held by someone Sammy knows through someone else, a connection no one can make any sense of, but it seems everyone is going. ('You have to come with me,' Camilla says, 'I can't face it alone if Marcus is there with *her*.') And so I find myself sitting with her and about thirty others in a room with a dark green carpet and murky green wallpaper, surrounded by old bikes, trolleys and beer cans, like a village pond full of sunken rubbish.

The conversation turns, as if forced by my silent will, to the subject of Leo Ford.

'I heard he was gay,' says one of the boys, with finality.

'Yeah, he's blatantly gay.'

'Oh, just shut up,' snaps Camilla, her drink slapping the side of her glass. 'Just because he's *cultured* and is ten times cleverer than any of you.'

Even the girls can't agree on what kind of a person Leo Ford is, however.

'I think he must be promiscuous,' says Sammy. 'He's got those flirty eyes.'

'No way,' Camilla says. 'He's a true romantic.'

'Speaking of romance, James is single now,' another girl says, with a look in my direction. I had wondered about this when James called me a few nights earlier.

'I'm back in London,' he said, as if I had been waiting for him. 'I'd like to see you. Just us.' I listened to his voice, the flat electric pulse of it, all his charm stripped away. The bones of his voice were easy to refuse.

Since his kiss with Camilla I have deconstructed him, like a psychologist conducting a study behind a one-way mirror, and concluded that aside from being good looking there is nothing astonishing about him. Without being stupid he isn't clever, without being unpleasant he isn't kind. He seemed interested in me without asking me any questions: rather, he made his own observations about me as if they were statements of fact. I marvel at how I went after him – walking through the dark towards the neon heart suspended ahead of me, but when I arrived, there was nothing there after all.

The room is smoggy with the heat of many people, the open window behind me breathing icily at my neck. I pull at my dress, worried it is sticking to my hot and cold skin. Tonight everything is exactly the same as it was before the holidays: here are all the usual materials of a party. The people dancing in the sitting room; a couple of overdressed girls in skirts and tall heels clinging erotically together, bracing each other. The girl sobbing on her phone in the wet garden. ('But why?' she cries.) The room from which issues the bittersweet, musty smell of marijuana and tobacco, the people doing lines on the sticky kitchen side. The drunk girl telling everyone about her messed-up past, her tragic tale, a boy being sick out of a window, a couple in a bedroom who have pushed furniture against the door, a couple in the bathroom, several people outside, shouting and knocking.

Camilla, next to me, smiles when I look at her. 'Great party!' she shouts.

'I'm going to get some air,' I say, and stand up. On the way out into the hall I find myself cornered by Marcus, who smiles as if in enjoyment of his own reputed villainy. Only the want of a moustache prevents him from twirling it.

'Are you on orders not to speak to me?' he asks. He inclines his head and I follow its direction, to see Camilla hurriedly turning away as if she is talking to the person next to her, and not watching us.

'No. Don't be silly.' I have always felt uncomfortable around Marcus, unwilling to flirt with him in the exaggerated, courtly way I flirt with the other boys of our group, not only aware of Camilla's feelings but cautious of his own uninterrupted gaze, the smirk of interest.

'I don't believe you. You always do what other people want you to. Like Camilla. She bosses you about. But then, you're sweet and nice, so you go along with it.'

'You know all this about me already?'

'Just guessing. Maybe you're not so nice underneath. Who knows? That nice thing might be a big act.' He raises his eyebrows, waiting for me to argue. He is standing too tall, angled too near.

'I'd better go,' I say, flustered and prim.

'Feel free to come back any time,' Marcus says, waving as I leave.

When I come back with a drink and sit back down again Camilla raises her eyebrows at me.

'You were having a lot of fun,' she says, with a pristine disapproval that only her blue eyes, blond hair and white skin allow her to pull off.

'Not really,' I say.

'Persephone,' Camilla says loftily, 'if you want to get together with Marcus, just do it. You don't have to lie about it to me.' Hurt, I don't say anything. After I finish my drink I leave early, reasoning that as I had only come out to support Camilla, my perceived failure in this task allows me a pass home.

When I get back I lie in my bed, half-drunk and exhausted by effort, staring through the dirty cold condensation out of the window. I thought I would love London, and I do love it, but in a sick way. I feel like I'm drowning in it. I saw on television that a day in London is equal to smoking fifteen cigarettes, that the pollution even makes it warmer, which is how escaped green parakeets can breed and form their flashy colonies in the parks, where the tops of buildings are still visible, the sounds of passing cars and the jabber of voices still audible. There is no silence, no stillness, no chance to think. The dark and gleam of London presses down on my eyelids and all over my body. It is making me ill, but I know it still has something in it I want, something I lack. I can sense it the way you can see a light through closed eyes, the way it glows through the skin.

I know that part of my sickness is the awareness that it has been almost a fortnight since I saw Michael, who hasn't called. The absence of a call makes me restless, jitters my fingers and tenses my mouth, until I take action and invite Sass back to Spook with me, along with another couple of girls from our course.

Camilla, who has been distant with me since the party, before apparently forgiving me, now seems inclined to jealousy.

'Why are you hanging out with that dozy bitch, Sass?' she asks. 'You know she only calls herself Sass because she can't spell Alexandra.'

'She's nice,' I say, then, feeling myself on safe ground: 'You should join us.'

'Is anyone else going? Sammy? The boys?'

'I don't think so.'

'I'd like to but I think I'd better give this one a miss,' Camilla says, adding unconvincingly. 'I've got work to do.'

Standing at the door of Spook that night I feel I am on the edge of something, like a girl in a fairy tale in stolen shoes, looking through a crack in a palace door, at the gold and velvet vista, the noise and splendour. Through the door is a land into which I will sail, in my sharp heels, the narrow, steel-colour trousers in which my legs scissor along the corridor, cutting up the distance between myself and Leo Ford.

This week the room which once held the silver balloons, scattered like bubbles through glass, has been transformed into a funeral parlour with coffins as tables and large arrangements of lilies. We sit on the upturned plush of the coffin lids and look around, but I know before I see him that Leo is there: the whole place seems altered, as if it is aware of him.

He is positioned at the convergence of everybody's surreptitious looks, sitting with his back to me at a dark corner table with a couple of other men and two women; one with a long string of pearls writhing down her body, the other a Japanese girl with black hair and a tiny nose like a Persian cat. In a club of good-looking people this group resonates the most, giving off a humming, tangible sparkle. But they keep it to themselves, talking closely, not once scanning the room in the same way as everyone else.

Michael is not with them; he doesn't appear to be anywhere in here. My hope contracts sharply and painfully in my chest.

'Have you seen something you like?' says one of the girls I am with, putting her chin over-familiarly on my shoulder and looking in the same direction as me. 'Aha.'

I resent this *Aha*.

'That man looks attractive,' I say.

'Don't you know who that is?' says the girl. 'That's Leo Ford. Attractive doesn't quite cover it.'

After several drinks, which I can barely taste, and a while of talking to the others, who I can barely hear, we go to a different room to dance. A song is playing that I like, crackling and billowing thunderously, top notes dropping on to the dance floor like sleet. I circle my hips, my hands skim my thighs, I dip and rise. For the first time that night my anxiety drops back and I realise I am actually enjoying myself. I feel a glow of good feeling towards the girls with me, even towards the men who periodically dance up to us and dance away, like investigative seagulls.

This room is full of solid darkness; even the light is dark. Empty shapes turn out to be people, people turn out to be mirrors. The music curls around the real and reflected shapes, moving them and jostling them like a gale in the trees. Through them I see Leo Ford, only a few feet away, glimpsed through people like a deer seen in the woods, in his group's own enchanted clearing. He isn't dancing with anyone particularly, looking away to that distant place people look when they are dancing, their gaze looping to somewhere internal, somewhere remembered or imagined. He dances well, undemonstrative but smooth-moving, salient. Every once in a while he glances up and smiles at one of his friends.

What I feel, looking at him, is more than attraction – it is almost fear, knowing the distance between myself and my want and how presumptuous it is to want it. The centre of my body is all emptiness, all demand. It is more than the chill of excitement I have felt before, it is an almost-heavy thing, an incapacity.

As if in response to me, Leo looks up again, directly at me. As soon as our eyes touch I look away, shocked at the contact, then horrified with myself for ending it. I dance for a moment with my eyes lowered, then look back. But he and his friends have gone.

I go to the bar for an excuse to look for him, waiting interminably for a drink, then check the coat queue and pretend to use the loos, but Leo's group are nowhere to be found. The Japanese girl and the pearl-wearing girl are obviously as swift at leaving as they are slow to get ready. Spook itself seems colder, emptier, as its clientele unconsciously register the departure of a necessary element of its magic. I myself am queasy with disappointment. The night is dead; it is a stamped moth, easily smashed.

All the way home and to bed, a persistent buzz runs through my body. I don't need to look at myself in the mirror to know that my eyes are skittish and intense. When I lie down and try to close them they open again, hot and dry. I have to go back, get closer to Leo, move somehow into the far edges of his orbit, like a revolving Io. Just to look at him; to wait for him to look at me.

I have an assessment with my personal tutor Dr Watkins the next day, sitting uncomfortably in his dim office, which is covered in books, sagging spider plants and random chairs. Dr Watkins, who has grey hair fanning out above each ear where it needs trimming, and a murky tweed coat, resembles the kind of dilapidated man I would avoid on the bus. He smiles at me kindly.

'So, Persephone. How have you found life in London?'

'I'm not sure yet,' I say.

'Yes, yes. It's great fun and it can be tempting not to leave. But have you been to the rest of England? The Cotswolds, for example. Some of the villages are very lovely.'

'I'll remember to look around before I go.'

'Do!' Considering the chitchat over, Dr Watkins opens up my folder. 'Now, your most recent essay results. How do you feel about them?' He leans his elbows on the desk and looks at me investigatively. He has a crumb in his beard.

'I could have done better, I suppose.' I say.

'Well, that's what I felt, given your first few very good grades. Has anything . . . knocked you off course this term? Did you have difficulty with anything?'

'Not really.'

'I hope there were no personal problems?'

'I just don't think I worked as hard,' I tell him.

'Oh. Well, not many people say that. Are you going to work harder, then, Persephone?'

'Yes. Yes, I will.'

'I'm glad to hear it. Because you are one of our high achievers, and I'm sure you want the best for yourself.'

'Oh, I do,' I say. 'I want that very much.'

At the same time as I am thinking about him, Michael calls me. Struck by the coincidence, I start to tell him about it, before realising my mistake, halting, and asking him how he is instead.

'I'm sorry it's been a while,' he says. 'I was away over Christmas.'

'Don't worry at all!' I chirrup.

'Have you got plans this evening? Would you like to meet at Spook again? At the same time?'

I hesitate, wondering if Sass, who said last time that she found Spook 'a bit . . . well, spooky' and suggested we try somewhere on the King's Road instead, might be persuaded to come with me tonight. Michael appears to read my silence as wariness and rushes to explain, 'I'm there with some friends. I thought this could be part of your planned emergence from the university bubble. Getting to know new London people. That sort of thing.'

'I *do* want to emerge. But won't they mind me tagging along? It's just – I'm not sure my friends are going out tonight.'

'God, no. We'll be there from nine. It should be fun. They are – honestly – very nice.'

'I'm sure they are,' I say, stupefied at my good fortune. 'I'll see you later.'

When Camilla hears my plans she looks at me curiously and a little sadly, as if I am a favourite jumper that has developed a hole: 'That place again? You haven't come out with *us* in ages.'

'I know. I'm sorry.'

'If you're trying to avoid James, you don't need to bother. He's sleeping with some girl on his course,' Camilla says. 'That's how long it's been since you were out.'

'Okay, okay. I'll come out with you on Thursday,' I offer.

'Good!' Camilla says, apparently satisfied, and starts talking about whether Laura might come out, or whether she'll decide to stay at home with her boyfriend, *again*.

I can barely concentrate on what she is saying, timing my responses by her frowns and eyebrow raises. I am thinking about meeting Leo. I try to replay the moment of eye contact at Spook, improbable and wonderful, but the more I think about it, try to inhabit it, the less real it seems: the colours no longer true, the image shrinking, flattening, into the familiar limits of a photograph or a screen.

I arrive at Spook wide eyed, intoxicated and alone, feeling oddly more lucky as a stray than if I were safe and forgettable in a group. The room with coffins has changed into a white-walled space station with pod-like chairs, kitsch control panels winking under a large screen on which stars whistle past, cocktails in improbable future colours served at the glowing white bar.

Leo Ford is here, standing at the bar with his greenish eyes lowered, listening to another man. There is the Japanese girl, and next to her the pearl-wearing girl, who has shed her pearls, her mermaid tears, and is wearing a huge pendant that lights her cleavage like a lamp. I watch the two women, both of whom are beautiful, either of whom could be with Leo. They glance around them occasionally with vague interest, not unfriendly but not approachable either. They have the great distance of women who have anything they want, and aren't sure that they want anything else.

As I watch, two of the men with Leo move and – as if a curtain has been drawn back slowly – I see Michael's enthusiastic hair. I walk quickly towards the bar without allowing myself to think too much about what I am doing, like a trapeze artist throwing herself out, smiling and terrified, into space, and then Michael catches my eye and I land safe.

'Persephone! I was only just looking around to see if you were here. Glad you made it. Let me introduce you to everyone.'

The closest person to us is Leo. 'Leo, this is Persephone, Persephone, Leo.'

Leo turns towards me, both of us standing in the strange light cast by the bar.

'Hello,' he says, smiling. Illuminated and clarified, looking exactly like himself; his long sexy mouth, underwater eyes with their narrow corners, are almost less believable for being so near.

A purely reactive 'Hello' appears from my mouth, bypassing the usual consultation with my brain, which has jumped ship in fright and left me standing alone.

Then I have to swing like an unwilling gate to the others as Michael says, 'Catherine . . . Emiko . . . Anthony . . . Max, this is Persephone. She's here studying at King's College.' I nod and smile at the curious-eyed Emiko, jewelled Catherine, and two good-looking men who don't compare to Leo, on blank autopilot, still absorbed in my three seconds of Leo, who has turned back to his original conversation. Though he was disturbingly close, his smile came from far away, wholly uninterested. I re-run his 'Hello': low pitched, with a suedish edge.

'What a pretty name,' Catherine says to me, waking me up. Up close she is very slender, her face as delicate and bright as a capuchin monkey's, her hair splendid around her face, autumnal fountains and cataracts. 'Do you have Greek heritage?'

'Oh no, none at all. I'm from Scotland. The Highlands.' I realise that I am – out of shyness and a desire to please – talking too quickly, and cut myself short before I can give her my full address and family history, or add a placatory 'sorry', for not having agreed that I do indeed have Greek heritage.

'I'd *love* to go there,' Catherine says. 'You know what I'd really like – to see a Highland cow. They're fascinating. Like bears with horns. I think they're lovely.'

'They need all the shaggy hair for weather-proofing,' I say. 'Cows here look naked to me. They don't realise how lucky they are.'

'And so frivolous in their black and white . . . so matchy matchy,' Catherine says, and I wonder if she is laughing at me, but no – she is kind eyed, and it seems I am in on the joke. 'Pampered Southern cows.'

'I do like it that cows here – and people obviously – can be dismissive of the weather. It's something I haven't experienced before. It feels like such a luxury.'

After that she and Emiko stand close and listen with delighted horror to my stories of the Assynt – of the hour's drive to town if we run out of milk, the week last Christmas that snow trapped us inside our houses, the ghosts of Ardvreck Castle on Loch Assynt: the Marquis of Montrose who was hung, drawn and quartered, the daughter of a McLeod chieftain who threw herself from the tower after she was betrothed to the devil.

As I speak I feel myself halving, falling into two pieces: one half abruptly back in the Highlands, sitting on a rock overlooking the whistling dam, the roll of the mountains, submerged in the stillness. The other, estranged, half standing in the dark heat of the bar, glass in hand, speaking over the music; struck by how odd her home really was.

As the two women smile at me my fingers relax around my glass and my tongue can clamber down from where it has been pressed nervously against my teeth. I take a sip of my cocktail for the first time, travelling up its straw to my lips like a neon light. Catherine and Emiko may appear diamond like but they are not cold, and I find it easy to talk to them. I like them – though it feels almost presumptuous to consider them in those terms: they are beyond my prosaic likes and dislikes.

I don't have the courage to address Leo that night. When he leaves early with no more than a wave and an already-absent smile, encompassing all of us, I pretend not to notice – though the night is ashes in my mouth – and I make sure I announce my own exit at least an hour afterwards.

'It was great to see you,' Michael says, kissing me on the cheek, not appearing to mind that we barely spoke. I smile at him with near-tearful gratitude, for not being attracted to me after all, for his kindness, in allowing me through a previously barred door.

Catherine and Emiko's eyes shoot codes: they smile at each other in agreement. Then Catherine says, 'Persephone, do you want to join us for lunch at mine tomorrow? If you're not busy, that is.'

I have essays to work on but I drop them like a pile of books and run open armed towards the school gate. 'I'm free,' I say, and I do feel free; floating, rising, like a loose balloon, whisking up towards the sun.

PART FOUR

Travelling downwards with the silent Hades in a rushing, roaring coldness, it is a long time before Persephone opens her eyes and looks around. When she does, she sees something impossible. A huge, coved darkness, a river made of diamonds, singing lights in the vaulted black sky. The wind strips her hair back from her face, as they head towards the palace.

Ivy Ford
Persephone and Hades

On Saturday morning when I wake up I am surprised to see our house looking the same as usual. There is the lachrymose cup of tea beside my bed, the light battering through the too-thin curtains, the faint voices from next door, the woman's shouts as abrupt as the barking of a dog. I feel I am seeing everything as new: the dingy stairwell with its heavy embossed wallpaper, coated many times over with cream paint, the patches on the grey carpet, the flowered curtain held up with string, the landing window that looks out only onto a brick wall, splashed with rain. Then the warm sitting room full of cups of tea and biscuit wrappers, the girls already in splendid residence, the Claires fled I know not where. I sit birdlike on the sofa arm in my dressing gown, feeling temporary.

'Is that your dinner from yesterday, Camilla?'

We all look at the plate of shrunken baked beans and toast-crusts at my feet.

'No, I don't think so,' says Camilla. The lie hangs in the air and gathers strength, until it cannot be challenged. 'Hangover?'

'Not too bad.'

'How was it?'

'It's good,' I say, worried my friends will decide they'd like to go. 'We really should all go.'

'But no one fun goes there,' says Sammy (by which she means, none of the boys). 'So anyway, I really thought Alastair was coming on to me on Thursday. I didn't think about Ben all night.'

'Oh, Alastair,' says Laura. 'Yeah, he's such a flirt, isn't he?' She conveys that she too, has received this attention. Sammy frowns.

'God, can we stop talking about men?' Camilla demands. 'I'm sick of men. I'm sick of everything being about *them*. We're what's important. Girls. Friends. We should be happy with that.'

There is an awkward silence then, because we all know the truth. We would all give each other up for men, though we say that is the last thing, the most unforgivable thing, that can be done. Because it *is* all about men: Camilla's anger is about men, my silence is about men, Sammy's good humour is about men. How close can we be, really? I know my girlfriends' emotional events; I know their crises, but so would anyone else who knew them for a week. It's all the same, it's all about their currents, the men they flow towards.

Later that afternoon I am standing, intimidated, in Catherine's road, a quiet, old street lined with formidable pale buildings, lavishly made, intricacies of stone and glass and steepled roofs. Here even the city-noise – while it never stops – at least dulls and hushes respectfully.

Catherine comes down to meet me and take me up to her apartment, talking excitedly about the things that have gone wrong with her ambitious lunch. 'I wanted to impress you with my cooking, and now I've just had to salvage bits and pieces that aren't burnt or undercooked, and make a salad and turn it into a sort of table picnic – Oh, I hope you don't mind. My intentions were pure.'

I am ushered through to a large kitchen with a table: though 'table' seems too commonplace a word for the deeply glossed, dark wood installation, with its single central orchid – a flower with an architectural purity, a precise, condensed beauty – and 'kitchen' an inadequate description of this twenty-first-century marvel, every surface fiercely shiny. Emiko is already sitting down, revolving a wine glass in her fingers and appearing preoccupied.

'Sorry for the sour face,' she says to me, gesturing in the general direction of her head. 'I've had a strange morning.'

'Emiko's psychoanalyst has gone mad,' Catherine explains.

'I'm not sure if they *can* go mad, can they?' Emiko asks. 'Isn't that meant to be the point? Surely they're certified and insured against madness.'

'*Anyone* can go mad,' Catherine says.

This hangs in the air, ominous, for a moment, before Emiko carries on. 'Well, mad or not, she's not my psychoanalyst any more. She called to tell me I betrayed her and said she never wanted to see me again.'

'Emiko started going to a new CBT practitioner and forgot to tell the psychoanalyst,' Catherine says.

'She said I forgot on purpose,' Emiko says with immense sorrow. 'Because I have deep-rooted issues when it comes to authority. And there was something about transference too . . . I said it was really that it took up too much time and I couldn't afford it. But she wasn't having that at all.'

'I'm sorry,' I say, unsure of what condolences are usual in these circumstances, but they seem satisfied with that and begin discussing whether Emiko ought to tell the CBT person the whole story and risk offending her too.

I study them while they are distracted. Emiko has a small, smooth face, completely symmetrical, a white oval in which her black eyes and eyebrows float as if painted. Catherine is so slender she is almost frail; her breasts shy on her narrow body, her upper arms soft and thin as shoots. But her hair is all the different colours of Allerlairauh, brown and red and pale and blond and dark underneath, lying pulsing over her shoulders like a dozing tiger. Though different, they both remind me of the orchid on the table, a beauty that is rare and ascetic, different from the jostling prettiness of the girls at university, like a clamorous cluster of tulips.

The conversation moves quickly. Catherine and Emiko are perfectly attuned to my presence, like well-calibrated barometers, explaining references I am not likely to understand, asking questions, teasing me gently: a toned-down version of the way they tease each other.

They don't talk about Leo until Catherine says, 'So, this is going to be boring for Persephone but I have to know what last night was like. Was it gruesome?'

'That's exactly the word. You really should have been there. It's impossible to explain. The best I can do is say that the canapés were tiny little burgers and hotdogs. You'll have to extrapolate the rest of the party from that. Oh, and our hostess cried.'

'Because of Leo?'

Emiko nods ruefully.

Catherine turns to me. 'At parties there is usually a girl crying over Leo. And Leo always says, "I haven't done anything," completely failing to see that this is why the poor girls are crying.'

They both look at me and I can tell they are wondering if I might be a girl who would cry over Leo.

'I thought it was just at university parties where girls cried about men,' I say.

'No,' says Emiko. 'It doesn't matter if you're a big girl or not. We all do it sooner or later.'

'At the very end,' says Catherine.

'I've cried over people and it hasn't ended,' says Emiko. 'Loads of times.'

Catherine shrugs. 'Oh, of course. But that's not the same kind of crying. When you *know* it's over, and it might not even be anything you can pin down, but you see that it's over for good. That's the kind of crying I mean. That's what makes you sit on the stairs or in the garden sobbing in front of everyone, because even if they all talk about you it can't be as bad as the black, sour horrible crying, knowing it's over.'

'I don't think I've cried like that yet,' I tell them.

'Lucky you,' says Catherine, with genuine envy. 'Maybe some girls never do. They might be out there, walking the earth with the rest of us, looking just like the rest of us, when really they are an entirely different species.'

'Do you feel like you might be a different species?' Emiko says to me.

'I think I'm just another crying episode waiting to happen,' I say, and they laugh.

When I leave I experience a fluttering, fearful moment on the steps, when I expect them to say, 'Well, we'll probably see you sometime,' casting me back to wherever I came from. But Catherine says, 'Can you come to my party, this Friday?' and there it is, their friendship: landing in my arms like a thrown bouquet. I clutch it against my chest as I walk back along her road, in the clearer light that seems peculiar to it – still February-grey, but a brighter, more silvery grey, beaming off the white stone, hovering above the well-shaped trees – thinking about Emiko and Catherine, and then about Leo, repeating his 'Hello', investing it with a warmth beyond politeness, until the original 'Hello', with whatever intonations it once had, is long gone.

'Do you want to be famous, Persephone?' Laura asks me, apropos of nothing.

I look up, startled and guilty. 'No. Why?'

'Me neither. Sammy says everyone wants to be famous whether they admit it or not. But I wouldn't want to.'

'If they said you could be on a reality TV show, you'd do it,' confirms Sammy.

'No, I wouldn't!' Laura protests.

'But it's so artificial,' I say to Sammy. 'They decide what you're going to be. The bitch. The boring one. The stupid but sweet one. The whore. It's always the same, no matter what show they're doing.'

'I'd be the whore, I suppose,' Sammy says glumly.

'I'd be the boring one,' Laura muses. 'Persephone would be the woman of mystery.'

'The woman of mystery? Do you really think I'm like that?' I ask. 'Camilla?'

'Definitely. I often feel like I don't know you very well,' Camilla says, very casual, as if she is saying something commonplace; as if she isn't meant to be – as she has always called herself – my best friend.

I sit thinking on the sofa while the flag of female conversation flies gaily above me. It strikes me that Camilla has probably done her best at being my best friend. I wanted to be a best friend but, in some critical way, it is me that has failed. How *could* she know me? I don't even know myself. When I try to see my identity as a whole, I fail; I am too cloudy, murky, a collection of particles filling into the shapes of Camilla, or Sass, or even Catherine and Emiko. I don't exactly mean to do it. I don't put on an act, but I do trim and tone my personality to suit my surroundings. I don't lie, but in my mouth the truth often becomes more supple, more pleasing.

Sometimes I feel discomforted by this; my ability to take on someone's shape like a glove, without pretence, just a willingness to realign the vagueness of my atoms. I wish I could be defined: I would like to be a brave, diligent, selfless girl, who enjoys visiting her grandparents, is committed to her course, plays some kind of sport with healthy gusto. I worry that my mother, who in life could see the dead, might be able to see the living now that she is dead. I want to be something she could love, but I am just a wisp in London, an itinerant poltergeist, a curl of smoke, rising in a bar. Connected to nothing, with nothing to catch on to and hold.

And yet – there is a freedom in formlessness. Ghostly, I can climb the dirty air to the stars: I can slip upwards, into the place where I want to be.

~

At night Catherine's street glows white under the rainy navy sky; black railings, wet flowers, cars drawing up and drawing away. People get out, drift up the steps, vanish inside. Once I have got out of my own taxi I have no time to stand outside on the pavement and become brave, in case my hesitation is noticed, and so I scurry up the steps of the house, taking a breath as I ring the bell, like someone bracing themselves to dive into a freezing lake.

I am relieved when Catherine herself comes to the door. She draws me in and gives me a glass like a prismatic bubble of ice. The wine inside it does not taste of anything so commonplace as a fruit: it tastes of distilled courtliness, old gold. Then she brings me for the first time into the main sitting room, lined with tall windows. The walls and chairs are in the cocoa spectrum, ranging from dark to paper-pale, the lamplights hang wells of warmer colour over the shadowy floors, the bowls of lilies, sofas with majestic heaps of cushions.

Catherine sits with me and points at people. 'That's Max, who you didn't see much of at Spook because he was making phone calls. He's a tour manager for that band . . . they did that song "La la la something something doo dee . . ." No, that's not how it goes. Anyway, you'll probably never have a conversation with him that isn't interrupted by his phone.' I look at Max, who has the sheen of hard work; there is something attentive and thorough about him even at the party, like a police dog, genial but alert. 'He's with Emiko, but they haven't moved in together or anything,' Catherine continues. 'Mainly because neither of them have enough time. Did you meet Anthony?' she says, pointing out the other good-looking man from Spook. In fact, if I hadn't seen Leo I would have been awed by Anthony. But it's too late for that now. 'He's bad with women, which I suppose means good with women, really. Oh, and here's Leo.'

A red carpet of silence rolls out before Leo as he enters the room. Catherine calls him to her first and gives him a kiss of friend-ownership on the cheek.

'It's Persephone, isn't it,' he says, and kisses my cheek lightly, more of a touch than a kiss. Then Emiko comes towards us and I step back a little. Leo's eyes follow me for a second – a skim – and then move on.

My hands and teeth clench with the enormity of my longing. I see how unavailable he is; the haze of it is all over him. He looks at no one in the room – not Catherine, not Emiko, not the several other attractive women – with need. Whereas I look at him and feel feverishly cold; almost sick with want.

I spend a lot of the evening talking to Michael, whose company is easy and amusing: I can stretch out in it and relax, relieved at – for once – a simple give and take of words, with no tiny cues to watch out for, no dangerous undertow, pulling me towards the rocks. But later in the night I am telling him about my friends, trying to hint that they might not be easily mixed with his own, and then he asks: 'Are you with anyone?' and I realise that he is looking at me like a reticent small bird, head slightly tilted, eyes hopeful, and I see that I was wrong about the absence of undercurrents.

I falter. I want to come back to these people – not only for Leo but for them – and for all this to carry on, without having to lie or mislead them. But I don't know if that's possible, so I say: 'No. I'm not really looking for that. I'm sort of . . . a student nun.'

He takes me seriously. 'You're religious?'

'Not exactly.'

'You know, I was reading an article about asexuality, and abstinence, and how increasing numbers of younger people are just finding it simpler to . . . sort of, not get involved with that side of . . . things. It's really quite a fascinating, and probably wise, thing to do.'

'I'm not asexual,' I say, alarmed. 'I actually liked someone at university – up until recently, anyway.'

'Oh! I understand. I didn't mean to pry – I'm sorry,' Michael says hurriedly.

'Don't be sorry! I'm okay. It wasn't exactly a great romance to begin with.'

He looks at me sympathetically, and I realise he thinks I am being brave.

'You don't have to pretend things are okay if they're not. You should talk about it. Burn photos of him. Change your hair. I don't know. Whatever the usual routines are.'

'None of that is necessary. Actually, just being away from my usual group has been lovely,' I say, then – inspired – 'I can honestly say I haven't even thought about him in the time I've spent with you guys.'

'You say it like you're planning not to see us again.'

'No, not at all!'

'Well, Catherine and Emiko are rather smitten with you. They phoned up just to tell me.' This is half directed at Emiko, who has wandered into the field of audibility.

'For God's sake, Michael,' she says, 'I told you we were playing it cool.'

Michael laughs and tops up my glass, his face returned to its usual cheerfulness, with no trace of its previous birdlike hope, and I am satisfied that, even if I showed only a corner of the truth – giving the tail of the elephant to the blind man – at least I didn't lie.

By four a.m the only people left are Catherine, Emiko, Max, Anthony and Leo. They are opening a fresh bottle of wine and Anthony is rolling a joint. I can tell by looking at them, the way they are with each other, that the other people at the party are merely the orbiters of the group, whereas this few are its centre, its pearly core. Intimidated, I murmur something about getting a taxi.

'Oh, you mustn't,' Emiko says from the end of her long sofa. Her hair has been taken down and curves in two smooth wings over her shoulders; she looks like a doll, left in the cushions. 'You haven't had a chance to get to know everyone. I'm staying tonight. You should stay.'

'Yes, stay,' Catherine cries. So I sit uncertainly on the other end of the sofa listening to the music, a mournful, pretty song, making a delicate path through the velvety density of the air. In the corner a black and white film is playing, though nobody pays much attention to it: it is only when I look at it properly that I realise it is an old porn film, a crimp-haired woman moving her shiny black mouth over a flickering white penis. Leo looks over at the screen for a moment, eyes slightly narrow. The juxtaposition of Leo and these images, just across from me, is more than I am prepared for: I turn my face away, flustered.

'*What* are we watching now?' Catherine says, noticing but misinterpreting my expression. 'Let's put something else on.' 'Let's watch a film about mistaken identity.'

'Let's watch a film from the baddie's point of view.'

'Let's watch *The Jungle Book*,' says Leo. 'What? I'm not joking. It has all the elements you need in a film. Danger. Love. Friendship. Humour. Who can argue with that?' Nobody can, but *The Jungle Book* is not to be found, so we put on a film from the baddie's point of view.

'It's funny how first-person narratives or films are so engaging,' I say. 'I always hope things will go well for the main character, even if they aren't very nice.' Leo smiles at me: the first time he has given me his full smile, wide and astounding. It is like a painful, sweet stab, that visceral sexiness.

'I'm going to write my next book in the first person,' he says. 'But I can't decide how much knowledge everyone should have. At one extreme you have a narrator who knows everything and a reader who knows nothing. Then there is the opposite extreme. I think maybe neither the narrator nor the reader should get to know what's going on. That would be the most realistic.'

'But you would know?' I ask him.

'That's another question.' Leo sinks lower in his chair with apparent enjoyment, unfurling his arm along its back. 'Maybe the author shouldn't know either.'

'That sounds like a lot of work for you, Michael,' Emiko observes.

'It sounds horrific,' Michael says, laughing. 'Please don't do that, Leo.'

'Maybe I won't, then,' Leo says equably.

'Speaking of art no one understands, remember Jimmy Z?' says Max. 'I saw him earlier today, talking to himself in Portobello Road.'

'We thought he was artistic but he's actually insane,' Catherine explains to me. 'Remember that time he stole a milkfloat and turned up at your house in it, Emiko?'

'Remember his racist dog?'

'No!'

'It got angry whenever it saw black people. It tried to bite Max. You *must* remember. It also hated dark-colour dogs.'

'The stupid thing was the dog was a beige pug with a black face, but it didn't realise as it could only see the rest of its body.'

As they discuss Jimmy Z and a few other people they are reminded of, I begin to realise that I am not the first new person the group has befriended. They seem to have known a lot of stray and impoverished film-makers, asylum seekers, graffiti artists – all the stories ending with something going wrong in the nascent friendship, something that baffles the group but that I understand perfectly. I, however, am determined to join seamlessly, to make myself necessary, if there is any chance of doing so.

When I first arrived in London I found it dirtily polluted, at times squalid, but with an uneasy excitement at its heart, more felt than seen: a hard, glimmering loveliness hiding in the slippery streets like a jewel in a fag-filled puddle. Now I see where that beauty originates from; flaring pure and ornate inside the sooty precipices of the bleary streets, the blare and drum of the frantic roads, the heavy rain darkly weighting the sky, the irritable, packed-in people.

I have a vision of the existence of Leo and his friends inside this secret city, wheeling in and out of each other's lives like the personages flitting around the ceiling of the Sistine Chapel. Languidly drunk, I can almost see the gold-coloured radiance that wreathes them, shining up in the morning dusk. I breathe its starry vapour; I let it enter me, like the light of an entrancing, mysterious sun.

The next morning, I wake up in the stiff white peaks of Catherine's spare bed. As the others aren't up and I don't have the confidence to make myself a cup of tea or put on the television to wait for them, I leave a grateful note and slip out.

I walk back to the tube under a clear silvery sky, before descending into the underground, which reminds me on some days of a gloomy rat's lair and on others of a tiled public lavatory. I rush and rattle through the tunnels as the dead, thick air coats me once again, plastering over any traces of the previous night. Then I emerge into a snappy rain and walk back to our house, stepping over an upturned and disembowelled rubbish bin, skirting the oily puddles, avoiding eye contact.

'Hello, dear,' says Sammy unexpectedly from the sofa when I get in. 'Camilla's in the shower and the Claires are in their rooms avoiding me. Where have you been?'

'I went out with that friend of mine from work experience,' I say.

'Is *he* the reason you keep going out without us? You must really like him.'

'We're just friends,' I say, 'Honestly.'

Sammy winks at me. 'Whatever you say. Hey, I saw James yesterday. He said you'd been avoiding him.'

'Isn't he with someone else now?' I say. 'He should focus on that.'

'You're his true love,' she says dramatically, throwing her arms out. 'The new girl won't last long. He's just on loan to her and she knows it. Every time we're out he's asking why you aren't with us.'

I sit down and rub my eyes, tired. The evidence of James's interest is like news from another country; I can't see what it has to do with me.

Camilla appears, steamed clean, cheeks bright as fruit, hair wrapped in a towel. 'Aha!' she says when she sees me. 'I almost texted you last night to check you were okay. But I didn't want to interrupt anything. Was he good?'

'Don't you think I'd tell you if I'd slept with someone?' I ask her.

'She's denying everything. They're just friends,' Sammy recites.

'Bullshit – you don't spend two hours getting ready to see a friend,' Camilla says.

I try not to lie because when I do I blush. I don't go pale, with spots of pink burning in my cheeks like a Victorian heroine; I turn comprehensively and brightly red. Camilla eyes me but misreads the colour. 'So you haven't slept with him yet, but you do like him, even if you won't admit it.'

'You two should interview criminals,' I say.

'We could specialise in sex criminals,' agrees Sammy. 'Cup of tea anyone?' The difficult moment is over: Sammy exits to the kitchen and Camilla begins switching through the television channels.

'Want to go to Moriarty's this week, or will you be out chasing Mr X?'

'Sure, I'll come,' I say, and Camilla smiles at me. I know this was a little test, and that I have passed it. But I'm not sure for how long I can keep passing tests: my concentration span is too short. I had to make an effort to actually remember Moriarty's; I was thinking only about last night, my head full of it, the rainy chill that wrapped Catherine's apartment, like a liner ballroom sunk in the Atlantic, the heat and light magically flaming inside.

Our group at university has its own celebrity – of a small and silly type, but one that I once enjoyed. Now, however, I have been near the exciting, frightening fame Leo possesses, of being the one who is the *most* wanted. His singing, his books, even his arrest for attempted murder: each public episode has elevated him more. He throws off light like the North Star; he is distant from having been loved too much, but he is more alive for it, more beautiful, more necessary. Finally, I have found my icon; there has never been anyone better than him to covet.

~

'I'm having my picture painted today,' Catherine says to me. Her voice is one of those unaffected by phone cables; it rolls mellifluously down the thin buzzing channel like melted bronze. 'Do you mind very much coming over for a drink and being entertaining while I sit and talk to you without moving my mouth? Excellent, I'll come and get you.'

Catherine arrives in a green vintage car, which she drives with slapdash gusto. 'I know everyone hates my driving,' she says. 'Emiko goes to see a psychic and she said the psychic told her that she ought to stay away from green cars.' She runs a red light and bounces off the kerb as she turns. 'But I'm sure she's making that up.' A ringing comes from her bag and I fish the phone out.

'It's Emiko,' I say.

'Would you mind sort of holding it to my ear?' Catherine's end of the conversation goes, 'Yeah. Yes. Did he? That's obscene. No, do. Jas is coming later. Perse's here. Hello, Perse, says Emiko . . . Do, do . . . See you then. Thanks darling,' Catherine says as I take the phone back. 'Emiko's coming too. I'll make us some cocktails. I did a course on how to make them and I haven't tested out my new skills yet. It is afternoon now, isn't it? What's the rule about alcohol again?'

'I didn't know there were alcohol rules,' I say with interest.

'You students,' Catherine says merrily, though she is not much older than a student herself.

I perch on a bar stool in Catherine's kitchen, admiring the way her long windows collect the chilly sunlight and let it slip, gentled and pearly, on to the polished floors, as Catherine, forehead clenched intently, bludgeons some ice with a rolling pin, going backward and forward between a row of bottles and her instructions. Then Emiko – who appears to have her own key – springs in like a black and white cat, depositing a wine bottle on the side, hanging up her coat and dropping her bag on the floor in a routine I envy for its familiarity.

'You have to look at these pictures quickly and tell me which to use on the website,' she says.

I had asked Emiko and Catherine about their jobs in my first meeting with them, the information barely registering in the adrenalin-lit febrility of being in Leo's presence, and now I don't remember what either of them do and can't ask again, confined to listening for clues. The photographs are all of children in a sunny village, holding spades and smiling widely at the cameras.

'For the charity!' I say and Emiko smiles, pleased at my enthusiasm.

'That one looks evil,' Catherine says, pointing. 'You should Photoshop him out. It might put people off.'

'Evil-looking children deserve our charity as much as cute ones,' Emiko says piously. 'If not more. Oh look – these are old.' She has clicked backwards into another set of photos on her laptop, in which Leo appears: not the closest to the camera, only half smiling, but instantly distinct from the other faces. I want to rush through the other pictures to let my eyes satisfy their gluttony for more of him, but Emiko flicks through at a measured pace, kindly trying to remember the names of various people for my benefit.

'Oh, there's Ivy,' Catherine says. 'She'll be back soon.'

Ivy is a crescent moon of a face, half obscured by another head. I can make out an eye corner, dark hair, a tailored eyebrow and a pretty mouth.

'Ivy is Leo's half-sister. She's on a research trip in Greece, she's a doctor of classics.'

I don't want to say that I have heard of Ivy, several times before. She was with Leo when he shot somebody. She represents an unknown side of Leo; something to collect up and remember. I examine the visible pieces of her more closely. 'What is she like?' I ask.

'Ivy is . . . a force to be reckoned with,' says Catherine.

'What kind of thing is that to say? Ivy is really lovely,' Emiko interrupts. 'She speaks Greek and Latin. Not that *that* makes her lovely, of course. Just clever. She's very clever.'

I want to ask more but at this point Jas, a small electrical-haired man, arrives and Catherine is arranged in a chair with a hat in her lap and a fluffy toy cat on her head.

'This cat doesn't look very real,' she says.

'What *is* real?' Jas asks, scratching his startled hair. 'Keep your face still, please.'

'Jas has just finished a "childhood immersion" piece,' Catherine says, rigid mouthed, to me.

'For example, when we know not to put toast in the DVD player,' says Jas, 'why don't we do it? It isn't common sense – it is because our parents have conditioned us not to. I'm trying to undo that conditioning.'

'Did you put toast in your DVD player?' I ask.

'No, in my parents' DVD player, of course,' says Jas.

'You wouldn't be able to play your films back if you ruined yours, anyway,' Catherine says. The cat wobble.

'I don't understand his films,' Emiko whispers to me. 'The last one was about a woman who cut off all her hair and then ate it. I *told* Catherine this picture would be silly. But she liked the idea of being immortalised. I suppose it serves her right that she's going to have a cat on her head for ever.'

'Why would you want to undo conditioning?' I ask, a little befuddled by the cocktails, the sun, the paint fumes.

'If you don't learn, you stay young,' Jas says, as if this is obvious. 'It's as close as we can get to eternal youth.'

I see more and more of Leo's friends in the weeks after that. Leo is not usually at these gatherings, something I am rationally used to, though I cannot train myself into detachment. When he does arrive – invariably late – I jangle like a dropped guitar; when he leaves – invariably early – there is a different sort of pain again, quick and sharp and personal.

Despite these ups and downs, Leo's friends are absorbing in themselves; not simply his backdrop, they have their own stage lights, their individuating colours and textures. From Leo's fame and Catherine's apartment I assumed at first that they were all rich, but I am relieved to find that this isn't so. Emiko lives with a housemate in a small apartment of Turkish carpets and bookshelves in North London, while Michael and Max share a vague flat somewhere south of the river. Confusingly, Anthony's apartment block – which the group refer to as 'the favela' – turns out to be a stacked expanse of prime City real estate.

The difficulty in identifying who has what is partly owing to the friends' horror of any discussion of money, names, or brands. Whenever one of them slips up the others swoop like gulls: on the copy of *Vogue* discovered at Catherine's apartment, or the time Emiko mentioned work that a celebrity had done for her charity (though Leo, interestingly, is exempt from this type of mockery: the friends implying an unshakeable understanding that Leo is not famous).

Part of their battle with materialism is the adoption of people who conform to their picturesque idea of the liminal, the culturally exotic: though their habit of doing so only highlights the difference between the group and the adoptees. Confident and generous, they don't understand that strays often have their own particular survival mechanisms, their own fears and resentments, which invariably cause the friendship to collapse under the weight of misunderstanding.

Now that I know I have not been included only as a potential girlfriend of Michael's, I have started to wonder if I am another stray: if they see something lost and undomesticated in *me*. Maybe I went too far with my stories about life in the mountains. This realisation has given me a low-level anxiety about my position in the group, which might be in question once they discover that I am an outsider only by circumstance: that all I want is to belong.

Belonging also has its own difficulties: the emphasis the friends place on authenticity and originality removing many of the tribal markers that define a group, the currency of survival with new people. I am not sure what to be in order to fit in with them. They champion the original, but I don't know which parts of myself are original and which are trained. I don't know, finally, how to take the metaphorical toast out of my DVD player.

March comes with what I suppose must be spring showers, merging seamlessly with the rain of January and February, so that the spring edition of the rain is indistinguishable from the rain of winter. I note the passing of the month with guilt: it has been a month of missed lectures (Sammy has begun to hand her lecture notes over to me with not exactly unwillingness, but a faint precursor of it) and excuses made while the other girls go out to parties and bars.

To make amends I have agreed to a girls' night in with Camilla, Laura and Sammy, even though Catherine and Emiko had invited me out that night. Camilla asked me challengingly if I would join them – as if making an accusation rather than an invitation – and seemed almost startled when I said yes. But here we all are with wine and chocolate, marijuana, crisps and dips: the paraphernalia of female bonding. We sit in the living room wrapped in smoke, fog billowing by the coving as if we are at a séance and the ersatz ghosts of our grandparents have stopped by.

In the film we are watching, misunderstandings have been keeping the leading lovers apart, as in so many other films. They struggle, they have to chase each other at the end at the airport or the train station or the chapel, before finally they are allowed what is implied to be their perfect bliss.

'Why does it have to be so difficult?' I ask. 'Is love difficult? And is it only difficult because films like this make people think it ought to be difficult?'

'I think this is a terrible film,' says Sammy. 'I told you we should've got a horror.'

'Love doesn't have to be difficult,' Laura says, warily, from her position of privilege. 'If you both like each other and you're suited to each other, then it *shouldn't* be difficult.'

'But,' says Camilla, 'some people might just take longer to decide what they want, and what if you give up just at the moment when they were about to decide they want *you*?'

'Oh come on!' Laura, waving her joint for emphasis, unshoulders her usual restraint. 'Who do you know – male or female – who has chased or waited for someone over a long period and that person, in the end, has turned out to be the perfect partner?'

No one knows.

'*Sex and the City*—' Camilla begins.

'In *real life*.'

'Okay then,' Camilla says, 'but it's not like you can switch your feelings on and off. You can't like someone for exactly a month, and if they don't reciprocate within the set time limit you just *move on*. What if you just can't stop liking them? What happens then?' When she finishes her eyes are brightly layered with tears and, though the mechanism of our friendship has got somewhat stiff and rusted of late, I shift over and put my arm round her gently. I feel ashamed that I haven't told her about Leo. At first it seemed like my meeting him was too new a shoot to be entrusted to anyone else, in case it got accidentally trampled. Then I got into the habit of guarding it, of holding it close and keeping everyone else away – and for what? For no reason at all.

Feeling remorseful, I am about to explain everything, but then Camilla turns to me then and says: 'So, have you fucked Mr X yet, Persephone?' lightly, combatively, and raises her eyebrows.

'No,' I say. 'Not yet.'

By the end of the night I am more stoned than I have ever been before: laughing so much that it is painful to draw breath, like a broken concertina. My mouth thickens up with dryness, my cheeks ache. Then once I stop laughing I can't think of what I was laughing at and sit puzzling over it.

'What were we laughing at?' I ask the others.

There is a silence.

'I can't remember.'

'What are we trying to remember?' Sammy is leaning her head back on the sofa, struggling to keep her eyes open, and as I watch her they slide closed with the finality of stage curtains. Her mouth tips open peacefully. Next is Camilla, then Laura, their movements slowing, their voices fading, until they lie as if dead on the sofa next to each other. I sit up in my chair, refusing sleep, feeling my thoughts struggling like ants in honey, drowning and drowsy.

Even in this state, I can see Leo, call him up like a magic spell, saying his name three times until he appears before me, all his edges bright and clear. I watch him for what seems like a long time, though really it can only be a few moments, before I lose him, folded into the thick snow of sleep.

'Do you miss your family when you're away from them?' I ask Leo. He is idling in Emiko's kitchen; I am pouring drinks, very slowly, in order to keep him for longer. In the sitting room the others, playing poker, don't seem inclined to come in and disturb us. A coolness makes its way through the open window, a misty lunar scent, a chill off the sky. It is my first real moment alone with him and I have been looking at him surreptitiously, trying to work out where in his face his beauty collects. It pools and condenses in his eyes, but it also resides in his eyebrows, the incline at the corners of his mouth, his jawline. When he looks up his eyes are a little too much for me – too much green, too much focus – and I have to redirect my gaze into the ice cubes.

'Thinking about home?' he asks.

'Maybe,' I lie.

'Is this the first time you've spent a long time away from your parents?'

'Just the one parent. My mother died when I was little. But yes, it's been six months now, when I don't think I've spent much more than six hours away from my father before.'

'That's not quite usual,' Leo says. 'Are you finding it difficult now?'

I start to say 'not really' but have to stop, embarrassed at the sudden quirk in my voice. I turn to the fridge, rummaging around for soda, raising my eyes up to the ceiling until the tears drop back. 'Your parents both live here?' I ask, trying to gather the conversation back up.

'My father lives in London. My mother lives in France. They've been divorced for a long time.'

'Oh, I didn't know that. You've never mentioned them before.'

'I can't imagine why anyone would want to hear about them,' he says. 'Do *you* want to hear about them?'

'Yes. Why not?'

'Well, William Ford is my father. He's taken over at Carson's Bank.'

'I know who that is. I've seen him on the news! Isn't he changing everything to make it fairer?'

'Supposedly,' Leo says.

'The plans sound wonderful,' I say hesitantly.

'Do you know wonderful didn't always used to be a term of approbation?' Leo says. 'My mother is called Tamara. She lives in Paris and spends her time enjoyably, if not usefully.'

'Do you miss her?'

'Aha,' Leo says. 'That's a difficult question coming from you. It would seem ungrateful of me to be dismissive of my mother. So I'm not going to answer that.' He says this with finality but remains leaning on the bar across from me, with a look of curiosity and humour, as if he expects me to ask something else, so I do.

'Where does your sister live?'

'Half-sister. On William's side. She lives here and there. I'm not entirely sure where, at the moment.'

'Don't you get along with her, either?' I say, meaning it as a joke, then remembering as I say it that Ivy's one-time position as an accessory to the attempted murder of her boyfriend might have strained the relationship. I blink, uncertain, my fingers curling unhappily under the counter.

'Now, who said I don't get along with anyone?' Leo asks, looking suddenly sharper, but no less amused. He says it gently enough but I flush and look back down at the forgotten elements of our drinks lined up on the bar between us. I can't help but be awed by him: his shoulders relaxed in the shirt that pulls intermittently across them, showing the outline of his body underneath; his long mouth, the green eyes, still watching me. 'In answer to your question, we do get along,' Leo continues. 'Though I am widely considered to be the nicer of the two of us.'

I smile, relieved, pouring the vodka. 'Did she bully you as a child?'

'Luckily for me, we didn't know each other as children. She bullies me now.'

'Really?'

'A little. Ivy doesn't believe in water under the bridge, brushing things under the carpet, or not rocking the boat. Not just with me – not with anyone. She . . . doesn't make things easy.'

'And you do?'

The drinks finished, he reaches across the bar and takes his glass. Our fingers don't touch but I get a chill, electrical, of longing. 'Oh, very easy,' he says, and laughs, and walks into the sitting room.

In the round lights of the silver lamps the others are playing a game where they have to tell a secret if their number of the dice comes up, or drink a shot.

'I slept with my cousin's boyfriend,' Emiko says, to delighted shock. 'She never found out, and now they're getting married.'

As there are already five players, I am assigned joint number six with Leo (a connection that I exult in despite its meaninglessness) and quickly have to think of a fictional secret I might tell them, being too new and too afraid to entrust them with one of my own.

As the dice rolls I hope our number comes up. I want a secret from Leo, to curl up in my heart like a pearl in an oyster. I know it would be ridiculous to expect him to say anything about the incident on the yacht, about picking up a sword in order – he must have believed – to kill somebody. What I most want is for him to say something about his sexual life, the dark land behind the curtain, a place no one seems to know anything about.

The dice lands five uppermost, prompting Max to confess that he once asked a friend to finish with a girlfriend for him. Then Anthony, unable to wait for his turn, tells a story about how he dated a girl who turned out to be 'crazy' – not funny crazy – bad crazy. 'After two dates she booked to go to the same place as me on holiday, then when I arrived she pretended it was a coincidence. Then I tried to finish with her and she just wouldn't accept it. So I got my brother to, er, tell her I was dead.'

'No!' Emiko cries. 'That's awful.'

'Did you have a mock funeral?' Leo asks.

'Fortunately, I didn't have to go that far. But I heard a few years later that she ended up with a restraining order.'

'Obviously from someone who wasn't quite as inventive as you,' Emiko says.

Then the conversation turns to ways of finishing with someone and the dice game is forgotten. I am disappointed at the loss of another prospective piece of Leo's soul, shining and priceless, to add to my collection of fragments to turn over and treasure in his absence.

Later Catherine says to Leo, 'We all had to tell a secret, Leo, and you completely got away with it!'

'Luck of the draw.' Leo shrugs.

'You should tell us one anyway,' says Catherine. 'Come on!' She is almost wheedling and I feel unreasonably annoyed with her, as if she is somehow giving away my feelings, as well as her own. I don't know why women do this – always speculating and trying to pin down what a man is, always trying to interpret what he does into the shape of themselves. At least men move on if a girl isn't exactly what they want, they pretend to be dead, or they cheat and wait to be caught. They don't push onwards into a still, blank day, holding out their hopes like kites, waiting for a wind to sweep them up, to carry them aloft.

I take the bus back to my house the next day, my body heavy and uncooperative after only three hours sleep, my head packed with greasy black feathers, through which a muffled pain seeps, my eyes bare and brittle, blinking in the thin, watery light of the window, the rotation of passengers like cuckoos, shuffling staccato down the aisle.

At a stop I have never got on or off at, a black spot on the route, a pack of girls throng aboard and blare down the aisle towards the back of the bus. I don't need Camilla to help me identify what tribe these girls belong to: I can tell there is a certain amount of danger contained within them, the way they talk loudly, challengingly, swivelling to assess their fellow passengers, even conducting combative eye-sweeps of the street beyond the bus windows.

I have something in common with them: the habit of staring. I know that at best it isn't polite and at worst it is an invitation to fight, and so I try to keep my eyes to myself, but I still feel the need to gaze, to see everything I can. My girlfriends at university do not look around much because nothing, to them, could possibly be more interesting than their own conversations. Catherine and Emiko, used to being stared at themselves, do not look at anybody. Even when walking, they don't appear to notice the presence of other people, moving as if with tiny sensors, cat whiskers, somehow avoiding collisions. But I watch everything almost frantically, trying to absorb every interesting flash of beauty – the shiny slick of hair falling over a woman's face, a laugh, an iridescent shoe, a well-formed and sexy mouth – as well as the grotesqueries: a man urinating against a wall, a black eye, a bulldog tattoo. I gather all I can until the object of my inspection turns, their eyes rising to mine as if by magic, at which point the game is up. I wonder if my habit of staring is another signifier of something more than my newness in London: if it indicates something feral in me, something stray.

''E says 'e's gonna finish wiv 'er,' one girl, waiting to pass my seat, shouts to another. Her hair, pulled back mercilessly, is retreating in defeat from her forehead, but her flesh flounces defiantly from every border of her tight top. The top reads 'Sexy,' in shamefaced pink writing. Then the girl turns abruptly and our eyes meet.

'What *you* lookin' at?' she asks me.

I stare at her uncertainly. Nobody has ever asked me this before. I sense what the girl needs: to hit something, to express her discontent with her receding hairline and her cheating boyfriend and her hopeful top. I realise that I could be the next target of the girl-gang violence that preoccupies the media; that palsied mobile phone footage of this act of violence might be distributed among the teens of London. I have no idea what to say to her. The other passengers around me fall silent.

'Come on,' her friend says, laughing, and pulls her away down the aisle. The crackle of the storm passes away with them and ease is restored to the bus. The other passengers look at me with sympathy and a few head shakes, as the girls assemble themselves at the back, drilling their cigarettes into their seats.

Sometimes it seems like the whole of the city, with its rushing people, its crashing, splashing advertising, is straining for something; everyone wants something, everyone is trying to escape something else. Even in the expensive areas, the other London, of white stone and flowers, this hunger still lingers, cooled and suspenseful, like a silent blanketed cage under which a bird waits to shriek again. Everyone is vulnerable to the hunger, and no one knows quite how to eat.

PART FIVE

From that night on Demeter is vertical. She does not sleep, she does not sit, she does not eat. She moves over the world like a great bird, borne by sadness, calling her daughter's name. Like a forgotten houseplant, nature suffers from its mistress's lack of attention. The seeds spoil in the earth and her salt tears blight the crops. Her sighs blow the leaves from the trees and the sky reflects the heavy grey of her despair. In the lofty heights of Olympus her seat is empty, and every day the gods look sidelong at Zeus, wondering when he might comment. But Zeus pretends not to notice.

Ivy Ford
Persephone and Hades

'So,' says Camilla, 'I hear you're friends with Leo Ford.'

'Hear from where?'

'Some of Sass's friends went back to that club you go to and saw you. You didn't notice them, apparently.'

I look up, startled, to where she sits opposite me, a pure spot of light in the stodgy, littered gloom of our sitting room. Her eyes are a thorough, simple blue, like those of a baby, clear and glossy.

'I'm not friends with him. I sort of got to know a couple of his friends. I barely know him.'

This is basically true, but Camilla sees through the layer of truth like a jeweller scrutinising a piece of silverware, instantly identifying the baser metal underneath. 'So you've met him and you didn't tell us?'

'There just wasn't much to tell,' I say.

For a moment I see it: curiosity and hurt, Camilla's pained mouth, and then the expression vanishes.

'That's cool,' she says. 'But honestly, Persephone, there's nothing wrong with having a crush. You don't need to be proud about it. We wouldn't tease you!'

I don't answer immediately. I think instead of the word 'crush'. There is a brutality to it, an implication of breakage, of ruin.

'You okay?' Camilla presses.

'Just a little tired. I might go to bed,' I say, moving towards the door, away from the range of her hostility.

'Sure,' Camilla laughs. 'I remember doing that – lying in bed fantasising that some celebrity was my boyfriend. Except I was like, thirteen at the time.'

This is when I realise what has happened. Without my intending it, I am on one side of the glass wall, and Camilla is on the other. I can't say anything to undo it, so I say nothing, and go to bed.

Later that night I lie awake listening to the familiar murm-murming of the voices on the television below, all their human meaning taken away by the intervening layers of plaster and wood. I pull the duvet over my head, blocking out the noise, my messy room, the heavy dark furniture, the old, cold smell and the leprous ceiling, the smattering sound of rain against the window. I press my face down into the pillow, clenched against my eyes and face, until I see a dull red colour. I lie there and feel sick of Camilla, then, unsatisfied with being sick only of her, I feel sick of Marcus, and Sass, and James, and even Laura and Sammy, until I am thoroughly sick of everything, and finally content.

Leo's house is positioned slightly off a square arranged around a caged sward of grass and flowers; a vivid imprisoned green. From the outside his house is much the same as Catherine's building – a white eggshell façade, railings like slender arrows – but inside it strays, it resists décor. The sitting room is full up with old things: faded carpets; a wall of books; three mismatched lion-footed sofas;

chandeliers like constellations of crystal; nymphs wandering over the fireplace; a globe of the world; lamps balanced on piles of yet more books; paintings which I am sure must be valuable, of naked women in chiaroscuro, their ivory-peach limbs glowing in the thick, soft darkness like deep sea fish.

Only a few rooms in the house appear to be colonised; the rest are maid-tidy but bare. The dining room is empty except for a Greek statue of a man, tragically dignified in the absence of his hands. In the bathroom there is a row of fossils on the windowsill, but no towel rail or loo-roll holder. Two of the rooms upstairs on the way to the bathroom contain beds but little else; three others are empty. The final door is closed.

Leo is slightly different in his own house, more present, I notice. He moves around his sitting room as if restless, quick to press drinks on us, or music, switching compulsively onwards to the tracks he wants us to listen to.The others themselves are, as usual, frequently getting up to smoke, or make drinks, or go to the loo, then returning and sitting down in new places, so that a sped-up recording would look like a frantic game of musical chairs, with me sitting in the middle, too unsure of myself to move. Eventually this revolving seating plan brings me into contact with Leo, who takes the seat next to me on the sofa, slipping into it with his customary grace of movement, animal-like, free of artifice or awkwardness.

I can't achieve the same ease. Even across a room eye contact with him can feel too overwhelming: now, sitting next to him, I am very aware of my eyes, as if they are giving me away, our faces too close, our connected gaze too fierce and naked. I avoid turning to talk to him directly; I tuck my leg up and curl my arm around it protectively, reducing my exposure to him. His arm rests near me, the colour of his whisky, of radiant honey, the smooth skin with its dark, feathery calligraphy of hairs. Looking at it brings back a memory of the hiker in the Assynt. He was like an early match flaring: now here is the conflagration.

'Are you ignoring me?' Leo asks.

I reluctantly draw my eyes up to his, embarrassed to realise that we are the only people on this side of the room. The withdrawal of a few people to either side of us has created an invisible boundary, slicing the conversation neatly into two halves like a grapefruit. Leo and I sit cradled in our half: I have his full attention. He is watching me with humorous curiosity.

'Sorry, I was daydreaming.'

'I'll try not to be insulted,' he says.

'Insulted . . . that reminds me of your interview,' I say, without thinking, then have to continue, 'you said it was an insult to an author to accuse them of putting someone they know straight into a book.'

'You watched that, did you?' Leo says.

'My housemate did,' I cheerfully sacrifice Camilla. 'She's a big fan. Er, I am too, now, of course. I just hadn't heard of you before then. Living in the middle of nowhere. These things take a while to filter through.'

'It must be nice,' Leo murmurs. I can see now that he is slightly drunk: his voice has that slow, careful quality. 'Living in the middle of nowhere. What's it like?'

'Not as nice as you think,' I say, dismissively. 'So, you never put anyone in your books?'

'It's just bad workmanship,' Leo says. 'Now, putting yourself into a book – that's different. A lot of my characters have something in common with me.'

'Didn't you tell the interviewer that there isn't anything of you in your books? Because she said that people will buy the books to see you.'

He looks interested. 'You paid too much attention to that interview. Well, Miss Marple, if someone *did* want to look for me, they wouldn't know where I was hiding. Not all the characters are like me. And they are only like me in some ways.'

'Very elusive,' I say, trying not to sound disappointed.

'But necessary.'

'You must be very controlled when you write?' I know I have asked too many questions already, but I can't stop. A frontiersman who has struck oil will not walk away, a child who has suddenly been handed an ice-cream will not leave it half-finished, and I will stay here listening to Leo, entranced, asking and asking, until something intervenes to stop me.

'I think writing is sometimes like dreaming. There's a school of thought that everything in a dream is an aspect of the self. It's not a conscious process. Writing isn't always entirely conscious either – the difficulty is becoming conscious.'

'I see,' I say. 'Like a lucid dream.'

'Exactly. The best kind of dream. You have them?'

'No. I have recurring dreams.'

'You know the first rule about dreams, don't you?' he asks.

'What?' I lean in to hear it.

'Our own dreams are endlessly fascinating. Other people's dreams are just as boring.'

'Oh,' I say, abashed.

'But there's one exception to that: people in unrequited love. They're always interested in what the object of their affection is dreaming about, because they hope it might be to do with them.'

He says this quietly, more intimately than usual, not looking away. There is something in it, his look, his near smile, which I can't understand.

I smile too but my lips are shaky. If there is a moment to say something flirtatious, this is it, but I am not brave enough. I look down. Then, as if a klaxon has sounded on a gameshow (*time's up!*) Emiko and Max rush over to retell something that had just happened outside, and all our closeness is broken up.

That night Catherine and I sleep over at Leo's, in the only bed with sheets on, the two of us folded into the pale linen, rustling like leaves of translucent paper. It takes me a long time to fall asleep, and when I do I dream about my mother, floating far away across a wide ocean. There are no curtains at the window and I wake up before seven o'clock with a cool, sober light filling up my eyes. Catherine's hair has slid over her face, like a thick mantle; she sleeps on, making only tiny noises of breathing.

I dress as quietly as I can and leave our room, pausing at the closed door: Leo's door, a solid shape of silence that casts its hush down the long landing. I try to imagine him lying asleep inside, try briefly to call up the breadth of his shoulders, the tan back, but I can't do it: as soon as he is out of my sight he moves off, into the realm of the impossible.

Mouse-like, I descend the wide and intimidating staircase to the kitchen. My own tapping feet are the only sounds in the house, slow and regular over the tiles. I go to the sink and drink a large glass of water in an attempt to rejuvenate my brain cells, which I imagine to be softly shrunken, like dead flowers. I contemplate putting my face under the cold tap for a moment: a liquid slap to wake myself up, and lower my face close to the water before quailing and pulling away.

After that I wander around the silent rooms of the house barefoot, clutching my glass. I find another, empty room at the back of the house, painted all in white so that its edges and corners seem to soften and melt, and a room with French windows looking on to a long, long garden. A cool haze sits on the bluish grass and trees like ice-vapour, lifting slowly, in a premonition of sun.

I try to open the doors but they are locked, which seems right: I didn't really expect to be able to cross into a place that looks so unreal, a dream garden. I put my face right up to the pane instead and peer out like a child, until the chilly sun springs over the trees at the end of the lawn, returning the grass to its usual colour, the beautiful vapour all gone.

I go back through to the kitchen, feeling a little worried that I am in Leo's house alone. I know if he were to come down, now that I am sober and self-conscious, my make-up stripped away, I wouldn't know what to say to him. I have an urge to go back and curl up next to Catherine, but I don't want to wake her, and I have the idea that now the door has closed on her she too is beyond my reach. The house has that feeling, of changeability and enchantment, conjuring its inhabitants away once out of sight.

I put the glass carefully by the sink with the amassed collection of others from last night, lipsticked and tide marked. The sound of the glass hitting the stone chimes through the kitchen, carrying too far in the quiet. Trying not to make any more noise, I find my shoes and leave a note for Leo and Catherine – a lie – to say I left early to hand an essay in. Then I open the front door – its heavy brass handle cold in my fingers – slip through, and pull it shut on the house, not without a faint, inexplicable feeling of relief.

Outside Leo's house the calm, verdant square, apparently deserted so early on a weekend morning, feels just as strange: there is a pang in the air, a near-sound, unidentifiable. A small, dandelion-headed dog runs out of the bushes, without a visible owner, then stops and looks at me solemnly with its Chinese dragon's face, until I turn and walk out on to the street.

To shake off the uncanniness that has ghosted me so far, I go into the nearest coffee shop to re-establish myself in its hot tropical aroma, little marble tables, copper piping, businesspeople in grey and black, sputtering steam noises, the Polish barista with a coffee stain on her apron. I stand in the queue and eye a glossy pastry until there is a cough behind me. I recognise this variety of cough as an 'excuse me', and turn around to see if I have offended someone.

The man I see startles me. It is as if the odd feeling of the morning has condensed as it follows me, gathering and coalescing into the shape of a figure, stepping after me into the coffee shop. Unease swirls round his body like heat waves, miasmic. He is only slightly taller than I am, consumptive-thin. His hair is black, his eyes are almost black; turning in their sockets with a painful, mournful light, like two burning drops of tar. They are sad eyes, in a sad, thin monkey's face. He looks at me with interest.

Embarrassed, I realise I must have misread the cough and turn back around. Then he says, 'Hello.'

I look back without turning and give him my best unwelcoming smile.

'Was it a good night?' he asks, undiscouraged. 'At Leo's?'

'Excuse me?'

He doesn't explain; he just smiles. His smile is pleasant, as is his voice, though his eyes remain sad.

'Have we met? Are you a friend of Leo's?' I ask.

'In a way. Martin.' He extends his hand. I take and shake.

'Persephone.'

'How do you do,' he says, in such a grave way that he might be asking, '*What is it you do? How on earth do you* do *it?*' This impression hangs for a moment before he continues; 'You have a very interesting name. Did your parents name you? Or did you name yourself?'

'My parents. My mother.'

'I hope she knew what she was doing,' Martin says. He looks bothered by this.

'She's dead,' I say. 'I can't really ask her. It's just a name.' I frown slightly at him, curious and waiting for him to explain himself, but he doesn't appear to notice.

'I suppose that's right,' he says. 'So, what's going on with you and Leo? What's the deal?'

'I'm sorry?'

'It *is* a deal, you know. Someone gets something, you get something back. But what if you give them some money and all you get is a bag of sugar? Metaphorically speaking.'

'I . . . don't know.' I stare at him.

'You give them forged notes, that's what.'

I get to the till then, grateful to be able to face the girl behind the counter and order my coffee, aware that he is still watching me. I realise that he must be a journalist.

'I'm sorry,' I say, taking the coffee too quickly and spilling it on to my hand. 'I have to go now.'

'Good to talk to you,' he says, with an obliging nod. As I get to the door and look back he waves politely, then turns away, becoming only a thin neutral back in a grey coat, so that afterwards I wonder if the encounter happened at all, or if it was just something I made up, a strange end to a strange morning.

When I get home the house is empty and dim. Without the motion of girls to stir the air there is a ghostly smell of old fat from whatever was cooked earlier in the day, and Camilla's perfume still hangs over the stairs. The clutter of the house is lifeless and cold without its makers: the drained wine glass and the open magazine lying next to the sofa could have been there for years. A distant *pang, pang* noise strikes at random intervals: I track it to the kitchen, where a leaking tap is dripping on to the steel drum heap of saucepans in the sink.

I do the washing-up in order to get at a mug at the bottom of the pile, then check my phone.

'Call me when you get back,' Sammy's recorded voice tells me. 'We're all at James's place. Camilla's here already, she said you weren't home. You have to come out – that's an order!' The voice is cheery but unconvinced, as if it already knows I won't come.

I am relieved to be alone at home, without having to talk to anyone, try to be anything. Since Sass's friends told people I knew Leo, my relationships with my friends have changed. Sammy and Laura ask about him with avidity, undeterred by my hesitant, unwilling answers. They ask if he is dating anyone, what he's really like, and if I could get them an invitation to his house, the next time I go. The way they see it, we are part of a syndicate and now that one person has picked the winning number, we can all share in the good fortune. But I hold on to my treasure selfishly, because it is not a fortune that can be divided, it is a seedling, unfolding luminous and fragile, and if we all rush towards it the new shoot will be trampled and crushed.

Camilla doesn't ask about Leo. Since our exchange the other night she has adopted an insincere friendliness, bright and artificial, keeping me back with her singsong hellos and goodbyes. She doesn't invite me to places and she doesn't confide in me, even after the telephone arguments with Marcus I hear through my ceiling. (I used to be able to sonically track the progress of these calls: the metal sigh of the bed as she sat down to begin the conversation, the raised voice, the angry creak of the floor as she jumped up to make her point, the voice becoming louder, the thud of her phone hitting the wall, the agitated glissando of her feet descending the staircase next to my wall, before, finally, the knock at my door.)

I pick up the post that has been propped outside my door. Amongst the bills and slick-surfaced promises from the magical land of direct marketing, whose inhabitants are silky skinned, lush haired and enjoy access to endless credit, I find a letter from my father:

> *Sadie and I thought it might be a good time to take a trip to London. Please be assured that we won't get under your feet, or ask awkward questions about how much you are drinking . . .*

I pause to wonder at my father, now apparently capable of laughing at his own fear of death.

. . . and we certainly won't demand to meet your friends or boyfriends (?). Anyway, I hope to hear from you soon. I won't book flights until I hear your opinion of the idea.

Your loving father, Evan

I put the letter down and try to think of what to do. I feel a strong antipathy to the idea of my father coming to London, out of his natural habitat, away from the wind-faded shutters and quiet classical music of the Assynt house. I don't want to see him here, superimposed upon the sights of London like a man in a doctored photograph, looking baffled and wrong.

And yet, I know that this isn't my real problem, because I do want to see him. I just don't want him to see me. I am afraid that he will notice the difference in me: my hunger, my spiritual thinness. He will wonder what his daughter has got herself into.

Finally, I write back to say how busy I am, citing coursework, lectures, approaching exams. I pick up his letter again, as if its quiet face might reflect something of my father, but the grey of the slate sky outside falls over the page, thrown off the dull and dirty street, and spoils it. The miry light floods my eyes, floods my room, in which the bits and pieces of my existence float as if under a fogged sea. Ashamed of myself, I seal the letter to my father and drop it into my bag, ready to post tomorrow.

This week Leo's group goes to a new bar, prompted by the arrival of paparazzi photographers at Spook.

'We'll go to a few different places for a couple of weeks, then go back to Spook,' Michael explains to me. 'We have to do it every now and again.'

Like a bandit Leo has to keep running: if he stays in one place for too long other celebrities inevitably follow, a trend begins, and things start to get constrictive. The air gets heavier, the stares more acquisitive. Finally, he'll step out of a club into a shower of camera flashes. The photographers shout like they are selling something at a market, 'Leo, Leo. Over here! How was your evening?' Leo gives them a smile: all they ever get, but they never get tired of it.

Michael tells me that every day Bendricks and Blake receive hundreds of letters for Leo: love letters, suicide threats, naked photos, a whole voodoo flood of ex-body parts: hair, nails, once a vial of blood. The letters are boxed and passed to a woman whose job is to sort them, a cardiganed taxonomist of female lust, female sadness. I think about these letter-writing women as I get ready: their ghostly forms surrounding my own shape in the mirror, hovering disappointed and yearning, calling up the past or the future, I don't know which.

Even in the new bar, a place called Casbah – pierced copper lanterns, arched ceilings and inlaid tables – there is no getting away from the effect of Leo. I know very well what women are thinking around him. They get hungry, low voices, they prowl and stalk, they rearrange their necklines, their legs, their hair, they stare at him, as if by looking they can consume him. When Leo walks over to join us I feel not pride that we have been selected from the crowd, but fear, that the crowd might take him away. I have the precarious privilege of an emperor's concubine – except minus the emperor, or any hope of him.

Leo is wearing a pale shirt that shows a slice of his collarbone. His eyes in the light from the bar have a sweltering beauty, a lazy flickering sexual presence, green, green, flaring nearly black at the iris rims in dark coronas, the gathered thick lashes. When they are not on me I search in them, but if they are pools, they are pools at night, and if they are windows, someone has drawn the curtains. He gives nothing away in the saunter of his body, his drowsy mouth.

Later in the night I get my time with Leo, a few minutes of him alone while the others are dancing, and I ask him: 'Do you know someone called Martin?'

Leo shakes his head. 'But then Martin isn't a very memorable name,' he says. 'You're not thinking of dating him, are you? I wouldn't bother. A Martin can only take you so far.'

'What name would you recommend?' I ask him.

Leo considers this. 'Archie.'

'Well, I'll keep an eye out for one. Anyway – I met a man called Martin who says he knows you. Or, well, he didn't exactly say he *knows* you.'

Leo looks at me patiently. 'I see,' he says. 'Or, well, I don't exactly see.'

'I think he was a journalist,' I said. 'I didn't say anything. About you, I mean. I think that's what he wanted.'

'What might you have said?' Leo asks. 'I need to know how far in your debt I am.'

I lower my face, wondering if every conversation I have with Leo is destined to end up this way: progressing confidently until I realise I am scrabbling at the edge of a steep drop, trying to recover safe ground. Perhaps every time I speak to him I can build up the time it takes for it to happen, until eventually I will be able to converse with him in a reasonable and intelligent manner for a full five minutes before reaching the edge and falling silent, flustered and flushing.

'I didn't mean to imply I was holding something back,' I say. 'I don't know you very well . . . I certainly don't have anything bad to say.'

'You must think I'm very boring,' Leo says. 'Remind me to tell you some awful secrets sometime.'

I laugh, relieved, and he smiles, and it seems suddenly that the air is thin on oxygen between us. Leaning together like this, braced against the music as if it is a storm, there is an intimacy, a thrill, which I feel like a change of temperature, though I'm not sure Leo notices it. Then a song begins that I know and love, a sinuous song with a heavy, slippery undertow: it seizes me, swings me up in a sudden alcoholic impulse.

'I have to dance to this,' I tell him, gulping my drink quickly: my throat stinging briefly and intensely, rushing to the dance floor to find the others, skirting and weaving between the revolving constellations of dancers, until I realise that they aren't there, and that Leo has followed me. I have only ever seen him dance in a group – another survival tactic, another evasion – but he is behind me now, and so I keep moving, across the dance floor which simmers and shimmers like a hot spring, the kaleidoscopes of shadow and brightness brushing over my arms and face, and like Orpheus I daren't turn and look at him until we are safely sheltered in the very centre of the crowd, facing each other.

It is too dark to see much except his eyes, still bright, glimmering and narrow-cornered. My hands clench, my bones ring like struck keys. The tide of the music roars in and out: dancing so close to him I can barely make it out, I just follow the bass, obedient as a cheerleader. His hand burns on my waist. I don't know what to do, but he is smiling, and rather than breathe, I step into the unyieldingly hard, warm feel of his body.

It lasts a second, not even that, before the fire alarm goes off, the music vanishes, the lights blaze, and we are all evacuated. As the crowd moves out of the club – bodies slipping against bodies like fish in a net – Leo falls back and I step out alone, into the rainy, spiteful night.

The next day I spend a few hours in the Chancery Lane library trying to finish a draft of a presentation about ethics in management. I had an enforced 'chat' this morning with my least favourite lecturer, who told me that my grades had slipped. He held up my last essay. 'This looks like it was written in an hour – at three in the morning.' I was intimidated by the way he waved it at me, like a war flag, and so I came straight to the library. Just sitting surrounded by books and quiet people has made me feel a little more virtuous already.

The exterior of the library has not changed in over a century: the many steps, the faceted stone, the tiny lead barred panes of glass that make up the towering gothic windows. Much of the interior, however, has been stripped and made prosaic: it is a maze of modernity, an artificial-carpeted, new-chair place that is the same as any other new building.

The library is in this way a microcosm of London itself, the Georgian towers and pinnacles, the stone façades above the electric bluster, the buses and reeking takeaways and neon posters and trails of cars. In some places history has collected – little pockets of forgotten time hidden in cellar bars and untouched marble halls – while in other places the older buildings have been destroyed entirely and steel and concrete blocks have sprung up in their place. Back in the primeval Assynt, man-made objects are denuded of their original meanings and swallowed into the land, but in London the eras physically fight it out. Human traces build up, layer on layer of man-made things, and anyone can add something of their own. This is the right place for Leo, I think; a place always ready for the next big thing.

Thinking about Leo has become a bad habit for me, something I drift into when I am not busy. Some people lose concentration and find themselves with their thumb or their hair in their mouth; I come to and realise I am picturing Leo. I think about him in the library, in my room, in the bars, in bed. I think about him at odd hours; at twelve at night, in the morning, at six, as the day comes loose from the dark husk of the night and I lie in bed, woken as always by the light bursting in through my thin, flowered curtains.

I have nothing of substance to daydream about but I go over the previous night anyway, adding my memory of him opposite me – the cloudy feverish sense of it, the briefness of his assured body, his hand resting on me – to the stockpile of my most treasured recollections. Once outside the club we were met by the others and got into different taxis, and that was the last I saw of him, a wave out of the rain-obscured window and a retreating smile.

I can't concentrate now, not when my body is sending its fractious messages of longing up my spinal cord. Slurry flows from my pen. I get up from my box of moth-colour light below the window, and put my face close to the glass to see the indecisive rain alternately crashing down in iron sheets, then faltering to a tremulous spatter.

After a while, I walk to another floor of the library and look up books about Leo's novels, written by critics. Failing to understand much of it, I follow a whim and look up his sister instead.

Ivy Ford's books are in the classics section and have titles such as *The Orthodoxy of Homer* and *Ovid's Final Distinctions*. I pull out one in a more modern, purple sleeve with the approachable title of *Darkness Makes Any Woman Fair: An Introduction to Feminism and the Classics*. This is only edited by Ivy Ford, but I notice she has written a foreword. The density of the foreword repels me – my eyes landing on terms such as *intratextuality*, *gender binary*, and skipping onwards – but later on in the book I find her own retelling of the story of Persephone. I was hoping to see something of Leo, and it is a surprise to instead encounter myself.

> *My version of this myth*, says Ivy, *has combined elements of Ovid, Diodorus and the Homeric hymn, as well as my own interpretation, in the great tradition of myth telling, which has never been a purist discipline.*

I turn the page, impatient for my own name:

> *Ovid's telling of the myth explores the balance of the symbolic and the personal: social ethics and the more personal 'coming of age' of its heroine. But more than this: the famously gynocentric nature of the myth allowed Ovid freedom to dwell on the contradictions inherent in the contemporary perceptions of femininity.*

I turn the page again:

> *. . . Persephone's own actions are interestingly contradictory. This element of the story is never fully explained by Ovid – was Persephone a true innocent, who eats the seeds without*

understanding the consequences? Or is it more likely that she is aware of the law decided by the Fates and invoked by Zeus, that eating the produce of the Underworld obliges the eater to remain in that land? Her initial fast would suggest so. The fast represents a refusal to accept; a conscious barricade against not only sensuous enjoyment and satisfaction but against entry, and symbolically against sexual entry. It is a determined attempt to delay adulthood, and Ovid makes it clear that the fasting Persephone is 'childlike' – wandering and ignorant – until the moment she eats the seeds.

I turn to the end of the chapter, hoping for a summation:

Ovid's Persephone is an image of power, sexuality, darkness and renewable nature, compelling in her complexity. (In comparison, Hades, the god of the Underworld, loses definition: holding little fascination for Ovid here.) Persephone has become 'other' – but only partly. Following her metamorphosis she is a double goddess, retaining her initial identity as well as her new self: one of the only figures who is able to do so. This duality has given Persephone a vivid, timeless resonance, leading to multiple interpretations of her myth from the early worshippers of her mysteries, scholars throughout history, and modern readers.

I find Ivy's refusal of any final explanation unsatisfying; though I couldn't say exactly what it is I expected from her. I feel an odd comradeship with my mythical namesake: I would like to extricate her from the dim ether of speculation. My mother, the modern reader, herself withdrew from anything more than a vague and flowery interpretation of the story, the celebratory cycle-of-nature stuff of primary school plays. I wonder now if her choice of name reflected something more uneasy: if she knew, or sensed, that her daughter would face some difficulty in life, some unhappy metamorphosis. It is painful to me that I can't ask Sylvia about it, that she won't explain. She has left the personal and become myth herself, eternally inaccessible.

For two weeks after the dance, Leo is gone, and nobody seems to know where.

'He said he was at White's last night,' Catherine says, to which Max replies, 'But I was there and I didn't see him.'

Or: 'He said he was working with Michael,' Emiko tells us, and Michael shakes his head and says: 'I wish he was.'

Leo's friends can laugh about the loss of him, speculating cheerfully about his whereabouts, but I want to cry 'It's not fair!' All I can see is Leo, as if the shape of him has been removed from me with a corer, an outline of absence, running through every cross section. All I can think of is that last, bright night when we danced. I don't know what it meant to him, but I know it is set apart, the only thing I have been given that the other women haven't. It stands out in my account book, like a misprint. I want him to come back and answer it.

No one knows that I danced with him. I wish they did. I wish Catherine, sitting here now with her head tilted in her hand and her hair attracting the light, could say, 'So, what's going on with you two?' just to make it feel real.

I am having lunch with Catherine and Emiko, on an awninged restaurant balcony under the rare spring sun, stirring my ice around in my drink and listening to them talk. It is Sunday, a day I have come to associate with disappointment, with waiting for another week to go by, before I can be delivered into the weekend: the door swinging open on to a night garden, a path lit with lanterns, as blue as the sea, promising any earthly delight for a girl wandering in off the street.

'I don't know what to do about Leo's ticket for this charity ball,' Emiko says eventually. 'I've set one aside for him and for Ivy but I can't get through to him and I don't have her number.'

'Should we be worried?' I ask, relieved that the matter is finally being treated seriously.

'Oh, no need to file a missing person's report yet,' Emiko says. 'This isn't unusual. Leo's not exactly reliable.'

But I can't bear that, I think. I try sometimes to convince myself that I am becoming more used to Leo, that my nerve endings are hardening up, when really they are like millions of filaments, lighting up painfully at the idea of him. Going out and pretending to look casual and happy when my stomach is weighted with a cold stone of suspicion that he won't come. Then the relief when he arrives – turning quickly to the anxiety of hopefulness – or the terrible dull, flat sensation when he doesn't come at all. I hate it but I can't stop it: I am too reactive, too hungry. An accomplished romantic, I am familiar now with these processes of longing; with the art of wanting.

'He's probably seeing someone,' Catherine says.

I blink at her, stricken.'If he had a girlfriend he wouldn't tell you?' I ask.

Catherine laughs. 'God, no. He's so private about it. There'll just be phases of him leaving things really early, or not turning up until midnight, or vanishing completely.'

'He's the famous disappearing man,' Emiko says.

'But he never admits it's actually a girlfriend?' I press.

'No. But there will be signs. Like last time, when Max saw him going into that hotel, then he denied having been there.'

'I think he has some sort of fetish that he can't admit to,' Emiko muses.

'Like what?'

'I don't know . . . Bearded ladies? Grandmothers?'

'No!' Catherine cries, wounded. 'Poor Leo. I think he's just trying to keep his love life out of the press so it's easier to keep it secret from everyone. I think it's romantic.'

'Who was the last girlfriend he admitted to?' I ask them.

'Hmmm, tricky. Probably that one in Italy?' Emiko looks at Catherine for confirmation.

'Yes, her. He went to Italy last year to write his book. He was with someone then, apparently; she must have lived there. We never met her. His Italian publisher visited him and told Michael that he saw a woman's clothes in Leo's apartment. Then Michael told us.'

'Maybe they were Leo's clothes?' Emiko says. 'And that's his big secret.'

I'm grateful when the lunch is over and I have the time to make my painful calculations: trying to add up how much I gave myself away, how much I flirted with him that night, to conclude how exposed I am now, how stupid I look. The results aren't good, so I turn to other, less realistic arithmetic: the probability of Leo actually being with someone else. The evidence so far is flimsy; a period of absence could mean several things. It doesn't necessarily have to mean – I tell myself – that Leo has a new girlfriend, who he now intends to keep as mysterious and hidden as his other girlfriends, and that it's all over for me.

Sometimes when I read what my mother wrote: *Even when they were not together, she was always in her mother's thoughts*, as if she were already writing to me from another place, I speculate that she might have understood that I would grow up without her: that there would be no Demeter for her Persephone.

It was common knowledge that my mother had psychic tendencies, inklings here and there, flashes of information. For example, one day my mother was inside the house when she stood up suddenly and said 'Something's happened to Gustav.'

Gustav was the dog they had brought to Scotland with them from Switzerland, an unusually stupid Newfoundland who spent most of his life under our silver birch chewing flowers, sighing up at the unfriendly birds. There is only one photo of him from these days, which looks as if someone has left an old black rug out in the garden.

My parents went out to the drive where they found that Gustav had been hit by their friends' car pulling up. Apparently he had decided to chase the car, in a rare fit of activity, and had hit his head on the bumper when the car abruptly stopped. It must have been pretty embarrassing for their visitors to have to present my parents with their dead dog – poor Gustav – not to mention confusing, as my mother had already rushed outside crying, 'Where is he? How has Gustav died?' before she had been shown any evidence of an accident.

'We lost touch with the McKenzies after that,' is what my father says.

Sylvia's flashes of second sight were random by nature, but she saw her dead mother, Ellen, more or less every week. Ellen Hill appeared each time in the blue and white spotted dress she was wearing when she died of a blood clot several years before.

'What does your mother want?' Evan asked Sylvia. (He was

possibly worried about not having his mother-in-law's posthumous approval.)

'She doesn't really say anything,' Sylvia said. 'She just wants to be with me.'

I wish my mother would come back like my grandmother did. But I don't simply want her silent presence. I want her to let me have the secret of her happiness. I want her to sit me down and give me a good talking to, something I suspect I could do with.

But then maybe she does come back, maybe she is talking, and I can't see or hear her. I am not psychic like she was; I am blind when it comes to the future. My predictions are complicated by my incessant dreams, and I never, ever, see trouble coming.

A week after my lunch with Catherine and Emiko, Leo is still missing. I speculate about it with the others, in the same amused way they do, and I speculate about him alone, pressing my hands against the side of my head in bafflement and distress.

Finally, I go into the sitting room of our house one morning to find Camilla sitting casually with a newspaper, which strikes me as unusual, firstly because she doesn't read newspapers, and secondly because she never reads anything without having the television on at the same time, a habit that enrages the Claires. ('Why can't we watch *Time Team*? You're not even watching the TV!' To which Camilla calmly replies that she is *half* watching, and she doesn't want to half watch *Time Team*.)

'Hi, Persephone,' she says now. 'Sorry to hear about Leo. You must be gutted.'

'What?' I ask quickly, knowing my curiosity is allowing her a victory, of sorts, and not caring.

Camilla holds up the paper to show me a large picture of Leo, a murky long-lens shot, taken at night. He is getting into a car in an anonymous London street. In the passenger seat there is a girl, her face obscured by the flash on the windscreen. The headline reads: 'Literary star Leo Ford romances new lady.'

'Oh,' I say.

'Or is this "mystery brunette" actually you?' Camilla asks drolly.

'No.' I turn around and head for the door. 'I'm going to do some work. See you later.'

When I get upstairs I lie in bed, allowing my body to drop into the pillows as if falling into deep water, expecting to sink into an airless despair, but the moment is anti-climactic, as if I am lying in a puddle. I am not happy, but I can't quite feel my unhappiness: it is flat, dulled. Any advice I have ever heard to do with 'moving on' or 'getting over' something requires sadness to be released, in a cathartic firework display of tears or rage. I have never been told what to do if the sadness refuses to be drawn out, settling low and dark and stubborn, because there was never anything real to be sad about in the first place.

~

When Camilla goes out a few hours later, I go downstairs and sit in our tiny concrete-walled garden under the pale sunset with a bottle of wine and a pack of cigarettes, something I haven't done since living in Scotland. The first bitter heat of the smoke makes me cough, until I get used to it and it sends its crackle through me again, waking me up a little, a chemical burst.

I bought the cigarettes from the shop near the Strand campus. As I stood in line James walked past the window with another boy and a girl I didn't recognise. The three of them had just stopped laughing at something and James was smiling, turning to his friend, his eyes moving over the spot where I stood behind the glass like a fish in a tank, falling short before reaching me.

I pour myself another glass of wine. I have heard – because my friends insist on updating me on his situation, in the same way that companies continue to send hopeful junk mail long after a sole transaction – that James is single again. He was sleeping with a girl I haven't met, it wasn't expected to last, and it didn't. Now he is laughing with another girl, and may start sleeping with her, something I expect I'll be updated on, in due course.

After the third glass of wine I am thinking more sadly about James, his good-natured, good-looking easiness. I had compared this campus hero to an unreal ideal and dismissed him, when I should have been grateful that he liked me. I moved the goalposts off the pitch and into the land of dreams, an impossible cinema heaven. I linger over the idea of him now, watching him pass the shop again, and then again, his hair blazing in the sharp daylight.

When the fourth glass stands empty, like an hourglass that has counted all its sand down, I go inside, call a taxi, shower, put on a short dress, brush my teeth, ruffle my hair, darken my eyelids, and get into the taxi. My momentum, uninterrupted, carries me out of the car and up some steps to a shiny black front door, which James answers, barefoot, blinking to distinguish me out from the dark outside the door, standing in his own pale segment of light.

'Persephone?'

'Hi, James. How are you?'

'I'm okay. I'm . . . confused.' He looks at me closer. 'Are you drunk?'

'Not especially. Can I come in?'

'Yes,' he says, and steps aside. As he follows me up the stairs his puzzlement makes the journey into the recent past, in which he believes he has wronged me.

'I tried to call you, you know. I wanted to explain about the Camilla thing. I was drunk that night. I made a mistake. Then you didn't answer any of my calls and completely avoided me and I didn't get the chance to tell you how—'

'Water under the bridge,' I say, opening the door to his room.

He follows me inside, still talking, 'It really didn't mean anything. And neither did anything since then. I hope you understand that. I know I really hurt you and I'd just like to show you that I'm not like that.'

'It's fine. Really. You don't have anything to apologise for.' I take my coat and shoes off and put them near the television, where some car crash-explosion-and-bikinied-women film is playing on. So this is what James watches when he's by himself, I note with amusement, and a little sadness.

'And I thought you were dating this famous writer now? Aren't you? What . . . what are you doing?'

'I'm not dating anyone.'

When I switch the television off the room falls dark, with only a foggy yellow light striking in from the street, a row of bay windows through the icy clear window: the outside peering in. It is unexpectedly tidy. It will do, I think.

I sit down on the bed and watch James standing uncertainly,

wondering what will fight its way to the fore: his attempts to convince me of his decency, or the sight of me taking off my dress, the lingering stimulation of the sex and violence he had been watching only a minute before I arrived, his sense of unfinished business. Then he comes over and kisses me, eager and abrupt, pushing me back on to the already-twisted ruck of his sheets on the bed, and I see my decision through with a flat, stubborn sense of achievement, like hanging up on someone, or slamming a door.

The sex itself is quick, slightly painful, exciting and thoughtless. He swears when he can't unfasten my bra, a hushed noise. I am slightly repulsed by the condom, like pallid fish skin, with a chemical smell like car oil. He takes his shirt off but in the haste he leaves his jeans at half-mast on his thighs. Afterwards, denim shackled, he isn't able to get up in time to stop me leaving.

'Where are you going?'

'Home,' I say, putting my knickers back on, wincing as the fabric makes contact with my sticky skin. 'I have a lecture tomorrow. And you have the rest of that film to watch.'

He looks at me with comprehending benevolence. 'No,' he says, 'you don't understand. I don't just want to have sex with you. I want to be with you.' He struggles back into his jeans, reaches up and catches my hand like a mouse.

'You don't,' I say, dismayed, pulling my hand away.

'I do.'

'I didn't realise . . .' I begin, then falter. I don't want to tell him that I came to visit him because I wanted to end something else – to drive out not only my longing for Leo, but the taint of innocence on me, of childhood, of being a wide-eyed country bumpkin from the Highlands saving herself for the love of her life.

As I stare at him, ashamed and increasingly panicked, he rushes to reassure me of his honourable intentions, his eyes gravely keeping hold of mine, staring at me with terrible sincerity.

'James, I'm sorry. I really am, but this is a . . . a misunderstanding,' I interrupt him. 'I didn't realise you felt like this. I don't want a relationship. It's really nice of you to offer. But I just thought this would be one night. That sort of thing.'

He sits on the bed looking stricken. 'Persephone, I don't get it.'

'I'm sorry,' I say again, and then, before he can decide on a reaction, gather my coat and shoes, closing the bedroom door behind me.

When I get home I shower, feeling thoughtful, but without quite knowing what I am thinking about. The hot water hits the commingled scent of James – some branded, sweet aftershave – and my own smells, the moisturiser and perfume I applied earlier in the night, the sharp-edged odour of alcohol, secreted by my skin. Then there is an undertow of unfamiliar scent: coppery, salty, a mineral and metal smell. The perfumes rise up together, expiring in the steam like the ghosts of intimacy. I wash and wash until they are vaporised in the strong synthetic peach of my shower gel, until I feel almost like a newly grown fruit again myself.

As I dry myself I put my hand between my legs investigatively. It feels as if something happened; the skin giving a slight flinch at my touch, but I don't feel exactly injured, either. Which is – I think – a fairly accurate reflection of the night's events.

I make a cup of tea and sit in bed with my legs steepled under the duvet, resting the mug on the peak of my knees, watching the heat rise off it into the chill of my bedroom, feeling guilty again. I had no sense of my own impact before tonight – my idea of myself was more as something hapless, haphazard, carrying no weight of my own, landing and flying off unnoticed, like an airborne particle, and the realisation that I do have a sort of power, over James's feelings, came as a surprise to me.

Despite this regret, I do feel better without my virginity – a virginity that, as far as I know, nobody knew about. I hadn't told anyone at university about my condition and no one had thought to ask. I'm not sure that even James realised what happened just now: I had been careful with my movements, left no red flags. But just knowing my own virginity made me feel awkward; dragging the fact of it around, clanging like a leper's bell. It attached too much importance to my every move, too much expectation, as if I might be hoping to marry whoever I slept with, like a lovelorn baby duck. I should have got rid of it a long time ago.

And, there it is, inevitably. Leo. I try not to think about him but I can't help it. I know he couldn't have responded to my virginity as anything but a pressure, a future guilt. If the unhappenable happened and he looked at me with interest – considered me – I would appear to him not as a dependant but as a woman, someone predefined and complete, asking nothing, offering nothing, and he wouldn't know that this wasn't true.

PART SIX

Persephone sees the Fields of Asphodel, the in-between land, a plain of flowers with no end in any direction, peopled by the ghosts of men. She sees the Elysian Islands, hovering blue-green above the water like sea dragons, hazy with distance. A music issues forth from the islands; beautiful, and not meant to be sad, but it is sad: endlessly so. She sees the gloomy walls of Tartarus beyond Phlegethon's flaming boundary, where her ancestors lie thousands of miles deep, dreaming of the days when they were Titans and the heavens reverberated with their tyranny. Here are the secret-tellers, the son-eaters, the father-killers, their punishments grown dull and blank with eternity. At last she sees Hades, not just for what he appears to be, but for what he is, and he sees her in turn.

Ivy Ford

Persephone and Hades

The next day, as if my ceremonial seppuku has broken a spell, Leo returns. We are at Catherine's house: I am sitting in one of her sculptural ivory sofas, as firm and curved as a rib. The dark slides through the windows, sinking coldly down over us like a silk sheet: it has been a strangely hot day but it is still too early in the year for the sun to survive the night. Catherine has half re-created it, in the warm beams of the candles, the dense bronze lamplight, the bowls of glass-grown flowers. Tonight was meant to be – as Catherine described it – 'a couple of drinks with the usual people'. But her insistence that she make us zombies has tilted and skewed this civilised arrangement, so that Max has passed out on the carpet, Emiko is dancing by herself on a table, Michael is laughing at nothing in particular, and Catherine is now confiding to Anthony in a liquid, slurred whisper that 'I just want to be loved by someone like Leo. Not Leo, because he's my friend. But someone just like him.'

'Pity he doesn't have a long-lost twin,' Michael, overhearing, murmurs to me.

'Long-lost twins are always evil,' I say. 'I think it's the rule.'

'Good point.'

'Why would it have to be a twin, anyway? Catherine and Leo would make a nice couple,' I say idly, hoping he will disagree.

'I don't think Leo sees her that way,' Michael said. 'He's known her for a year or so now. If something was going to happen, it would have happened. But then – what do I know. Leo doesn't give much away.'

'He's only known Catherine for a year?'

'Didn't you know that? Catherine is Emiko's friend. Emiko is with Max. Max went to school with me. I work with Leo. That's how the collection of drunkards you see today was formed.'

This is a shock to me. I had always thought the group, perfect and pristine, must have existed in the same state for years and years before my arrival. I wonder who Leo's friends were, in the time before. Band friends? Drugs friends?

'So you're the hub,' I say, smiling at him.

'No,' Michael says, 'Leo's always the hub. Whether he likes it or not, he can't get away from the spokes.'

'Poor Leo,' I say absently, thinking about what Michael has said, putting it over my picture of the group like a piece of tracing paper, finding that the lines still match up. I have noticed before that though Catherine and Emiko appear to be Leo's closest friends, they are shy of him. They discuss him too laconically; this manner can only be artificial. And when he isn't around they are visibly more relaxed: noisier, more playful. For example, when Leo walks into the room now, Emiko – who is still standing on her table singing, *'Non, je ne regrette rien'* – gets down abruptly, like a ten year old caught out by her parents.

But it is clear that Leo is as drunk as the rest of us, dishevelled and extremely vague. He makes unsteadily and politely for Catherine.

'*I'll be a bit late?*' Catherine quotes incredulously. 'It's four o'clock.'

'Is it?' Leo says, looking startled. He looks outside, where the sky is gradually bleaching to a pale grey. Catherine sighs and hands him a drink, rolling her eyes as if they are married and she is a long-suffering wife, a pretence I know she enjoys, having seen it before.

Leo sits down on the sofa next to me, and whether it is alcohol-clumsiness or simply that he is more familiar with me now, his leg rests against my folded knee. I can smell his scent, piercing and grassy, like sweet mint, with an overlay of whisky and a faint smokiness from wherever he has come from.

I don't try to talk to him, wanting to pull in every sense of him without interruption, just for a moment. I watch his tilted profile as he talks to Catherine opposite – the shadows of the lashes on his cheek, the edge of his mouth – and I get that longing, that stinging, acrid longing that I am nearly used to now. The warmth of his skin gathers on mine; I feel a waking feeling creep up from the touch; along my thigh, until finally he reaches for his glass and moves his leg, and my skin cools again.

'Leo!' Catherine says suddenly. 'Your face!'

I lean forward and there, on the other side of his profile, is the smouldering residue of a bruise, seal coloured, close to his eye.

'Have you been brawling?' Max asks.

'I have no idea what with,' Leo says cheerfully. 'I drank too much last week and woke up on my bathroom floor with a sore face. The sink is the prime suspect, but it won't admit to anything.'

'Bullshit,' Anthony cries. 'That's a punch. A husband's punch.'

'A pregnant girl's punch,' Max hypothesises.

Leo laughs and says nothing.

'I reckon she hit him because he tried to go the "wrong way",' Anthony suggests.

'Or he shouted the wrong name.'

'Yeah – his own.'

'Or he came in her eye.'

They continue their suggestions of what Leo might have done to anger his unknown lover, becoming increasingly ridiculous and obscene, and Leo just laughs, until they give up and change the subject. No one seems to expect to find out what really happened, and I know I can't ask now, either.

My father always calls exactly at the time he says he will. Someone else might say, 'Will you be home tomorrow if I call? Say, five?' and they might call at ten to, or ten past, and this will be understood by the person taking the call. If my father says five, the telephone will start ringing at exactly 5 p.m., which leads me to picture him sitting, receiver in hand, watching the big hand of the clock ascend to its zenith, at which point he dials.

'Hi, Dad.'

'Hello, Persephone. I'm not disturbing you, am I?'

'No, Dad. I was expecting the call, remember? How are you?'

'Oh, very well. Things are much the same here. Well, I suppose much the same as the past few months have been. Not the same as the past few years.'

Neither of us say: *The time before Sadie*, or, *Before you left for university* in case these references are taken as a reproach.

'I suppose the big news is that I thought I might put in a new kitchen,' my father says. 'I thought I might do it myself but I don't really have the tools. Someone called Will is coming on Thursday to have a look at it. I think he feels sorry for me. Then I was thinking that now he's coming I might as well ask about a skylight.'

I remember the old kitchen with its dulled pine surfaces and scarred worktop; the way light coming from the north window used to struggle to fill it, so that the room appeared gently suspended in shade through the year. The wood table where the hiker sat with his arm outstretched on its surface; the muscles interweaving close under his skin, running together, tapering to his wrist, the burnt brown colour of him.

A cast-iron casserole dish occurs to me next, too heavy for Sylvia to lift, bought as a wedding present for my parents on the grounds that it would outlast them both: a promise already half fulfilled. Then my father, trying to cook, getting it nearly right, turning round from the oven abashed and mildly annoyed, two plates held out.

Distracted by the life of the kitchen flashing before my eyes, I am unprepared for his announcement that he is going to visit one weekend after Easter (Sadie's voice excited in the background: 'We can't wait to see you! We'll take you for afternoon tea at the Ritz!') and reply without thinking, 'Yes, that would be lovely,' and it is agreed: my father is going to come to London and see his daughter, and what he will make of her I have no idea.

As one of Emiko's closest friends I am obliged to buy a ticket to a charity ball she has organised, which I don't want to go to at all.

My new friends' dislike of pomp and pretension has sheltered me from the full brightness of London's money, like someone squinting up at the sun behind a cloud and through sunglasses, yet still blinking at the fierceness of it. But money isn't simply the petrol of the city – powering it like an engine – it is an incarnation in its own right, demanding obeisance, and Emiko has to pay court to it in the halls where it blazes in thousands of reflective surfaces – sequins and jewels, precious metal and crystal – before it will allow itself to be sent to children in developing countries.

Walking up the steps of the ornate and crenellated hotel, diamantine windows blinking in the chilly blue of the night, I feel my nervousness sharp against me as I hand over my coat and stand alone in my nakedly thin dress and spindly shoes. I am relieved when I find Michael: I can stay with him as the others swoop from known person to known person, ebbing and flowing under the chandeliers, as champagne wheels round to us on silver platters held by black and white staff whom I don't know whether to smile at or not.

'You look worried,' Michael says.

'I've never been to anything like this before. I've never seen so many famous people . . . it's like Madame Tussaud's has come to life.'

'You know, all your references are straight horror staples,' he remarks, laughing. 'Evil twins, living waxworks . . .'

'Well, I'm frightened.'

'Dutch Courage!' Michael cries, ambushing a champagne-carrier. 'Did you know that refers to gin? Invented by the Dutch, apparently.'

After a few glasses of champagne and a reassuring monologue

from Michael on the topic of alcohol, a soothing murmur that works as it would on a frightened horse, Leo appears on the stairs, sees us, and makes his way over. He is holding a glass of champagne in each hand, which I have realised is a trick of his to avoid being stopped by people. Leo's escapes: performed so often I'm not sure that they are even conscious any more. Sometimes it seems he does it before even registering the person talking to him, waving across a bar, tapping his arm. They think they have him, and then with a murmur, an apologetic smile, he is gone, as if in a puff of smoke.

'I heard my favourite Ford is back from Greece,' Michael says to him.

Leo nods. 'She's here somewhere. We arrived together, but I haven't seen her all night. I think I've been shaken off.'

'Ivy's here?' I ask. What little I have heard of Ivy Ford – primarily through her writing and what is written about her – has given me the feeling that we are in a strange and one-sided relationship. Though she has no idea of my existence, she knows more about Leo than I do, and more about my namesake than I do, thus commanding privileged access not only to the object of my affections, but also to my own identity. My uncomfortable half-sisterhood with her can only be balanced by meeting her.

'It says something that someone who's been away for three months can't tolerate being reunited with their brother for three minutes,' Michael says, then widens his eyes. 'Speak of the devil.'

Even if Michael hadn't said anything I would have understood that the woman arriving now is Ivy, because she couldn't be anyone else. She creates the same awareness that Leo does: people move out of her way with the same slyness, covertly looking. She wears a long dress in a gleaming ginger colour, red-gold; her hair is a lit brown. She has his green eyes, very bright, flickering like butterfly wings. Her eyes have the same, more sightful gaze as his, the same resistance to interpretation. However, as I look at her for longer, I can see that her physical similarity to Leo only extends as far as her eyes, the rest of the resemblance being a trick of manner, existing in her movements only. They both arrange themselves in a similar way; relaxed but held back. Even their interest, their friendliness seems to arrive across a distance, like aviators waving down at their spectators, from a great height.

'Hello, Ivy. Long time! We missed you,' Michael says as she kisses him. 'In fact – we had to replace you. This is Persephone.'

Ivy smiles and takes my wavering hand. Her hand is slender but her fingers feel strong, cool as ceramic.

'You're my replacement?' she says. 'I suppose that makes us enemies.' I open my mouth, flustered, but she is laughing. 'Persephone is a lovely name. I haven't met a real life Persephone before.'

'Apparently,' Leo says, 'Ancient Greeks were superstitious about actually saying the name Persephone. They used other names instead.'

'Nice of you to enlighten Persephone on the subject of her own name.' Ivy raises her eyebrows at me, inviting me to join her casual mockery of Leo, as if that is something I am capable of.

'I actually know hardly anything about the myth,' I admit, curling a little at the edges, feeling – not for the first time – embarrassed at having aspired to a name without any academic knowledge of it. 'Why didn't they say her name?'

'She was a goddess of death,' Ivy says. I must look dismayed because she adds quickly, 'Also one of renewal and fertility.'

'It reminds me of that *Macbeth* superstition,' I say. 'Maybe I should tell everyone to call me the Scottish Girl.'

'I prefer Persephone,' Leo says. 'But then, I like to live dangerously.'

What he says isn't technically flirtatious; it is flirtation's distant relative, bearing only the faintest family resemblance. But I respond as if it is the real thing, and am too self-conscious to reply. I have noticed that of all the new friends I have made in England it is Leo who has never shortened my name to Perse or Pers: he is the only one who gives it so much time in his mouth. But whether this is a sign of his appreciation for it (and perhaps its owner) or whether he is simply preserving a protective cellophane layer of formality between us, I can't tell.

'Ivy! There you are!' Catherine rushes up to us. 'You didn't tell us you were back. I heard you've been in the UK for a while? Were you avoiding us?'

'It's been busy,' Ivy says with an apologetic tilt of the lips, and Catherine brightens, as mollified as if Ivy had been far more affectionate.

'Well, I hope you're ready to resume full duties now,' she says.

As if on cue, a photographer appears and we arrange ourselves in an uncomfortable row. Michael and I exchange the glances of non-famous people who are likely to be cropped out. Leo and Ivy exchange a glance of indeterminate meaning. Catherine, the most civilised of us, stands in the middle with an obligingly wide smile. I glance at Ivy next to me and am grateful for the prospect of being neatly sliced off the picture like the crust-end of a loaf of bread. Next to Ivy's fiery, leafy dress and her colourful eyes, my ashen silk and sun-starved skin must give me the appearance of a drowned Pre-Raphaelite girl. I skulk uncomfortably in my own body, wishing I could go home and start again.

When the photographer moves away I take advantage of Ivy's proximity to ask, 'So, you and Leo are half-siblings?'

'We have the mutual bad luck of sharing a father,' Ivy says.

'Oh, I'm sorry.'

'Please don't be. I've only had two years' exposure. I moved in with Leo and William when I was sixteen and left when I was eighteen. That was enough.'

'It must be a difficult thing to deal with,' I venture.

'Not particularly. Family is just a genetic coincidence. We're only socialised into treating it as sacred. So I don't see William as a failed father. He's just a man I met a long time ago, and didn't much like.'

I try for a moment to think of my father – greying, worrying, his puzzle of picture frames, his one Ravel record, sitting in the garden looking hopefully at the barren magnolia tree – as a genetic coincidence.

'Anything beyond that is just attaching unnecessary and artificial meaning to the relationship,' Ivy says, giving me a sudden, almost coquettish smile behind her wine glass, as if in sympathy with my inability to understand her.

'Where were your mothers?' I ask, fascinated.

'Mine was dead,' Ivy says, 'Leo's had emigrated. And we didn't have any spares.'

'I remember the day Ivy arrived,' Leo reminisces. 'She was a little bitch. She broke my nose throwing a book at me.'

'He who lives by the sword,' Catherine says wittily, then frowns, then goes red. There is a moment's pause as the air cools in a halo around her.

'It was genre fiction too,' Ivy says wryly, 'adding insult to injury,' and we can all laugh.

I'd like to talk more to Ivy, but she is quickly accosted by someone she knows, and though I look out for her throughout the rest of the ball, it isn't easy with the changeable crowds, sifting and shifting, and the rising tide of champagne that eventually closes over my head, so that I view the party as if I am underwater, through an entrancing, shimmering haze, until finally I wake up in daylight in Catherine's house with my feet hurting from dancing to music I didn't recognise and my stomach hurting from laughing at jokes I can't remember, without having seen her again.

When I go back home the next day, I realise that I have no food of my own in the house, and I can't afford to buy more, having spent most of my allowance on the dress for last night. I walk to the local fish and chip shop, whose greenish tiles and fluorescent lighting remind me of a public swimming pool. I pass two men who are leaving, arms and legs angled outward as if to occupy as much room as possible, both of whom give me an exaggerated once-over. I look at the ground until I have passed them. There seems to be a point of etiquette among this type of male, that the moment a woman is behind them – no matter how close she still is – comments may be passed freely and loudly about her face, body, sexual preferences and so on, and this is exactly what happens now.

As I wait for my own grease-shiny parcel from the stern Chinese woman behind the counter I am joined on the row of plastic chairs, under the chlorine glare of the lights, by two young teenage girls in identical pink tracksuits, who rifle impatiently through a magazine, taking in images and the occasional word at high speed.

'He's fit,' one pronounces. Her finger comes down on the page. I glance across. Under her pink fingernail is Leo's face. The picture was taken last night, at the ball. I am surprised at how quickly the media works, that I can follow the actual Leo into print, and back in the flesh again, as if he is passing in and out of real life.

The girl doodles her nail over Leo's mouth. 'I would.'

'A writer? A *book writer*?' the other observes, pulling a strained face.

'Still would. Still got money. Doesn't matter how he got it.'

'My cousin's a pap. *He* has one of them white four-by-fours. White leather interior. Custom rims.' She pronounces it as if reading from the catalogue.

'No.'

'Yeah,' the first says, with finality, and they fall silent, in mutual contemplation of this heavenly white vision.

I had never seen a paparazzo before I met Leo, and I find it hard to adopt the attitude the others have towards them, that they are just something in life, like sudden rain showers or punctured car tyres, that must intermittently be borne. They stand on the opposite pavement to whatever bar their quarry is emerging from, a welcome party with flashes and shouts. 'Hello, Leo! Over here, mate! Good evening, was it?' But at other times someone less popular, or someone scandalous, will appear and their cheeky friendliness is abandoned, the school-boyish effrontery, and they turn jeeringly righteous. 'Who is she then, eh? Where's the money? How's the wife? Did you do it? Did you?'

The paparazzi frighten me: leaking from one half of London to the other, bringing with them the smog, the dark, choked greyness across which I skim uneasily, making the journey towards the bright. They are bottom feeders, with a hatred for the celebrities who feed them, as if wanting to eat them entirely. Though the people might look down on the paparazzi, they are an expression of the people, their dense envy, their hunger.

Coming from a vast nowhere-land, this aspect of London worries me. The way people flow down the streets like wasps; living packed in, like termites in towers. I can't help but think that, if provoked, they will rush out; they will mob and hurt someone, even the nicer people. They will all be caught up in it; they will not be able to stop themselves.

'I think he's definitely sleeping with her,' Sammy says. 'They said they were going out to get cigarettes and they took, like, an hour. And they looked really shifty when they got back.'

It is a few days before the Easter holiday and Sammy, Camilla, Laura and I are sitting outside a café, at a little silver table that shifts each time a cup is put down on it, trying to snatch as much as we can of the scanty sunlight. Having been invited by Laura and not being able to think of a good reason why not, I came. Now I sit and reflect on the several good reasons why not that have occurred to me since I sat down, while trying to follow an ongoing soap opera of a conversation I dropped a long time back. Of course, it is the same conversation it has always been, some familiar names; some new.

'You could spy on him!' Camilla suggests. 'We could dress up and follow him and see what he does.'

'Do you really want to be with him?' Laura asks. 'It's only been two weeks and this is the third big argument over him flirting with other girls.'

'Fourth, if you count that abusive text I sent him,' Sammy corrects her.

'Well, then. Anyway. I'm not going to say anything else. Everyone ignores my advice anyway.'

'It's because you've been lucky and you don't have to go through all this shit,' Camilla says, without unkindness.

I look at her with interest, wondering at the change in temperature. Camilla has been noticeably friendlier to Laura since our estrangement and I wonder whether this represents a genuine acceptance of Laura's betrayal (in getting a boyfriend), or simply prudence on her part, because getting rid of both me and Laura would leave her with a significant friend shortfall, and so she has decided to pardon the less offensive of our two crimes. Sometimes I wonder if I have hurt her feelings, but I can't tell whether she is hurt by the loss of me, for myself, or for the loss of her listener and her sidekick.

'I haven't been lucky! I've met guys who flirt with other women or are rude or jealous or don't pay you any attention or are just more interested in other things, and I *didn't date them*.'

Sammy shrugs, not listening, and turns to me, 'So, any Leo Ford updates?'

'Nothing much. I barely know him.'

The sceptical look Sammy and Camilla exchange now shows how unreliable they consider me to be. I investigate my feelings about this, and find I have none either way.

'Did you see him at that ball?' Sammy asks.

'Briefly.'

'Is he single? What about that woman he was with? In that picture?'

'I don't know if he's single, and I don't know who the woman is.'

'Maybe you should give him my number just in case,' Sammy says, undeterred.

Camilla listens coolly while I am questioned about Leo, with a faint, irritating smile as if she feels sorry for me. Then she says, 'So, Marcus and I are thinking of going on a holiday together this summer.' With this familiar tactic – a conspicuous change of the subject – she imagines she is puncturing my pretensions, not knowing that I'm grateful for her intervention. Before I met Leo I would have expected that I'd enjoy being questioned about him: the chance to flash his name around, like a credit card. But I'm not interested in doing it after all: not because I have attained any kind of philosophical calm about such things – more that, these days, I have different people to impress.

Feeling tiredness well behind my eyes, I put my hand up to my mouth discreetly but Camilla, still talking about holiday destinations, notices and I have to arrest the yawn, finally managing to swallow it.

After lunch I walk to the tube station with Laura, who also has a lecture to go to.

'Are you okay?' she asks me, unexpectedly.

'How do you mean?'

'Look, I know you slept with James. He told Ben, and Ben told Alex. Nobody else knows,' she adds, 'I haven't said anything. I was just wondering why? He was a bit depressed about it.'

'I didn't promise him anything,' I say defensively, reminded of my guilt about James.

'I'm not criticising you. I just didn't know why you'd suddenly sleep with him, when you said before you didn't like him. And now you don't like him again. It's just a bit . . . random.'

We walk in silence for a moment, and I consider telling her about Leo, and his absence, and my unwanted virginity, but I just can't do it. I have no practice in confiding, or revealing: my mouth stiff as an unused tap.

'I was drunk and muddled,' I say. 'I didn't intend to sleep with him but I did, and then afterwards it all seemed so wrong.'

'I understand,' Laura says, and changes the subject, but not quickly enough that I don't notice her frown. I know she doesn't understand at all, but has decided to accept what I say, because what else can she do?

I say goodbye to her and walk home looking forward to the Easter holidays, when I can be alone in the house, the emptied rooms refilling with my own expectations, my own wonderings. I won't have to give my attention to anything, the scanty attention I have left, sputtering and dying like champagne froth. I won't have to come down and gaily greet the girls when our house is chosen as the venue for an afternoon drinking session, or make my excuses and wave them off when they clatter perfumed and colourful into their taxis.

I wish I had better reasons for the neglect of my former best friends. The only reasons are nots and not quites. Not enough in common. Not quite close enough to begin with. And now I have discovered Leo, and it seems they can just fall away, like ash from something burning.

Martin finds me as I am walking from the clotted tube station towards Catherine's house, down a long narrow street into which the sun slots, hard and impassive, beating on to the many heads of the pedestrians, who tuck their faces down and battle onwards as if it is another rainy day. Moving crosswise through frowns and glares, a sooty-colour coat emerges, and ends up next to me.

'Hello,' Martin says.

I hadn't expected to see him again and stare at him with suspicion. Martin occupies a dark and indistinct category: not yet a danger, certainly not a friend.

'I haven't met you – aside from the other week – have I?' I say to him accusingly.

'No.'

'And you aren't a friend of Leo's.'

'No.'

Despite this admission, Martin keeps pace with me anyway. I stare ahead, intending to ignore him.

'So, you're not dating Leo,' he says, as if informing me of this sad fact. I don't answer but he accepts this as confirmation and gives me a rueful look from his soft, dark eyes. 'I thought you'd be a faster operator,' he says.

'What are you suggesting?' I ask, though I know I shouldn't ask questions. I imagine myself in the police station trying to explain that I have a stalker. ('So you asked this person *questions*, Miss Triebold? Did you think that was a sensible course of action?') But I can't help myself, and I don't feel threatened by him, his smallness, vulnerable neck and neat suit. The heat, which toughens everyone else, seems to sap and shrink him. He moves frailly, glancing at people as they pass. The density of the crowd under the staring sunlight also reassures me, though I could well imagine the pedestrians clunking impassively on as Martin stabs or shoots me, turning their faces away, tracking my blood up the road in hundreds of footprints.

'You're good looking, you're clever. I have a suspicion you are a nice person. It shouldn't take long for a man to fall in love with you. Why don't you make your move?'

'What are you, some sort of freelance dating coach?' I ask. 'If you think I'm going to discuss this with you, you're mistaken.'

'That's okay,' Martin says equably.

'What do you *want*?' I ask. 'Are you a journalist? Who are you?'

'I'm Martin Black and I'm a book reviewer,' Martin says. 'I've interviewed Leo before. I don't expect he would remember.'

'So, if he doesn't remember you, and you've only met him once, why are we talking about him? Why are you talking to me?'

'I like a good conversation.'

'You want to write an article about him, don't you?' I ask, suspicious. 'You're hoping I'll let something slip.'

'Have you met his sister yet?' Martin asks.

'As it happens, yes.'

'Don't be uptight, I'm not going to ask you about her. I know what you think about her.'

'How?' I know I have asked too many questions. The correct thing to do would be to avoid eye contact and say, 'You're bothering me. Leave me alone.' I will say it, soon. We are only a few roads from Catherine's house and I don't want him to know where I am going, in case he waits in order to follow me when I come back out.

'You wonder what sort of woman she is, to date a man who

shoots her brother. Or a man whom her brother attacks with a sword. Because it hasn't been established, of course, what happened first – shooting or stabbing.'

He is right, which annoys me.

'So that's what you want,' I snap, stopping to face him. Someone behind nearly falls over me, then the people ripple, tutting, around us and move on in the current. 'You're digging. You want to do an exposé or something.'

We stare at each other. He shrugs, as if apologetic.

'Why are you talking to me?'

'I just need a few . . . finishing touches. And anyway, I like you.'

'Well, I don't like you. Why would you want to ruin someone's life?'

'You assume that what I know will ruin his life?' To which I can't reply, frustrated at being talked into a corner. His eyes' acknowledgement of this victory is sorrowful, his smile strained, as if his face isn't made for it. It is partly this air of sorrow that makes him appear so small and fragile, like an ant in a glass of water, floating in sadness.

We face each other in the heaving crowd; a little patch of silence in between us. Then I say, 'You're bothering me. Leave me alone,' and walk away.

He doesn't try to follow me, and when I get further down the road and look back, he has gone.

When I get to Catherine's I am red and sweating, from walking too fast in the clinging heat, away from the encounter with Martin.

'You look flustered,' she says. 'Are you okay?'

I sit down and take deep breaths, generous scoops of air, allowing the wide space of her apartment to calm me. She gives me a glass of water, frosted with chill.

'I just saw a local lunatic,' I say. 'I seem to attract them.'

'God, that's happened to me so many times! Last week some drunk jumped out at me, then ran away. I think he just wanted to make me jump.'

'Was this around here?' I ask. I feel oddly protective of Catherine in her flowery white street, which ought to be inviolable, an ivory enclave.

'No. It's a bit quieter in this part of town, fortunately.'

Eventually we talk about the ball and I can eagerly listen as Catherine deconstructs it, as if watching a carnival float stripped – the lights and bright paper picked away, revealing the base assembly of metal. Listening to her now, talking about charity board feuds, erratic celebrity behaviour and catering disasters, I wonder how the ball ever intimidated me.

'But on the whole Em was pleased,' she concludes.

Sensing that Catherine might be about to change the subject, something she does with swift finality, I say: 'Ivy seemed really nice.'

'She's not your typical academic, is she?' Catherine says. 'I always expected her to be a librarian type, you know – spectacles and cobwebbed vagina. I was quite stunned when I first met her. She definitely has the family looks.'

'I don't understand how she only met Leo and William when she was older,' I say, hoping Catherine, who enjoys telling a good story, will pick up the trail.

'Yes, it's a weird set-up, isn't it?' she says, leaning in now with enthusiasm. 'I don't know all that much about it, but apparently Ivy's mother hated William. They weren't married – William cheated on Leo's mother with Ivy's mother. When she got pregnant she finished with him, so William wouldn't know he had a daughter. Except she was an alcoholic and so they didn't have any money. Then Ivy's mother killed herself.'

'God.'

'Yeah, Ivy was fifteen. She was meant to go to live with William but she ran away and lived for a while with some dealers in a squat in Hackney. Completely dropped out of school, everything. She only came back when they got raided by the police and her friends went to prison. She had to live with William and Leo. Leo's mother was long gone by then, which probably made it slightly less awkward. But not much.'

'William doesn't seem to have a great history with wives.'

'No – I understand he's an utter cunt,' Catherine says. 'Leo and Ivy didn't get along at first but I think they were united by William. A sort of "common enemy" thing.'

'How old was Leo?'

'Well, he's a year older than her so he must have been seventeen. He signed a record deal not long after that. So he and Ivy were as different as they could possibly be.'

I nod but I don't see it that way: I think Leo and Ivy had found themselves in strangely similar situations. Leo was on the way to fame, Ivy had been living in the dim drug hinterlands. Both of them had grown up already: without any peers, anything to compare themselves to. They couldn't help but stand out.

'How awful for Ivy. I wish I hadn't mentioned any of it at the ball.'

'She won't mind. I've never seen Ivy offended. I think she's been through enough genuinely awful stuff not to worry about one of her friends putting their foot in it. Like what I said about living by the sword . . . !' She puts her head in her hands exaggeratedly.

Hearing this now, the first mention of the yacht incident by one of Leo's friends, electrifies me. I feel like a wildlife photographer must when – after sitting uncomfortably for months in the cold and wind, hopelessly waiting – a snow leopard hoves into view.

'No one ever talks about that, do they?' I ask.

'I heard Max made a joke about it to Leo a while ago, but it didn't get a very good reception. The subject is *verboten*, basically. I've never asked him about it and neither has Emiko. It all happened before we knew him.'

'You're not curious about it?'

'Of course we are,' Catherine cries, hands opening helplessly. 'Nobody knows why Bruce tried to shoot him. None of them said anything in court. They all wanted to drop the case. And as far as I know, no one has said anything since. It's not the kind of topic where we might say, "Hey, Leo, what was that yacht palaver all about, eh?"'

'I guess not.'

'Everyone knows it has to be something to do with drugs. Ivy was into them at the time, which must have been how she met Yelland. But again, I don't know Ivy all that well and I've never asked her about it.'

'Clearly there aren't any hard feelings between her and Leo,' I observe.

'No, it's obviously Bruce who was the bad guy. Some people say maybe Leo was the first person to . . . attack him –' she pauses and I can tell we are both trying to picture the same thing, the thing that can't be pictured. After meeting Leo, the yacht incident had travelled down the rankings of my thoughts, displaced by the disorientating presence of Leo himself. It is impossible to imagine how this Leo could attack somebody with a sword. He must have moved forward so quickly. Did he pull the sword back afterwards, or let it go as Yelland fell? The blood there must have been, on both of them. '– but Leo would never have done that,' Catherine concludes.

'Oh, definitely,' I agree.

Though I don't say it to Catherine, I think I can see one of the reasons why Leo and his friends have fallen in together. Catherine and the others are not the kind of people to show their curiosity: they are too civilised, they don't show direct emotion or need. When they do talk about the personal, it is in a neat and conversational form, presented either as a joke or as something historical, to be treated with detachment. Used to my father's reticence, I had to adjust to the noisy, ragged immediacy of my university friends' feelings – their demanding force – but now I find myself in familiar territory again. There is something reassuring in my new friends' layer of urbanity, of social grace. They don't question me with, 'So who do you fancy?' like Camilla might, they don't beg for advice on some crisis that I have no idea how to solve, they don't expect more revelations from me than I am capable of. It is this quality, too, that must appeal to Leo, allowing him to elude, to remain slightly apart, to keep his secrets.

~

That night I dress according to my want, which reaches out to Leo; an ache stretching across London. It cries out; it twists and yells. I put on a long silver pendant that trails down the diving V of my crows-wing top, black patent stilettos, shiny as liquorice. I apply dark make-up, then more, my eyelids plum-like, a dark sheen under a sulky frost. I do all this in a house emptied of housemates; my own noises – rustling fabric, the whine of a zip – the only sound. Finally, I go out into the night that seems to hover, indecisive, between the possibilities of rain or calm. It gives me the feeling that I am in a parallel plane, located off to one side of real life, different in countless significant ways.

When we arrive at Spook its revolving room has changed again, having a German fairy-tale theme; a hazy lamplit bar, mirrored trees ringing the walls, reflecting the shadowy interior like an enchanted black forest. Another room has been opened up beyond that, as if the unnamed owners of Spook are tunnelling further below London like goblins, expanding their territory. This room is cavernous, hundreds of tiny lanterns hanging from its ceilings, shaping the dark walls into new and indistinct forms.

'In the Hall of the Mountain King,' Catherine explains. 'That's what it is this month.'

'How do you know?'

'Max used to work with the owners. That's how we always get in free.' She laughs at my surprise. 'Didn't you think that was peculiar?'

I hadn't wondered: the free entry seemed simply part of the group's enchanted existence, moving past queues and barriers, passing from hidden space to hidden space, the world shifting itself to one side to make room for them.

The evening in this alternate reality follows an unusual course. Emiko and Max, normally so at ease in their relationship, are irritable, jarring at angles where they usually fit together, and finally leave early, wrapped in a thick layer of pending rage. Michael, normally a reassuring presence, is absent with a cold. Leo talks to me and Catherine only briefly, before drifting out into peripheral vision, and finally vanishing, and Catherine for once doesn't look after him. She suggests we dance, and I accompany her until I realise she is aiming her dancing at a man nearby, who watches her, smiling, so I excuse myself and go to the bar.

As if influenced by Catherine's disloyalty, I scan the room myself, looking for someone attractive. I am tired of not having anyone to touch, to be solid next to me and reassure me that I still exist. It occurs to me that I could find Anthony, who has a history of ambushing the girls who come innocently after Leo, then making them miserable. I have heard he is good in bed, and I know he couldn't make me any more miserable than – drunk and self-pitying – I already consider myself to be.

Sleeping with Anthony would be to officially fold, declare myself out. Perhaps then there would be an end to this anxious state, existing nervily, my senses heightened, strung out between desire and disappointment. I could move back into the time before I'd heard of Leo, when things seemed more under control. And surely this is the night to do it, while everything is off-kilter, like a leap year, a small tear in the regularity of life, through which I might slip.

I finish my drink and put the glass on the bar with finality, intending to look for Anthony before I can change my mind.

'Persephone.'

Leo is standing next to me. 'Catherine just left with some guy and she couldn't find you,' he says. 'She said she is very sorry and gave me her key to give to you. I can share a taxi back with you. We're practically neighbours.'

'Oh, okay,' I say, taken aback. 'When did you want to leave?'

'Whenever.' He tips his hands up.

'Well, I don't mind when we go either.'

We stare at each other for a moment, as if both refusing to give in and state a preference.

'Then how about now?' he says, turning around and walking away. Realising I will be left behind, I run after Leo into the street, where it is raining after all. As he hails a taxi I notice something impatient about him, sending the keys flying with a metallic chime up from his hand, catching them again sharply.

Once in the back of the car, I feel too drunk and fractious to talk. I press my lips together and sit in silence. Leo seems to have no interest in conversation either. He doesn't appear to be drunk: his eyes are watchful, looking out of the window at the houses that roll by, pillared and stony. I sit with him like this for what seems like a long time and no time at all, suspended in a twilight of strangeness and impossibility, stretching in all directions, around and beyond the two of us.

When we stop at Catherine's house he gets out after me, and pays the driver.

'I'll walk from here,' he explains.

We both stand for a moment in front of the dim night steps of the house, the rain having stopped, and watch the taxi roll away with a solemn sense of occasion, as if it is the last car in the world – which it might well be, there being no other traffic at this time of night. The idea of this makes me smile. He notices but doesn't say anything. My smile drops off my face.

I don't understand why we are standing here together, how it has happened, but I understand that I am exposed, simply by facing him like this, not smiling, not ending the silence. I look up at him, his unveiled eyes, their underwater green, without hiding myself. He looks back at me with a slight frown, a seriousness, and then he kisses me.

It is a shock: so much so that I can't fully feel his mouth on mine. I have the sensation of freezing, of falling: there is a crazy exhilaration, like a soldier must feel who has got over the top of his trench and is running and realising he hasn't been shot. After a moment my body comes back to me: I can feel the pressure of his hand on my back, his skin under the creased fabric of his shirt, hot in the cold air. I can tell his kiss is skilful, it is demanding, it isn't offering anything except its own immediacy. Leo Ford, I think, trying to comprehend it. Leo Ford is kissing me. But the name floats free far above me, detached from all sense, clear and bright like a road sign.

When Leo moves back I nearly lose my balance: I must have been leaning into him. His frown has gone, supplanted by a hard-to-interpret smile.

'So, Michael tells me you're mourning some undergraduate.'

'Oh, no,' I say. 'No, no.' I am horrified that this has been passed on to Leo. 'It was nothing. I mean, I used to like him, but not any more.'

'Poor guy,' Leo says, amused. I wish I could take up this tone myself, but it seems I am doomed to play the straight man.

'Shall I call you, then?' he says, taking my hand. Very slowly, as if half awake, I realise he is giving me the house key. I am all outward facing like a mirror, holding nothing but his reflected, ambiguous expression, tipsy and shaken and bewildered, but I get myself together just for that moment and manage a nonchalant mouth lilt, if not quite a smile.

'Why not,' I say.

He laughs. 'Bye, Persephone.'

I move away first, making it up the steps without tripping, unlocking the door without fumbling, going inside without looking to check whether he is standing below me or whether he has already walked away. Then I sit down abruptly on the white and black marble-tiled floor of Catherine's apartment, like a chess piece, held in suspension. I put my hand up to my mouth as if the skin of my lips still holds some charge, some trace of what happened, and lean my head against the front door. I don't know how long I sit there, unable to even think anything, to fit events to the shape of my mind. I watch the light on the tiles dim and recede like water: the glass of the door filtering the harsh street light into a purer gold, lighting up my skin like a halo, like a transfiguration.

PART SEVEN

'Tell her I did not want to steal her against her will, but I am unable to regret my dishonest act. And though I bow to the decree of my brother, she must know that if I had been her husband she would have not one cause for anger or tears. I would have kept her as safely as if she were in the sheltered glades. I would have given her anything she asked for. No creature would have failed in its duty towards her. No star of the mines would not have shone on her. No expression of love would have been denied her. Wait – do not say these things. Just tell her . . . I am sorry.' Hades gestures: away. His smile is grim.

Ivy Ford

Persephone and Hades

For five days after the kiss, silence follows, and I exist in a place where it is all there is, one kiss, on repeat. Sometimes I consider the run-up to it, Leo's behaviour that evening: which hand movement, which side swipe of the eye, might indicate that the kiss was planned and not a moment of madness. I refer to the events of the night – he chose to get out of the taxi rather than travelling on to his house; he could have given me the key at the bar, but decided to leave with me. I even reread a text message from him sent the week before, saved in my phone's memory like a dried flower in a book, though I know it word for word – 'You left your scarf here. Catherine has it. Leo X' – seizing on the X as a direct signifier of our eventual kiss. And on I go, left to myself in the vacant rooms of my house, ringing with the erratic dripping of the kitchen tap, building my case for pre-meditation half out of hard fact and half out of longing, a sparkling and unstable confection.

On the other side of this is my worry, which expands the more space I allow it, diffuse and comprehensive. What if Leo and Catherine are sleeping together? Or Leo and Emiko? What if he and Ivy are still in trouble with Bruce Yelland and have to flee the country? Or there is the other option – the one I don't want to even consider – that he has changed his mind and wants to forget the whole thing. I couldn't bear it if he came to me, like a boy came to Sammy once at university, and said, 'About last night, er, sorry.' The tarry shame of having that said to you.

When I hear the periodic sharp tones of my phone I get a little fearful chill of excitement, like drinking cold water quickly and feeling it travel to the stomach. My heart clenches; it is almost painful. It is never him calling.

I can't discuss it with anybody, not even Catherine and Emiko, not yet. I might have expected something like this to feel like a victorious secret, but it seems that in something secret there can be no truth. The kiss that nobody sees is the sound of a tree falling in the empty forest; its reality is questionable.

I wonder what my mother would say to me, if she were here to give advice. I suspect she would be disappointed. In her world, governed by the ideals of parity and female empowerment, a woman would not sit miserably watching reality shows on television, glancing every few minutes at the lifeless mobile phone beside her, like a relative at a coma patient's bedside. 'Pick up the phone yourself,' I imagine my mother saying. She is wearing the dress she got married in, bell-sleeved, cheap but lacily romantic, giving her the appearance of a seventies angel. Her hair sways around her indistinct face, flowers grow where she stands. 'I can't,' I say. 'Then he's not right for you,' she says earnestly, before fading out, to the strains of 'Stairway to Heaven'.

I recognise the validity of this, but also, I can't apply her robust feminist logic to my situation. Leo may not be right for me but he isn't wrong for me either: unreachable and impossible, he isn't *for* me at all. I may as well wonder about the good sense of dating Rhett Butler or Mr Darcy. Her advice is for women who love real and present men, men met in everyday situations. It is not meant for somebody like me, given a shot at something extraordinary.

By the end of the five days I am half convinced that the night really was a strange sort of hiatus in reality, a dream of an alternate Persephone. The re-run memory of him kissing me becomes a desperate thing, more like mourning something. In my real dreams, we stand in a decaying house, with creepers coming in at the windows, an empty bar with the lights off, an unflown aeroplane. In these dreams, whether something happens or not, I wake with my leg muscles tightened, my fists rolled, hollow with want, want, want.

On the sixth day, Leo calls, leaving a disturbing, sudden voicemail asking me if I'd like to do something on Wednesday afternoon, at a time which would usually be reserved for lunch, but without mentioning lunch itself, leaving me no idea what to expect.

I get his message as I am getting ready to meet Catherine and Emiko for drinks. Mindful of what happened with Camilla, I don't want to hide anything from them, so once we are all sitting on Catherine's balcony under the wisteria, I say, 'Something's happened with me and Leo.'

'Something? How do you mean?' Emiko asks, trying to fish a fly out of her glass.

'Well, we kissed. After that night out last week.'

Emiko's eyes become very large and her mouth very small. She takes a swallow of her wine and drinks the fly.

Catherine is obviously bewildered; her mouth tips slightly, as she says, 'I didn't know you liked him?'

'It sort of . . . developed gradually,' I say.

'God, how exciting! So what happened?' Emiko demands. I can tell she doesn't want to seem impolitely surprised, but can't keep the incredulous yelp out of her voice. I don't blame her; I am incredulous myself. 'Was it good?'

'I don't have much to compare it to, but yes, it was good. It was strange.'

'Strange how?'

'Well . . . sort of, not knowing what he was thinking, and it was so quiet, and I was drunk . . .' In difficulties, I tail off. Our three wine glasses sit abandoned on the table, as if on board the *Marie Celeste*. 'But now he's asked if I'm free Wednesday.'

'Free Wednesday!' Emiko repeats with enjoyment.

'Which I am, but I don't know if he meant just us, or everyone.'

'I hadn't heard anything about Wednesday,' Catherine, startled quiet at first, says finally. She touches my hand, reassuring. 'I'm sure it's just the two of you.'

At this generosity I feel an abrupt surfeit of gratitude, though I can't thank Catherine without acknowledging her own feelings for Leo. I smile at her instead.

'And we all thought you were devoted to the memory of an ex-boyfriend at uni,' Emiko says.

'That got exaggerated in the retelling,' I say quickly.

'So you don't know what you're doing yet on Wednesday?'

'I don't know anything,' I say. 'I don't even know what Leo thinks about me,' and though they must catch the note of supplication, they can't enlighten me. I'd like to ask them what – if anything – Leo has said about me before now, but the conversation is governed by the usual rules of Leo's friends, prohibiting such obviousness. For the first time I find I miss the interrogative techniques of university chat.

'This will be the first time we've known a girlfriend of Leo's,' Catherine says, growing thoughtful. 'He might tell you about the you-know-what on the yacht.'

'Do you think?'

Emiko shakes her head. 'I'm not sure he'd tell anyone that. It's not just to do with him, is it? You don't want to put him in that position – to betray Ivy's confidence or to not be honest with you.'

'I think we're getting ahead of ourselves,' I say. 'I certainly wouldn't want to do anything that Ivy wouldn't like, anyway.'

'That's for sure,' Catherine agrees.

'Anyway!' Emiko says brightly, 'this is a momentous day. Leo has finally given in to romance. The days of wondering where on earth he is or whether he's going to answer our invitations are over. It's like having an insider at the KGB!'

But just before I leave, Emiko looks at me with a kind of grave worry, the way you might look at someone who has suffered a death but is acting as if nothing has happened; a concern for their glassy high spirits. I wonder later if she was trying to kindly, subtly warn me that Leo will not give in to romance, that I will not know where on earth he is, and I will not be an insider, just a more privileged type of outsider, sitting above the stalls in a private balcony, but watching all the same.

'Persephone,' says Martin Black when I pick up my mobile phone. 'How are you?'

'How did you get this number?'

'I'm a journalist. Are you angry?'

'Of course I am.' I am mainly relieved: I was frightened it might be Leo, calling off our date later. 'I don't want to talk to you.'

'Please,' he says. His voice down the line is gentle, cottony. He sounds serious but not threatening, even when he says, 'Just because I plan to write something about Leo? I don't see why that should affect our friendship.'

'Go away.'

'Okay, I didn't want to get . . . *heavy* about this, but if you hang up, I'll just publish tomorrow. I've got enough material.'

'You're bluffing.'

'I don't think you'll call my bluff. Have you asked Leo about what happened that night?'

'It's none of your business.'

'I bet you haven't. If it was any other man you'd have asked him straight away. You'd want to check you're not about to get involved with a sociopath. But with Leo you know he wouldn't want to tell you, and you're worried that if you so much as mention it, you'll lose him. And you like him so much you can't risk it.'

This is so stingingly true that I snap, 'Maybe I'm not interested in what happened.'

'Rubbish. Just remember, if this is so obvious to me, it'll be equally obvious to him. You've set out with a very unequal power balance.'

'Supposing that were the case,' I say, 'and I don't know what happened, and I won't ask, what exactly do you want from me? I'm not going to be very useful to you.'

'I told you, finishing touches. I want to reveal what Leo's fragrant girlfriend thinks of the whole contretemps.'

'You're mad,' I say with interest. 'When are you going to tell me what happened?'

'When I know it all. Not yet.' A slight pause. The faint noise of cars begins when his voice ends. I look out of the window and down the road, it having occurred to me that he might be outside the house.

'Have you been following me?'

'No. And don't get the wrong idea: I like you, but not like that.'

'Well, I have a rape alarm. And I often carry a knife.'

He laughs. 'That won't be much use if you're dating Leo Ford. Blades are his speciality. I'd suggest a handgun.'

'Very funny.'

'Well,' Martin says, switching tone to something light and unlikely, mocking me, 'this has been a lovely chat but I must dash. I'm sure we'll meet again soon.'

'I don't seem to have much choice in that.'

'Not really.'

'You won't get anything out of me.'

That's okay.'

'Goodbye, Martin.'

'Goodbye.'

I'd planned a meticulous costume and make-up schedule to allow myself enough time to prepare for Leo's arrival but not enough time to get too nervous, and Martin's call has made me late. I don't have time to think about what he said, or the ability to separate my worry from my longing, so, with the uneasy opposing forces of Leo, distant and shining, and Martin, dark and low lying, fighting it out in the grey marshes at the back of my mind, I focus on the mechanics of getting dressed. Putting my legs into the silk underwear, embroidered birds criss-crossing its deep blue sky. Aiming perfume at my neck. Groping awkwardly across my back for the zip of the short, lead-colour wool dress. Unspooling the black opaque tights, sheathing my toes that look as hesitant, suddenly, as if they are dipping into dark water; watching my pale legs disappear. Struggling briefly to get my arms inside my blazer. Putting on a silver pendant, removing it, putting it back on: a deliberation that only ends when the bell rings, leaving me no time to decide on shoes.

I pick up a pair of heels and run downstairs. Claire Hetson has come back from the Easter break early in order to study, so I call as I go, 'It's for me, don't worry, leave it, it's for me,' to stop her reaching the door before me. The hurry of this flusters me, as does Leo's shape, visible through the molten forms within the glass door panels. I drop my keys before I can unlock the door, then find it impossible to get my feet into my shoes, as if I have expanded with fright, like a blowfish. Then I get the door open and he is there, standing in his own astonishing Leo-ness, looking at me curiously.

'Is everything all right? I heard shouting.'

'Everything's perfect,' I say emphatically, as if I can force it to be so, and it works: he smiles. Then I step out of the house with a slight shudder of the air, as if I have passed through a looking glass, into a new and welcome world.

'I hope you don't mind the afternoon slot,' Leo says once in the car. 'I'm having dinner with my agent tonight and I can't cancel him. He looks like Father Christmas. I can't stand to let him down.'

'He might put you on the naughty list,' I say.

'I've been on that list for a while,' Leo says, laughing. 'I was going to make us some late lunch at my place. Or we could go out, if you prefer.'

'Your place is good.'

'We just need to make one stop on the way. Sorry. It's my father's house, but he's not home, so no need to worry. I'll be two minutes.'

'Are you dropping something off?'

'No. It's tactical.'

But the traffic slows and gathers like a snake pulling itself together, and Leo, though he asks me about the work I'm doing for my course, and makes several remarks – uninformed but penetrating, to the extent that I begin to question not just my latest essay, but the validity of the essay question – is clearly irritated by the delay. 'Come on,' he murmurs at a red light. He checks his watch. 'Should be okay,' he says, more to himself than me.

Leo says 'house' but really the place is a mansion, blanketed by tall dense trees and iron gates. When he rings the bell I can hear the sound travelling, low and ponderous, through the vast rooms within. A housekeeper answers.

'Your father went out to meet you,' she says when she sees Leo.

'Really?' Leo says, appearing suddenly dismayed. 'What a disaster. I thought he said to meet here. He went to a restaurant? Oh dear, well, tell him I called round.' He turns to leave.

'But he's home now,' the housekeeper says. 'He got back just a minute ago.'

'Oh,' Leo says, looking, for the first time, genuinely thrown. 'What luck.' He frowns and whispers 'Sorry,' to me, as the woman shows us inside.

My curiosity to see inside the home of Leo's father is cowed at once by the interior, like a cat that wanders into the lair of a bear; catches the scent of the unfamiliar animal, and abruptly changes direction. My high heels knock brutally on the tiles and echo up to the ceiling with the sound of rifles firing as we are ushered along the hall. The house is dark and rich and ornate as a Fabergé egg, adhering to a kind of cliché I have never seen except on television, with its Persian carpets and towering sombre draperies, a library I see through a door-crack. The furniture is something dark – walnut or rosewood or mahogany – and deeply shiny; the cabinets and bureaus reflecting my passing face, bowed and frightened.

I know some of the words of this house; chinoiserie, Aubussons, girandoles, but it is a language I am unfamiliar with, and I am worried I will slip up unforgivably. I know that Leo's own house is full of antiques, but it is done in a laissez-faire, eclectic way. Here ancestry and money has settled and grown denser and denser over the years, until even the dull light coming in at the great windows is old and distilled, pressed dark like oil. Pictures hang on the walls of people's faces and shoulders, rising out of heaps of fabric according to long-deceased fashions. Their tepid, foggy eyes look as if they have given up trying to see in the costly gloom, and are now blind as bats.

'What do you think?' says Leo.

'It's so old,' I say.

'It's like death in here,' he says, and he does not smile.

We go into a large room in which the sofas sit silently in

gatherings, like guests at an uncomfortable party. I have no idea which to sit on so I hang back, pretending to look at a vase, then choose one next to Leo. Beyond the French windows there is a hazy garden, like the backgrounds of the unlit oil paintings. I perch on my sofa as if I have sneaked under a red rope in a stately home and a tour guide might arrive at any moment to evict me. Leo says nothing to ease this feeling.

At this moment the double doors open dramatically and William Ford, wide shouldered, tall and thick haired, stands in their frame, appearing to fill the available space as if his edges extend out beyond his skin. He beats a newspaper against his leg and wears a powerful frown.

'What were you playing at today?' he snaps at Leo. 'I don't see you for months and now you don't show up at the restaurant. Last time you cancelled. The time before that you pretended you had the time wrong.'

'I thought I was meant to meet you here,' Leo said.

'Well you can piss off now, I've made other plans. I've got a girl coming over.' Anger gives way, for a moment, to a hint of self-congratulation, before reclaiming its rightful place on the face of William Ford.

'Call girl?' Leo asks.

'She may as well be. When you're old and rich, like me, you've always got to pay.'

'Unless you date someone of your own age and appearance,' Leo murmurs.

'And *why*,' asks William, 'would I want to do that?'

'On that note,' Leo says, 'Persephone, this is my father, William. Before you mistake her for the call girl.'

'How do you do,' says William, extending a hand.

'How do you do,' I murmur back, grateful that my old tutor Mrs Farquhar, though she wasn't useful in much else, had a traditional sense of etiquette. The rest of the world had moved on since she was a genteel girl of twenty and men stood when she left the room, but frozen in her house next to the singing lake, she hadn't realised.

After removing his hand from mine William crosses the room, pours himself something from a decanter, then sits and stares out of the windows, making it quite clear that his part in any conversation is over.

'Well, then, I'll leave you to your afternoon engagement,' Leo says to him, adopting the kindly tone of a nurse in a care home. William flinches with irritation like a stung horse.

'Engagement . . . my least favourite word,' he says. 'Goodbye, Persephone. It was a pleasure meeting you. Leo, call my secretary if you find time in your schedule for another lunch. Though maybe next time I'll stand *you* up. Ungrateful shit.'

'Bye, William,' Leo calls, taking my hand and drawing me out of the room. As we walk through the hall of the house the darkness of its innermost rooms fades and the light permeating the leaded-glass windows strengthens, giving the impression of leaving a subterranean tunnel, and the same sensation of alleviated claustrophobia.

'Persephone, forgive me,' Leo says once we are outside. 'That backfired. Still, perhaps it isn't a bad thing for you to see the elder Ford – originator, fount, template. Now you know what you're dealing with. What do you think?'

I hesitate. Criticising a parent is the exclusive right of the child, but if I say something insincere about William, Leo is likely to laugh at me. I say instead, 'It wouldn't be fair to make a judgement without seeing your mother,' and he smiles.

Having never been on a date before, my expectations of them are derived mainly from television and films, in which dates tend to follow three paths. There is the disastrous date, usually necessitating some sort of escape via faked phone call or lavatory window. The date that is so sexually charged that the participants interrupt their activities, rushing towards each other hurriedly, desperately. And finally, the date that goes perfectly, crowned with a chaste and romantic kiss at the end. I am not sure which date I am on. The appearance of William Ford indicates the first type, but it is not too late, I hope, for it to turn into the second type.

As I am considering this, Leo glances at me and smiles, and my body tips as if the car has turned over, lurching into longing that I can't believe is invisible to him. His hand rests lightly on the wheel, his profile – solemn for the moment – is bright at the edges, shadowed on the side that faces me, before he makes the turning into his own road and the whole is brought into the light.

He pulls to a stop outside his house, just behind a dark car.

'Ah. . .Ivy's here,' he says, and frowns. 'This wasn't meant to turn into "Meet the Fords".'

'It's okay. It'll be good to see Ivy,' I say, though the sight of her car, dark and anonymous, gives me an unexplained pang of nervousness. I expect her to be waiting inside it but as we approach I see it is empty. She opens the door of the house instead, wearing jeans and a loose pullover that make my dress and tailored jacket look immediately foolish: a schoolgirl's idea of style.

Even prepared for Ivy's presence I am startled by her. Her beauty has the immediacy of Leo's, something about its colour perhaps;

the bright eyes, bright hair. Ivy, for her part, seems just as surprised to see me.

'Leo, I needed to—'she has begun to say, then stops when she realises I am behind him. 'Oh! Persephone. How lovely to see you again.'

She drops back as we enter the hall, kissing me lightly, in a quick movement, and I realise that this must be as close as Ivy gets to discomfort.

'I've dropped a proof in for you, Leo,' she says now. 'You caught me just as I was leaving.'

'But you should stay!' I say, compelled to ease the moment of awkwardness. Both Leo and Ivy look at me as if I have suggested something outlandish. 'It would be really nice.'

'Would you like some lunch?' Leo asks, turning towards the kitchen, so that Ivy, who looks at him curiously, fails to meet his eye.

'Ah . . . why not?' she says eventually, and smiles, and I feel again like a schoolgirl, one whose favourite teacher has patted them on the head.

Ivy and I sit in the kitchen and watch Leo chop various ingredients, his knife flashing like a fish. Watching him stirs the pool of my stomach until the want rises up again, circulating fitfully.

'We just had an accidental encounter with our common parent,' Leo says to Ivy.

'You and Persephone?' she asks, turning to me. 'How was that?'

'She's too polite to answer that one,' Leo says.

Ivy raises her eyebrows. 'Maybe that'll teach you to stop playing these games with him. If you don't want to see him, just tell him. And your mother too, for that matter.' She addresses this partly to me, and I get the impression this isn't the first time she has said this to Leo, but the point is being repeated now either for my benefit, or simply to make him uncomfortable.

'I don't like confrontation,' Leo says, shrugging, playing, like Ivy, to the audience.

'Keep hiding, then,' Ivy says. 'Like the Wizard of Oz.' She gets up and looks in the fridge for wine as Leo, behind her, frowns. I wonder if this last line is part of the usual routine.

'So, you're writing another book?' I ask Ivy. 'What's it about?'

'Very roughly, it's about sight,' she tells me. 'Clytie looking at Apollo, Semele looking at Zeus. There were disastrous consequences for all of them; as women, they simply weren't able to view the full male glory. But in the myths in which men saw goddesses, such as Athene and Artemis, the goddesses both made a decision to administer punishment to their presumptuous male viewers. They weren't fatally dazzling in themselves.'

'What about Orpheus and Eurydice?' Leo asks.

'That just confirms it. Hades and Persephone told Orpheus that he could lead his wife back from the Underworld so long as he didn't look back at her. It was the male gaze that had the power to make Eurydice vanish. Orpheus emerged unscathed.'

'Not quite,' Leo says.

'That was unfair of them,' I say.

'Who?'

'Hades and Persephone. If they were going to give Orpheus his wife back they shouldn't have added conditions.'

'That's the Greek gods for you,' Ivy says. 'Fair doesn't come into it.'

I sip my wine, admiring Ivy intensely. She is so different to many of the female lecturers I have encountered at university, who seem – old or young – a little like dried flowers; awkward, dusty, enslaved to their leathery old knowledge. Ivy's knowledge is, like her, mobile, colourful, slightly disturbing.

That afternoon I barely taste the food in my efforts to keep up with what is said. Leo and Ivy talk about books, plays, art, politics and history without pretension, and I can tell this is the sort of talk Leo is used to: a breadth of reference I could never offer. When they mention the friends we have in common, discussing Anthony's current affair with a married woman, they connect it back to a known history that I can't follow. Even when Ivy asks me about my course, which I have begun to hate, I feel at a loss, ashamed of disparaging my chosen field in the presence of two people with such bright and pressing vocations. Alone in Scotland I felt exceptional, at uni I felt less so, and now I feel as if I have been picked up, a tiny little fish, and thrown into the open ocean, to try to survive with the dolphins and sharks.

Trying to match their conversational pace, I don't notice the time until Ivy says suddenly, 'Is it really six o'clock?'

'No!' I cry, but it is. I don't know how the time has been lost: it seems unfairly taken.

'Shit,' Leo says. 'What happened?'

We all look at each other, each with our own dismay, Leo and Ivy's purely practical, mine more complex.

'I have to go – I have dinner plans,' Ivy says.

'I've got to meet my agent.' Leo frowns. 'Persephone, I'll drive you back now if that's okay.'

'You don't have time,' I say. 'It's rush hour. You'll never get across

London and back. I can take the tube easily. I've got to make a couple of stops on the way back, anyway.'

'Are you sure?' Leo asks, visibly relieved. He follows us to the front door but seems distracted: a reticence familiar to me has settled back into his mouth, his eyes are lowered, sheltering the brilliant hazy irises. He offers me the same brotherly kiss on the cheek that Ivy receives, before retreating without hesitation or delay back into his house, at which point I realise that this was the first type of date, after all.

The day after the strange afternoon with the Fords I am not sure whether I ought to call Leo and thank him for the lunch; as if I, too, hadn't expected anything more than a casual afternoon. My hand even makes it to the phone several times before dropping back, slack and uncertain.

I spend an uneasy and unproductive day on the sofa, reading through a guide to Greek mythology, swinging between its characters and my own regrets. The regret of losing Leo is uppermost. Second to that is regret that I told Emiko and Catherine about Leo, and now face the prospect of issuing a retraction. I have a superstitious sense that speaking about my love too soon has caused it to be taken away. My book tells me that Psyche lost her husband Cupid through impatience, trying to take more of him than he had offered. He only appeared to her in the dark, but goaded by her jealous sisters, she lit a lamp to see him in the light, whereupon he vanished.

But then, I think, it wasn't fair that Psyche wasn't allowed to see Cupid, just as it wasn't fair that Orpheus couldn't look at his wife. My sympathies are with the humans, battling within the limits set by the inexplicable gods. I can't help but cast the Ford family as the pantheon, the ones who decide the rules, while I, a human, can only try to guess what they are. Like Semele, I am fatally dazzled: by the imperious dark of William's house, by Ivy, the sleeves pushed up her lovely arms, her mobile eyebrows, quick and mocking, and most of all by Leo, his presence next to me, only seen in halves, in quarters, the profile that never turns enough towards me.

Early that evening Leo calls. I can hear a few voices in the background, though I can't tell if they are coming from a television or from other people.

'What a ridiculous day,' he says, which doesn't allow me to guess in what way he found it ridiculous. 'So, Catherine said we were all going out tonight. You and I included.'

'I think so,' I say, swimming luxuriantly in the *you and I*.

'Great. So I'll see you later?'

'Okay,' I say, and he rings off, and I get up and run, panicking, to the shower.

At Spook I arrive before Leo and hurriedly order a shot; wanting to be drunk, to unshackle my nerves, slip out of my shyness like a set of uncomfortable clothes. In the mirror overlooking our table, right next to me, my face swims like the moon reflected in glimmering water. I turn away and watch people dance, suspended in the music that rises up warmly, its erotic pulse. I can feel the gentle pressure of Michael's eyes, across the table, but I keep my head dipped towards my drink. Finally, he moves to the seat next to me and asks: 'So – you're with Leo?'

I shake my head. 'I don't know. Nothing's really happened.'

'He's coming tonight?'

'I think so,' I say, though it is almost midnight and the implied intimacy of *you and I* is fading with distance. 'Michael, have you known any of Leo's previous girlfriends?'

'No. I know they've existed. I don't know who any of them were.' I catch a little concern, or possibly disapproval, in his expression.

'Can I ask you something? And tell me honestly. Do you think it's a good idea to get involved with Leo?' I ask. Hearing myself say it, the words sudden and clumsy, I realise how drunk I must be.

He looks uneasy. 'Honestly, I don't know.'

'Oh.'

'It's just – Leo tends to spoil plans. I've seen him do it. Not just in terms of his work but with his personal life. There are a lot of people out there who have been disappointed by Leo. He won't *mean* to spoil a plan, but he invariably does.'

'My plans,' I say with amusement, finishing my drink. I have no plans.

'But then, I haven't seen Leo with anyone before,' Michael continues. 'He keeps his girlfriends and his friends separate. The fact that he isn't doing that now is probably significant.'

'He won't be able to avoid me if he breaks my heart, so he's less likely to do it?' I ask. 'Well, that's sort of reassuring.' We sit in silence for a moment, watching the dance floor, on which two girls are undulating awkwardly, self-conscious, going through their calculated moves. I turn away, not liking to see even such a small failure; something tried and not pulled off.

'Leo!' cries Catherine. As I watch him, arriving at the table with all the lights raining down on him, I realise that people are looking from him to me, more curious than usual. The pressure of it weighs me in my seat, my hand sets stony around my glass. I get the same smile from him he has always given me: alluring, narrow eyed, unspecific. My own smile sets and separates from my face like curds.

Instead of waiting for him to complete his circuit of everyone at the table, I go to the empty lavatories and lean my elbows on the chilly marble around the sink. I moan out loud, a sound which surprises me with its muffled, baffled need. I rework my make-up, put my head upside down and agitate my hands through my hair so that it falls into waves and slopes around my face, hovering – as beautiful as it has ever been – in the icy Venetian glass, the ivory light. Still, I am not satisfied with the face, with what Leo might see in it.

When I get back he is sitting next to my empty chair, smiling at me.

'Did you deliberately arrive at midnight?' I ask, showing him my watch.

'Like a backwards Cinderella,' Michael says.

'I was a pumpkin up until a few minutes ago,' Leo says. 'Hence the lateness.'

In my absence the group has apparently reached the agreement that they want to play poker: either at Catherine's flat, or at Michael's, where the neighbours are less likely to complain about noise, so we all exit into the spitting wet night and stand, debating, on the pavement outside.

'Let's go,' Leo says in my ear.

'What?'

'Let's just go home. There's a cab just there.' He indicates it with a sly gesture. I stare at him, realising that I am suddenly on the inside of Leo's elusive manoeuvres; that if I hold his hand I can vanish along with him.

'Okay,' I say, and we step into the car with hardly a goodbye to the others, who start to protest, and then the door closes and the interior of the taxi with its friendly gloom rolls around us both, the high-pitched, virulent sounds of the street muffled and dimmed, the driver a blank behind his window. Leo kisses me, and I am surprised at how close and demanding the kiss is, from someone so far and detached. I bring myself as near to him as I can, transported with either desire or relief, not knowing which.

There are two moments apart: the few minutes in which he pays the taxi driver, then another hasty moment in the hall where we shake out of our clothes, like wild creatures that have been dressed up unwillingly. Then I follow him, up the stairs, down the long landing, and, at last, into his room.

In bed I don't feel enjoyment so much as shock. It is all too much – I am too excited, too shaky, as if I could come loose from my body and look down on his back with its visible muscles like a sculptural river, a dipped, classical coil, his shoulder, sleek and brown as a hazelnut, the obviousness of the scar, a white gather in the well of his collarbone.

Afterwards I lie and look out into the murky soft light of the open window. He goes to sleep easily, but I need the brightening hours to shake away the conviction that something quite close to real life has happened, but not quite real, all the same. I hadn't come; I was too uncomprehending. It was an alignment of casings only – of outsides – without the involvement of my night-struck, baffled consciousness.

Now I re-run it, trying to make his body familiar, to feel it, remembering the way my own enclosed it, three times, like a spell that had to be repeated. I smell the flat, salty scent of sex on my hands; a smell that seemed almost nauseous when I slept with James, queasy as a bad oyster, but has now, in the aftermath of Leo, become arousing.

I wonder if there can be anything better than exactly this time. So long as he is asleep next to me, his arm crossing my body, fingers upcurled, I can't be disappointed. So I lie awake, trying to hold back the morning with my open eyes.

Despite my efforts not to fall asleep, I wake up late, alone except for a note. I repeat its contents the next evening at Catherine's house, pretending to vagueness, though I can recite it word for word:

> *Had to go to book fair. Apparently it's too late in my career to do a Pynchon. Help yourself to food, alcohol, anything. Will call you tomorrow. L x*

'What a nice note!' Emiko exclaims.

I am dismayed to realise the note is where I left it, lying on the highly polished wood of the table next to the bed, overlooking the storm-wrecked sheets and pillows, like a letter found after some disaster or disappearance. I wish I'd kept it, to have something tangible in the absence of Leo.

'Did you sleep together?' Catherine asks. I nod. The right thing to do in this situation is to return the openness the two women have previously shown me: cheerfully deconstructing every movement and measurement of their own sex lives. I know what I should be recounting for them: the way his body lived up to his face – its smooth-hilled strength showing down his arms, his legs, his arrow head-shaped torso – the dimensions of his silky, blunt penis (Leo's ego and his penis enjoying a mutually beneficial relationship). But I am a nervous beginner, and I'm not sure where to start.

Below us the doorbell tolls decorously.

'Let's postpone this,' Emiko says. 'That's Ivy. I'm pretty sure she won't want to discuss her half-brother's sexual prowess.'

My feelings about Ivy joining us today have been in a state of flux. In one way I am glad of her presence because she is connected to Leo, and being friends with her adds extra fortification to my relationship with him, a new beam raised to support it. But at the same time she makes me feel not frightened, exactly – but something further down that spectrum. Being around her necessitates a higher degree of alertness, in order to stay above water. And I want Ivy to like me: I want to feel the brilliance of her approval.

'Persephone – I'm so sorry about taking over your afternoon the other day,' she says to me as soon as she comes in. 'I don't know quite what happened.'

'No, no, it was good to meet you properly,' I say.

'You *are* polite, aren't you?' Ivy marvels, turning to Catherine and Emiko. 'How did you two end up with such a nice friend?'

'She's just moved here from the Highlands,' Catherine explains. 'She has nothing to compare us to.'

'That explains a lot,' Ivy says. 'So, what have I missed?'

As Emiko and Catherine talk over the outlines that their relationships do not quite fill, I watch Ivy, trying to pin down the secret of her preternatural self-possession. It is partly in her long, level stares, that cool green light, but also partly in the simplicity of her manner: the absence of tics, hesitation, sidelong movements.

'So I thought he was interested after we went for a drink,' Catherine is saying. 'And he sent flowers the next day. Then I called him to make another date, which he cancelled the day before. He said his mother was in town and was staying. Then I didn't hear from him for a couple of months. But then yesterday we were emailing each other – very flirtatiously – almost the entire day. I got no work done at all. He didn't mention another date though.'

'He's one of *them*,' cries Emiko. 'You'll never know with him.'

'I suppose the right woman must know,' Catherine says. 'The one who understands them. They're the main act. And you're just a . . . fluffer.' She tells a story about dating a married male boss, who subsequently left his wife, but not for Catherine. 'It was like an interview process. And she got the job.'

'Crumbs,' Emiko says.

'I have such bad luck with men,' Catherine says sadly. 'They always fool me.'

'You *want* them to fool you,' Ivy says. 'Or you wouldn't be fooled. You want to see something in them, and you see it.'

I look between the two of them, startled at this disregard for the usual protocol. Ivy doesn't seem to notice that she has said anything unusual. She gives Catherine a sympathetic smile; a shrugging lift of her lips, as if to say, *I cannot tell a lie*; as if it is harder to lie than it is to tell the truth – which is not true at all.

The rain as I leave Catherine's nearly blinds me, so I get into the first taxi I see. As I am closing the door an indistinct person darts towards it from the watery street and opens it again, getting inside.

'For fuck's sake,' I say, angrily.

'I'll pay for the cab, how's that?' Martin offers. Rain has pressed his dark hair down over his skull, revealing its uneven, frail structure. He looks thinner than the last time I saw him. His skin has the unusual quality of seeming pale on the surface only, like thin muslin covering a night window. I draw away from the radius of his dripping coat.

'Were you waiting outside for me?' I ask, then, as it occurs to me that he must have known the start point of my journey, 'Do you know where I live?'

'Of course.'

I rest my head against the hard back of the seat, not knowing what to do.

'Well, this is an awkward silence,' Martin says, which almost makes me laugh. It must be the perceived safety of the cab that cushions me from being afraid of him, as rationally I ought to be. Either that or the fact that since spending the night at Leo's, the worries of the world – rape, murder – seem smaller, less real, compared to the fear that Leo might not want to see me again.

'What do you want now?' I ask.

He removes an envelope from his coat, takes out some pictures, and hands them to me. For a moment I think it is Leo in the pictures, and my heart dulls, brakes heavily, before I realise the man looks nothing like him. It is a famous actor, in fact: a man with a wife and children. In the dark space of the picture he is suspended as if crucified, pale and marked. The marks have presumably been made by the woman standing in front of him, holding a riding crop.

'What is this? Why are you showing me this?' I drop the pictures, where they lie on the seat between us.

Martin picks them up and returns them to the interior of his coat.

'I thought it might interest you,' he says. 'The public judge it interesting, anyway.'

'What are you going to do with it?'

'I've sold the story to a national paper. I work freelance for them.'

'Is this what you do?' I say. 'Making the world worse?'

'I'm not changing anything. I'm just showing the world what it is.'

'Showing this man's family.'

'Wouldn't you rather know, if you were his wife?'

'Maybe. But not like this. It's not fair.' As I say it I realise how childish this sounds.

Martin looks at me with sympathy.

'This man is part of an industry that promotes him as better than reality. They tell us he is perfect. There are risks inherent with making claims like that. Everything has to balance. When you shout, "I'm good," there will always be an echo that says, "No, you're not." When Leo, for example, gives a magazine interview presenting himself one way, he must know there will be an answer to that, a negative of himself, and only half of each is true.'

'So you're part of some cosmic yin and yang principle?' I say.

'No, I'm just a man about to make several thousand pounds from pictures of a celebrity being whipped.'

'Is this what you're going to do to Leo?' I ask.

'I don't have any pictures of him in a brothel,' Martin says. 'Though I live in hope.'

I turn away to the window, steamed opaque by the rain rising off our wet clothes, and wipe a hole looking out into London. The streets I see tell me I'm nowhere near home yet.

'Don't look so miserable,' Martin says.

'You're trying to ruin Leo!'

'You keep saying that, but I don't expect I will. If I were to find out something bad, Leo – as a media figure – will only be strengthened by it. Look at all the things that come out about Princess Diana or Elvis or Marilyn. People just love them more for it. Because that's what people want. We don't want God. The concept of ultimate goodness and perfection is boring, as well as being a lie. What we really want is the old myths. We worship celebrities because they are like the Greek and Roman gods. We want our gods flawed and complex and unfair because life is flawed and complex and unfair.'

'But some people are almost entirely good,' I say. 'And you might never find a real, serious flaw in one of those people, because they *are* worthy of looking up to.'

'Want to make a bet?' he asks. '"Leo is good" versus "Leo is seriously flawed"?'

'We've made that bet already, really, haven't we?' I say, and he turns up his hands, and laughs.

The Easter holiday comes to an end and the house fills up again, first with Claire Brayne, then Camilla, returning tanned and aloof from a holiday in France, then with Sammy and the others. Though Camilla has maintained her artificial, reflective politeness (a front that also makes it almost impossible to confront her when she uses the last of the loo roll), the other girls ask about Leo avidly: 'What's going on! Seriously!'

'Can I meet him?'

'Have you slept with him?'

'Well, have you?'

'Come on, Pers!'

There isn't much genuine congratulation in their voices; rather, they sound almost aggressive, acquisitive. I doubt they think me deserving – I have simply been lucky. If *they* had known him, they think, it would have been them. They have the arrogance of all pretty girls, only just adults, so ready with their brash, undented sexuality.

Catherine and Emiko ask me, more gracefully, how things are going.

'I'm seeing him tomorrow,' I tell Catherine on the phone.

'At his house or going out?'

'Just over to his.'

'Intimate,' Catherine pronounces. 'That's good.'

'Is it? I can't tell if I'm seeing him, or with him, or going out with him, or if he's my boyfriend, or what the exact differences are between any of those things. I don't know if it's . . . anything. Is it too early to know what it is?'

'Maybe see how it goes tomorrow, then ask? But don't take my advice. I always get these things wrong.'

'Okay,' I say. 'Thanks.'

When I arrive at his house the next night he kisses me at the door. 'Hello, Persephone. Drink?' But the drink isn't made: we have sex on the sofa instead, too impatient to take the stairs to bed. With him I feel suspended over a drop, as if I have to hold on: if

I let go I would fall away. Every moment, even this close together, I am aware that my time with him might end; the chill of this runs all over me, ecstatic but terrified.

Afterwards, lying together, he says: 'I forgot to buy anything for dinner. I've been reading a book about Harry Houdini all day and I haven't left the house. Do you want a takeaway?'

'I've eaten,' I say, which isn't true, but eating in his company isn't easy: like swallowing wet cement, the food sits in the bottom of my stomach, heavy and uncomfortable. With Leo even my body becomes unreliable, forgetting its own basic functions – digestion, inhalation, circulation – as if rendered as stunned and torpid as my conscious mind.

'Did you know Houdini almost died when he was buried alive?' Leo asks. 'He was six feet under and he had almost dug himself free when he passed out.'

'That's horrible.' I reach for my dress and pull it primly over my breasts, unsettled by Leo's evocation of death, and by my own nakedness in the face of it.

'His hand made it to the surface so they pulled him out. Apparently he panicked once he was buried. He didn't anticipate how claustrophobic the soil would be. Or how heavy.'

'Why would anyone do that to themselves?' I ask.

Leo appears to count this question – which was serious – as rhetorical, and continues enthusiastically: 'Houdini was actually one of the earliest advertisers. He had links with companies. For example, he'd be trapped inside a beer barrel and then disappear from it. But the barrel would be promoting a brewery.'

From my ongoing observation of Leo, I have noticed that the other side of his elusiveness is an intense and committed fascination with random subjects: the Hundred Years War, Mata Hari, the Galapagos Islands; sitting up at night reading about them online, or saying, apropos of nothing: 'Did you know that there wasn't really a table found laid out for breakfast on the *Mary Celeste*? No half-full cups of tea. No cooling toast. Isn't that disappointing?'

At times he becomes completely occupied with certain people. Some spark of their conversation will catch him and he'll lean in, absorbed with questioning them, ignoring everything else around them. I imagine him at these times as a ghost. If I tried to touch him my hand would pass through his body, just as the rest of us must seem like ghosts to him, silently moving, silently speaking, like a pattern of light shifting and falling around him. The last time I lost Leo to another conversation it was with an elderly man who used to be a burglar. The worst time was when it was a younger woman, a pretty Australian girl whose hand had been bitten off by a crocodile. ('A crocodile. *Really*?' I said to Catherine.)

Really, I am envious of these obsessions of his, though I know they never usually last longer than a day or two. Like a caterpillar moving from leaf to leaf Leo will mentally chew up his passions – Plato, Kipling, Fellini – one after the other, then rarely mention them again. But in the brief time before he drops whatever it is that interests him, he gives it his full focus, intense and complete. Even if I divide the quantity of attention I have had over the days I have known him, and compare the result to the quantity given to one of his obsessions in twenty-four hours, the sum does not work in my favour.

Whether it is my frustration with Houdini, or the way his hand rests on my collarbone, as easy as if it is his own body, or because my head is on his shoulder and our eyes don't meet – because eye to eye my nerve fades – something springs my mouth open, and it asks him, 'Are we in a relationship?'

I think I can feel a smile, in the contact between his jaw and my temple. Then he says, 'Relationship is a broad word. We have a relationship to each other. Sexual relations are something different altogether.'

'Is that what I am?' I ask. 'A sexual relation?' I pull myself on to my elbow so I can see him, but his eyes are too strong, too green, as he looks back at me.

'No,' he says. 'Not simply that. Not to me.'

'Are we exclusive?'

'Another abused word,' Leo says. 'This is the problem with modern language. A word is so perfect when it expresses something singular. But we try to take that away, to beat everything down into an inarticulate, senseless soup. We say jealous instead of envious, or infamous instead of notorious. We have made disinterested mean the same as uninterested. We are reducing our own capacity for saying what we mean.'

I look away, unable to press him further, and he blinks as if returning himself to me. 'Sorry. What you're asking me is do I sleep around?'

'Do you?'

'I wouldn't eat a sweet I found on the street,' Leo said, 'And I don't sleep with people unless I know them. It's unsanitary.'

'So what am I?' I say. 'A known sweet?'

Leo laughs. 'You have a preoccupation with deciding what you are.'

There is a silence and I lie back, to turn my disappointed face away from his line of sight.

'Persephone, you shouldn't ask too much of yourself, in terms of monogamy. You're young, you're at university, you're new here. I don't expect you not to enjoy yourself.'

I imagine 'enjoying myself' without Leo – the cider and black, the sticky dance floors, the cigarettes smoked half hanging out of the window of the student halls, moving between boys like musical chairs: boys who throw up over themselves, or laugh with each other about how their one-night stands performed, down to the last detail, what was allowed in, and where.

'Okay,' I say. 'I'll keep that in mind.'

Later that week I am sitting in a bar with Leo and the others, though the 'others' are no more defined than that for me: I have ended up in between Leo and Ivy, who are having not quite an argument, but a conversation that, like a boat in choppy water, keeps threatening to veer into the rocks. It takes all my attention to keep up, to stay ready for a sudden appeal or reference that might include me.

'I just don't understand why famous or public figures are asked personal questions in interviews,' Leo is saying. 'Why are the normal rules of polite interaction thrown out of the window the moment you are talking to a . . .' he pauses – 'I don't know what, a celebrity? A "media figure"? What depressing terms. But anyway, I wouldn't ask a woman I'd just met about her sex life. So why does some journalist think it's acceptable to ask *me*?'

'You're being disingenuous,' Ivy says.

'How? The idea that famous people somehow owe it to us to

give up any element of their personal life is ludicrous. You pay money and you get to watch a film. There's no contract that states you are entitled to hear about the lead actor's divorce proceedings. Or even to see pictures of him at the premiere. When I buy meat from the butcher I don't ask him for a photo of him and his wife. What is it about the arts that provokes such interest?'

I almost answer – quoting Martin – 'What we want is the old myths,' but I stay quiet.

'It's perceived as glamorous,' Ivy says, as if bored: as if reciting lines we should all know. 'Higher proportion of young, good-looking and wealthy people.' Leo frowns. 'No one really thinks they are entitled to know about celebrities' personal lives,' she continues. 'The media know it and the public know it. But they want it and they're going to beg or steal it anyway. And you co-operate with it. You fuel their interest when you appear on television or in magazines.'

Leo leans back and crosses his arms. He and Ivy look at each other for a moment, without speaking. I have the urge to slip under the table, crawl through the copse of legs beneath, and emerge into safety.

'I like to talk about my books,' Leo says finally, in a neutral voice that I haven't heard before.

'But you're talking about yourself too. You're perpetuating the chase.' Ivy is leaning forward, visibly irritated, and I realise Leo's even, muted tone is as close as he is likely to get to his own display of anger.

'I can outrun it.'

Ivy makes a dismissive gesture. 'You can't outrun women. Aren't you on the cover of a magazine this month? Every desperate female in London is going to be able to identify you. It's like a Wanted poster.' She doesn't look at me when she says this, which gives me the uncomfortable feeling that she includes me in this category: of desperate women. Then she stands up, says, 'I'm going to the bar,' and removes herself cleanly from the conversation.

And of course the girls *are* desperate. This is the first night I am out in a public place with Leo, and I have noticed how badly the women treat me. They can freeze me off his arm with their stares; their eyes cling to him. They are shameless; they ask him the time, or say they know someone in common, or just say, 'So, how about it?' Some women have even struck up conversations with me, to get to him. The questions and the stares, the accidental touches, patter over us like rain, a deluge of female attention.

'Do you agree with her?' Leo asks me.

'Well,' I say. 'You do seem to be . . . wanted.'

'They want me because they don't know me,' Leo says, smiling. 'It's a cheap trick, isn't it? I'm a blank to them. They see what they want to see.'

But I don't know you, I want to say, but I stay silent, again. He looks at me for a moment, then leans back to allow Emiko to include us in the wider conversation, dissolving our intimacy.

I try to judge carefully but I never know what reaction he wants from me; I always feel I have given the wrong one. With him I am always on my best behaviour, always making an effort. I am worried that he can sense this like an animal picking up on the pheromones subtly leaching off me into the air, sharp and acidic as sweat, a bouquet of fear, and of need.

The next day, Camilla and I have an argument, beginning with her arriving in the sitting room, mouth held tensely curled, little cartoon flares of annoyance sizzling off her, levelling an empty carton of milk like a jouster's lance. The argument moves swiftly from the milk to the noise I made with my keys at four in the morning, and finally from the keys to my ultimate failure as a friend.

'I really didn't finish your milk,' I say.

'Fuck the milk,' Camilla says, and starts to cry.

This unexpected turn in the argument surprises and confounds me. The long weeks of polite, hostile exchanges with Camilla have hardened into something glacial between us that can't be melted, can't be crossed. I stand helpless in the doorway of the kitchen, unable even to offer her a tissue because – after a standoff between the three factions of the house: Camilla, me and the two Claires – there is no loo roll.

'You've changed,' Camilla says, wiping her eyes with her jumper sleeve. 'I thought you were my best friend. Then you meet Leo Ford and now we aren't good enough for you any more.'

I wonder briefly if Camilla actually thinks these things or whether they are just lines that have suggested themselves from the inchoate casserole of cultural references that is her unconscious, peopled by the characters of films, television and snippets from magazine advice columns, lines so well used they have almost no meaning left, like a worn-out toy that has lost its squeak.

'It's not like that,' I say. 'It's . . .'

But even this small note of disagreement, intended to placate, seems to spur her, lighting her up, and she raises her voice: 'How can you say that? You kept him a secret from the start because you were ashamed of us. We're just your embarrassing university friends. It's so obvious! I'm not the only one who's noticed, you know.'

'I don't see you as an embarrassment,' I say, trying to be soothing, but Camilla, her voice clotted with anger and tears, isn't listening.

'I should have realised it when you flirted with Marcus. And broke James's heart. You don't really care about other people.'

'But I never flirted with Marcus! I didn't even like Marcus. I liked James.' I falter and stop, unwilling to add '– and you kissed him', in case it makes her angrier, heightening an argument I would like to sidestep, if at all possible.

Apparently it is too late for sidestepping, or conciliation. Camilla abruptly slams the milk carton on to the side, knocking her hand as it crumples. The unfair pain of this, rather than distracting her, seems to add force to her sense of injustice.

'I suppose that's a dig at me? How was I meant to know you liked James? Whenever we asked you about it you played it down. I thought maybe you did but I didn't know. And I was drunk. I thought you'd forgiven me but you've obviously been holding a grudge. Is that why you've just shut me out? You can't just secretly hold a grudge and not tell anybody! You never give anything away. No one understands you. Like now! I'm devastated and you're standing there saying nothing.'

I stand silenced. Camilla is crying more quietly now, more sadly, and I don't have the will to argue with her. I don't even really understand what went wrong between us. A lack of trust, without a defined betrayal. A lack of kindness, without any bad intentions.

She sniffs and looks up, and in the moment that her tears drop back I catch sight of something regretful and tender, peering at me suddenly, and I think, for a moment, that she might make one of her old, extravagant gestures of affection, cross the kitchen and hug me. Then she says:

'Fine, just turn your back on us for Leo Ford. I suppose that was always the plan. That work experience – I thought it was weird at the time – and Sass told me it was your idea to keep going back to that club. You went after him from the beginning, I guess, because we were too boring for you, because we're your own age and we aren't famous? You're crazy, you know. He's dangerous. He stabbed somebody, for fuck's sake! Do you even know anything about him? You'd ditch all of us for a – a *murderer*.' She doesn't wait for an answer: she walks past me, out of the kitchen. 'Good luck with that,' she calls back as she goes up the stairs. After a few moments I hear her door crash closed.

I pick up the milk carton and put it into the bin, then go up to my own room. Leo had an early morning appointment and hadn't invited me to stay last night, so I had got a taxi home from the bar and spent the rest of the night in a drunk, sleepless state of misery, pitching from side to side in the bed like a seafarer, without any hope of getting comfortable enough for my eyes to close. I sit on the edge of the bed now and put my face in my hands, pressing my fingers into the curve of the skull under my skin, feeling how close it is to the surface.

Despite my irritation at Camilla's reliance on television and film, we take our references from a common pool, and I am reminded now of the trope in which a character leads a double life, and as the action of the plot becomes more complex, more frantic, the protagonist forgets themselves and slips into the wrong character at the wrong time. I was a different person with my university friends to the person I am with Leo and his friends, and at times I forget which

I am, and say something at odds with my situation. The first Persephone would apologise to Camilla; the second Persephone would tell her that what she said was wrong and unfair and only partly true. But standing in the kitchen watching Camilla's eyes spill black on to her jumper sleeves I found myself hovering, stymied, between the two selves, unable to do anything.

Of course, there is another Persephone, a third girl, the self I had in Scotland: an authentic self, taken for granted and unconsciously owned – but such a new, raw self that it was unsustainable, being more a chrysalis, a temporary housing. Perhaps if I had never left the Assynt I would have been able to live within it for ever, unchanging and pure. But it's too late: none of the three selves feels right to me now. I can't fully inhabit any of them.

I tell Catherine and Emiko about the situation with Camilla and they offer the appropriate murmurs and eye-widenings of sympathy. Then Emiko interrupts the routine, struck by an idea.

'Our friend Leni is going to spend the summer in Sweden and is looking for a house-sitter. She'd pay you to stay at her flat. It's just around the corner from me.'

'Much safer than your area, Perse.'

'Really?' I ask. 'That would be perfect. Thank you.'

'I'll text her now and see if it's available . . .' Emiko carries on talking, her finger flickering over the screen of her phone as if moving independently of her body. 'Oh, didn't I tell you, Persephone, about the last time I picked you up from your house? About the woman with the dog?'

'What happened?'

'This really old woman came past with a dog, and then right next to my car, her dog shat on the pavement. Then she started walking away! I got out and said to her, "That's so antisocial." She turned around and gave me the finger, and said "Up your pipe".'

'Oh, is *that* why you're all saying that?'

'Isn't it a great expression? Really covers a wide variety of situations.'

'Up your pipe,' Catherine repeats, with relish.

I can't join in with their joke. The early days of summer seem to have brought out the drunks, the disturbed, and the gangs of angry teens like wasps. The heat rises smoky and cloudy over the tall flats, the gaseous leviathan roads, the dirty windows. It crouches in the streets, with a palpable hostility, as the city-people hurry and sweat. And the people get irritable; they shout into their phones, throw their cigarettes at passing legs, key the endless line of their anger on expensive cars, scratch and rail at each other. I see several fights in a week, one at the tube station, one in the night road, one outside a fast food outlet, chips flying everywhere like startled birds.

Leo's friends laugh at all this, but I don't find it quite so funny. I sense a malevolence to London, more apparent in my neighbourhood than in theirs, a frantic ill will that swirls with the rain and the grey smoke. Catherine and Emiko move through London with their slender bones and good looks, conspicuous as Siamese cats, risking the envy, the need, that might catch them in a sudden, random gust.

It is this ill will that blows a postcard with a picture of a yacht on it through the letterbox of my house. I throw the postcard away, before it occurs to me that it might be a good idea to have Martin's fingerprints, and I pick it back out of the bin and put it in a bag.

Do you know yet? it asks.

PART EIGHT

'You can go back to Enna now, Persephone,' Hermes announces grandly. 'Your foul imprisonment has come to an end.'

Persephone, collecting her thoughts, wonders if he can see the change in her. But Hermes is occupied with an exaggerated re-telling of how he forced his way past Hades and stormed heroically to her bedchamber.

'One moment,' she tells him. 'And I'll be ready to go with you.'

Hermes stands on her balcony gazing around him at the glowing spires of the palace, while Persephone goes out into the hall, to a window, leans out and plucks a pomegranate from one of the slender dark-growing trees.

Ivy Ford
Persephone and Hades

The beginnings of a morning sunshine have rapidly given out, trembling and breaking up into a sulky rain, large heavy droplets that burst on the windows and roof like water balloons, dousing me as I run from the taxi into Leo's house, trickling from my hair and over my face, swept off with his fingers, in an odd echo of my meeting with Alex the tourist, back in the Assynt.

Inside we lie on the sofa and watch the rain striking the glass; the room dim with the changed light, a weighty, wet light, rolling over us like a flood.

'This reminds me of home,' I say, stroking his brown forearm, lustred with hairs, gold like a fine metal filigree.

'I want to hear about your home,' he says. 'What's your father like?'

'He's nice,' I say.

'Do you realise how much happiness is needed in one's upbringing, to have the luxury of being able to say, so casually, "He's nice"?'

'Well, he *is* nice. Nice, and sad. He's always missed my mother. He gets worried easily.'

'No other family in Scotland?'

'No. And no friends. Unless you count my old tutor Mrs Farquhar.'

'And what sort of woman might Mrs Farquhar be? I'm guessing a retired good-time girl with some fake diamonds and a romantic past.'

I laugh. 'She's more like a mouse. A Victorian mouse. She lives in a tall house next to a deserted dam.'

'So who were your boyfriends?'

'I didn't have any.'

He laughs, not unkindly, but unconvinced, so I tell him the three stories of my early experiences with love, then I tell him more and more, up to and including the arrival of Sadie.

'I *thought* it was like that,' he says, finally.

'Like what?'

'Your childhood was basically a sociological experiment.' Now I recognise that flare in his voice, the excitement of his curiosity. 'The isolation. The way your encounters with society have been disappointing. The fraudulence of people. You're like Candide. Or Gulliver. Or a noble savage—'

'Hold on,' I protest. 'I'm not some simple-minded yokel.'

'That's not what I meant. But anyway, you've lost that innocence by coming to London: socialising, consuming, *wanting*. Once the innocent begins to want he becomes corrupt. That's Western society for you.'

'I did have a television. We had the Internet,' I say crossly. 'I watched films and I had magazine subscriptions.'

'So perhaps you were a little corrupt before you even arrived,' Leo says, matter-of-factly. 'Maybe that's what brought you here. No, it's your father that really interests me. That's a man who wants nothing. You couldn't offer him any amount of worldly spoils to do something he didn't want to do.'

'Maybe you should write a book about him,' I mutter.

Leo gives me a diffuse smile then, and changes the subject, but he is only half with me, and I know he's thinking about the Highlands, and about Voltaire, and it isn't long before he has found *Candide* and is reading me excerpts from it.

I wonder whether this is the attraction I have for Leo: the process rather than the product, or even the raw material. Perhaps to him I am just a curio: something to appreciate in the abstract rather than the personal, like Darwin inspecting a tortoise from the Galapagos Islands. Even lying with him now – his arm resting against my shoulder, my hand in his hair, listening to the faint sound of his breathing – I can't feel his interest as anything more than scientific.

I tell Camilla and the Claires that I am moving out to house-sit for a friend, but that I'll still pay rent on my room for the remaining months of term. I explain that the move is for financial reasons. This isn't exactly a lie: the money Leni is paying me will cover the rent, with a little extra.

'Hope it all goes well,' Camilla says, in an arctic voice.

Laura and Sammy receive the news with unsurprised dismay: making sad mouths, they tell me we have to keep in touch.

'Of course,' I say. 'It's not like I'm really going anywhere, anyway.'

In truth we know that there is an awkwardness between the three of us now. *No one understands you*, Camilla said, from which she must mean I have been debated and discussed, and this was the conclusion.

I'm sorry that I didn't spend more time with Sammy and Laura on their own, building autonomous friendships with them, but it's too late now. Camilla always managed to be in the middle of us all; we were moons orbiting her, and now that she and I are opponents the others in our group can only hover and flit between us like fish, eyes wide. The closeness I had with them, that hair-stroking, clothes-sharing intimacy is over. After I move, they text me a few times, and then there is silence.

The first night in my new home, which is as spacious and tasteful as I have been led to expect, is an unsettling one. I lie in Leni's large bed with my eyes as dry as sand, refusing to close, my head burning bright like a lightbulb. When my wakefulness fizzles into an uncomfortable sleep, I dream I am at my grandparents' house in Dorset, looking at the photograph of my mother above the fireplace. Even though it is dark in the room and the curtains are drawn against the cold thickness of remembered white outside, Sylvia's picture is visible, hanging like a lit window. She is watching me.

'What is wrong with me?' I ask her.

She looks sorrowfully at me, but kindly. I try to tell her what I worry; that I am unmoored. I am a white-out like the snow, I am nothing but a longing. Then I see it isn't a picture of my mother at all, but of Ivy: that slanting hair, the irradiated eyes.

'What is wrong with me?' she repeats, mocking me. I realise then that I am not really in Dorset. I am half asleep, and when I see that I am half asleep, I am not asleep at all but back in my new bed, and the picture is gone, except for Ivy's smile, which has followed me out of the dream and stays, disturbingly, with me for the rest of the night.

It's Leo's thirtieth birthday, and he and his father have been drawn reluctantly together to celebrate. I have no idea that I am to be one of the party until Leo phones me while I am sitting in a pair of pyjamas trying to see a spot on the back of my neck by holding up mirrors.

'Are you sure you want me there?' I ask. 'What time should I meet you?'

'I'm outside now.'

I go to the window, horrified, to see him waving up at me outside his car. 'Don't be long,' he says, mouth moving distantly, his voice electronically close. Rivulets of pedestrians stare at him, then up at me as they pass. I draw the curtains.

Hot under the arms, I find a knee-length skirt and a white cardigan, make a cowboy job of my make-up, and run downstairs.

'You look like you're appearing in court,' Leo says delightedly, starting the car.

'Oh God. What are we even doing?'

'Dinner at William's. Don't look so stricken. It'll be funny.'

I think this is extremely unlikely, but say nothing.

Flickering uncertainly behind Leo, I am led by the housekeeper once more out of the daylight into William's house, folded into its grand darkness, passing into the long night of the dining room. As my vision gradually sharpens up I can make out more of the room, its dark wood coffin-panelling, ghostly towers of lilies, marble busts. The silver and crystal on the tables catches the heavy light from the high, moulded ceiling like unmined treasure in a cavern. I sit stiffly and self-consciously at the table. The window nearest me emits a draught that rolls in over my feet like a cold tide, soaking swiftly up my legs.

'Is Ivy coming?' I ask, hoping to suddenly see her appear, bright as a deer, or fox, against the dark of the wood.

'No. She doesn't see William. Hasn't for years.'

'Oh. She must really . . .' I tail off, faced with the largeness of the word 'hate'.

'Indeed,' says Leo.

'So . . . where's William?' I ask, when it becomes apparent that this information is not going to be volunteered. Hope flaps in my chest: perhaps William isn't coming after all.

'He's often late. Probably cashing up.'

It is a favourite conceit of Leo's that William works behind the counter at his bank, dealing with bad cheques and savings accounts, harassing his female colleagues and starting feuds over missing Biros. It has taken me a while, consequently, to understand what he actually does do. 'He lies about money,' is how Leo explains it, reminding me of Martin. They both say *money* in the same way – slightly bitter, slightly amused, slightly rueful.

'Hello,' calls William, walking in looking both cheerful and unfriendly, with a newspaper in his hand and a red glisten on his nose. 'A very favourable response indeed,' he says.

Leo doesn't give him a cue to continue, and I am too hesitant, but William, dent-proof, carries on as if he has been asked anyway.

'To my speech at the press conference.' He unfolds the paper on the table. 'The media loved it. "William Ford is a charismatic voice of authority, going some way towards reassuring the public that the banks are fundamentally altering their attitude to the consumer and small business owner alike".'

'Are you sure "authority" is the right word?' Leo asks.

'What else would it be?' William says, not really listening.

'Bathos?' suggests Leo. 'Sophistry?'

William looks up with a malevolence surprising in its suddenness.

'Shut up,' he snaps.

'Pseudery,' Leo decides, with satisfaction.

I wonder if I could deal with a father in the way that Leo does; ignoring him or baiting him, but always treating him like a harmless fool, an impotently raging Lear, which seems to infuriate him all the more. For his part, William doesn't seem to like Leo either, or expect to be liked by him. He just seems to assume that they have to spend time together.

'I hope you know what you're getting into,' William says, turning to me. 'For years I've had to deal with this. Not just Leo but his bloody sister. Bonnie and Clyde. I suppose you know about that attempted murder or "accident" or whatever the hell it was – which, by the way, has never been explained to me, or the slightest consideration given to its haunting of *my* career.' He gazes around the table, before hissing, stagily: 'Ingratitude!'

'Happy birthday to me,' Leo sings under his breath. I am almost annoyed by his blitheness myself. I could tell that when William started to speak Leo was angry, or concerned, but whenever he looks as if he is about to act on a feeling, his next impulse is to bat it away. Whatever I saw clarifying in his eyes, emitting its own peculiar light, he has ducked and avoided.

William changes the subject when the housekeeper brings in the first course. I gaze longingly after her as she exits the room, as if she might take me with her, out into the coloured-in world beyond the house. But I have to stay where I am, and eat three courses while William talks animatedly and without interruption about money: who wants money, who needs money, and why he considers it his personal duty to prevent them from getting their hands on any of it.

I pretend to listen and think about Ivy, who has become more prominent by her absence. She appears straightforward enough, but in a way that is almost too seamless: she is never clumsy, never embarrassed, never excited or angry or sad. It is hard to tell whether she has lost these things – if they have been cast off in the speed of her growing up, the rush of time – or if she keeps them hidden, vivid and hot. I can't imagine the things I have heard about her: the drugs house, the episodes of running away, the cause of the fight on the boat. The clean, clever sweep of her hands, her flawless skin and eyes as shiny as green glass, admit no cracks, no seediness.

But sometimes around her I feel wary, as if I am walking on a sunny day and have seen a shadow pass behind me like a wavering of ink, a fault line. Then she will look up or say something, and the shiver of it vanishes, and I feel stupid, and prosaic, for being alarmed by something simply because it is different.

When Leo and I drive back to his house, the rain is pouring again, slushing through the streets, the umbrellas scurrying past like black beetles.

'Well that was fun,' I say.

His profile smiles, lines of rain moving over it in the steely light from the windscreen.

'You don't have to come to these things,' he says. 'This afternoon is a good illustration of how politeness will get you in trouble.'

I wonder if he really believes that it is politeness that leads me after him, following him, both waiting for him and trying to catch him up.

'Will you see your mother?' I ask.

'I don't think so. She'll send a card.'

'When did she move to France?'

'After divorcing William and having me. The two things happened at almost the same time. She never forgave him for knocking her up.'

'Did you live there with her when you were young?'

'No, I lived in England.' He exhales – almost a sigh – and I lean forward, wondering if he will confide something, unearth some emotion from the past, something I can keep as evidence of our growing closeness. But he doesn't add anything more.

'So William did raise you alone?' I ask.

'Oh no,' Leo says with amusement. 'I had nannies. Several of them, in fact, before I went to boarding school. William kept sleeping with them and then sacking them. I was used to nannies arriving, crying a lot, then leaving. I thought that was how everybody grew up.'

'So did you miss your mother?'

'I never knew her. I went to stay with her in the holidays when I was eleven. She had birds in cages in the house. They were miserable there and reminded me of the nannies, so I let them all go. After that I wasn't invited to stay again.'

'That's awful,' I say, and Leo looks at me with a small smile, as if he had expected me to react this way, to be tritely shocked and sorry, so that I can't ask him anything else.

'Do you remember your mother?' he asks.

I try to picture Sylvia, who seems further away the longer I stay in London. When I was in Scotland I felt that she was completely missing, but now I see that she was more present there than she is here.

She is always somewhere behind me, growing more and more distant.

'I wish I did,' I say. 'But I was so young when she died. I have a sort of memory of her, that she was . . . I don't know. Warm. And her hair smelled sweet. But I'm not sure whether that's just something I've convinced myself into remembering.'

'Isn't everything?' Leo says, serious for once, but without looking away from the road, and the rain.

'Why haven't you gone back to visit Scotland?' Martin asks me. We are sitting in a park near Leni's flat, a scrubby expanse of grass punctuated by benches, litter bins, and caged trees, in an evening floating in the residual warmth of the day, the last-minute drying of the rain.

'I haven't been away long,' I say. 'Not even twelve months.'

'I thought you were going to tell me it was none of my business. But now I see you're defensive about it. Guilty conscience?'

'None of your business,' I say, and he laughs.

'I suppose you've asked me here to discuss Leo.' Intending to sound coldly formal, I am dismayed by the petulant slenderness of my voice; the sound of playacting. I cough, then continue: 'So let's discuss him. What do *you* think happened on the yacht?'

'Well, of my various theories, my personal favourite is as follows. Ivy is sleeping with Bruce Yelland for convenience – in terms of her supply, I mean. Leo's protective of her, so he agrees to join the couple on holiday. Bruce attacks Ivy in a drug-fuelled rage. Leo stabs him. Then Bruce shoots him. This seems to be the most plausible scenario for various reasons. Firstly, Bruce Yelland is a well-known thug. He's attacked women, employees, police and anyone else who bothers him. Secondly, I can't see Leo lifting a sword *after* being shot. He's a writer, not a trained assassin.'

'Do you have any evidence for any of this?'

'I have evidence that Ivy was taking drugs. I have evidence that Bruce has assaulted people associated with him. I'd like to track down Bruce Yelland or, failing that, the captain of the boat, who was also on board at the time.'

'But this doesn't even make Leo look bad,' I say. 'In your version of events he's a hero.'

'So you were worried about what I might find out.'

'Not at all,' I say, leaning back on the bench with relief.

Martin looks at me for a while. I am aware of being assessed: a gentle scrutiny moving over my face. Finally, he says, as if surprised, 'You don't have a mother.'

'What?' I sit up sharply. 'How did you know that?'

'Just a guess.'

'Stop guessing. You're not writing about me. You don't need to know anything about me.'

'Sorry. I'm on a lot of medication. I get distracted easily.'

'Why are you on medication?'

'I'm dying.'

'I don't believe you,' I say. But when I look at him I can believe it. His eyes are faded; the skin around them is grey, folded, in his cigarette-paper face. Under his coat he hunches as if cold, even in the dusty twilight heat.

'I don't tell lies. Not many, anyway. Or, at least, not about death.'

'Dying of what?' I ask.

'The usual.' He shrugs.

'I'm sorry,' I say hesitantly.

'Don't be. You've got bigger things to worry about. Like your situation.'

'Oh, my situation. I suppose you're about to make another guess. Fine – what *is* my situation?'

Instead of answering, Martin stands up. I watch him curiously. Previously I have cut off our conversations, but this time it is he who gives me a strange little salute, says, 'Bye for now, Persephone,' and wanders off, down the bare path and through the gate.

That night I stay up late, raking and turning over the detritus of the Internet, looking for anything to do with the yacht incident. I am relieved to see that the two men Martin would like to find – Bruce Yelland and the captain of the yacht – seem just as determined to remain lost. The captain couldn't be tracked down as a witness, while Bruce fled various drugs charges and remains at large. All Martin knows is that Ivy took drugs, something I doubt anyone would find either interesting or surprising.

As a final check, like a security guard half-heartedly making his torch-lit way around a secure perimeter fence, the enclosure in which I believe Leo to be safe, I ask Michael at lunch the next day if he was working with Leo at the time.

'No. I started working with him the year after.'

'You don't know anything about it?'

Michael looks unhappy. 'Look, Persephone, I told you things with Leo wouldn't be simple.'

I recognise the truth of this and feel abruptly ashamed, for asking Michael awkward questions, and because I can't imagine asking Leo about what happened myself: why he tried to kill somebody, and what Ivy had to do with it. My eyes unexpectedly under pressure, I turn my head away.

'I'm sorry,' he says. 'I don't mean to sound cold. But I'm in the same position as anyone else: I really don't know anything about it. Whatever I think about it is just speculation.'

'More informed speculation than mine.'

'I don't think I've ever been as intimate with Leo as you are,' Michael says drily.

'But you know Ivy. I think the whole thing has more to do with her than with Leo. Which is why I don't want to ask him about it. It was *her* boyfriend, after all—'

'Not necessarily,' Michael says. 'I don't think Ivy, even then, would have involved herself like that . . . with a man like him.'

'Then why were they all on holiday together?'

Michael puts his hands up to his face and his fingers wend into his hair as if attempting to hide there, burrow into safety. 'If I tell you what I think about it, will you tell Leo what I said?'

'Of course not.' I am indignant.

'Okay. Well, this is conjecture. Nothing more. I think Ivy and Bruce's relationship was strictly business. Even though she went to public school and Oxford and all that, she used to be quite . . . outside the normal operations of society. But wild, rather than feral. A feral creature was once tame, and Ivy didn't start out that way. It's only further down the line that she acquired a veneer of civilisation. I mean this in a nice way. I admire and like Ivy a lot. But in her early life she was basically a petty criminal. I think she was dealing too. Hence – Bruce Yelland. Her lifestyle may have changed by then, but she hadn't. She probably sought him out rather than the other way around.'

'I thought maybe Leo was protecting her,' I say.

'I think so too. But I'd say something went wrong from the money side of things. Bruce was a pretty nasty guy. Paranoid, aggressive. He probably thought Ivy was messing him around, something like that. Hence the "incident".'

'No one knows for sure if Ivy was dealing drugs?'

'No. It's fairly common – if unofficial – knowledge that she used to take a lot. God knows how she did it and aced all her courses. That's Ivy, I suppose. But people don't know that she sold them. Which is why it's so important that you don't mention any of this.'

'She could still be in trouble with the police if they found out?'

'Yes, if it's true. But fortunately everyone who was involved that day won't say anything, and no one else knows anything.'

'I can't really believe it of her,' I say. I think of the day that

Anthony was talking about drugs and Ivy walked in. ('Drugs make boring people fun,' Anthony said, 'but once you get addicted to anything it's boring. Films about it are boring: "I'll just try a little bit." "Maybe some more." "Where is my money/family/love-life?" Then they either die, or go through rehab and become even more boring because all they can talk about is how they used to be an addict. . .') I remember the awkwardness that doused us, cold and clammy, when he eventually realised Ivy had joined us and tailed off, but she just laughed.

'Ivy's complicated,' Michael says. 'Remember that black eye Leo had? He got that the night Ivy came home from Greece. I was with him in the evening when she arrived, clearly pissed off about something. It was tense so I excused myself. The next day he had a black eye.'

'What could he have done?' I ask, shocked.

'I have no idea. They often disagree but they don't argue. I know there are . . . family issues. I don't understand why Leo speaks to William and Ivy doesn't. I don't pretend I understand Ivy, and I don't know much about her past. The more you wonder about her history the more you feel like an archaeologist, finding some bones that don't make sense, a tablet with half the words missing. Fuck knows what really happened.'

'Leo knows,' I say.

'And I think you're probably right not to ask him,' Michael says.

After I leave Michael I go back to the Internet, to a paparazzi image I found of Leo and Ivy at the time of the trial. They walk through a galaxy of cameras, both of them looking younger, their skin glowing white in the flashes. Ivy's face is barely visible beyond a protective swag of hair. Leo looks wary, but vivid, riled, as if cornered, ready to bite or run. *Wild rather than feral*, Michael said, and I can see it here, in both of them. The scene is primitive: comparable to nothing but the tropes of a wildlife documentary, the wild creatures of a natural aristocracy falling foul of an opportunistic pack: two young hawks mobbed by seagulls, a pair of foxes chased by dogs.

Later I sit outside on the small terrace of Leni's flat. Around me the spiky plants make their complex shadows, figurations of leaves, on the warmed flagstones: the road noise, the snarling of London, has dimmed now that its people are home from work, the traffic sounds at low tide. It is peaceful, but I am not at peace. I am worried that Martin will find out about Ivy's past, and publish, and then not only her charmed life, but Leo's, and then mine, will come abruptly to an end.

I tell my father and Sadie that I'll meet them in Hyde Park because, firstly, the sun has come out and the whole of London seems to be in a bacchanalian good humour – emptying off-licence shelves, sprawling its keen white flesh across any available grass – and secondly, because the Italian Gardens are a good place to start my precisely planned tour of 'unmissable city sights', most of which I have so far missed.

Really I meet them in Hyde Park because I'm not sure how to explain my occupancy of Leni's comfortable apartment, and the tour is an exercise in distraction: if I can keep up an unrelenting presentation of columns, statues and façades over the course of two days, my father won't have time to ask me any questions, or look at me too closely. I inspect my face myself the night before they arrive, as if it really might show its loss of innocence – a hardening of the eyes, a knowing mouth-curl, a haggardly guilty brow – but it looks the same as always: smooth and blank and slightly uncertain, like a passport photo. A face in transit.

Crossing Hyde Park I see my father and Sadie sitting on one of the stone benches, reading something. I haven't seen my father as one of a pair before: the way he politely holds the book open for Sadie to read, one hand resting on her back, is oddly difficult to watch. They seem like a couple who have had longer together, absorbing each other's movements, following each other's angles. They look as if they have been married for thirty years, and are waiting not for me, but for their own daughter, Paige, a bright blonde studying medicine, whose good-natured boyfriend they will be meeting later.

I hesitate by the fountain until my father looks up and I have to move forward, waving furiously and calling a vivacious, 'Dad! Sadie! Hi!' to cover my unsettlement.

'Perse . . . are you all right?' he asks, unfooled.

'Oh yes, sorry, I was running late, so I ran across the park, and I'm out of breath.'

'Running in those shoes?' my father begins, but is interrupted by Sadie, still perky under the weight of a bulky camera, rucksack, sunglasses and sensible jacket, demanding a 'huge hug!' and telling me the shoes are just gorgeous, and if I can run around in them, I darn well should, because there's nothing like running around in the sun when you're young enough to look good doing it.

'Well, quite,' says my father.

Over afternoon tea I inspect him, reaching uncertainly for a small purple cake, trying to separate the new vision – the clarity of estrangement – that allows me to see his age for the first time, from genuine wear and tear. His face is still folded in the usual places, but softer, more tanned than I remember. His hair has been recently trimmed; even his eyebrows, in fact, are neater than they once were.

'You look well, Dad,' I say. (Could Sadie have asked him to trim his eyebrows?)

'Do you think? I suppose I've been more active lately. I was thinking about getting a dog. We haven't had a dog since Gustav – and you never met him. You always used to want a dog when you were young, do you remember?'

'Yes. You were worried it would bite me.'

'Well, perhaps that was an overreaction.'

'Well, better late than never,' I say. 'Get a dog. Why not.'

'But there are other things to consider. If we had a dog, for example, we'd need a house with a garden. It would rule out the possibility of, ah, living in a flat.'

'Thinking about moving to London?' I ask, beginning a smile, before I notice his glance at Sadie. 'You're thinking about moving? I thought you were redoing the kitchen?'

'No, well, I wasn't sure, so I put that on hold. I'm not definitely thinking of moving, either. Just ideas floating around. Thinking about getting older . . . the practicalities. Stair lifts. Retirement bungalows. And so on. That sort of thing. I've come to think that perhaps the Highlands are a little . . . too isolated.'

I stare at him until he blinks, uncomfortable, and offers, 'You always told me we should live nearer civilisation.'

'These are all just ideas, Evan,' Sadie interrupts. 'Now you've worried Persephone. It's her childhood home, after all. Her mother's home. You can't just drop this on her.' She turns to me. 'Don't you worry, hon. Nothing's going to happen to the Scotland house.'

Annoyed that Sadie has so accurately judged my mood, I shake my head, say, 'I don't mind what you do. It doesn't bother me at all,' and take a mouthful of the nearest cream cake, which turns out to be full of caramel – a taste I hate – but with both of them watching me, concerned and guilty looking, I have to chew and swallow it anyway, and it settles down in my stomach, to become a too-sweet, oily presence, for the rest of the afternoon.

On the last day of Evan and Sadie's stay, my busy itinerary takes us past a hotel that my father stops at, taken aback.

'Oh! I remember this place,' he says. 'I stayed here once, in the eighties. With your mother. We were on the way to visit Jack and Ellen and we thought we'd spend a day in London. We went to the National Gallery and then we stayed here.'

We all look solemnly at the neat window boxes of the white façade for a moment, as the bipolar spring weather, previously sunny, lapses into rain.

'Well, would you look at that sky! Why don't we go inside?' Sadie asks. 'Obviously we were fated to pass by here. We could look around. Have a cup of tea.'

My father hesitates, but she is on the steps already, one hand on her camera, and so he follows her, with a 'Why not, I suppose', and I follow him. But once we are all standing in the lobby, a smooth vista of taupe and ivory, long-blocked sofas and glass tubes of light, he looks around with bafflement.

'I don't think this is the same place at all,' he says. 'It's not what I remember, anyway.'

'Maybe it's had a refurb?' Sadie suggests.

'Maybe.' He looks at the row of rainforest plants, the gently pinging lift, and the marble floor, frowning, then finally at the front desk and the receptionist, who, to her credit, pretends to be busy moving paper around.

'Well,' I say, after a while of contemplation, 'it's either not the same place to begin with, or it isn't any more, so let's go and get lunch.'

There is a moment of silence outside, ruffled by the unfurling of umbrellas and raincoats. I look at my father, who seems subdued, his mouth lowered into the familiar shape of our life in Scotland, a thoughtful line.

'Ah, what a shame,' Sadie says, then, brightening, 'I guess not many things have stayed the same over the last twenty years, hey? I sure wish my face had!'

In the end, the visit didn't go as I thought it would. Working so hard to remain cheerful yet unreadable – avoiding questions about my course, my friends and my romantic life, which didn't leave me with a lot – I hadn't expected that my father might have his own shy truths to keep back. The trip finishes with him still on the back foot; his awkward guilt at the airport, his tentative kiss. When I put my arms around him he smells the same as always, of dry wood and glue, a faint soapy sweetness, the sameness of it disturbing me as much as if Sadie had doused him in something new.

The prospective house move is mentioned only once more, my father saying, tentatively: 'I haven't decided anything about the house, Perse. I wanted to ask you what you thought first. We've spent a long time there, after all.'

'Dad, don't be ridiculous,' I say, more energetically than I intend. 'I've always told you to move. Anyway, it's your house. It's completely up to you.'

'We'll discuss it when you're back over the summer,' he says, but I cut him short:

'Nothing to discuss.'

After I wave him and Sadie through their grey plastic airport gate, I wait to watch the large window, filmed with the murk outside, the fog the planes move in and out of, until their own plane makes its way up into the clouds with a long, desolate wail. Then I walk back through the concourse, sit on a train, leave the train station and get into a cab, watching the day darken around me, as if I am carried on a slow-moving river, floating without volition in the night stream.

I am relieved that with a delicate choreography of evasion, silence and outright lying, I was able to keep the hemispheres of London and the Assynt separate. My father, predictably, didn't ask me anything about my love life, though Sadie allowed herself a warm and winking interrogation in the powder room at the Ritz. *Girl talk*, she hopefully called it, which made me think she was going to give me a tutorial on tampon usage. I told her that, being shy around boys, I had only been on a couple of dates so far.

'Jeez,' Sadie said, aghast. 'A girl as pretty as you can't be sitting at home studying on Friday nights. Why don't you go to the disco? Or you could join a club? I met a gorgeous guy at college through a book club, believe it or not.'

'Maybe a book club would be a good idea,' I agreed smirkingly, enjoying my closeness to the wind.

'You don't even have to read the books these days. You can get synopses online if you want to impress a literary guy. I remember I got my date by talking vaguely about the "ambiguity of the voice". It didn't last, of course. But it sure was fun for a while.'

I told Leo and the others that I was working all weekend on an overdue essay, out of concern that Leo – who had previously shown signs of making my father one of his obsessions – would demand to meet him. Nobody questioned me: nodding with sympathetically sage mouths – the 'of course' expression they reserve for anything work related – giving my own work far more consideration than I ever have.

When I get out of the taxi I stand briefly outside Leo's house in the pale cone below the lamp-post, reacquainting myself with the end-of-the-world feeling his street has at these times, the sky over the rooftops lowered by the uniform cloud, starless and moonless, the clear pavement, the noise of distant traffic. Then I knock on his door with the usual fear of him not opening it, before the light inside is turned on and hope takes hold of my mouth, making a smile of fixed, helpless adoration. I watch his shape in the glass, forming, becoming more real the closer he gets, until the door is opened and he is there, as preposterously beautiful as ever, and not real looking at all.

Leo's bedroom is a place in which, after several visits, I am still not entirely comfortable. It is a room of contradictions, of collisions and tension, between what I want and what I am afraid of. This conflict extends into the room's own composition: even its wallpaper, an unexpected and not entirely lovely floral print. Its flowers do not behave as flowers should; they writhe on the walls, they have their own demanding life, green vines, white stamens, purple petal mouths, red lips, flickering voraciously in the movement of light from the rainy window.

Leo says that the paper was made by William Morris and accords it a reverence I rarely see directed at anyone human. When he and Ivy viewed the house she said he had to buy it, if for nothing else than the wallpaper. I suspect that in the floating, imagined future in which Leo and I live together, the wallpaper has already won the impending war.

In the centre of the room is a vast Jacobean four-poster bed. The woman who comes, invisibly, to clean Leo's house invariably draws its claret curtains, so that the bed stands ominously like a magic trick, a great red-cloaked chest. Once inside it the drapes turn to theatre curtains, drawn back for the grand performance. The bed itself is dark and deep, with weighty, carved posts, a flotilla of pillows. Its red roof is a thick shadowiness above me, something I am not used to. In my own room I can see the light moving on my white ceiling, a landscape on plaster, the reflection of the car headlights at night wheeling like stars across the sky.

I lie here now next to Leo, unable to sleep as usual, counting the ways he disappears. The first way is physical disappearance. He has told me that most of the times people believe he has gone away, he is simply at home writing and not answering his phone or the door. But it suits him for people to think he's unreachable, doing something secret and debauched, otherwise they harass him. ('The more successful a writer you are, the less time people allow you to write,' Leo said. 'Better not to get published. Live on a pittance. Have all the time in the world.'

'Having no money can't be as romantic as it sounds.'

He frowned. 'I wouldn't do it for the romance.')

The second way is his intellectual disappearance. I have noticed how difficult others find it to pin Leo down to any discussion of ethics, politics, religion and academic theories. He sidesteps serious debate with a joke or a conversational diversion.

'My interest is in the personal, not the abstract,' he has claimed more than once.

'That's nonsense,' Ivy said, on an occasion when he made this statement in front of her, and I have to agree with her. Leo dodges the personal as warily as anything else that appears to demand something of him: like Rumpelstiltskin he gives nothing away. Asking him about himself is like trying to hold water: the harder the grip, the faster it runs away. This is the third way: emotional disappearance. Just like Ivy, I have never seen him cry, or even look as if he might be about to. I have never seen him laugh uncontrollably. I have never seen him in a heated argument, and sometimes I crave a quarrel with him: I want him to raise his voice, punch a wall. To make him angry would be a form of connection, an inescapable solidity of feeling.

The fourth and final way Leo vanishes is not quite the same as the rest except in its effect, because it is an unconscious disappearance: sleep, the unanswerable removal. Leo falls asleep so fast it is almost impolite, as if he can't wait to be away from me. He lies on his back facing God, with a careless vulnerability. I myself am a side sleeper, I prefer to shelter, leg crooked. Before he falls asleep he usually has an arm around me, which he takes back with an irritable sound once he is dreaming. Other than this he doesn't move, he doesn't murmur, sigh or talk: inhaling and exhaling with admirable deepness and regularity, as if he were getting the utmost out of his rest. Sometimes, like now, I feel lonely in bed with him, then stupid, for reading sleep as rejection.

Lying here in the bed with its dark curtains cradling me, I feel like something archetypal, storyfied. Yet I suspect I do not make a good fairy-tale heroine. Heroines are innocent and brave. They don't fantasise or flirt or manoeuvre. They don't vacillate, they don't compete or resent. They don't lie next to their prince and feel annoyed that he is asleep. But then, if Leo is a fairy-tale prince, he is the kind that operates under a spell or a curse, an enchantment I don't know how to remove: *All the women in the land will love you, and you will love none of them.*

Martin calls me on a day when I am feeling particularly ill at ease with myself, having tried to read Barthes and finding myself unable to understand most of it. I had better luck with another of Leo's interests: Plato – Leo himself representing the perfect form, the template that no one else can meet – but by the time I finished my guide to Plato, Leo had moved on to something else.

I take Martin's call out on to the bamboo-bordered seclusion of Leni's balcony, as if the interior of the flat might be under surveillance. The sun has drummed onto the silvered wooden decking all morning and its slats are hot under my feet, shocking my soles.

I sit down and tuck the phone under my ear, stretching my legs out to meet the light.

'Hello, Persephone,' Martin says. 'Lovely day, isn't it? Are you outside?'

'Are you watching me?' I look across at the facing windows of the next block, anonymously mirroring the sunlight.

'I can hear the traffic.'

'Oh. Okay. Well, why are you phoning? I'm very busy.'

'Just wondering what you thought of William now that you've met him. He's a character, isn't he?'

'Pff,' I say, noncommittally. The question is, as usual with Martin, a well-targeted one, because William is the reason I bought a collection of Barthes' essays. I had been reading one of Leo's books, in which a father – falsely – tells his daughter she is adopted. The father claims that he is ending the parent-child relationship of dependency and blame, effectively unsubscribing from his role of father. 'Only the parentless are truly free,' he tells her. This is so similar to what Ivy herself has said about William that I asked Leo what had inspired the character.

Leo looked at me for a long time, as if sorrowful, disappointment radiating through all the agate colour-graduations of his eyes, a circular ripple of impact.

'Persephone,' he says. 'There really is no excuse for this squinting through a text, trying to see out the other side. Not now that post-structuralism has happened.'

'Post-structuralism?'

'Barthes compared a text to an onion. Let me see if I remember it. "A construction of layers, whose body contains, finally, no heart, no kernel, no secret, no irreducible principle, nothing except the infinity of its own envelopes, which envelop nothing other than the unity of its own surfaces."'

That shut me up.

It is with this sense of failed comprehension and points missed that I ask Martin now, curiously, 'What do *you* think of William?'

'I don't know yet. I was just making conversation really. I'm not sure if he interests me or not. His relationship with Leo is an odd one. Ivy, so far as I'm aware, hasn't spoken to him for over ten years. Leo, apparently, is on good terms with him, but there is an interview from a few years back in which it becomes clear that William doesn't know that his son has had a book published. I think it suits the Fords to hide the extent of the family rift.'

'But why would they do that?'

'All of them are publicly visible. They might want to avoid prying. It's understandable.'

Martin's tone – dismissive and already vague, as if he is about to lead into another subject – prompts me to clutch at the disappearing strand of the conversation.

'I asked Leo about William,' I say, 'and he quoted a line of Barthes I don't understand. And can't really remember. Something about onions.'

Martin laughs, an unexpected, textured sound, surprising me with its sudden pulse in the receiver.

'It's only the terminology that's deflecting you,' he says. 'You're more than capable of grasping the concept. I think you probably have already.'

'What's the concept?'

'That literary criticism used to focus on trying to find out a single meaning for a book – the message of an "Author-God", as

Barthes put it. He said that there was no use trying to examine writing in an attempt to get the message. Rather, a text is a soup of writings and quotations and cultural associations. This is why he said "The space of writing is to be ranged over, not pierced." In other words, enjoy its surfaces.'

'So is writing a soup or an onion? Or is it onion soup?'

'Soup was my own little excursion into analogy. I shan't bother next time.'

'Sorry. Only joking.'

'So, Barthes went on to say that if you look at it like this, a reader has his own role as a producer of the meanings of a text. This is what he referred to – most famously – as the birth of the reader, and the death of the author.'

'Leo *likes* this metaphor? The death of the author?'

'Derrida said something similar,' Martin continues. 'A piece of writing doesn't have one true meaning that originates from the writer's pure consciousness. Which is helpful when you consider a long-dead writer such as Ovid. We don't have any access to his consciousness. We have to make sense of his writing in our own way.'

'I understand,' I say, then, curious: 'Why are you helping me, anyway?'

'I don't like to see anyone in the dark,' he says. 'And on that note, why do you think Leo chose this particular quote for you?'

'To confuse me? To stop me asking annoying questions?'

'No. I'll tell you. He's writing himself. You're the reader.'

'Now you're back to teasing me,' I say. I lie back on the balcony, my face tipped to the sun, to catch it like the bowl of a flower.

There is a silence, heavy and sudden, as if a hand has been held over the receiver. When I press the phone to my ear I can hear the cough on the other side of his fingers.

'Are you okay?' I ask.

Martin's voice, when it returns, is leaner, gentler. 'Just the smog. Gets into me on days like this. You ought to be careful yourself. You must have noticed the black pollution in your nose. Wipe your skin and see for yourself. That's London all over you.'

'You sound like my father,' I say lightly, then stop, dismayed that I have been eased into the personal. Martin, for his part, doesn't appear to notice.

'Apologies, Persephone, but I have to go,' he says.

'Oh,' I say, feeling myself abruptly dropped and wondering what has happened, at his end of the wire. 'Well, ah, thanks for the explanation.'

'Any time,' he says, and I can picture the accompanying shrug, the momentary gentility of his sparse, scuffed shoulders. 'Have a nice day.'

'You too,' I say.

I hang up, lie back and shut my eyes, through which the sun still permeates, lighting my eyelids like stained glass – red and black and violet – half dozing eventually but still trying to work it all out: what Leo meant, what Martin meant, what Martin might be up to; what I, myself, am up to.

Later that month Leo's new book is nominated for a prize, and he invites me to the awards ceremony. 'It'll be funny,' he says on the telephone. 'And you'll like being photographed.'

I do like being photographed, though I have never told Leo this. A couple of pictures of the two of us have appeared in newspapers and magazines over the past month, in which I was the 'stunning brunette', the 'brainy beauty', and even the 'posh student'. I like seeing my grainy, crepuscular self on the arm of my printed lover, looking far more lovely than I have ever felt in life. People might look at me and think they saw Leo's muse, someone myth-like, someone adored.

But then this thrill only lasts so long; it's a short mephedrone moment, blinking out and leaving me in a cold, low place. It ends when Leo laughs at the pictures of us, or when a reporter calls and asks me to do a 'kiss and tell', and I realise that even if I wanted to, I have nothing to tell.

'You should think about whether you want this,' Leo said when the first picture of me appeared. 'Once you cross the line from private to public, it's not easy to go back.'

'I don't mind,' I said quickly, worried he might be tempted to finish with me simply to spare me unwanted celebrity.

'That's because it's new. Wait until every time you do or say something you hear an echo that no one else hears – "What if this gets out". Or worse, the echo arrives before you can act, and you end up living a life without any authenticity.'

'But everyone has to have some forethought. Even if you're not famous you can still be seen and heard by other people.'

'But the moment passes. It isn't recorded. The things public figures do solidify around them. Life is a gradual process of becoming sealed up in amber.'

I am thinking of this conversation when I ask him now, 'Will anyone ask me about the book?' The book, Leo's latest, is hard to trap and understand. There is confusion about the identity of the narrator, and whether or not he might be dreaming. I gave up on puzzling it out and scanned the pages compulsively and guiltily for hints of Leo's personality – which, I imagined, might run through the novel like the silver thread of a banknote – but it turns out that the book *is* very like him, in that I don't understand any of it.

'I shouldn't think anyone would be so crass,' Leo says, and laughs.

I prepare myself carefully for the ceremony, paying a hairdresser to steeple my hair, eviscerating my bank account to buy a cloudy, silvery dress, which shifts waywardly over my body whenever I move. By the time I arrive into the room of more sensibly dressed people, my breasts on display like a bakery counter, I am regretting my decision.

The only other exposed breasts in the room belong to a young female author, another prize-winner. She is attractive but looks only half pulled together; messy gilt hair, a lax, disorderly cleavage. Still, I am uneasy as she talks to Leo. I can imagine that he might be able to love another writer. Their literary powers will converge and produce genius offspring, hold soirees, learn obscure new languages. I watch her miserably, unable to defend my position next to Leo, our structure of intimacy.

'My favourite novel is *Women In Love*,' she tells him in a flowery voice. 'That imagery! So sensuous and complex. I do wonder if our choices are revealing of something in ourselves? What's your favourite novel?'

'*The Very Hungry Caterpillar*,' Leo says, and I can relax. This writer will join the shadowy numbers of one-time encounters, of people who ask more of Leo than he wants to show.

I predict, and then watch, Leo go from quiet to vague, as if becoming gradually more translucent, until eventually the author can't find anything to grip or hold and is forced to give up.

I eat some of the canapés that do not look like any kind of food, and are accordingly uncertain eating. One thing crackles and burns, another collapses on my tongue like a dying butterfly. The final offering tastes of the sea, a desolate salty coolness in my mouth. To take the feel of it away I go to the bar, where an older man with a clotted drunk voice leans in too close to talk to me.

'Cheer up,' he says. 'I think you're the best-looking girl in here.'

My mother would say, *What's so important about looks?*

Ivy would say, *What does it matter what you think?*

When I leave the bar, I realise Martin is standing not far from me, apparently without having noticed my presence. I cross the room hurriedly to meet him, facing each other for a moment in the half-light beneath a towering arrangement of flowers, which give off a hot jungle odour. Martin is enveloped in his stiff suit; his eyes have retreated further into their sheltering hollows. He looks tired.

'You look very lovely,' he says.

'Why are you here?'

'I'm a journalist, remember. I'm covering this epic logroll.'

Across the room I see Leo look over at us.

'Fuck,' I say crossly. 'Now I'm going to have to invent a conversation I'm having with you.'

'Don't worry,' Martin says. 'He won't ask.'

'I can't talk to you here,' I say, turning around so quickly I step on the train of a woman's dress. He takes my arm. 'Stop it,' I say, trying to whisper, and pull my arm back sharply, nearly unbalancing him. I see now that he had been leaning on a stick.

'Hello,' Leo says, appearing at my side, apparently without noticing the hasty pas de deux we have just executed. He smiles warmly at Martin, and I am alarmed, because if Leo notices Martin's walking stick, he might start talking to him. Leo is often more friendly towards people he perceives as disadvantaged or weak, because he has never been close to being either of those things. He doesn't understand that the weak can still do him harm.

Martin, with a purposeful handshake, introduces himself as Eric Bridges.

'Have we met before?' Leo asks, looking at him.

'Unfortunately not, as I'm a devoted follower of yours. I work for Amazon.' He inclines his hand politely in my direction, 'I've just had the privilege of meeting your lovely companion Persephone. We've been having a rather heated discussion about art.'

Panicked, I can feel my mouth setting tight, my hands drawing up at my sides. I drop them and smile, not meeting Martin's friendly eye.

'A broad topic,' Leo says, apparently amused.

'We were discussing Duchamp's *Fountain*,' Martin explains, as I burn, silently, next to him. 'The acceptance of the ready-made urinal as art, and the moment the definition of art changed. Before that it involved skill and creation. After that, what is art?'

'What did you decide?' Leo asks me.

'I . . . hadn't arrived at any conclusions yet,' I say. 'That was when you came along. I was hoping you might have been to the bar. I'm *so* thirsty.'

'I was about to say that art has become simply a statement,' Martin says, before I can get rid of Leo, 'an act.'

'But that means that everything we do is art,' I say.

'And some of us are better artists than others,' Martin replies.

'What would you define as better?' Leo asks, leaning in with a look of interest, and I see the door out of this conversation closing.

'Perhaps an act that is – if not pure – at least aware of its own nature, as a starting point. I see Persephone is frowning . . . Let me give you an example. What is it you said you were studying?'

'Management.'

'Do you know what it is you want to manage?'

'No.'

'In that case, we can consider the abstract concept of management, which suits the purposes of the point better. Management is an act. Of course, it's not an autonomous – or pure – act because you are trying to make someone else act, and are usually yourself under the direction of someone else. You are living off the acts of others. Essentially, you are a parasite. But you may or may not be conscious of that position.'

'A parasite,' I say, with a sharp, laugh-like huff of breath, 'so much for small talk.'

'That isn't a necessarily negative word,' Martin says. 'And I do hope I haven't offended you.'

'Not at all,' I manage.

'We're all parasites in one way or another. I feed on culture, or more specifically, on the Western literary tradition, as, to some extent, does Leo. There are no truly independent acts. Just greater or lesser degrees of awareness of them.'

'What about bakers?' I say. Both men look at me, not understanding. 'Are bakers parasites?'

'Bakers use recipes,' Leo says, to my annoyance.

'Okay. Then what if I were, say, to hit somebody? Wouldn't that be a pure and independent act?'

'No,' Martin says, remaining genial. 'An emotional act isn't a pure act. Why might somebody want to hit someone else? Because they want something they have been conditioned to want. Then they get angry because something goes against these pre-conditioned ideas of what they want.'

I am so angry by this time that my anger makes a harsh sound in my throat, which I turn into a cough, then – struck by inspiration – keep coughing, until Leo looks at me with consternation.

'Are you all right?'

'Just a dry throat.' I make a helpless face. 'I've had a cough lately. Probably London pollution, or something.'

'I'd say the only truly pure act is a bodily act,' Leo says, 'and on that note, I'm going to excuse myself and find Persephone a glass of water.' With a polite nod – nearly a bow – in Martin's direction, he turns easily and vanishes in the crowd, moving quickly and sideways as always, oblique as a chess bishop.

I turn to Martin, who has found a little gilt and velvet chair to sit on and is looking suddenly pained. For a moment I almost feel I should ask if he needs help. Instead I say, quietly, with the jabbing emphasis used by angry wives at dinner parties, 'This is absolutely over. What the fuck was that? I'm going to tell Leo what you're doing.'

'Don't do that,' Martin says. I ignore him and turn away, but he continues, loud enough to be heard, 'I know Ivy was selling drugs at that time. And yes, I've got evidence.'

I stand dismayed. 'You didn't say that before.'

'Of course I didn't. I'm only telling you now because you're forcing my hand.'

There is a moment of silence, in which he looks at me closely, and then says, sadly, 'Oh, Persephone. You thought I'd be honest?'

I don't reply.

'I'm sorry. But you have to let me finish what I'm doing. If you don't, I'll have to go public with this.'

'If that were true, would Ivy go to prison? Would her career be over? She hasn't done anything to you!'

'I agree it seems harsh. But she is Leo's sister.'

'Half sister,' I say automatically. I am close to tears, the stem of my glass sliding in my hot fingers. 'I thought this was about proving Leo is flawed. This doesn't prove anything.'

'I told you, I'm not finished yet,' Martin says. 'I need you to give me some time to finish my story. Some more of *your* time. It works for you because you delay the blow. Anyway, if you're lucky I might even die before I find out what I need.'

He is small under the overarching, barbaric flowers, small and ill.

'Here's hoping,' I say, then I turn away and walk back to find Leo.

~

When the night is over and Leo has claimed his award, we leave with a model, an insectile blonde who promptly starts talking to the paparazzi outside about getting in touch with the creative spirit while we side-step into Leo's car.

'Like a human shield,' I say.

'There never used to be so many models and actors here,' Leo says, baffled. 'And the press follow them.'

I know, but don't say, that it is because of him. The glamour of him attracts them, he has lit a lamp in a darkened corner of the arts and after him they come, a glittery slipstream, dancing and taking drugs, like moths whirling in his intoxicating light. I lean my head back instead, watching the city wheel and recede in the car's windows, overlaid by our ghosts, our partial colours.

I sit and sit with my question, letting it grow larger and hungrier, until it forces its own way out.

'What happened that night that you were shot?' I ask.

'Oh, that night,' Leo says, with his eyes still on the road. 'What do you mean? What happened from beginning to end?'

'Uh . . . yes,' I say, startled.

'Well, we went away with Bruce Yelland, who was Ivy's . . . let me think of a word. He was her friend – though he wasn't really what you'd traditionally define as a friend – and her dealer, but not just a dealer, because she was selling drugs on for him, to our "friends" at the time, so perhaps business partner is the correct word. *Associate*. That's better. So Ivy took him up on his offer of a holiday, and I went along, mainly because I was young and stupid.'

He glances at me but I am blinking and static like a stalled appliance at his casual revelations, and so he continues:

'So that night we had a drunken falling out, so drunken that I struggle to remember what started the whole thing. But Bruce accused Ivy of stealing from him, that was part of it. The whole thing got out of hand – Bruce pushed Ivy, I hit him, then he brought out a gun. I – absurdly – got that sword off the wall and, around the same time that he shot me, I stabbed it at him. Luckily we both missed anything important. The whole thing was really quite embarrassing. Poor Bruce was so embarrassed he left the country and hasn't been seen since. And there you have it.'

'Good lord,' I say, and laugh.

'You seem relieved.'

'It's just . . . I was so worried about asking you.'

'Why worried?'

'I'd heard the subject was off limits. That you never discussed it.'

'No one asked,' Leo says. 'Except strangers. And William, but I didn't tell him because it seemed funnier not to. It still annoys him.'

'Does Ivy mind you talking about it?'

'Well, Ivy was in an . . . indecisive state around that time, but since then she's metamorphosed into a respectable academic. For her it's like a discussion about someone else.'

'But nobody knows about her dealing?'

'Not really. She was under some suspicion when she first became a lecturer, I think. But nothing has ever been confirmed.'

'Don't you worry that someone – some journalist – might try to pursue it, just because she's connected to you?'

'No one has so far,' Leo says. 'Do you want to get a takeaway? I'm starving. Every time I got near any canapés someone would interrupt me and I'd have to watch them carried away, like Tantalus.'

'Sure,' I say.

We sit in silence for a while as he fiddles with the car stereo.

I watch the sparks from a thrown cigarette skitter across the black road ahead of us like a smashed star, sitting deep in the hum of the night road, the radio flickering in between channels, feeling my faith return to wrap and warm me. Leo has done something noble to protect someone else and I realise I have to do something noble too – not only to protect Ivy, but also to connect the three of us; earn a place in their intimacy, their pact of silence.

In June, Leo leaves London for Los Angeles. He is supposed to be talking about making a film of his latest book, which the studio heads want to change. They don't like the ambiguity, they want to know who the star is. They demand answers. Leo doesn't like it, but the film is being made anyway, so he goes to talk to them over croissants and coffee, watching their white snappy teeth eating up his story. They would ideally like Leo to act in the film; in a brilliant crystallisation of publicity. Short of that, they want him to do interviews, promotional events. They want contracts, to fix him in place. He calls once to say that he is tired of films, is coming back. Then no one hears from him for another week. The world is closing in on Leo, I think, and I worry that he will disappear altogether in his efforts not to be bought.

I talk about it with Michael and the others.

'Bendricks and Blake let Leo do whatever he wants,' Michael says. 'Mostly because he will anyway. He's politely unco-operative. He doesn't meet deadlines – we have to change our schedules for him. Doesn't do signings, doesn't do interviews . . .'

'He did that TV interview.'

'Which is likely to be his last. He didn't like that at all. But in America he's less of a celebrity and more of a commodity.'

'Maybe it will be good for Leo to be told what to do for once,' I say lightly.

'Yes!' Emiko laughs. 'He hates being told what to do.'

'More like, he hates being pinned down to anything.'

'I think he sees promotional work as undignified,' Michael says charitably.

'I think he's worried what the press might find out,' Ivy says, and there is a moment in which everyone looks at her uneasily, before she smiles, and we can all laugh. As the conversation goes on I see her turn away slightly, shruggingly, with a resigned expression, as if bored with us all, for pretending that she was making a joke.

Other than this night I haven't spent a lot of time with Catherine, Emiko and the others recently. This isn't their fault, but mine: with Leo away I feel tired and quiet, unable to find and dust off my old self for them, to be lively and sweet. Even their talk about Leo reminds me how little I can contribute to it. I have got, gradually, to a point where without him the light vanishes, the curtain is down, and there is no point to my performance.

I don't enjoy my solitude either. Being alone with myself is like sitting in an empty dressing room; one with no windows, an electric light, and an unflattering mirror. I spend most of my time in the library or at my computer, working mechanically through essays and recommended reading, inexorable and lonely, until I become the unexpected darling of the most disapproving lecturers. I rarely meet my university friends in the corridors of campus, but the less

I see of the girls the more worried I am about seeing them, until the sight of them comes with a jolt of near-superstitious fear. When we do cross paths I change direction, tilt my head down, side-step into empty lecture rooms or lavatories, until the danger has passed.

Even so, I find I have no shortage of friends at university. Girls often try to sit with me or talk to me, reaching through me to snatch something of Leo. The better I become at shutting them off – giving an unenthusiastic smile instead of a real one, pretending I have to be somewhere else – the more I understand his warning about fame. It fires you hard and sets you aside, like a precious artefact in a glass case. I remember how it was to be on the other side of the glass, standing with all the other girls, looking in. Talking to them carries the uncomfortable reminder that I could be back there with them, back on the outside, more easily than I would like.

As the weeks of solitude settle like snow around me, covering my house, piling on to the quiet roof, I decide on my noble act. I am going to make better friends with Martin, and find out more about what he knows.

I haven't heard from Martin while Leo has been away, and I am curious about what he is up to, whether he tailed Leo to America, or is still here, flapping thinly around London in his dark coat, like a weary jackdaw. I look online for his address or phone number, but there are no contact details. I do manage to find a few of his articles, on various subjects. He writes well – sober and almost affectionate – with the air of a slightly battered travel writer, who still retains gentle enthusiasm for the countries in which he was lost or maltreated.

After a few days Martin calls me himself, asking to meet. I go to see him in a small café in a forgotten block of London, a sad place in grimy, bleached-out circus colours, red and yellow and white, the greying floor tiles and shiny tablecloths with their small plastic salt and vinegars. The air is oily, making the proprietor gleam like a baked ham. The early afternoon sun outside lights the dirt on the windows with a flash on the grime, a sharp eye.

'I thought you might enjoy it here,' Martin says when I sit down. He has a plate of untouched chips in front of him. 'I don't recommend the food, but the atmosphere is unparalleled.'

'How's the exposé going?'

'Slowly.' He rests his head in his hands and smiles.

'You're not a very good investigative journalist, are you?' I say nastily, before I remember I am meant to be insinuating myself into Martin's confidence.

'How's your course?' he retorts. 'I hope you're working hard. You get distracted easily.'

'I'm working fine, thank you,' I say.

'In the absence of Leo?'

'Yes.'

'Reading Ovid?' He gestures at my bag, which has collapsed open, exposing its contents.

'It's good. I've got up to the bit where Hades is hit by the arrow.'

'Ah yes,' he says. 'One thing it has in common with Ivy's story, if I remember correctly – and I always do. The idea of not having control of love. Love as injury, invasion.'

'I like that. Because you can't help whom you love. And sometimes it might not seem reasonable or fair that you love them.' I notice his expression. 'I'm talking about "you" as in "one". Not as in me.'

'Sure. Ivy's Hades is more like that. He isn't Ovid's predator, though he behaves like it. He has conflicting feelings. He doesn't want Persephone but he loves her anyway: he is compelled to take her but he feels guilty for it. He is a victim of love – unfair, and irrational.'

'I'm not sure either of them are right,' I say. 'I think Hades had the whole thing planned. He knows he's going to get hit by an arrow at some point. It's fate. But he values his bachelor lifestyle too. So he and Zeus agree the whole thing in advance and they choose Persephone because they know Demeter will cause a scene and take her back.'

'No, no, you've got it wrong. Hades is the mark. Persephone wants to escape Enna, where she's condemned to sing and pick flowers with her friends, sexually frustrated, bored out of her mind. She meets Aphrodite and comes to an arrangement with her. She sets up the hit and the narcissus. She is waiting for Hades before he even knows who she is. And there you go: Queen of the Underworld, for half the year, anyway.'

'Oh fuck off, Martin,' I say good naturedly. 'I know what you're getting at.'

'In any case, it seems Ivy is the true romantic. At least her version is a love story.'

'Who's to say ours aren't?' I ask, and he smiles at me, with something hard to identify passing over the frangible land of his face, a temporary slip or cave-in, close to paternal, but not quite. His face itself is slightly less coloured than it appeared at the book awards ceremony, though his eyes in their bruised niches have their own radiance, like dark roses blooming.

'Tell me about your father,' he says then, picking up, as usual, on my own tracks. 'Is he alone, or did he remarry?'

I hesitate. I don't want to discuss my family with Martin but I would like to find out more about his own personal life, and so I proffer Evan, like something I made at school, for his inspection.

'Neither. He's met somebody. Not long ago. So he isn't all alone in the Highlands, and you needn't worry about him.'

'Has it been long since your mother died?' He asks this solemnly, looking as sad as if he is talking about his own mother.

'A very long time. I don't really remember her.'

'So this is a big change for your father.'

'I guess.' And here it is: the sudden water in my voice, rising to my eyes. I squint against it angrily. 'Where are your parents?' I ask. 'Are they alive?'

'In a way. They're locked up in a retirement home. They're both at different stages of senility. One of them will have a lucid moment while the other is lost in the past. But they get along all right.'

'Do you visit them much?'

'Why not,' he says. 'Yes, I visit every week and take them some of their favourite brand of jam. It's one of the only things they remember.'

We sit and look at each other for a moment.'You're lying to me,' I say.

'Does it matter if I am?'

'I thought—' I say, then stop, frustrated. 'Never mind.' I say nothing for a while, staring out of the window at the lunchtime crowds. There is a crossing outside where people do battle with cars; forcing their way across the road through sheer numbers. Then for a moment the bleating cars will win and reclaim their strip of tar, before being beaten back again by the milling, tumbling pedestrians. Once on this pavement the people pass close to me, separated only by the soundless glass, their profiles whisking past like phantoms. I half enjoy the feel of it but for the times when someone looks in and meets my eye, an abruptly uncomfortable contact, as if we have collided.

'You must be very passionate about management for it to take you so far from your father,' Martin observes, watching me. 'What's the career plan?'

'I'm not going to sit here and tell you all about myself,' I say, because we both know that I'm not passionate about management, and I don't have a career plan. 'It's not fair. It's one sided.'

'Suit yourself,' Martin says. 'Would you like a chip?'

'No thanks,' I say primly. 'I'd better leave now. Unless there was something you needed to discuss?'

'Not really,' Martin says, smiling sorrowfully. 'My motives were purely sociable.'

As we leave the café the effort of opening the door for me appears to wind Martin. He takes a deep breath that hoots like a split concertina as it reaches its apex, then gives a dreadful cough, cracking and knocking at first like nuts and bolts shaken in a barrel, then whipping out in sticky, hacking noises, before declining into a rattling, rasping finale. The proprietor looks up at us with dubious respect.

'God.' I am shocked, my hand left hovering in mid-air, not knowing whether to take his arm. 'What is it you've got?'

'Lung cancer,' he says, drawing his breath back gratefully. 'Well, it started there. It's all over the shop now.'

'I'm sorry,' I say quietly.

'Ah.' For a moment he looks angry. 'You should know better. Don't be sorry.'

'Well I *am* sorry. Which way are you going? Do you need me to see you into a taxi?' I say.

He waves irritably: no.

'Suit yourself. Bye, then,' I say, turning away.

'One last question for you,' he says. 'Why hasn't he told you he loves you?'

'How do you know that?' I ask. 'Have you tapped something . . . done something . . .?'

The wind rises and whisks my voice away in its hoarse complaint. It sounds painful; as if it issues from Martin himself; his sick breath. 'I know it now,' he says, but he doesn't sound triumphant. 'Goodbye, Persephone.'

At first I walk in the opposite direction to Martin, and then I turn around and follow him, his black back, moving delicately through the blundering bulk of the crowd. As I walk I tie my hair back and put on a pair of sunglasses and a jacket: an unnecessary precaution, because he doesn't look back.

My main worry is that he will get into a taxi, because I don't feel up to jumping in another and shouting, 'Follow that cab!' But he keeps to the street, passing taxis, bus stops, and the Underground station, and I realise that he is going to walk to wherever it is he is going. We move away from the busier streets into neglected residential roads, where he skirts a group of children sitting on some steps in the sun, gathered around a whimpering electronic device, a couple of teenagers proceeding in a stately matrimonial rhythm down the road, talking intensely and incomprehensibly.

I follow on, getting more and more uncomfortable in my jacket. The sun has flickered on and off in the past few days, like a faulty fluorescent light starting up, flaring finally into a choking heat, marshmallowy with smog, pressing down on me like the murmur of engines, the clouded buzz and mumble of the traffic.

Finally, Martin turns down a nearly empty street of thin, terraced Victorian houses. I follow, realise my mistake, then scurry back behind a building, worried about being seen. When I put my head around the corner he is stepping inside one of the houses. The door closes, the sound of its latch rattling along the quiet street.

I wait for a while around the side of his house, which ends the row, then walk coolly and slowly to the door to read the panel of handwritten inhabitants. Nowak in the basement. Hendry on the first floor. Black on the second. Leaning in, I am startled by a darkness moving down the rippled glass panel that looks on to the inner staircase and have to retreat down the steps and around the side of the house, where I duck behind a phalanx of wheelie bins.

I am in time to watch Martin pass me, walking quickly along the pavement in the same coat as before, moving with the same breakable edginess, as if made of glass spindles. Facing forward, he doesn't notice me half huddled behind the bins, but it takes several minutes for me to become bold enough to come out again. When I do, the road is empty. Martin has left to pursue whatever business he is doing; the riddle of him lost once again in the jangling streets.

I go back past the bins to the side gate I became familiar with while in hiding. It pushes open easily to allow me to follow the narrow concrete path – littered with old snail shells, bare of the smallest scrap of foliage – that insinuates itself between the two houses. The path takes me to a courtyard garden at the rear of Martin's building, which, though it ascends in one vertical line at the front, is not so impassable here. A patio table leads on to the roof of a small outdoor lean-to, which leads just as conveniently onto a single-storey extension with spider plants in the windows, and, more reassuringly, no sign of any Hendry.

A window – Martin's window – hangs above me where I balance on the hot tiles of the extension roof.

I crouch where I am for a moment and look at my hands, marked with bird shit from the gutters of the roof I hauled myself on to, hearing my own breathing, which sounds remarkably loud in the warm afternoon. Ridiculous as my position is, it would be more ridiculous to climb back down without looking in the window, so I step slowly across the tiles and pull myself on to the sill, where I can sit and peer inside.

The window doesn't open, contrary to my expectations. It is also dirty, and I can't wipe it, so I have to put my face close to the glass and wait for the room to coalesce in my limited vision. The room, when it appears, is almost bare. There is a futon in the corner with sheets and a pillow on it. A laptop sits on the floor at a tidy right angle to the head of the futon. In the corner stands a piece of equipment that I take at first for a modernist lamp, before I realise it is an oxygen tank. There is nothing else on the walls or the floor: no rugs, no shelves, no pictures, no evidence of any human decorative impulse. I climb down in disappointment and the awareness of the ridiculousness of what I am doing, leave the denuded garden and walk back in the direction of the nearest tube station.

I wasn't sure what I had expected to find at Martin's flat – a memory stick, camera film, a recording? Some evidence of Leo's or Ivy's wrongdoing, that I could destroy? The other idea in my mind was that I might find out something about Martin himself. Some photos or diary revealing the tragedy of Martin Black, which might be palliated, leaving him at peace and without any desire to expose the Fords' secrets. Or, failing that, something I could blackmail him with. The easy endings of cinema: those were what I had hoped for.

And what had I found instead? A room that reminds me, uncomfortably, of my own. Is this what I am – the same as Martin – an outward-facing person, nest-less and restless? No wonder Martin is drawn to me; he is the only one who understands my situation: knowing what it is like to wait for something – to long for it, to not exist without it.

A few days later, Leo is home. He calls later in the afternoon, four painfully counted hours after the time his flight lands: 'Hello, Persephone. The Americans have half killed me, but I made it back. Want to come over and celebrate?'

When I arrive at his house I am disregarded by the paparazzi until I am on the front step, and ducking my head under the hail of their shouts; what seem to me to be jumbled, poetic words. 'Ivy,' they call at first. 'How are you, Ivy? How's Leo?' Then they realise their mistake and call, 'Hey, love . . . love. How's Leo? You and Leo . . . is it love?'

I smile and peer through the glass of the door, biting at my tongue with my old fear that the door won't open and I will have to turn around and walk back. Then the door opens and Leo appears. 'Good afternoon,' he says to the paparazzi.

'Afternoon, Leo,' they shout, like children at assembly. He brings me gently inside, closing the door on their questions.

When we go into the sitting room Ivy is already on one of the sofas in a dark glossy dress, her hair drawn back, looking both beautiful and unapproachable. But she raises her eyebrows humorously at me when I come in, and says, 'What a palaver,' by way of a greeting.

'Has something happened?' I ask. 'Why are there so many photographers around?'

'I'm home, of course,' Leo says. 'Some British hostage has been released from the Middle East today, but never mind that when there's a niche author at the airport. Drink? Whisky?'

I notice he and Ivy both have a whisky themselves. In fact, the whole atmosphere is a little tight, drawn; there is a vibrancy in the air, as if someone has just plucked a chord and the after-sound is still being felt. I realise with a sad drop of the stomach that Leo is not going to kiss me; not yet, anyway.

'Yes, please,' I say. Leo nods and leaves the room.

'What a strange situation,' I say to Ivy, staying safe and platitudinous.

'How do you mean?' Ivy asks.

Under investigation, I become hesitant. 'I mean, the situation that Leo is in . . . all that attention. He never asked for it. He tries to avoid it. But it happens anyway.'

'You admire his efforts to avoid it?' Ivy asks. I look at her but she appears to be genuinely curious, her mouth and eye corners softer, in the absence of their family irony.

'Well, of course. He has to work hard not to sell out. Not to be owned by everyone.'

'How do you think he's done that?'

'Uh . . . by not giving anyone any information about himself? Or' – I correct myself – 'only giving them the bare minimum.'

'So, giving them only a little of what they want . . . You know there's a word for that?' She is smiling, but I glance at the door anyway, in the hope of rescue.

'I didn't mean to say Leo's a *tease* –'

'I know you didn't. But it's true. The problem with being a tease is whether something real is actually being deferred. Or whether you get beyond the initial promise and find . . . only a blank.'

'You're saying Leo is a blank?' I laugh, startled.

'He certainly gives every appearance of being one, doesn't he?' Ivy says. 'Where the performance ends is anyone's guess.'

'Ah,' Leo says, coming in and handing me my drink. 'Ivy is wearing an unpleasant smile. Persephone looks distressed. What have you two been talking about?'

'A new book,' Ivy says. 'An affair. A train crash. You choose.'

Despite what Ivy says I see no performance in Leo. Both of them lack the need for self-promotion; they are inexplicable and seamless, proceeding not as most people do, from insecurity and need, but from other, inscrutable motives. Maybe this is because of their past, the way fame got hold of them early on, in a savage and unprovoked attack. Perhaps they haven't entirely recovered. And now Leo has to talk to the press and Ivy tries to stop him, like a horror film in which one survivor returns to a dangerous place, while the other cries out; 'No!'

'I read your version of the Persephone and Hades myth,' I offer, hopeful, to Ivy.

'Did you like it?'

'I liked what it said about love,' I say, losing my grip on the ideas that seemed so available when I was with Martin, streaming away from me in the wind tunnel of Ivy's full attention.

'Love . . .' Ivy says, as if she is saying 'Death'.

'You make it sound so bleak,' I say.

'It is bleak. Look at all the women who love the wrong men, men who beat them up, or cheat on them, or men who don't care for them at all.'

'But – that's not love. Surely . . .'

'Isn't it? They need that person, they long for them, they are happy when he wants them. What's the difference?'

I have to think of how to answer. 'I suppose, that it's more of a need, than a love. To have someone to be with you, to want you, even if he treats you badly. They're frightened of not being loved.'

'Aren't all women like that?' Ivy says.

'That's a . . . cynical way of looking at it,' I say, diminuendo.

Leo has picked some papers off the table as if he has heard all this before. From his lowered, vague eyes I can tell he isn't listening. He has abandoned me.

'Women want men to qualify them,' Ivy continues. 'They give everything they have in exchange for an emotional pay-out.'

I feel as if Ivy has seen *my* heart; she has walked on its grubby carpet, surveyed its teen posters, its teddy bears, and she is contemptuous. I can't reply. I sit and fiddle with my necklace like a child.

'So, what do men want?' Leo asks her suddenly. He has been listening, after all.

'You tell us,' Ivy answers, but Leo looks away again, and says nothing.

I leave Leo's a little later, making my excuses, receiving a kiss at last by his front door: a kiss like a pat on the shoulder, a brush-off. The paparazzi have finally gone away, for dinner probably, and I can walk through the park opposite Leo's house, the civilised greenness, the straight trees like debutantes at a dance.

I could tell something was wrong at Leo's – Ivy sharper than usual, Leo deliberately diffuse, like a smoke figure – almost as if they have picked up the scent of approaching trouble, rolling low along the horizon like the black clouds of the Assynt. I am worried they know about Martin somehow, but, unable to ask about it, I am confined to watching them, the jostle and crackle of their hidden stress.

At this point my train of thought is derailed abruptly by its object: Martin, sitting on a bench in front of me, under the trees, enfolded in the leafy dark as if it is a shadow cast by him, by his illness. He sits up straight but he is as thin as a line drawing. I can see the blackness of his eye casings from here. He raises his hand up in a languid salute.

I go over to join him and sit down next to him.

'You don't look very well,' I say. 'Are you being . . . looked after?'

'I'm being groomed ready for death,' Martin says. 'Like a pharaoh. The nurses are getting ready to take out my insides, to parcel up and give to the god of the NHS.'

'And yet you still haven't given up on Leo,' I say, putting on my jacket. The late sunlight is not strong enough, dilute as watercolour, and in the shade it vanishes altogether. 'You should be going on holiday, not pursuing this. What about hot air balloons? Swimming with dolphins?'

'Is that the kind of thing you want to do before you die?' he asks.

'Of course it is. Who wouldn't be happy swimming with a dolphin?'

'It depends on your capacity for happiness,' he says. 'On how much one goes in for feeling . . . its ups, its downs.'

I am trying to work out whether he knows that I have been at his house, but he gives no sign of it.

'What brings you here?' I ask. 'Leo's not doing anything exciting today. Even the paparazzi are all gone.'

'I came to give you something,' he says. He takes an envelope out of his coat, removes a photocopied newspaper article from the envelope and hands it to me.

Expecting to see Leo, I am startled to see that the picture is of my mother, in a full shot, with her feathered hair and long skirt blowing slightly. She is standing with some children and there is bunting behind her. It all looks very English: cake stalls, grass, balloons, the children squinting innocently at the camera, under their lemonade sun.

The top of the page says *Dorchester News*, and the rest of it is about how my mother and the other people at the shop where she worked raised money at a fête for some swings and slides for the local children.

'Where on earth did you get this?'

'I found it in the archives,' he says. 'Thought you might like it. You can keep it.'

'Thank you.' I put it into my bag and sit next to him, confounded, listening to the difficult whistle of his breath.

'She looks like you,' Martin observes. 'Was she like you?'

'Not really,' I say. 'She was . . . pure. And good. Not materialistic. She cared about things . . . things that matter.'

'You don't think you're like that?'

'I'd like to be. But I'm just not. I might try hard not to spend hundreds of pounds on a pair of shoes, but I'd still want them. My mother would walk past the shop window and she wouldn't even see them. She'd think the window frame was painted a nice colour, or something.'

'Wanting shoes doesn't mean you're not good.'

'But I want so much!' I say, more passionately than I mean to, almost a cry, loud under the trees.

'Still . . .' Martin opens his hands up. 'Maybe your mother did too when she was your age. Or she made other mistakes. Or . . . maybe you're right and she was a saint. But it seems unlikely.'

I smile, then look at him more severely, remembering myself. 'I don't know why I'm talking to you about it.'

'Consider it off the record,' he says.

'Thanks.'

'It's not a huge favour, you know. The market for stories about charitable dead mothers is a slow one.'

We sit for a while, falling into a soundless, half-sad companionship, until he says abruptly, 'I find myself in an unexpected dilemma.'

'Which is?'

'I'd rather not hurt you.' He looks away, to where the grass ends neatly, hemmed by its wrought-iron fence. 'There isn't any chance you'd be tempted to bail, is there? Let Leo go? Go back to drinking at the student bars, with friends your own age?'

I shake my head.

He shrugs. 'I suppose not. Well, so long as you're happy.'

When we leave the park and go home in different directions, I think about what he said. Am I happy? I am excited, or stressed, exhilarated or deeply miserable. I am a patch of static. I am a firework. I am a falling rain, a sunken ship. I am a moth, hunting for the bright, money-coloured moon.What I am not, is happy.

PART NINE

Persephone would not have expected to see her father Zeus – and accordingly he is nowhere to be seen – but Demeter is waiting for her at the gate of her flowery temple, and covers her with tears of gratitude. As she holds her daughter her grief flows out of her, her exhausted body becomes strong and dignified as an oak, her hair lustrous, her eyes bright. And Persephone cries with happiness to be returned to her beloved mother, though in her heart there springs a tiny fear, of what will and will not be discovered in the days to come.

Ivy Ford
Persephone and Hades

The next day I go to Leo's. It is just the two of us at last, afloat in his bed like a pirate's dark-sailed galleon. The moon hovers in the window above the dark smoke of the garden. I am relieved to be here with him, though below the relief there are layers of worry that have not lifted, and the relief of sex has only revealed these worries, lit them in its sudden light.

In bed Leo loses some of his dense elusiveness; his eyes are clearer, closer, his mouth more immediate. But despite this, and despite his flawless technique (almost disconcertingly flawless in its attentiveness, forensic attunement, its deliberately measured pace), there is a lack of passion. I can't help but compare him to James, my only other point of reference. I wouldn't want to sleep with James again, but I miss the feeling of hunger; the idea that someone's need for me is so great that it could make them rushed or inconsiderate or awkward. With Leo I sometimes have the sense that he's just being polite.

Lying uncomfortably with my comparison, I ask Leo who his first love was.

He laughs. 'Someone else in the music business. She was called Sophie.'

'Was she very beautiful?' I ask mournfully.

'Not without her make-up. Not as beautiful as you. She was . . . glamorous. Studiedly so. A cigarette holder and false eyelashes.'

I note the compliment; clutching it as I do all his compliments, locking it away.

'Why did you break up?' I asked.

'Various reasons. I was nineteen. She was twenty-five. I was indie, she was pop. I was going up, her career had stalled after her first single. We liked different things. She and Ivy didn't get along.'

'Didn't they?'

'To the point of being unable to share a room. Back then Ivy could be a little . . . unforgiving in her condemnation of bullshit. And Sophie was a bit of a bullshit artist. She had a whole fake backstory, fake name, the lot.'

'How can you be with someone like that?' I ask. 'Surely you don't really know them.'

'That's what Ivy said. But at the time I found it fascinating.'

'Who broke up with whom?'

'She broke up with me, though she might not have seen it that way. She liked to be the main event. When I told her I couldn't sacrifice other things in my life for her it became . . . difficult.'

'Have you been very hurt in love before?' I ask, as he seems less evasive than usual.

'Of course. I was hurt then. I've been hurt in several relationships since.'

'Who hurt you most?'

But it is too late, Leo's faint smile is back, and the door is shut.

'That's impossible to answer because there is no true comparison. Things appear to mean more the younger you are. A pain that lasts a month is a larger proportion of the life of a twenty year old than it is of a forty year old. Also, you don't have any frame of reference. Being dumped for the first time has the shock of the new along with its own pain.'

'Okay,' I say, thwarted.

'But really I think youth and innocence make us hard. Like apples. We soften as we get older; we absorb knocks more. When you're a teenager you think you're devastated but you recover quickly. Then when you're older you might convince yourself that you're okay, but really you're bruised more than you can see, for longer than you expect.'

'Hmm,' I say.

He laughs, looking at me closely. 'But of course this all sounds patronising to you.'

'Especially coming from a thirty year old.'

'Fair point.'

'So what about if someone gets to forty and they have never been in a relationship or been in love. Then they fall in love and they get hurt. How much does that hurt?'

'What do you want, a graph? I can't quantify that.'

'That is what I want. I'd like a formula for the least amount of hurt. I suppose I'm young, so that's on my side, right? Even if I'm devastated I won't *really* be devastated, so that's okay. But I don't have any experience. I've got no protection there.'

'Why are you so worried about hurt?' he asks, with a tone I can't interpret, turning towards me. I remain on my back, eyes tilted to the ceiling, out of range.

'It'd just be nice to avoid it, if at all possible. Maybe it isn't possible.' This is a question, but he chooses not to answer it.

In the silence that follows I imagine Sophie, who in my mind has stark blond hair and red lips, wielding her cigarette holder like a blade, cavalierly demanding that Leo renounce everything for her. I am envious of her bravery: her readiness to gamble. But then, Sophie isn't with Leo any more. Sophie, who presumably asked Leo to choose her over Ivy, isn't lying in Leo's bed now; two heads come to rest next to each other on the same pillow, one sneaking small glances at the beauty of the other's profile.

And his beauty is astounding; there is still nothing like it. Even the sharpest light falters when it reaches him, gentles when it touches his skin. I wonder whether, if he wasn't quite so exceptional, things would be different. I remember before we were together I was weighted by the feeling of being outside, longing to cross the boundary separating our bodies. But now, having crossed it, I am still on the outside. Even lying like this I am still chasing him, still longing for him. Camilla used to say about people at university: 'Tries too hard.' It was instant damnation. But with Leo, I am always trying.

'I'm not sure I believe in all this,' says Catherine to me, quietly, so Emiko can't hear. We are waiting at the front door of Emiko's psychic, who charges nearly fifty pounds an hour to talk to the dead. It comes as a surprise to me that a price can be found for something so metaphysical, so miraculous if it is true: yet this woman, Maud Blake, has found it.

Maud Blake, when she opens the door, turns out to be a small, modest-looking woman with a small, modest house, not the incense-heavy cavern of crystals and ethnic wall hangings I might have expected. She makes us tea and takes us into a sitting room with cream sofas and a large orange cat.

'You've booked in for one reading,' she says. 'I don't have many appointments this afternoon, so I could do another, if one of you would like?'

'No, thank you,' Catherine says quickly.

Maud Blake nods as if expecting to hear this. 'It's not for everyone,' she says. She has a deliberately calm way of speaking, like a nurse at a children's hospital. 'Would you like a reading?' she asks me.

I intend to shake my head, but my head, surprisingly, stays still and says yes. I sit down on one of the cream sofas and feel angry at my head's abrupt abandonment of common sense, while Maud tells Emiko that a little boy – a brother? A cousin? A family friend? Yes, a family friend – wants to talk to her.

'He says he is happy now; it was his time to leave,' she tells Emiko, who cries a lot at hearing this.

'I was so mean to him,' Emiko sobs. 'I never shared my toys.'

After a little while of this, Emiko hears some general common sense about her path in life and learning to trust in a wider fate. Then it is my turn.

I sit, feeling uncomfortable, while Maud Blake looks at me. As I look back at her I try to find something in her strawberries-and-cream complexion, her brown hair, that might indicate either fraudulence or heavenliness.

'There is . . . a woman,' Maud Blake says.

'Yes,' I say, looking down. I don't want to say anything telling; I have heard that psychics pick up on their clients' tiniest physical cues. I keep a bland face and wait, though I am feeling hot under my skin, prickles springing up on my chest and neck.

'She is worried about you,' Maud tells me, still looking right at me, not above my head or far away, like I would expect her to do. 'She says there is something, in which . . . you need to find your way. Is this your . . . mother? She says – she says she loves you very much.'

She continues talking, but I don't hear her, and only when I notice that she has stopped, and Emiko and Catherine are looking at me with concern, do I realise the reading is over.

'Are you all right, Persephone?' Emiko says.

I sit back and cough, and drink my tea. Emiko puts her hand on my arm, then it seems a very short time before we are leaving and Catherine is leaning back in Emiko's passenger seat to put her hand on mine, saying, 'What on earth are you paying that woman for, Emiko, to scare the shit out of people! It's not real, darling,' she says to me. 'You know that, don't you? It's all guesswork.'

I tell Leo about my experience at Maud Blake's, leaving out the part where Maud told me I needed to find my way, in case Leo interprets this as him not being my way, and decides to do the honourable thing and get rid of me.

'Houdini didn't believe in psychics,' Leo says. 'It was a hobby of his to expose frauds. Even after death he wanted to prove his point. He and his wife agreed that after his death she would hold séances for him. They agreed a code word that his spirit would use to prove that it was really him appearing. *Rosabelle, believe*. It was a line from a play she had acted in.'

'Was he really trying to prove it was all fake?' I say. 'Don't you think he and his wife must have secretly hoped it was true?'

'The whole thing unfortunately got completely confused,' Leo said. 'His wife claimed that he did come back, then retracted it. So nobody really knows.'

'Right,' I say, impatient for a point, but it seems Leo is just enjoying telling me about Houdini, like someone telling a friend what their mutual friend has been up to.

'What's funny is that Sir Arthur Conan Doyle believed that Houdini was actually a top psychic and he used his powers to carry out his tricks,' Leo says now. 'Which just goes to show, for all the trouble he took, he couldn't force people to stop believing.'

In Leo's bathroom I sit on the curled edge of the bath and take the newspaper image of my mother out of my bag. I smooth the fold that halves her face. I look for something new, but her world remains fixed: laughing children, wind-caught bunting, evenly distributed sunlight.

It isn't really what Maud Blake has told me that bothers me: I have always expected that my mother would be worried about me if she could see me. It is what my mother might be *doing* that I am most bothered by. Does she spend her time hanging around in some murky half-place, in the half-light, waiting to be contacted? If I were trapped like that I would not send postcard messages of love and advice. I would be frightened and incensed. *Your mother says, Where am I? Get me out of here.*

My father has raised me to believe that the spirits of the dead exist somewhere, though he is not quite sure where. Clearly this was something my grandmother Ellen neglected to tell Sylvia when she dropped by. Or maybe she knew Sylvia would see for herself, soon enough. 'Not hell,' he said firmly to me, though Sylvia was borderline pagan and Ellen was lapsed. 'There's no such thing as hell.' On the subject of heaven he wasn't so certain.

I don't believe in hell either: it is too primitive, a child's drawing with crayon flames. I'm not sure I believe in reincarnation either. I find it uncomfortable imagining myself living other lives and being people I can't remember. It reminds me of the disorientating occasions where I drank too much and had to be told the next day what I'd said or done. Which takes me back around to heaven: an afterlife of bright light and perfection. This is in itself worrying. After death most religions would have it that the soul is stripped back and purified, becoming something perfect and beautiful, but if everyone was perfectly understanding and wise and generous and loving then they would all be the same. How can you tell one angel from another? And if I meet my mother again how will I recognise her? Would her immortal soul still wear tatty denim shorts? Would she still like Led Zeppelin? Or the ironic-lame jokes my father attributes to her: *What do you call a man with a seagull on his head? Cliff.* My mother's flawless ghost would look at me blankly, and not laugh.

I don't have long at Leo's before the others arrive for the night: my pleasure at being effectively a hostess in Leo's home – wifely and helpful, taking coats to hang up and offering drinks – balanced by my disappointment that in the few hours we spent alone he still hasn't told me he loves me.

Ivy arrives late, moves people over in order to sit next to me, and says, 'I heard about your foray into the spirit world. Catherine was quite worried about you.'

'Oh, it was silly,' I say, embarrassed. 'I think I was just tired. And it was hot in there.'

'What did the woman tell you?'

'Nothing specific. Just some nice things, really. Things you could say safely to anyone.'

'I'm not sure my mother would be available for a chat,' Ivy said. 'I'm not sure I'd want her to be. Not because I wouldn't like to speak to her again. I think I'd rather she was doing other things. Something better.'

I want to take her hand, my own hands eager with relief, but though her eyes are sincere, resting on me gently, I hesitate. Instead I say, 'Houdini's wife Bess said that. Before her death she told her friends not to bother trying to contact her spirit. She said she wouldn't be coming back.'

Ivy looks surprised for a moment, then asks, 'How did your mother die?'

'Cancer. Though I don't remember it – I was too young. What about yours?'

'Suicide. I was a teenager at the time. I remember coming home with a hangover in the afternoon and there were police at the house. She'd done it in the car apparently. She rented a car for the day because she'd already sold ours. I was surprised at how organised she'd been, in the end. I started drinking again when I heard the news and I went to her funeral after taking acid. It was open casket. I tried to shake her and wake her up. It must have been grisly.'

'Oh no,' I am horrified. I realise the absurdity of trying to compare notes with Ivy. I'd have liked to talk about life without a mother. I could have told her about getting my period without my mother around (I felt I had been pragmatic; researching online, buying my own tampons from the 'feminine hygiene' shelves at the supermarket). I could have told her about my first bra: bought optimistically oversized, destined never to be filled. But Ivy hadn't done things like this. Ivy took acid, ran away and lived in a squat, then did her A-levels in half the time, to catch up and get an Oxford scholarship. Ivy opted out of teenage pamphlets, of the 'roller-coaster' of emotions, of prosaic greasy hair and braces and first kisses at school dances.

'I'm sorry,' I start to say, but Ivy is laughing.

'Don't be. I think she would have wanted that. She liked to make a scene. William ditched her partly because of her temper. She used to break plates over his head, have screaming fits, and so on. I used to make sure we didn't buy anything in glass bottles or jars – we ate from paper plates most days. It was almost a compulsion with her, to break whatever could be broken. She didn't leave many possessions behind.'

'Nor did my mother. But just because she wasn't very materialistic.'

'So the only direct bequests we have from either of our mothers are our names,' Ivy says.

'I don't even know why my mother called me Persephone.' I think of the story: a slippery, crowded story, with no moral, a multiplicity of shadowy, inconsistent meanings, as in a dream.

'I used to hate my name,' Ivy says, gently. 'I thought my mother had put a curse on me. You know, poison Ivy. Later I found out it was her grandmother's name. I looked it up myself after she died.

Around that time I would have welcomed a séance. I needed her to be answerable, just briefly.'

'But not any more?'

'No. It's not easy when you're young and you don't have a mother. Human nature is comparative, and I didn't have that primary female comparison. I made a lot of mistakes before I realised what kind of woman I wanted to be.'

'How did you realise?' I ask her.

She pauses and looks across the room at Leo, who is talking animatedly to Catherine, putting down his glass in order to gesture more freely. From Catherine's frown I guess that Leo is telling her about his new passion: string theory.

'Meeting Leo helped. When I met him I was doing anything I could to dissolve any connection to anyone or anything. As if I could prevent any kind of cause and effect. If I had no friends, nobody could judge me. If I was drugged, I couldn't judge myself. Leo made it difficult to do that. He persistently and quietly got in my way.' She pauses, her eyes different: brighter, as if newer. I don't say anything, taken aback by what I realise is a moment of emotional connection between us – at last – and unsure what to do in the sudden intimacy. Then she raises her eyebrows again, wry. 'But don't tell him I said that. He'll be insufferable.'

It has been a week since I heard from Martin, which – in the condensed time of London, in which relationships are cemented or ended in a few days – is unusual. Always caller withheld, always appearing from nowhere, he has made our communications one way only. I check newspapers online for signs of his story but all is quiet. I check my mobile's voicemail, even the few letters I get in the post – bedded in their layers of gleaming junk mail – more frequently than usual. I walk to his house, which is silent, and peer through the muddled glass of its front door, until a woman comes out of the house next door and leans pointedly on her wall, looking at me with undecided suspicion.

I don't know why I am upset that my stalker has cooled off on me. I'd like to talk to Leo about it, but he has cooled off on me too. We've slept together only once since he got back from America; not that sex brings much reassurance. Its brief heat is like a fire: a few steps back from the fire there is near-complete cold. I can't even be near him, no matter how inappropriate the circumstances, without wanting him to touch me, without that shivering, that depthless longing.

Finally, after another tedious week, I receive a Sincerest Condolences card, with a picture of lilies on the front. It reads: 'I know you have a thing for lost causes, so you should visit me. M.' The address of a hospital is written underneath.

I am supposed to be at a lecture that day, then seeing Leo in the evening, but I have enough time to miss the lecture and go to the hospital, with time to spare. I take a taxi through the tepid, polluted rain, arriving at the expressionless glass doors of Martin's wing. I walk through a corridor trying not to look through the open doors of each private room, but seeing anyway: each inhabitant shrouded in white sheets, unmoving.

When I get to Martin's room, a sensible sage-green chamber, brimming with usefulness, he looks much the same as the other residents, static in his white bed, wreathed in wires and tubes. His face, as I get closer, has become concave in the wrong places, oddly shadowed. I can hear the whistles and creaks as he breathes, like wind in dead tree branches. He notices me and waves cheerfully.

'Oh, Martin,' I say, with horror.

'Hello,' he says, static disrupting the familiar notes of his voice. 'Thanks for calling on me the other day. I appreciate the thought.'

'What's happening? Are you. . .?' I sit down on a plastic chair.

'Dying,' he confirms.

Used to the to and fro of my meetings with Martin – the tricks, the slides into familiarity, only to be mocked and knocked back, the repeated retreats – the open finality of his situation now is a shock: more of a shock than I could have expected. Silenced, I curl my fingers against the grainy, used plastic of the chair and watch him.

'Oh dear,' he says. 'I thought I could rely on you not to be sentimental.'

'I wasn't prepared for this. I thought . . . I didn't know. You never tell the truth.'

'You have a point. I'll excuse you for not having brought flowers, or grapes, or Scrabble,' he says.

'How long are you going to be here?'

'Until I die, you mean? I don't know. They're coy about times. I suppose if they promise I'll die tomorrow and I don't, I might get awkward about it and sue. So if they know, they're not telling.'

'Not like you not to have the inside scoop,' I say, and he smiles.

'That's more like it.'

As if each word has taken a little bite out of him, he sighs and lets his head turn on the pillow, up to the moon-pocked tiles of the ceiling. 'Apologies. I'm not quite myself.'

'Don't tire yourself out,' I say. 'I'm just going out to make a call. Do you need anything?'

A head shake, economical in its motion.

'I'll be back in a second.'

I go out into the corridor, call Leo, and ask if we could see each other tomorrow instead of tonight. I don't need to use my prepared lie: Leo doesn't ask me for a reason, accepting my presence or absence with equanimity, requiring no adjustment of himself.

When I go back into Martin's room, he has fallen asleep on the bed. I lean over him and look at his eyelids, lines running through their clouded dark like a blueprint, water stained. His face without him in it is oddly uncertain: his unconscious mouth less adult than usual. Then it occurs to me that this is what he is going to look like after he dies, and I shift back in dismay, sitting back down.

I watch the light fade on the hospital wall as Martin sleeps on. I read a little of Ovid, the only book I have with me, but my attention is faulty, fusing and sparking. I think of Leo, and for the first time I don't care what he is doing without me. I think of him for the first time not as Leo Ford, but just a man, doing something at his computer, eating, talking, having a drink, just like anyone else. When Martin wakes up it is just past midnight. He turns his head, sleep clearing slowly away from him, and focuses on me with muddy curiosity.

'Persephone? You're still here?'

'I thought you might like some company,' I say.

'You should have used the opportunity to put a pillow over my face.'

'Are you ever going to take this seriously?'

He chooses not to answer, eyes investigating the upturned book in my lap. 'What are you reading?'

'Ovid. Still. I'm a slow reader.'

'Read some to me,' he says, so I read him the story of Arachne, who knew she was a great weaver and refused to pretend otherwise or credit her gift to Athena. Athena, outraged, turns up to take Arachne up on her claim that she could outweave the goddess herself, and, after some pointless arguing with Athena in the form of a pensioner, the two women duel on their looms. Athena produces a rather stale piece featuring the gods sitting about, looking majestic, bordered with warnings of the terrible fates that met the humans who challenged the status quo. Arachne answers with a tapestry showing the gods as they really are: greedy, sexually incontinent, lazily enforcing their droit de seigneur.

Though Arachne's tapestry is better – both in truth and skill – she can't win this one. Athena tears up the tapestry, hits Arachne, and the unfortunate girl is driven to attempt suicide. Athena's final concession is to turn her into a spider, and in this form act as a warning to any other aspiring radicals.

'Uh . . . not many of these stories end well,' I apologise. 'I wasn't trying to make a point.'

'I had assumed you were thinking about yourself,' he says.

'What? I'm not the one writing about celebrities.'

'I don't mean you're Arachne. You're Athena. All your creative energy going in one direction; maintaining the pantheon. Protecting the male gods, in what is – let's face it – an entirely one-sided relationship. If Athena were really the Goddess of Wisdom she'd turn her back on the lot of them. Then she might have a chance of producing an original tapestry.'

'I thought there was no such thing as original.'

'It's all relative.'

'Come on,' I say, becoming angry, 'you're not Arachne! You're not a revolutionary. You're not overturning the gods. You said it yourself. You're just someone who makes money out of pictures of people being whipped.'

Martin looks at me, thoughtful, though it is impossible to tell the direction of the thoughts.

'You aren't even going to be able to spend the money,' I add. 'You're just going to hurt some people. More than they've been hurt already.'

'And you,' Martin says.

'And me.'

Martin seems to understand, or, at least, I think he does. His mouth moves towards a smile, he says 'Hm' and then he goes to sleep with such suddenness that I jump up, horrified, to check that he isn't dead. After I have held my finger under his nose long enough to feel the slight movement of his breath, I go back to sitting next to the bed, waiting, turning away the nurses who come from time to time to ask if I need anything. 'How . . . long has he got?' I ask one.

'Not long now,' she says, as if reassuring me. It reminds me of the car journeys with my father, always a long journey, no matter where we were going. *Are we nearly there yet? Not long now.*

As I sit there with him, I become aware of the silence of the hospital room at midnight. It reminds me of the closeness of the silence of the Assynt. In its very vastness it seemed airless; there was a pressure to it. This is the first time I have felt it since coming to London. If I close my eyes, the dawdling buzz of the electrical equipment might be a bee, trawling nearby over the brown heather; the movement of Martin's breath the occasional stir of wind, passing over us like an old memory, hushing us both into the dark.

~

I wake up startled, cast rigid into the shape in which I fell asleep, the texture of the chair imprinted on to my face. Outside it appears to be almost dawn, the night greying at the edges, the purplish light illuminating the utilitarian garden outside. Martin is awake and looking at me with apparent consternation.

'You're alive,' is what I say, surprised.

'You're here,' he replies. 'Why?'

I look at him, trying to find the feeling of the night before, but something has gone with morning, the invisible contact that enclosed us has blinked out, as if it were artificial to begin with, a drug warmth, an alcohol love. I stand now on a wide, sober plain, Martin watching me, with an expression that worries me.

'I didn't want you to be by yourself,' I say.

'I'm sorry to break this to you,' Martin says. 'Because I know in a moment you're going to regret your charitable vigil, and hate me for it.'

'What do you mean?'

'Fortunately or unfortunately, depending on how you look at it, I've found out what happened on the boat.'

'How?'

'I spoke to the captain.'

I stare at him with dismay. We look at each other for a long time, alone together in the cold light, without speaking, the only sounds the hum of his monitors, the turning of distant metal wheels, the strange clamour of the birds outside. In the collapsed pools of his face there is no triumph, not even satisfaction.

'What happened? Are you going to publish?'

He rests his head back on the pillow and closes his eyes, with a long intake of breath, answering with them still closed.

'It's not what you think, Persephone.'

'Then tell me what it is.' I am trying not to feel panicked but my eyes crackle, about to spill. His face in the bed blurs, as if moving past at speed.

'You have to do something,' he says, laboriously.

'Tell me.' I lean closer.

'You have to stop fighting this. Turn your back.'

'Martin. Please don't do this. Don't publish it, whatever it is.'

He ignores me and continues, 'You need to think of . . . what your mother would have wanted. For you. That's how you stay close to her.'

'My mother?' I push back my chair, surprised and angry. 'How dare you bring up my mother?'

There is a noise in the doorway, making me aware of my own volume, that I am standing over Martin, in the vibrating quiet left by the end of my voice. A nurse holding a tray watches me with concern. I pick up my things and hurry past her, not stopping to say anything to her or to the receptionist I pass as I leave, who looks at me with compassion, imagining perhaps that I am Martin's girlfriend, or his sister, and feeling sorry for my impending loss.

When I arrive at Leo's, almost half an hour late after falling asleep in the bath, I am nearly run over by his car, pulling at speed out on to the road.

'What's happening?' I ask, when he stops and opens his door.

'William's had a heart attack,' Leo says pleasantly. 'I'm going to the hospital.'

'Oh, God.' I stand next to the car, wavering, unsure of what my place in this drama is.

'Come on,' Leo says. 'You're not getting out of this.'

And so I find myself on the way back to the hospital, walking through the corridors to a ward not far from Martin's, too rushed and startled to say anything sensible, worrying that somebody will recognise me and say something. The first time Leo himself speaks is when we are waiting outside William's room for admittance.

'He might die,' Leo says, with a puzzled expression.

I am trying to think of what to say when Ivy appears, improbably, at the end of the corridor. She must have been on her way somewhere; she is wearing a purple dress, a deep rich colour against the scuffed white of the wall; the grey tiled floor. She looks like a butterfly in a refrigerator.

'What are you doing here?' Leo asks.

Ivy stands next to us and rubs her hand over her face. When she takes her hand away I can see how tired she looks. Her eyes, with their dark make-up, rest steady on him, as if waiting for him to answer. Then she blinks and says, 'I don't even know.'

Leo doesn't reply. He sits down on one of the chairs and looks at the wall, without discernible expression. After a moment Ivy does the same, then I copy them and take another chair, so that the three of us are arranged in a row like filmgoers, waiting for the feature to begin. I feel my own presence acutely; how unnecessary it is. I notice that I am wearing all grey, the same colour as the floor, the sky outside, where the rain has stopped for the moment. Even in the composition of the scene I am background to Ivy's purple dress, Leo's red scarf, their green eyes, turned the colour of absinthe in the disinfected, medical light.

We all flinch when the door to William's room opens and a nurse – a large woman, with a tremulous manner – appears.

'Would you like to go inside?' she asks.

Leo looks at Ivy, who shakes her head.

'I'll go,' he says.

'I'll wait here,' I offer, not wanting to be left alone with Ivy, silenced and strange, but wanting less to go inside and be confronted with William, in whatever state he might be in. Leo nods.

'Are you okay?' I ask Ivy, once the door has closed behind Leo.

She turns, with the same slowness that has characterised her movement since she arrived, and it occurs to me that it may not simply be the soporific effect of grief – that she might have taken drugs.

'Not really,' she says, after a moment. 'I don't know if I should stay. I know I can't go inside. I have the urge to just wait behind the door. I'll know where he is but he won't know where I am.'

It seems as if she is hunting for something, not exactly from me; her eyes have come to rest in my direction, even if I'm not their subject, because I am the only person here.

'Forgive me, Ivy. I don't want to be presumptuous. I don't know anything about you and William. Any of the history. But would you feel sorry if you didn't talk to him now? If this was really over for him?'

She considers this, her eyes still on me, sharpening. Her pupils are so large that I can see myself in them, a tiny shape in the blackness, like a girl in a well.

'Persephone,' she says, 'you're a lovely girl. But this isn't the usual sort of family. It's not a *good* family.'

'I know William isn't—' I start, but she cuts me off.

'You have no idea.'

She shakes her head, fiercely, and stands up. 'Please tell Leo I said goodbye. And don't tell William I was here. You should leave yourself, you know. You don't have to be part of this.' And then she is gone, back to her usual speed, walking with finality back down the corridor and around the corner, and I can't ask whether she meant part of this – here, now – or part of the Ford family in general.

Left alone on the row of seats, I think about Martin Black, with no real purpose, compulsively returning to the sight of him talking, looking like a ruined paper boat, folded in on himself. I almost wonder if I should take the opportunity to pretend to use the lavatory and go back to Martin's room instead, to ask him what he is planning. But there's no point. I have been comprehensively outwitted. I thought I had some influence over Martin, some personal connection, and he must have seen my clumsy machinations for what they were and indulged them, carrying on in the pursuit of his exposé. I feel ashamed to think of how ridiculous my efforts must have looked to him. I even allowed his declining body to convince me of his vulnerability, his need, like mine, for love of some sort.

After a long time of thinking about Ivy, William, Leo and Martin until they all seem inextricably connected – Martin himself a missing

Ford, a brother, or a lost son – I decide to speak to Leo, who doesn't know that Ivy has left, and might be waiting for her inside. I knock, then put my head around the door in what I hope is a tactful manner.

Leo looks up, standing by the bed.

'Persephone. Are you alone? Come in.'

The room is larger than Martin's, with blue curtains and a large painting of some jauntily coloured fruit on the wall opposite. William lies sturdily in the bed, his face like a ripe apple that has rolled out of the picture, crowned by vigorous white eyebrows. Even his wrinkles appear decisive, adding extra emphasis where none is needed. His head blazes on the same regulation white sheets that had appeared to swallow Martin's dust-colour face, as though he were being obscured by a blizzard; his outlines under the sheet like a handful of dropped matches.

Leo stands by the bedside, unaware that he looks like a not-very-kind prison warden. I hang back, keeping an escape route to the door open.

'Is he asleep?' I mouth.

As if hearing me, William opens his eyes. They are the unexpected green of a spring lawn, lacking their previous critical glossiness. He looks at Leo, then me, and then at the picture of the fruit, which appears to make him sad.

'I am going to die,' he says to Leo.

'Nobody knows anything yet,' Leo says, rather unhelpfully.

William gazes unhappily at the picture. 'I am alone,' he says. 'I'm going to die unloved.'

Leo and I exchange baffled looks over his head, but William saves us the necessity of a reply, by shutting his eyes and going back to sleep.

'He's on a lot of medication,' the doctor explains outside William's room. 'He's not going to die. Considering the amount he smokes and drinks, he's really very healthy. But he won't hear of it.'

'Oh,' Leo says. 'Okay.'

After this news Leo's calmness seems to harden into a tenser state, condensed into stillness, humming with unapproachable energy. In the car on the way home he uses his horn for the first time, hitting the wheel sharply, startling me. I realise then that the perception of Leo I had before, in Martin's room, has entirely slipped away. I have lost – and can't recover – the sense that he is anything ordinary. How can I tell him about Martin Black? One of Leo's favourite topics is that of his own disappearance: leaving the country, becoming a hermit. I remember asking him once, before we were together, why, when he loved dogs, didn't he get one? 'I couldn't meet its expectations,' he said. 'I'd only end up letting it down.'

'Why would you let it down?'

'When I do my bunk,' he said, and laughed, but I recognised the warning. I am worried now that he is delicately, uneasily balanced, like a man on a wall, arms out, and that if I tell him what Martin is planning it will be the final push, and he will vanish.

The next time I see Leo he shows me out to sit in his long, evenly grassed garden, under the sun. A fan of Sunday newspapers is spread out on the table. When he goes inside to make drinks I close my eyes and imagine, experimentally, that I am in back in the Assynt: the stillness of the air, the silence, with its occasional flurry of birdsong. It doesn't work, or at least not as it worked in Martin's hospital room. Rather than feeling myself back at home, I see myself from a distance, sitting outside the house – drinking, smoking, and waiting. I am reminded of the film *Alice in Wonderland*; Alice watching her own dreaming self lying under the tree, asleep and at peace, as her dream-world convulses and fragments. But while Alice was having a nightmare, I don't want to wake up from my dream. I am in Oz, and I don't want to go home.

Leo comes back, a deeply dark shape with flaming edges, like a pitch man set alight, standing in front of the sun holding a glass for me.

'I can't see you,' I say. 'The sun is in my eyes.'

'It's lit them up,' he says. 'They're fiery brown now.'

'I hate my eyes. They're too dark. They look like currants. Or lumps of coal.'

'I like them,' he says, moving so the sun shows him clearly; sweeping with reverence over his face.

William is still in the hospital after a week, recovering noisily, half buried under flowers and cards ('The wages of corporate fear,' Leo says). After the first visit Leo has avoided going back, telling William that he is out of the country – as indeed he will be in only a couple more weeks. First he is to go to Dublin to sell his newest book to Irish people, then Sydney, to sell it to the Australians, then to other cities, for almost a month.

'Are you looking forward to your trip?' I ask, hoping he'll say he will miss me.

'Not particularly,' Leo says. 'When I was younger I used to

associate planes and airports with freedom – escaping. Now they're a commute. I want to travel in the best sense of the word. Just set off and not know where I'm going. Write under a different name. End up living on a small island. Like Skye. I'd like that.'

'Surely not,' I say, dismayed.

'Didn't you like that?' he asks. 'When you were a girl in the middle of nowhere? I could be just a man in the middle of nowhere.'

No, I want to say. *Not you.*

'Maybe Easter Island,' he says, not realising that I haven't answered, 'or Tahiti. Or the Galapagos Islands. Though I don't believe they encourage immigration. Maybe I could get an exemption if I write about tortoises. Do you know they have found traces of DNA from a species of giant tortoise previously presumed extinct? The existence of the DNA in other tortoises means it's likely that members of the extinct species are hiding out somewhere in the Galapagos –' he pauses, thoughtfully, turning the pages of his newspaper as he talks. 'But really, how hard can it be to find a tortoise?'

I realise this is what I must represent to him – the isolation from society that he craves – and the thought frightens me. The idea of him living entirely alone feels absolutely wrong. Even if I were to join him on Easter Island it would still be wrong. Though Leo resists it, his place is in the populated world: he is a cultural being, a social being. He knows the only way he can stop being an object of desire is to be alone, but that's impossible: as soon as he has any number of other people around him, context will return and he will be shown up as what he is – something extraordinary.

Leo pauses in his shuffle through the newspaper. 'Martin Black . . .' he says with surprise, and the start of a frown.

I am halfway through putting my drink down, but my fingers forget their task and the glass drops the final inch to the table, landing with a loud bang.

'Martin Black?'

'What was that person at the awards called? This looks like him, but I'm sure he wasn't called Martin Black . . .' Leo continues to look at the page, as if concerned. I lean abruptly across to see it. But Martin isn't at the front of the paper, with his name in bold and a photo of Leo. He is at the back, in a black-edged box, above a glowing précis of his life, written by someone who obviously never knew him.

'No, it doesn't say anything here about Amazon either. It must just be a resemblance.' Leo notices my expression. 'What's up?

I shake my head.

He smiles with bafflement, and says gently, 'It *is* shocking, I suppose. He wasn't old. Very sad.'

The next day William is brought home. Leo tells me this on the phone, with the same dry, cool neutrality with which he informed me that William had been taken to hospital, but I deliberately misunderstand his tone. 'I'll come over,' I say. 'I'd like to give you some flowers to take to him, if that's all right? And a card.'

I hang up feeling slightly ashamed of using William's ill health as an excuse to see Leo – to be out of Leni's flat where my fears have expanded to fill the available space, with no room left over for my physical presence – and ashamed that I still need these excuses, these ruses.

When I arrive at Leo's I realise my mistake. Ivy is already at his house and when I enter the two of them appear stressed, moving in a snappish silence, punctuated by the sounds of the house next door being renovated. Not long after I arrive, the sound of metal beating on metal begins, ringing through the air like brass plates falling. Then a drill starts and adds to the clamour.

Despite this, the two of them quickly become sociable – almost artificially so – in my company. Leo cooks lunch with overt good humour, as Ivy tells a story about a student in one of her lectures, a story bowed down under its own footnotes – each term and in-joke having to be explained to me – until she finally gives up and laughs. 'Fuck it. It wasn't that funny anyway.'

'I'm going to write about katabasis in the next book,' Leo announces.

'What's that?' I ask timorously, aware that this is my fourth 'what's that' of the conversation.

'The epic convention of a character – a hero – going on a trip to the Underworld. Like Odysseus did. Anabasis is when they come back up.'

He glances at Ivy for confirmation and she gives a slight nod, adding, 'Not many people come back.'

'What is it called when you've always lived in the Underworld, but you decide to leave?' Leo asks. 'That's what I'd like to do.'

'Oh God, not the hermit again,' Ivy says.

'I can be a hermit if I want to be,' Leo says, frowning. 'Living happily in my mountain cave.'

'That's a bear, not a hermit. Hermits still live in houses.'

'Fine. Living happily in my mountain house. Alone.'

'If you are alone, Leo, you're not real,' says Ivy, without kindness. 'All you are is an idea in the heads of hundreds of women.'

'Thousands,' says Leo, and they both laugh, in the same restrained, angry way.

He turns to me: 'In English, we were given an extract from a book and asked questions about it. Why was the woman on the cliff? Why was she upset? That sort of thing. I got in trouble for writing: *The woman is not real.* I was trying to get out of the homework. At the time I got an F and had to redo it. But then the other day I read that it has since been presented as evidence that I was an early postmodernist.'

He turns back to the cooking, brings his knife down, and cuts his finger. 'Motherfucker,' he says sharply, more viciously than I would have expected.

'Are you all right?' I ask him.

'Why is Leo on the cliff?' he says, ignoring me. 'Why is he upset?'

Sensing that Leo's usual gentle amusement with my presence has become something less tolerant, I stay silent. Ivy watches him running his finger under the tap with her eyebrows somewhere between surprised and sarcastic. '*Really*,' she murmurs. It is as if something is unravelling, some previously wound-up anger is crackling around the room, as if the prospective death of William, who in life united Leo and Ivy against him, has disrupted this alliance.

When my phone rings – a call from my bank, which I would usually ignore – I rush out into the garden to take it, relieved to be in the green space, the blankness of the air, free of human undercurrents. The vaguely foreign, mellifluous voice of the call centre employee warning me that I am near my overdraft limit and liable to incur charges, and following that up with an offer for a credit card, is unexpectedly soothing.

As I go back inside I realise that I left the door to the garden ajar. The handle of the door is over a hundred years old, and can't be opened or closed without making a distinctive, owlish screech. Perhaps it is the absence of this screech that means Leo and Ivy do not hear me re-enter the house, and this is why, standing in the kitchen about to close the door, I hear Ivy say, 'No, I don't!'

Her voice is perfectly clear, sweeping through both the closed door of the sitting room and the open door between the dining room and kitchen. I understand, without hearing anything specific, that Ivy is saying something deeply personal: something she does not expect to be heard by me. For that reason, I stand still, not moving, quickly making a deal with my conscience: I will not creep nearer to the door and *actively* eavesdrop, but also, I won't announce my presence by closing the garden door or going inside.

Leo's voice has the kind of smooth lowness that is harder to overhear. He says something like, 'Rather he was dead?'

'How can I not?' Ivy asks.

Leo's reply is inaudible.

'I can accept that he exists. That's as far as it goes. That's not easy in itself.'

Again, though I lean forward anxiously on my feet, as if to cheat my own rule, I can't hear Leo's reply. I'm not sure if he *has* replied. There is a long period of silence. It occurs to me that Leo and Ivy might have realised I am listening. I am about to signal my presence with a screech of the door when Ivy laughs abruptly and says, 'What, like you? Smiling and keeping quiet. Delaying. Hiding.'

I make out the words 'end' and 'no point' in Leo's reply. Then

Ivy says, 'What about Persephone? You haven't told her anything, have you?' There is a pause, and then she says, more quietly, 'I thought not,' and there is the sound of a different, distant door – I guess the door to the entrance hall – being vehemently closed.

I wait for a while, then move like an automaton to the back door and pull the handle gratingly into its locking position. Then I make myself a glass of water and walk back in with it, phone in hand, trying to remember what expression my face might have had, before I overheard the conversation. It is a shoddy approximation at best, but Leo doesn't appear to notice.

'Ivy's got a headache,' he tells me, wearing his own mock-casual expression, far better than my own. If I didn't know it was only a replica I never would have guessed. This is disturbing in itself, but coming now it is only a tremor in the wider ripples of disturbance spreading out from my heart, which has fallen like a stone into cold water. 'She's going to head home,' Leo says.

'I'll say goodbye,' I tell him, following Ivy before Leo, who looks suddenly perturbed, can stop me. I don't know why I feel the need to chase Ivy: only that I have the sense of impending loss, a complete and precipitous loss. With this perspective, whatever I do doesn't matter now, and if I'm going to go down it won't be with my eyes closed, not even knowing what hit me.

Ivy is standing in the hall putting her coat on, turning as she hears me approach. Expecting a devastating unveiling of her contempt for me, I am startled instead by her tears, her eyes widened, bluish in the cool light of the hall, that appears in the window filtered by layers of cloud, all its warm tones stripped away.

'Ivy, what's wrong?' Surprise removes my awe of her and I put my hand on her arm, wrapped in its soft red sleeve. I can barely feel her solidity under the fabric.

'Just self-pity.' Her mouth quirks, despairing and contemptuous. 'Nothing very original.'

I am not sure what to say. I stroke the wool of her coat, then feel self-conscious and take my hand off her.

'I'm sorry, Persephone,' she says, wiping her nose with the back of her hand, a childlike gesture, which I find oddly intimate. 'You must be wondering what on earth is wrong with me. I just – I can't stand it here any more.'

'I'm sure things will be okay,' I say, with no idea what I am talking about.

'Yes, they will. I'm going to Prague.'

'Prague?'

'I've been offered a teaching post there. I can't live in one place for too long. And London will drive me mad if I stay here any longer.'

After this, with my questions all having fled my head, Ivy wishes me a politely tired goodbye, and leaves. I watch her through the door panes; her swift, balletic walk, pushing her hair back away from her marked eyes. I have no idea what to think. The reasons for her and Leo arguing, or for her tears now, run too deeply for analysis, like rivers underground, unfathomable by me.

I go back inside and stand in the doorway, looking at Leo, who doesn't appear to notice. Without Ivy the tension in the room has gone, leaving a wide distance, a space, like the garden, emptied of any intent. Leo is looking out of the window into the decayed light, his eyes vague, their unreadable, unreachable green. I wonder if this is the image I will be left with, when it all ends: the two of us a little apart, the foreign look in Leo's eyes, me, always watching him. I want to make him love me but I don't understand him, which is why he doesn't love me.

I wonder what happened to them, with William, with their mothers, with the drugs, with the vanished Bruce Yelland. What the 'anything' is that Leo hasn't told me. What the captain said to Martin. I suppose I will know soon enough, when Martin's posthumous story appears, like a malicious dog, snapping darkly out of the papers. I almost want it to happen, just so that I can finally locate Leo; to know where in that time he is hiding.

All the next week there is no sun; just a hot, miserable grey. Grey on grey, heaps of grey in the sky like a filthy snow, grey on the faces of the buildings, grey smog outside the window like curtains. The sun is a pale disc glimpsed through many layers; a distant, dusty sun. Finally, on the last day, it gathers itself and burns the greyness away, commencing a heatwave that gathers up London in a fierce grip, pressing itself against the people like a lonely man on the bus. Whether they complain, move, or bear it uneasily, there is no getting away from the intimacy of the heat.

I sit in my room, sweating, and try to read my course notes for my exams, which are only a couple of weeks away. I try not to feel anything, but it isn't working. I try not to cry, but I do, and when I do my tears are not soothing, they are hot, and sour.

I feel a kind of panic when I look out at London now. Without Martin to tell me how lost I am here, I feel genuinely lost. I feel like a child whose parents have crossed the street without them;

suddenly everything is blaring and hostile and the pressure of the crowd is unbearable. The density of London oppresses me, its air laden with the accumulated breath of hundreds of people for hundreds of years, making it harder to feel my own existence. I stepped so casually into it, in a rush, hastily immersing myself. Now I can't get my head to the surface.

After Ivy left Leo's house we ate a horribly polite lunch, before he indicated that he might like to write, at which point I left hurriedly, falsely upbeat. Since then I haven't heard from him. I lie on my bed now and remember things he said or did, as though I am tracking down the relationship, chasing a scent as it gets fainter and colder; trying to find something that is long gone. For the first time it occurs to me that I might be happier if I didn't love him. My body has arranged itself around its love; flesh cloaking a coal, a frightened palsied beating of the heart. A body heavy with exhaustion, and sadness, deathly tired, because it takes a lot out of you, to keep such a hopeful heart.

Finally Emiko calls me excitedly one morning, inviting me to a party. 'Tell Leo too,' she adds, before she hangs up.

I don't want to tell her that I haven't heard from him for days. There are a lot of things – little and larger failures – which I have never told Catherine or Emiko about because I can't allow myself to give them the weight of sound, bring them into the world of spoken history. Because of these omissions the group have come to assume I am a kind of oracle for Leo; able to interpret and predict his mysterious movements, pass on messages, and suchlike.

I call Leo, telling myself that I have to call him to invite him to the party, but he doesn't answer, or call back. As the day winds slowly down to the hour of Emiko's party I am uncomfortable in the knowledge that the missed call, and my thin, chirpy voicemail, are lying on the display of his phone like a dropped handkerchief, something that can only grow more pitiful as time passes.

Finally, he calls back, and at his 'How are you?' I sense the disappointment travelling electrically towards me. Accordingly he tells me that he is going to spend the evening writing.

'Are you sure?'

'Yes. Sorry. I wish I could come. Have a good time. I'll call you tomorrow and you can tell me how much everyone missed me.' He sounds flippant but weary, of his routine, and of me.

Emiko has hung paper lanterns around her house, which swing faintly in the soft air, coloured like butterflies. There are people I recognise, and new people, new foundlings, dancing together on the glossy, paper-lit floor. Catherine is making some complicated drinks with rum and sugar, laughing at another girl who is dancing on the long table in a short, glowing white dress, spinning and showing her bare feet and legs, sending provocative looks down at a man who watches her.

'She likes to think she's really wild,' Catherine says to me. 'She went travelling to the Andes to show what a free spirit she was, but she hated it. She came home early and went straight to the hairdresser.'

I laugh, but as with the other jokes of the evening, as soon as the laugh leaves me I feel my eyes slide downwards, my mouth settle into a sorrowful, bowed shape, weighted by the absence of Leo.

'Are you okay?' Catherine asks me, noticing. She puts her hand on my arm and waits, prepared to stroke and console.

I don't know why I can't do it: effortlessly accept and give support like other women do. When I am comforting someone who is upset it feels artificial: I worry I am doing it wrong, that in the face of such open emotion it will be apparent that I am shy and out of my depth, like an awkward bachelor holding a baby. In the same way, to allow myself to cry on someone else's shoulder, damp faced and uninhibited, is too much for me. I blink, raise my eyebrows ruefully and tell Catherine I'm worried about my upcoming exams, then have to accept her earnest sympathies with a feeling of guilt.

In the end several of Catherine's drinks and the general high spirits of the party begin to convince me that I have reasons to be optimistic. Though he is more and more distant, vaguer and vaguer, Leo hasn't actually finished with me. Though Martin has warned me of his impending exposé, it hasn't actually been printed. There is a distance – though it may be short – between the spot where I stand, and the end of the land, the gloomy future.

In this mood, I tell the taxi driver taking me home to go to Leo's house instead. It is 4 a.m. and I am drunk. Thoughts skitter through my head like pebbles thrown on to water: they skip, skip, then vanish. I worry briefly about having stagnant wine breath and eat a mint. I remember a joke Anthony told and smile to myself. I worry that Leo won't be at home. I check my mirror, struggling to see my face in the mauvish slightness of the light. I smooth my dress. I wonder if I should have brought a coat.

'Might get some rain tonight,' the driver says. 'Put an end to this bloody heatwave.'

When I get out of the car I can tell what he means. Though the beginning of the day around me is warm, the sky is full of massed, musky clouds, crowding together, murmuring amongst themselves. There is a density in the air, a sullenness. I stand on the pavement for a moment feeling the turmoil of the air coil and billow, wondering what on earth I am doing. My jokes at the party about Leo ('He's got very boring, hasn't he?'), my merry instructions to the taxi driver: these were actions that now seem to belong to a different occasion. I am familiar with the tradition of the drunk girlfriend turning up at her boyfriend's door, bothering him with her exaggerated affections, to be laughed at in the morning. *Why not me?* I thought. But, looking at Leo's house shimmering like a blank projection in the curious pewter light, I know very well why not.

As it's too late to call the taxi back now – or worse, Leo might have already seen me from the front-facing window of his study – I decide to go inside, ascending the steps to his door with my fear following me closely, and am taken aback to see that the door is already open. I stare at it, hovering ajar, unmoving in the lack of wind, as if the air is too thick for motion. The door indicates murderers and burglars, or hasty morning departures. Fight or flight. Believing the second more likely, I go inside, into the stillness of the house, to find out the worst.

I move quietly across the hall, trying to see in the dimness, making out items like the relics left scattered in the underwater rooms of the *Titanic*. The balusters of the stairs like jointed finger bones, the complex shadow of the chandelier frozen over the wall. Here are Ivy's shoes lying on the floor; there, Ivy's coat collapsed on to the stairs. Whatever trouble may have caused her to rush inside is no longer in evidence. When I stop to listen, no sound passes from any of the rooms into the shadowy hall. There is no sound from the street outside; it being too late for the night, and too early for the morning.

I walk as silently as I can to the sitting room, the doors of which are half open, and look into the apparently empty room, its curtains drawn. It is the feel of the room that compels me to continue looking, rather than turning away to carry on my search: the air is overwrought, as though full of ghosts. And the longer I look the more I see of them, half sitting, half lying, on a sofa, still clothed. Ivy's abandoned hand thrown over the sofa back, Leo above her, her other hand on his back. Neither of their faces visible, hidden because they are turned together, so that all I can see is Ivy's hair which moves slightly, lapping their shoulders and arms, like pouring water.

The air around them is impenetrable; they do not see me or sense me. I back out and stand in the hall just outside the door, where I put my hands to my face and get a shock from their coldness. I stand there, too limp to leave, heavy, unable to pick each foot up in sequence to move away. Then I hear Leo; an exhausted, passionate sound, an exhalation I have never heard before. It breaks the spell and I run out of the house, the front door wavering soundlessly, the tall white house receding behind me but still present, like something I can feel.

Once I get home, standing on the doorstep with my key in my hand, fingers still cold and hard to operate, my feet blistered from walking to find a taxi in the silk shoes now flayed and greyed by the cobbles, the evening shivers, shakes, and gives in to rain. It has succumbed to its misery, I think. At last.

PART TEN

And when all the gods are gone, here and there to their own loves and wars, Persephone is left alone to sit thoughtfully in the great hall, silently counting: one, two, three, four, five, six months. Half a year until the time when she will take her journey down into the strangely lit underworld, be carried across the Acheron, cross the fields of Asphodel, and enter the silver palace, where Hades waits.

Ivy Ford
Persephone and Hades

The next day I find a card, previously disregarded, partially hidden under an electricity bill on the doormat, informing me that an attempt has been made to deliver a letter to me. I go to the post office to collect it. No séances for Martin Black: the dead, it seems, favour next-day recorded delivery.

Martin's note is brief, written in an effortful hand:

Persephone – I'm not going to publish this. There are no other copies.
This is for you if you want to know.
Martin.

Inside the letter is another envelope, containing a CD recording and a transcript of Martin's interview with the captain of the yacht, from whatever remote tropic his wariness of Bruce Yelland had sent him to; a location he wanted to remain unknown. It is apparent that he has been well paid for the interview, his previous income having dried up. He makes a reference to the demeaning state he finds himself in at present, working in a local bar.

The captain, who spoke with a European accent I found hard to place, was used to unusual requests from Bruce Yelland, he said.

He had seen various unlikely and illegal goings-on on the yacht, which he minded but didn't mind because his generous wages allowed him to live well and save for his own future, perhaps as the owner of a small sightseeing boat in the Mediterranean, calling at the coves and bays of small islands like a bus, distributing its passengers across the sand, rounding them up again, carrying them home.

The captain hadn't met Ivy or Leo before this trip, but understood that Ivy and Bruce had been conducting a chaste business relationship selling cocaine to fastidious middle-class Londoners, who viewed Ivy as an acceptable representative of organised crime. Ivy herself seemed to view the trip as nothing so much as an office party; a perk of the job.

The captain said that his experience working for Bruce had given him a thorough schooling in the signs of imminent trouble, at which he was expected to make himself scarce: hear nothing, see nothing. From the moment Leo stepped on to the yacht behind his sister and Bruce muttered an insincere welcome, he recognised trouble coming. When he saw Ivy stretched out on the deck, the band of her bikini pulled taut between each hip-bone so that a shadow ran the length of her darkening stomach, he got a shiver of trouble. When Bruce watched her at dinner, tapping his fork sullenly against his plate with thwarted lust, there it was again. The day he saw Leo reach across to where Ivy sat and move her hair, a wilful slip of it, out of her eyes, with the gentle, unconscious intimacy of a honeymooner.

And finally, there came the day when Bruce was meant to be ashore in Sardinia, replenishing the champagne supply, but came back early, and found his young protégée and her half-brother not fucking – but almost fucking – excuse the captain's language – in the yacht's control room.

The subsequent argument ran the length of the boat and ended in the lounge, under the mounted swords. Bruce shot Leo. Then Ivy stabbed Bruce with one of the swords. Someone outside, passing the docked boat, heard the noise and called the police. This was the moment the captain judged it a good idea to leave the boat and take a train out of town.

The captain said that at first he thought Ivy couldn't have been taking drugs herself, because she seemed so calm, and so miserable. When it turned out that she was as addicted to cocaine as Bruce he was startled. But he reasoned later that her love for Leo, the burden of the wrongness of it – condemned by God himself – must have outweighed the chemical stimulant. He could see – and here his voice was not without sympathy – that they really did love one another.

After that day I float low in the flat, like a fog, diffuse and inactive. Even going out to the post office is an ordeal: the people there too compact and vital and frightening to be dealt with. The sudden noises of my phone or the doorbell come and go, too quick to follow. I brought the scattered elements of myself close enough together to send Leo a text message, telling him I need to lock myself away in order to revise. He called back and left a voice message, to say he understood. He wished me luck, in his light voice; quick, as always, to let me go.

I don't know what to do when the exams end, so I decide I will deal with that when it happens, in an effort to break the reality of my new world into manageable portions: first revision, then exams, then speaking to Leo.

Having portioned out the future, I am less successful at dealing with the past. I try to guess which of the times when he was missing or busy he was really with her. I go over the times Leo and Ivy were angry with each other, the times they seemed most at ease: trying to chart the wax and wane of their secret relationship.

I theorise, eventually, that they must have separated before I arrived. Perhaps it wasn't a mutually decided separation. I remember Leo's black eye, the night Ivy came back. Perhaps I was the reason for the argument: Ivy got back and Leo told her there was someone else. Thinking about this gives me a backdated moment of horror: that Ivy must have met me and known that I was her rival. But she was welcoming to me, even to the end, when I caught her before she left and she was not resentful but kind, her final smile that of someone who has played a hard match, has been defeated, and is gracious in defeat.

I try to imagine Leo and Ivy when they first met, two beautiful, hard teenagers, pushed together, found that they were the only ones who *could* be together. They must have thought it was so unfair. The idea of William's death must have seemed like a sort of freedom to them – the disappearance of their common genetic heritage. In Leo's books, I realise, the lovers always gave each other up, one way or another: the men let the women – Athena, Anna, Dolores – go, even though they were mad to do it.

I spend the next weeks revising in the flat, the windows open onto bright, polluted sunlight, letting in only stillness, until I buy a fan to stir the air. Each night I work until late, closing my books and turning my laptop off in the silent room, listening to its rill of music, then a dying whir before the screen fizzles and crackles, falling dark. The laptop has slowed in the heat, becoming laborious, venting so loudly that I hear its continual hum even when it isn't turned on. I have slowed down too, struggling through texts and theories that ought to be in my memory, accessible, but aren't. I make trips to the library and heave my books home in the wheeled oven of the bus. The underground is even more unbearable. There is a poster at its entrance reading: 'In the summer months the Underground can become very hot. Please read the following advice: 1) Don't take the Underground.' I think that I am going to fail my exams, that I deserve to fail, and that I don't care if I do fail.

What I think about as I ride the bus, or whenever I look up from the screen, or while I lie unsleeping in the sluggish nights, is Leo. Though officially Leo and I are still a couple, I carry out the traditional break-up rituals. I gather my mementos of him: a skimpy pile, not enough evidence to convict us of a relationship. A magazine article with a picture of the two of us together at the charity ball. An etiolated white flower from his garden, dry as tissue. A tie he removed and forgot he left in a handbag of mine. A photo Catherine emailed to me, of an unfocused dance floor. Nobody is aware that a picture has been taken. Emiko and Anthony are embracing. Leo is laughing at something out of shot. Next to him, I look as if I am concentrating, mouth serious, arm raised like a statue of a martial leader. I can tell from the picture exactly what I am thinking: how to make him love me. And there he is, looking at something else, smiling as if nothing in the world could ever involve him.

With me he could smile like that. It was Ivy with whom he had the desperate, doomed love, the thwarted, exhausting passion. She was his monumental affair and his muse. I only had a part of Leo, his play-acting, a leftover. This is where all my thoughts about Leo end, as if obeying a strict chronology. Every time I think of him I inevitably find myself back at his house, standing back from the doorway, with all that dreaming, all the waiting and wanting, come abruptly to an end.

The high stress level of the exam period has faded it in my memory, as if under intense light, but certain things stand out: rushing to the lavatory of the supermarket and just sitting and crying in a cubicle, breathing disinfectant, the locks snapping back and forth like gunshots, feet clattering across the white tiled floor in my low rectangle of vision. Falling asleep at the desk and waking up with a pen-lid embedded in my cheek, then staring at myself in the mirror with slow horror, not realising at first what had happened. Looking at the first page of the first exam so intently that I couldn't actually see the words. Walking past a bar I used to go to with Leo, its high studded wooden door closed to the daylight, and thinking about the spaces accessible to Leo but not now to me: the places like jewels, hard and brilliant, pillared and mirrored and bordered with their arching glittering windows, turning their cold, fierce faces on to me, standing outside unrecognised.

When I am not revising I watch the television, staring at anything dramatic enough to occupy my attention but not intelligent enough to force me to think. I watch constructed reality shows as I eat my lunch. I watch talk shows as I brush my teeth. The funny thing about the talk shows is that no guest seems self-conscious or shy; they are at home on the stage. 'You don't know me,' they shout, as the lie detector results are read out. 'Whatever.' Perhaps the presence of a physical audience just merges comfortably into our own assumption that we are important: that everyone *is* watching us.

At times the heat in the flat becomes intolerable; the dusty thick air, the night like a clinging blanket. It is relieved, occasionally, by the dull din of rain, washing the sky dark ink-blue. I fluctuate in the same way; sometimes dry and aching, at others melancholic and self-pitying. I languish, I wallow in my incomprehension. At the worst times I feel pain reverberating all through me, as if I am boneless, an exposed, nervy heart, and I hear Leo saying: 'You think you're devastated, but you recover quickly.'

I remember being nine and having a fever, the sick darkness of it, out of which revolved a mesh of white points, constellated and buzzing. When I look out of the window at night the fever is there; gripping the city in its sparkling net. I start sleeping with an eye-mask, to keep out the lights. It works a little, but not well enough. After one exam I am so tired that when I put down my pen and drop my face into my hands I think I can actually see Leo opposite me in the dark of my fingers, looking away with his unconcerned smile, eyes blue-green and cool.

When the exams are over I refuse drinks with the other people on my course and walk to the bus stop. As I am leaving the campus I run into Camilla, sauntering in with her sunny head and large black sunglasses. When she turns to me it is like being displayed on two television screens. I smile when I see her, though I know something has gone wrong with my smile recently. It is as if my face has set, like wet plaster, into an expressionless face, its movements heavy and unnatural.

Camilla doesn't appear to notice and kisses me on each cheek with every sign of delight. 'Have you finished your exams?' she asks.

'Just now. How about you?'

'This is my last one.' She makes an exaggerated mouth of worry. I wish her luck, expecting this to end the conversation, but she shifts her bag in her arms, unmoving, and looks at me through the sunglasses. I can only see the shape of her eyes, not their content.

'I saw you and Leo in a magazine the other day. You looked stunning. As usual. I wanted to say I'm really happy for you, Persephone.'

I try again to see into the sunglasses, looking for insincerity, but I can't tell if there is any, and she continues, rushing, as if I might interrupt: 'I know I was a bitch. I was upset and I was really childish about it. I suppose I proved you were right to find some more grown-up friends.'

'Camilla—' I say, but she is already speaking again. From under the rim of one black lens a tear drops, making its haphazard way down her face, unnoticed. If I cry I hold tissues against my eyes, applying pressure, as if to stop a cut bleeding. But it never did occur to Camilla to blot or wipe; letting her tears drop wherever they landed, carrying eyeliner and dissolved mascara along with them like silt, staining her face and clothes, dampening the shoulders she presses her face into.

'I wanted to say I was stupid about Marcus too. I know you wouldn't really have flirted with him. I just . . . I thought he was so wonderful that nobody would be able to help themselves.'

There is a moment of near suspension, a delicate seesawing between us, then we both laugh.

'I know better now,' Camilla adds.

'University's good for finding these things out. In the space of a few months rather than years. It's like it was faster than real life.'

'You sound like it's finished for good,' she says, and I don't answer, asking her instead what I have missed. Camilla is still eager to package, wrap and hand over the lives of our friends to me, picking out moments of particular note, without asking whether I deserve a 'best of' clip show when I haven't shown any commitment to the series.

'Sammy's new boyfriend is flying back to America. I think she might go out there with him for the summer.'

'Sammy's new boyfriend?'

'Yeah, she's been with this guy for a month or two now. He actually seems nice. Not the usual pricks Sammy used to go for. Remember that one with the gelled hair? Nate.'

'And his R&B nights at the Ice Bar.'

'The Ice Bar! How could I have forgotten that!'

We both laugh, then Camilla says, with a hesitancy that I might have read as awkwardness in anyone else, 'So, I'm seeing James now.'

'James Cass?'

'Yeah . . . Isn't that funny? He's actually a lot cleverer than any of us gave him credit for.'

I realise she is awkward, and a little defensive, so I say: 'I always thought he was clever. It was only you that didn't think so.'

'Huh, yeah, I suppose it was,' she says, looking pleased.

After a little longer I ask her when her exam starts, and she yelps with amusement. 'I'm such an idiot. I could stand here all day. It's so nice to see you though, Perse. We should do something . . .'

'Yes,' I say.

'I'm going travelling this summer,' she says, suddenly. 'You could come? If you wanted to? I know you must be busy.'

'Not really. I'm not with Leo any more. I have to work, though. Perhaps if I save enough I could meet you for a little bit.'

'Not with Leo? But only the other week I saw the magazine . . .'

'It's a recent break-up. But we were never on the same level. I just didn't realise that for a while. I got carried away.'

'It happens,' she says, and gives me a smile and a shrug, making them sympathetic rather than dismissive, a gesture of solidarity. We stand for a moment peering at each other with something like humour; survivors of nothing very bad.

'You really had better go,' I say, noticing the students coming out of the exam that is just finishing. 'Good luck for the exam.'

She kisses me on the cheek when I put my arms around her, tentatively, and grips me back enthusiastically. Then we move apart, carried easily in different directions by the twin flows of people in and out of the doors. Standing outside afterwards, once everybody has left or arrived, there is a moment of silence in which I feel the beginnings of a new sadness. My usual sadness shuffles over to accommodate it, making polite room.

I don't know exactly what shape mine and Camilla's friendship will be in future – it being another of the things I have temporarily put aside to 'think about later' – though even if we don't speak again I know there will still be a shape, filled up with the past.

I think of Camilla, Laura and Sammy, not as individuals but as the group we were. The way we used to sit on each others' beds with cups of tea in the morning; waiting for the rumpled, lipstick-stained faces to appear from the sheets and tell their stories of horror and triumph. The wine drunk from mugs, the strung fairy lights over the bedposts. Inspecting each others' backs for fake tan marks, awry clothes labels, visible bra straps. The time we danced round the house, holding on to each others' waists, before Camilla sprang on to the sofa, lost her balance and fell over the back of it.

The group only exists now in pictures, saved in memory cards and distant data centres. Four girls electronically frozen in time, with their dancing shoes, their aniseed-tasting shots and their lovely, dishevelled bedrooms of heaped clothes and magazines. Already they seem like something I just made up.

~

When I arrive back at the flat, Leo is waiting for me outside, sitting on the wall reading a book. I see him before he sees me, my surprise slowing my pace. I stare at him where he sits, the sun turning his hair the livid brown of Ivy's hair, making a simple woodcut of his face, stark in its perfection, like a blueprint of a man. I should have been suspicious of his beauty; its unearthliness. He never looked like something attainable, and he wasn't.

He looks up and smiles. 'What's wrong?' he asks. 'Your exams are over, aren't they? I thought we could celebrate.'

The street is almost empty in the afternoon lull but people are still passing, their faces clenched against the sunlight, which hides us from their notice. They are not friendly looking. They look busy, and tired. They are full of impatience. These are the people who love Leo – who would hate him if their idea of him were too rudely disassembled.

I take him inside, not up to the flat, but to stand in the hall at the foot of the staircase, under an old clock with one loud tick and a nearly silent tock, giving the impression that time is passing slower here; slow and off-balance.

Leo, perceptive as always, doesn't say anything. He looks at me curiously, ready for my explanation.

'I'm going back to Scotland,' I say. 'I mean – I'm not coming back to London.'

He is quiet for a moment: not surprised, but almost sympathetic, doctorly, as if the test results are in and his early diagnosis has been confirmed.

Then he asks, 'Why?'

'I've failed my course. I'm pretty sure I have anyway. But that's not the reason. You and I—'

There is another silence, which seems longer under the limping tick of the clock, the weight of his gaze. I wasn't prepared to see him so soon, or for him to be so unusually intent. I expected eye-evading relief from him, happiness to see me shrink tidily back into the low-maintenance shape of a former lover, an old friend. But he is watching me closely – waiting – and I can barely look at him.

'You and I?' he prompts.

'Not you and I. You and Ivy –' I hesitate, abruptly in dark water, deep water. 'I know about you two.'

His stillness becomes stiller, in the way that a final frame of a TV show freezes before the credits make their entrance; the minute adjustments between life and image. He stares at me, shocked at what I have said, and I look back helplessly, shocked at having said it. I am waiting for him to take a position: something I can take my own cue from – dropping gratefully into outrage, or tears; some known feeling. But it is obvious that neither of us know what to do.

His face is still. He asks, 'How?'

'A journalist was investigating you. He approached me to ask about you and we sort of . . . well, we didn't become friends. But we spoke. I was trying to put him off, to find out what he was going to do. I wasn't helping him, or anything.'

Leo blinks. 'The book awards,' he says. 'That was him.'

'Yes.'

'The obituary.'

I have the sense of being on the back foot now, though I'm not exactly sure how it happened. 'Yes. He died. He sent me an interview with the captain of that yacht, before—'

Leo interrupts me, and now his stillness is gone; his eyes, his hands, even his clothing, seem to be in motion, like a man running; a man on fire. He is angry; lit bright with it. 'And you met this journalist before you were with me?'

'I *met* you first,' I say hastily. 'I met him afterwards. But it was before we started – anything. He was just harassing me, at first. He followed me.'

'So you did the sensible thing, and befriended him?'

'We weren't friends!' I cry, but I lack conviction, and stop, wordless.

Leo steps back. 'Jesus Christ,' he says quietly. 'So what are you going to do now – sell it? I suppose you deserve the money. You've earned it.'

We stare at each other for a moment. His mouth has become a line of white, like a scar. His eyes are no longer like water, or distant horizons, they have the reflective hardness of glass. His anger is frightening; I become smaller under its suppressed violence, the radiant fury of it. Only in the moment after, a moment in which he doesn't walk away or hit me, am I able to locate myself.

'How could you?' I say, not meaning to shout, but near shouting. The noise of it billows up the layers of the staircase, raining back down on us. 'How could you say that to me? I didn't plan any of it! I fucking *saved* you. He was my friend, in the end, and you're lucky he was, or you'd really have to disappear to Easter Island, instead of just pretending. I stopped him publishing – he sent his material to me, not to the papers, and I got rid of it. I would never tell anyone about it. I'm not interested in selling you out. Or myself.'

Leo is surprised now, holding up his hands, saying, 'Persephone,' to try to calm me – and it's true, I have started to cry, in irregular, loud gulps – but I won't stop talking: 'Martin was the only person I ever actually had something truthful with. He told me I couldn't trust him and I couldn't. Then he told me I could and he was right. I knew what was happening with him. I never knew what the truth was with *you*.'

'Persephone, please—'

'Let me *finish*. How could you imply I was some sort of spy – some sort of, of honeytrap? It was so painfully obvious how much I wanted to be with you. And that you didn't feel the same way. You were wrong to let me love you when you didn't want me. You let me think there were possibilities. You should never have made me hope . . .'

In the end only the need to blow my nose stops me talking, and once I have located a tissue, wiped my face, and become aware of the silence in the stairwell now that my own voice has vacated it, I fall silent myself, quashed. As if watching – detached – from behind my own face, I see tears chase each other along the edge of my nose, falling on to my hands, which do not move to stem them.

'Persephone,' Leo has put his hands to his face, 'I'm sorry. I wasn't expecting this. I shouldn't have said that. I know it's not the truth. Please . . .' but there he stops, as if he doesn't know what he might be about to ask me for.

'I wasn't expecting this either,' I say, combative, but my anger is dying.

'I'm so sorry,' he repeats. 'Believe me. I was hopeful too. I was wrong, but I didn't know that.'

He moves to stand close to me, and puts his hand on mine. I look at the hands resting together, calm as doves, the curled white fingers. I don't look at his face. Still not a familiar face to me, not even now. Not something I can run my eyes over casually, proprietarily.

'I know this doesn't excuse it, but I want you to know that virtually nothing happened with Ivy –' he almost stalls over the name – 'while I was with you.'

'You don't need to explain.' I shake my head. 'You never promised me anything. In fact, you warned me.'

'Still, it wasn't fair.'

'I knew you couldn't love me. I realised there wasn't any . . . spare. I just didn't know why.'

'I did want to,' he says, so plainly and desolately that I do look up at him, his expression unlike anything I am used to seeing.

It lets me ask: 'But *why*? That's what baffles me. I never understood why you wanted to.'

'I don't know. It wasn't reason over instinct. It was just a different instinct. I suppose I was fascinated by your newness. Not your youth, exactly. It was your air of being on the edge of something, about to become something – anything – but still undecided. Your readiness for it. I want to go back, to that moment, when *I* had it, and didn't know that's what it was.'

He looks away from me now, the lids drawn down over the colour of his eyes. 'I wish I'd met you in the Highlands. Both of us young. I'd have met your father. Sheep wandering past the bedroom window . . . the quiet. I wouldn't have left.'

His fingers draw closer around mine, as if they are hunting for something. 'I would have been happy.'

There is a while of silence, then I say, 'I'd have hated it.'

He looks up, then laughs. 'I just want to undo it all,' he says. 'Go back, turn the other way. That's all.'

'I'm sorry.'

'You're being remarkably understanding,' he observes.

I bow my head, acknowledging this. Strangely, I do feel understanding. Possibly because I always understood, in one way or another. Even when I first saw them together, under my shock there was no disbelief. I had no grip on any sense of betrayal. Their relationship doesn't seem wrong; any more than London could seem wrong. It is what it is, predating me, outlasting me.

In the silence that follows I catch a glimpse of my old dream; myself at Spook, holding court below the city, Leo at my side. A diamond on my hand, lighting up the drink I hold. Darkness over my shoulders like a cloak. A dream – yes – a dream of nothing at all. But still, I had to do it – get around the other side of it, before I could understand that it was only a picture.

'I want you to be happy,' I say.

He looks away, without answering. His hands drop away. I half see, half guess at the thoughts that surface in his expression. Exhaustion, or sadness, or regret. His eyes could be teared or it could be the light, colliding and sliding away.

'You don't have to forgive this,' he says, finally.

'But I have. I didn't decide to. I just realise it's happened.'

'Thank you. And not just for that. For the newspaper – for everything. If there's ever anything I can do for you . . . you'll tell me?'

I am reminded of the fairy stories where a simple character unwittingly does a witch or some other fantastical creature a good turn. They would be given a horn to blow, a song to sing, or a name to call, whenever they were in need. The likelihood of me calling Leo for future help seems almost as improbable, but I nod anyway.

When he leaves I am shivering. In the door he stops and gives me a brief, solemn smile, before pulling it shut behind him. I go to the window, where I watch him walk down the street and around the corner, without stopping or looking back. As often happens when I make comparisons with Leo, I think of television footage of wild animals; in this case the ones taken in by humans and released back into their own habitat, moving swiftly out of sight, face to the future. Half an hour, from his arrival to the turn at the corner. That's how long it takes to end a relationship you don't have.

After a number of lopsided ticks of the clock, too many for

anything else to happen, I sit down on the floor and cry again. My tears flare and rise like a fire, emerging from my eyes hot and bitter, too quickly for me to breathe properly, too deep for me to sob. It must be the big cry: the one Catherine and Emiko told me about, the first time I met them.

It isn't all for Leo. Some of it is for myself; for my own wilful stupefaction, for closing my eyes and walking forward as if in a dream. Some of it is for the absence from my father, on patient standby, waiting for the time when he will say: 'No need to apologise at all,' and forgive me for delaying my trips home and missing his calls. Some of it is for my mother, standing in the sun at her charity fête, raising money for other people's children.

Finally, it is for Martin, who could have been remembered for ever for his story about Leo – the leader of the revolution, the burned books and media pitchforks – but will never be heard of again. I didn't speak to him, I didn't thank him. I didn't realise that he was less selfish than me: that it would be him, in the end, who did the noble thing.

Catherine insists on organising going-away drinks so I can say goodbye to her and the rest of Leo's friends, without Leo. It's a sweet idea, but in practice the conspicuous absence of Leo and Ivy, or even the mention of their names, makes the rest of our talk artificially light, shallow flowing and strange.

When Catherine, Emiko and I are alone, the two of them exchange glances, as if the pleasantries are over, and now we need to discuss business.

'Are you really sure you want to quit?' Emiko begins. 'Is the course so bad?'

It turned out that I passed my exams: not with any distinction – a selection of 2:2s and thirds accompany my name on the posted sheets of results – but passing was more than I expected. Finding myself able to stay, I realised that I had been looking forward to being thrown out.

'I hate the course,' I say now, firmly. 'I'd rather start again and do something I'd actually enjoy.'

'Do you know what that is?' Catherine asks. 'It's just – forgive us for questioning you, Perse – but you know what it's like when you have a. . . shit time. You want to throw everything out and then nothing will remind you of it again. We just want to make sure you hate the course for what it is and not for . . . other reasons.'

'I'm not trying to get rid of any reminders of Leo,' I say. Both women blink. We hadn't any of us expected to mention his name – at least not so soon. 'Ironically, I think I want to study classics.'

Emiko holds up her hands, 'Then we'll stop questioning you.'

'Except to say – might you come back to London?' Catherine asks.

'I don't know about London. Maybe not now. I can't pretend I'm not throwing anything out at all. London might be collateral damage.'

As if I have said something more emotional – or as if my light tone didn't quite come off – Emiko reaches out and puts her hand on my arm. 'Oh Perse. I'm so sorry.'

'No, it's fine. It's nothing to be sorry about. I just liked him more than he liked me. I thought I was in love with him. Maybe I was. I don't know. But he definitely didn't love me. It was just me, making things up in my head. I suppose I realised I can't carry on doing that. It's too tiring. It's too . . . upsetting.'

I hadn't meant to say all this, but the pressure of it, once given its vent, won't allow me to stop, and I start to cry. Despite my fears about crying in public, it turns out not to be such a bad experience. The two women move into place as if part of a well-rehearsed ballet: Catherine using her body to interrupt the line of sight between me and the rest of the group, Emiko holding out tissues. Then they begin a crooning, reassuring chorus, stroking my arm, waiting until the tears dry up, then easing off, beginning to joke again, until I can laugh along with them.

'Sorry,' I say. 'That was embarrassing.'

'We've all been there,' Catherine said. 'Under much sillier circumstances. I cried in a restaurant a few weeks ago telling Em about a sad film.'

Emiko laughs. 'I was the worst person to tell because I cry when other people cry. Like yawning. I see someone else crying and my own eyes well up. It's completely involuntary. So we both ended up sniffling at this restaurant and the waiters were approaching us then realising and veering away.'

Only after I am more composed does Catherine say, quietly, 'I think he really cared for you, Persephone. He's just different to other people.'

I nod. I don't need to tell her how far her rightness extends; into what dim and obscure corners it has accidentally reached.

'We'll all stay friends, of course,' she says, later, but she already sounds regretful, because we all know we're not likely to see each other again. I want to be friends with Catherine and Emiko, but there is no future in which I come back to London and take it in turns to see them on the nights Leo isn't around. We all kiss and announce our good intentions but the impending loss of the friendship hangs over the rest of the evening like a pall, a dampening fog.

When I leave early, pleading the need to pack, Michael accompanies me out to find a taxi. We stand together for a moment in the yellow light of the bar window, next to a group of smokers, the scent of their cigarettes crossing vaguely over to us.

Michael pulls his hand awkwardly through his hair and looks at me with worried affection. His face in the depleted light appears younger than it is, his eyes wider.

'I'm sorry about what happened,' he says.

I laugh, 'Well, don't be. You did try to warn me.'

'Are you okay?'

'Sort of.' I look at him more closely, wondering whether he knew about Leo and Ivy. I say, experimentally, 'It was funny how we all avoided talking about Leo tonight. Or Ivy, for that matter.'

'You haven't spoken to Ivy?' Michael asks, surprised, and I see that he doesn't know.

'No, why? She called me just before my exams but I didn't return the call. I did mean to speak to her, then things ended with Leo . . .'

'She probably called you just before she left for Prague – to say goodbye. She's been living there for a few weeks now.'

'Oh, right.' I puzzle over this for a moment. 'Well, good for her. I know she was bored of London.'

'I think it was partly William's heart attack too. I know she and Leo thought he was an idiot, but I think his possible death really shocked them. You never know how things with parents will affect you. Hence them both leaving so suddenly.'

'Leo's left?'

'You didn't know?' Michael says, startled. 'Well, he isn't on his book tours. The publishers are hysterical. Nobody knows where he is. He sent us a postcard from the Galapagos Islands. I don't know if that was a joke . . . We're going to have to make up some excuses for him.'

'Ha,' I say, able – strangely – to find this funny. So that's Ivy gone, and Leo gone too. It is an odd feeling, the idea of London without them, deserted and anticlimactic, like the closing hours of a party that the hosts have left.

We stand for a moment, as if thinking of the death of London, while the smokers next to us drop the last of their cigarettes and buffet each other genially back into the bar. A thin wind has channelled through the street, sifting the litter like autumn leaves, rearranging Michael's protean hair into new and startling shapes. The whistle of the air; the sudden emptiness of the night pavement feels like pressure – to leave, or say something worthwhile. As if sensing it, Michael shifts on his feet like someone preparing to start running; his words arrive in a hurry, delivered with too much force.

'I hope it doesn't take you long to be happy again.'

'Ah. Thanks,' I say, taken aback.

'Remember when we met each other at the photocopier?'

'Of course. It wasn't long ago,' I say, which is technically true.

'Does it feel like only a short time, to you?' Michael asks.

'Time goes slower when you're young because you've had less of it. It's all relative. Pain hurts more because you've had less of it, apparently.'

He looks confused.

'But you know, I looked it up and I found this study . . . and people watching a clip from an emotional film who were told to be neutral and suppress their feelings estimated that the clip lasted longer than people who just watched it naturally. So if you feel things, time goes faster. If you let things happen to you, and react to them . . . without thinking it all through first. Time must go very slowly if you refuse to take part at all. That's what I should have said.' I stop, noticing the way he is looking at me. 'Sorry. You were saying – the photocopier?'

'I was just going to say you seemed happier then.'

'Well, that's true. But I'm going to get it back. It'll be an informed happiness this time. Not a brand new, silly happiness. I was just rushing to do something back then. I was over-excited. I got carried away.'

He laughs. 'I remember you saying you wanted to meet new people.'

'That backfired, didn't it? Actually, I blame you for all of this.'

He looks more serious then, and when he asks, 'Do you regret ever meeting me?' I realise that I was more stupid than I previously gave myself credit for: I overlooked Michael in my auditing of my mistakes. A mark in the debit column. It wasn't even humility that stopped me realising what he felt, but self-involvement.

'Of course I don't.'

There is a short silence. Michael breathes as if he is about to sigh, then stops and lets the accumulated air slowly go. I put my hand on his arm, with the intention of telling him something: *I'm sorry*. Or, *I got it all wrong*. But the turning I missed is too far back to find again, and the two of us are enveloped in the overarching end of it all, caught out too late in the evening, looking at each other under the day that has begun to collapse, folding solemnly over us, like a circus tent after the last act.

As if it has been waiting for this sense of finality, the taxi I called earlier appears now and sits muttering at the kerb.

'I'd suppose I'd better go,' I say. 'Thank you for everything.'

He looks awkward, almost pained.

'I didn't do anything a friend wouldn't do.'

'Thank you for being my friend.'

Michael looks uncertain for a moment, then he puts his arms around me and I put my head on his shoulder, allowing myself its brief solidity, before tears start to gather in the corners of my eyes (this is, evidently, my fate, to be another public crier) and I move back and get into the taxi, smiling, waving unconvincingly with my head dipped. He waves, then turns and goes back inside the bar: sheltering, like everyone else, from the city night, from the open street.

~

On the plane at night I can almost imagine I am over water: London a host of spangled barnacles on a black rock, in a glittering coal sea, before the sea itself appears in the oval picture; a vista like a sky, darker and denser than the dark land. I spread my father's last letter out on the little cream fold-down table, where it looks like a battered artefact in a spaceship . . . *We're looking forward to your arrival. I have missed you very much.*

I put it away when the plane commences its bird-of-prey screaming; its cries of rage as it is forced down to the indistinct land. Sitting up in my seat while children start crying and people take off their belts too early, I have to remember where exactly I am arriving to, as if the flight has made me feel I am no longer a denizen of any landmass. I can't see any of Scotland from the window; just the lights of the airfield; the black flatness and the bag handlers and shuttles circling like the birds that clean the teeth of crocodiles; moving in diffidently, expectantly.

I stand in the bus-crush with the other passengers, who stare with demented tiredness all round them, clinging on to their plastic straps, swaying like seaweed. Then I collect my rotating cases, wheeling them out into the palely lit, tiled space of the airport, which sleeplessness has turned into a dreamlike other-world, a shifting space. A woman in front of me, thin, with glimmering hair, startles me until she turns and shows an unfamiliar profile. Then she faces away, and becomes Ivy again.

Though I am expecting it, it is strange to see my own name, Persephone Triebold, handwritten and held by a taxi driver. I repeat it to myself as I get into the car, *Persephone Triebold*, as if it has become estranged from me, a name loosed into the world, floating free and disconnected, and by saying it I am trying to bring it back, hold on to it again.

The taxi moves through the familiar, unlit land of the Highlands like an otter slipping easily through river water, following the flow of the road as familiarly as I follow it myself, remembering it as we go. Finally, at nearly midnight, we drive up an apparently absent road, towards the bright-windowed house at the end.

~

After I get home I work selling stamps and petrol and milk at the only shop in Achiltibuie in the week, dispensing alcohol to tourists and elderly locals at a Fort William pub at weekends, and babysitting the McLeods' five children in the evenings, which takes up so much of my time that it is nearly a month before I have a free day in which to unpack. I haven't actually needed any of my accumulated London possessions since I got back and my three cases have come to rest on the landing, undisturbed until today.

The noise of my hauling the cases across the wooden floorboards into my room draws Sadie up the stairs, offering help.

'It's okay,' I say. 'I don't even know why I'm bothering now. It hardly seems worth it for a month.'

'You've got to mentally unpack, hon,' Sadie says. 'This is important. It's a coming-home ritual.'

I nod and try not to mind the sentimentality. Really, I hardly notice it now. It's just another language barrier. Sadie speaks self-help, chick flick: I translate, recognising that the feeling behind it is authentic.

'Hey, your dad framed that newspaper photo of Sylvia. It's wonderful. You never said where you got it from.'

'A friend found it for me.'

'Oh now, that's nice. That's real nice. I guess you'll be seeing them when you get back? Bath isn't far from London.'

I evade this. 'I still have no idea if I'll get on to the course. It's very last minute, applying now. Hopefully classics won't be a very popular choice.'

'The gods favour the bold,' Sadie says, unexpectedly. 'Isn't that Ovid?'

'No idea. But if I'm accepted I can find out and let you know.'

'Well, whoever it was, they were right,' Sadie says. 'It was brave of you to change your course. Admitting that it isn't for you. I have a sixth sense that we'll be visiting you in Bath next year. Ah, all those Georgian sandstone buildings. And the pump rooms! I have very fond memories of Bath. It's quieter than London, though, isn't it? You sure it'll be exciting enough?'

'London was . . . too exciting. I think I'll like a change.'

At this point my father appears on the stairs, flushed from cooking, which has always slightly flustered him, turning him pink and grave, until the food is on the table and he can safely dissociate from it, like a man abandoning himself to fate.

'There won't be any courgettes, I'm afraid,' he informs us. 'They went off in the bottom of the fridge when I wasn't paying attention. I hope runner beans will do?'

'Beans are great.'

'I'm not really sure about leaving the meat so rare,' my father continues. 'I read an article about a parasite that lives in uncooked beef . . .'

'I'll come and help,' Sadie offers, following him back downstairs, and I am left alone with my unpacking.

With the cases lined up in my bedroom, the movability of my life – leaving home, returning home – reminds me of my childhood books about sporty English girls at boarding school. The books always started with the girls going in ready to get the 'corners knocked off them' as the head girl commented cheerfully. I imagined a kind of production line with the various girls (secretive, angry, sexy, melodramatic, untruthful, vain) going in one end and coming out the other without their corners. Healthy, good sorts, squeaky haired and buff skinned, with their naked eyelids and fingernails, clutching hockey sticks. I don't think any corners got knocked off me while I was away. I think, if anything, I gained some corners.

When I open the cases, the smell of London comes out, rising from my clothes, the scents of the mildewed tall yellow house of Camilla and the two Claires, Leni's flat with its rubber plants and bookshelves, Leo's rainy-windowed white palace. It is the scent of stinging tequila and the heavy fog of marijuana and the slick pavements under my heels, of fear-filled dance floors, of grey, insistent glamour. It feels like a dream, a cold, dark dream, drawing in as I inhale.

I pull out the clothes and shake them out; thinking of which night each of them saw. Who unbuttoned them, who looked at them, who they slid up against. I shake and shake until the smell of London leaves their seams and bones.

Aside from the clothes there isn't much else in my cases. I sold my university books online, along with two books of Leo's. A postcard with a yacht on it, I keep, putting it into a drawer. In amongst some papers I find a fashion magazine, which I put on the old pile by my bed. I look at this pile, then I spread its layers out across the floor, so that all the brightly lit female faces on the covers are looking up at me. Their faces remind me of my own: that look of trying. Everyone trying to be something, thinking they are nothing. Believing that if they have someone like Leo they will have the secret of being something.

This is Hades. Hades is something that is dark, but so bright that no one ordinary can see it. It is money, and beauty, and fame, but it is more than the sum of these parts – it is alive – magnified by imagination, indefinable and infinitely promising. It is an opiate, a hallucination, a vision, something to be swept up in. It is exciting because no one can ever have it: it carries with it the promise of its own loss, its death, the thrill of that fear.

An unwilling man has been given Hades as his portion, but it is his curse. He is lonely because he is known, he is invisible because he is visible. He is iconic because he is arranged around one idea, drawn in a simple outline; too simple to fit a real man inside. He is blank because when women look at him all they see is their own idea of him, a thousand different ideas, one for each woman, depending on what she wants to be: all hopeful, all wrong.

I pick up the stack and take it downstairs, to put in the recycling.

On the way back through the garden to the house I stop at the bush by the door, kneel down, and put my hand investigatively inside. The shape of a wine bottle, still half full, meets my fingers. I leave it there and sit instead on the bench, looking out past the green frame of our garden into the mountains, still soundly asleep. My arrival home – dazed and electrified, bringing the city soot and buzz with me – hasn't been noticed by the Assynt. I am not even a prickle, a mosquito, or any other thing that irritates someone awake. In a strange way, this is reassuring.

The air around me is still warm, still motionless, trapped in the bowl of the hills. I could swim up through it, but I float suspended in its water, coloured brown, grey, then blue above the rim of the bowl. I close my eyes and listen to the routines of the bees, passing over the flower beds, the bare magnolia, then back over the wall to the heather.

'Perse?'My father stands at a politely judged distance, leaning rather than stepping forward to see my face, like a man peering over an invisible wall. 'Oh, you're awake. I thought you might have snoozed off. It's been very balmy this last week. Lethargic. I fell asleep in the garden myself the other day.'

'I wasn't asleep. Come and sit down.'

He smiles and takes the place next to me with his usual hesitancy. I consider producing the bottle of wine from the bush and offering him a swig, but instead I say: 'I thought more might have changed here, since I left.'

'How do you mean?'

'I don't know. You might have redecorated. Painted the walls. Put the new kitchen in.'

'It's hard to know what to do with the house,' Evan says. 'It's been the same way for a long time. I don't know exactly how to explain it. It's as if there was a time to redecorate, but it's been left too long to do it now. I get the drill out occasionally and then I put it off.' He pauses, gives a small wince. 'That sounds ridiculous.'

'Not really. I understand.'

I know what has happened to the house: the same thing that has happened to the abandoned crofts, the derelict cars in the fields, the tracing of stone walls over the hills. Its flux time – the time of Sylvia and new babies and parties – is over: without human attention it has joined the comatose mountains, started its sink into the land.

'I suppose I ought to get somebody in. To fix the roof, at least,' my father says.

'Look, Dad—'

'I remember when your mother and I moved in we had to clear out a lot of things from the attic of the house – generations of accumulated things. It was like an archaeological dig through the family history. At the bottom I found your great-grand-uncle Louis's things. Do you remember I told you about him? He loved a girl but she decided not to marry him after all. He kept all her letters in a box. Not just letters – everything to do with her. Things that wouldn't have made sense beyond the two of them, like train tickets. I thought it was highly romantic at the time. But Sylvia said it was a sad thing. She didn't want to read any of it. She said, "He died alone. This is his loneliness."'

I can't see my father's eyes under the faded hat, which he puts on just to step out in the evening sun, the dim fringing of his grey hair. I put my hand on top of his instead, closing it over the awkward knuckle bones, the raised veining under the thin skin.

'You have to move.'

He sighs. 'Sadie says she likes it here. But she hasn't been here for very long. I'm not sure it's . . . conducive to a healthy mental state.'

We take in the blank billow of the brown and grey above us.

'Sell up,' I urge. 'Take our stuff. Take the box of letters. Sylvia's things. Then get out of here.'

'But where to?'

'I don't know. Anywhere. You could go to the countryside. Or the coast. Somewhere with villages and shops and public transport links.'

There is a pause while he thinks about this, a slow near-nod. Then he asks: 'But what about you, Perse? Everything will be very different if you change course and move house at the same time.'

'I like that. Something . . . different.'

The hat tilts up. We exchange something – not quite a wink, because the Triebolds are not that demonstrative yet. Not tears. But a signal, nonetheless, of understanding.